Katherine's Wheel

Rebecca Gregson is a freelance journalist and former radio presenter for BBC Radio Cornwall. She lives with her husband and two young children in Cornwall, where she is currently working on her second novel.

Katherine's Wheel

Rebecca Gregson

**POCKET
BOOKS**

LONDON · SYDNEY · NEW YORK · TOKYO · SINGAPORE · TORONTO

First published in Great Britain by Pocket Books, 1999
An imprint of Simon & Schuster Ltd
A Viacom Company

Simon & Schuster Ltd
West Garden Place
Kendal Street
London W2 2AQ

SIMON & SCHUSTER AUSTRALIA
SYDNEY

A CIP catalogue record for this book is available
from the British Library

3 5 7 9 10 8 6 4 2

ISBN 0-671-01593-1

Typeset in 11/13.5pt Sabon by
Palimpsest Book Production Limited, Polmont, Stirlingshire
Printed and bound in Great Britain by
Cox & Wyman, Reading, Berkshire

For Sophie, of course

Katherine's Wheel would not exist were it not for my friend Sophie Hosking, whose original idea formed the basis for this story and whose motivation and help in further shaping the story line makes this book very much a joint effort.

Time has no divisions to mark its passage, there is never a thunderstorm or a blare of trumpets to announce the beginning of a new month or year. Even when a new century begins, it is only we mortals who ring bells and fire off pistols.

Thomas Mann (1875-1955)

Prologue

At ten minutes past noon on Wednesday, 11 August 1999, one hundred and forty-two days before the beginning of a new millennium, Cornwall succumbed to a pitch black darkness. One million visitors, seduced by media hype to see the first total eclipse of the sun in Britain for seventy-two years, had more than trebled the county's summertime population. Everyone agreed that to experience this 'midnight at midday' was a once-in-a-lifetime chance – a fitting finish to the twentieth century, and when an opportunity like that came your way . . . well then, who cared if you were being stung for a fortune by an enterprising farmer in return for a small patch of field in which to pitch your tent?

Tremewan, a rambling community neither coastal nor pretty but situated at the heart of the eclipse, was being forced into a role for which it was hardly fit. More at home when the summer visitors took the by-pass on their way to the beaches and the harbours and the country houses of the guide books, it was now *the* place everyone wanted to be. The terraced granite-faced cottages lining its wide main street suddenly discovered the potential to be guest-houses after all, just like

1

their more marketable whitewashed cousins dotted with random perfection around the harbour of the neighbouring fishing village. Even Tremewan's rickety old clock-tower, spurned for years by villagers as being dangerously unstable and a drain on the parish purse, was managing to persuade the exploitable visitors it was a building of note. 'Take a picture of me under this, Bill. We can send it to Jean in Australia.'

This was agricultural Cornwall, where the rush of main-road traffic could only be heard if the wind was in the wrong direction, and where a single tractor could make an entire hamlet late for work if it had the mind. Narrow lanes, bordered by high banks of Cornish stone-and-earth hedging, were dressed now in their summer guise of foxgloves and campion, holding back a well-kept secret from anyone indifferent enough not to take a look over the intermittent and usually broken five-bar gates. In more ordinary times, curiosity would have been rewarded with rolling fields that took the eye as far as it could see, a vista divided only by more grassy walls and the occasional cluster of woodland. Now though, that same measureless countryside was under siege from an invasion of gaudy Gore-Tex tents, like a makeshift camp for an unwanted cavalry drafted in to help the natives in a showdown no one was ever going to win. Even the battery of telescopes, aimed with precision towards their target, looked ready to shoot anyone who might step out of line.

For months, huge maps of the village layout had been pinned to office walls at County Hall marking out road closures, one-way traffic systems and car parking facilities. Men in grey suits with long wooden rules had spent weeks indicating strategic positions to the troops during daily briefings, re-confirming to themselves that everything was under control.

2

Whether it liked it or not, Tremewan had no choice but to smile for the camera until the moment had passed. All this for two minutes of day-time night!

On the day itself, as the sun began to surrender to the usurping shadow of the moon, villagers and strangers marched in silence up the hill towards the appointed battlefield, keeping to a neat file on the pavement, nodding recognition at their shared vulnerability. It was a measure of the operation's success, which had been co-ordinated specifically to discourage individual behaviour, that not many had thought to watch the darkness from their own gardens or tents. The message had come across loud and clear. 'The eclipse will commence at 11.10 a.m. British Summer Time, be total for two minutes at 12.10 p.m. and finish at 12.31 p.m. *from the playing field.*'

The door to the Miners Inn was propped open with a beer crate as usual, but the bar was deserted. A few children originally intending to shake off parental supervision hung quietly over the climbing frame in the school playground waiting for a familiar adult to show as the sky grew inky and fearful. Even members of the Eclipse Committee – who should have been rhapsodic at the triumph of their complicated traffic flow plans – found it hard to loosen up. The smoke-free barbecue was smoke-free, the television cameras were out in force and the cloudless sky was an astronomer's prayer . . . but the oppressive sense of unease was tangible.

When the black-out finally came, there wasn't a soul in Tremewan who didn't feel a personal darkness. Those who could, opted for quiet family hugs – and those who couldn't, waited passively as the sausages hissed, sizzled and spat in the silence.

For Katherine Bates, it was almost too much, as if her

own world were closing in on her, like a huge pillow bearing down on her slowly and relentlessly, cramming itself into her face. So this was what a panic attack was, she told herself calmly, inhaling slowly for as long as she could, and reaching her arm casually around her daughter Hattie. Feeling the slim little shoulders of a child still hanging on to pre-adolescence made her grateful and she bent to kiss the crown of dark short hair.

Hattie, who wished she could lift her head back and let her mum cradle away her tears, wanted to talk about being on the edge of something, knowing what was going to happen but not being able to stop it. Instead, she bowed her head believing her mother was not yet ready to hear that even she, a child, had felt another darkness seeping into their lives, one that wouldn't fade away. She looked for her brother in the crowd and saw him standing across the field, their father's arms either side of his shoulders. Is this the way it is going to be soon? she wondered. Dad with Seth, me with Mum. Two and two not making four.

At the same time, on the other side of the Atlantic in Hoboken, New Jersey, Patrick Seal awoke too early. Lying in the half light, his bedroom blind blocking out all but a flickering frame of sunshine around its edges, his first few moments were kind to him. In the nano-second before he was fully conscious, he willed himself to sink back into the haven his dreams had created but then, as he turned, he felt the warm, smooth curve of Dido's thigh and he was awake.

Through the reluctant slit of an eye he saw her pink linen skirt over the back of his chair, the navy blue cotton vest on top and a wash bag dumped on the crumpled towel, like the debris from a hundred casual stay-overs

4

of a current lover – except of course, that this was anything but.

'Time for us to claim each other,' she had said last night, dragging her words after a transatlantic flight and a bottle of wine. When he'd opened his mouth to tell her why it wasn't, and why it could never be, not one sound had come. She'd looked so vital and emphatic, standing there that he'd decided it could wait. Now, in the light of the day, he thought it could perhaps wait just a little longer.

At half past twelve Cornwall time, full daylight was restored. In New Jersey, Patrick's darkness was only just beginning.

Chapter 1

THREE MONTHS TO GO

The Times, 1 October, 1999: A leading coroner has blamed 'millennium mania' for the death of a man who plunged over cliffs during
the total eclipse of the sun in August. A verdict of suicide was recorded
on Caleb Mitchell of Truro, bringing the number of 'eclipse' suicides
in Cornwall to four. Coroner Mr John Moore said the case had 'all
the hallmarks of millennium mania'. He was in no doubt that Mr
Mitchell had killed himself because of his inability to cope with the
growing momentum surrounding the approach of the 21st century,
and he appealed to the media to stop the hype. An inquest into the
death of a woman whose body was found hanging from her cottage
beams in Falmouth, Cornwall, an hour after daylight was restored,
will be held next week.

For all the privacy afforded them by the village, Katherine
might as well have put a poster in the shop window – 'Johnny
and Katherine Bates have agreed to a trial separation and
he will be leaving on Friday, 27 August, once the children
have gone to bed' – although no doubt by now she would
have been asked to take it down to make room for something more pressing. A missing cat perhaps, or a surfboard
for sale.

Their days as fodder for village gossip were over. She
hadn't been on the receiving end of any over-friendly smiles
for days, and even the trumped up invitations to dinner
had stopped. Five weeks into the split of their thirteen-year

marriage and the Bates were old news, such was the turn-around of information these days.

Katherine helped herself to another glass of wine and peered into the small driftwood mirror on her kitchen wall. She expected to look paler or more lined, but her face was reassuringly unchanged by the horrible events of the last two hours which had somehow seemed even more horrible than the accumulated events of the last two months. Sometimes, when her hair was clean and her make-up had worked, she felt almost attractive, although her inadvertent talent for occasionally managing to look remarkable always passed her by. Tonight however, her eyes were dull and her hair was flat.

'Old,' she said out loud before walking away, remembering how, in the bath last night, the skin around her elbow crease had reminded her of her mother's.

It was Johnny's weekend to have the children, and when he had the children he also had the car – a classic case of God giving with one hand and taking away with the other. She had been both childless and carless for six whole days in the last two months and still couldn't decide if this was a blessing or a curse. The main point in its favour was undoubtedly that it gave her the perfect excuse for not going out and grabbing her new single life by the balls like she knew she was expected to.

When she was in these moods, she taunted herself with a conversation she'd had the day after Johnny left. 'I remember that overwhelming sense of freedom when my husband finally went,' her friend Penny Shepherd's sister had enthused, 'as if a huge cloud that had been sitting over our house for years had finally been blown away. You must be feeling incredibly released.'

'Liberated, yes,' Katherine had mumbled in reply. In truth,

freedom was the last thing she was experiencing, and if she was continuing to be truthful, it was the last thing she wanted to experience too. If anything positive came out of the breakdown of her marriage, it might signal a permanence she wasn't ready for, so instead she preferred to wallow in the murky present.

It was a lot easier like that – or would have been, if the future wasn't currently *the* hot issue. As the world pitched and rolled towards a new millennium, Katherine was growing more and more seasick. Irritated by the idea that one tiny tick of the clock could change anything, she also found herself believing that she and Johnny might have survived if the year of their impasse had been anything other than 1999 – not that she had ever voiced such a flimsy theory.

Why did the house always seem emptier and quieter when the children were with Johnny than it did when they were at school? It was tidier too, and of all the things a home should be, tidy was not one of them, not in her book anyway. Her aversion to neatness came as a direct result of growing up in a house where she was constantly nagged to take her feet off the furniture, or put away her school bag, or use a plate if she helped herself to a biscuit. Stray crumbs had never featured in her mother's house, and it was with some alarm that she looked across the surface of her own limed oak kitchen now and realised how clean it all was. However much she aspired to the same artistic clutter that seemed to seed itself in Loveday's half of the cottage next door, she never quite achieved it. She would get so far and then she would suddenly be swamped with irritation at the accumulating piles of rubbish everywhere and out would come the bin bag. The fact that she had spent twenty minutes frantically wiping down all the units before Johnny had arrived tonight said it all, unless it was simply to prove to him that she could cope.

Her inability to strike the right balance between civilised disorder and clinical arrangement in the cottage annoyed her. It made her feel as if she was failing the spirit of the place in some way, especially when she thought back to the days before she was married and mortgaged, when it was all one long meandering house and she used to stay there as a student friend of Loveday's daughter Beth. It had been her first glimpse, at the age of eighteen, into the bohemian world her best friend Beth had always taken for granted, and Katherine could still remember the shock of being hit by a sudden contempt for the formality of her own suburban upbringing.

How anyone could rattle in a cottage with such thick granite walls she didn't know, but rattle she did. She could almost hear herself. To mask the noise of loneliness, she would usually put on some music and assume a casual pose, lying on the sofa or up to her neck in bubble bath and question herself over her weekend hibernations. Were they a subconscious fear of creating a new and separate identity for herself, or a conscious effort to hang on to the one she already had? Was she being an ostrich, or could it be argued that she was confronting the crisis head-on? Tonight, she simply wondered why the two glasses of wine on an empty stomach were not hauling her out of her self-analysis like they usually did.

On the painted blue dresser lay Johnny's biking gloves, stuffed in the upturned padded black crash helmet. The ignition keys, attached to a fob shaped like a tiny leather jacket she had put in his Christmas stocking only ten months ago, were next to them – an invitation to use his bike if she wanted to.

She tried to make a case for using her recently acquired licence to go to Truro tomorrow and wander aimlessly round the shops and cathedral like she had longed to do for years, or to drive to the cliffs of the north coast and stand on the wall of an old tin mine while the Cornish wind whipped the maudlin out of her, or be expansive and go to an art exhibition at the Tate in St Ives like Penny Shepherd had been trying to persuade her to. All around her lay a hundred possibilities but only one reality – she would stay put, in the safe confines of her deserted home.

Katherine removed herself and the bottle of wine from the kitchen to the sitting room, saying in a weary whisper directed at the helmet, 'You stupid bloody bike.' Then she shut the door on the lot of it.

One day last year, when Johnny was at the foothills of his mid-life crisis, he had walked back from the Miners after an uncharacteristically early evening drink, crossed the road to where his nearly-new royal blue four-seater hatchback was parked ready to take him to his standard issue local government office desk the next day, and delivered a swift but feeling kick to its front wheel to pay it back for what he thought it said about his life. Katherine, who had watched him do it from the kitchen window and felt an icy jab beneath her ribs as his shoe hit the tyre, said nothing.

The next day, without consulting his wife or bank balance, he had swapped the car for a Triumph Daytona 1200cc motorbike and used the argument that since she always did the ferrying around, there was little point in them running two sensible cars, and one of them at least might as well have some fun. As soon as she saw the bike, Katherine said, 'So you want a life other than the one you have, do you?' and he had muttered something about a bit of freedom. Well, he had it now, if that's what you could call living in a damp rented cottage surrounded by someone else's furniture two miles away from your own home, even if it was Nick and Penny Shepherd's furniture.

Katherine remembered the time she had stayed overnight there herself, when Nick and Penny were in it while their farmhouse was being re-wired and re-roofed. It was five years ago and she had only been there the once, but she could draw the layout now – kitchen to the left of the front door, sitting room to the right. She hadn't seen it since Johnny had moved in, he hadn't asked her, but she could imagine him there, and that made her feel that he wasn't entirely in alien country. In fact, you could say he was just staying with friends for a while. No, you couldn't – of course you couldn't! What you *could* say was that he had left her and that their marriage was over. She flumped on the worn linen sofa, feeling at least as old and exhausted as the springs that creaked beneath her.

Tonight's pick-up had been the worst so far, made all the more traumatic in its aftermath for the terrifying discovery of an urge to go after them and snatch them all back, Johnny included. What made it so awful in the first place was the politeness. True to their mutual promise never to make things awkward for either Hattie or Seth, Johnny had hovered in the kitchen doorway, as if he had been banned from crossing the threshold, and she had replied to his tactful enquiries with bland diplomacy. The two of them assumed the roles of parents meeting at the school gates – sociable but insignificant chatter. They had pulled it off before, but just not tonight.

Katherine pinpointed the start of the trouble back to when Seth had decided he was starving, half an hour before Johnny was due.

'You'll have to wait for Dad. He won't be long.'

'But we had to go to the supermarket before supper last time. He didn't have any food in the house, just drink. Honest. I saw cans and cans of it in the fridge when we got there. I feel faint. What if I faint and he's only got lager? I could die.'

'Don't be ridiculous, Seth.'

'But I'm feeling funny. Just a bit of bread then. Please.'

So Katherine had sent him sprinting up the hill to get fish and chips for three, thinking she could help Johnny out and feed him and the children before they left, but of course he had arrived shouting about an enormous pizza he had carried on the back of his motorbike all the way from Truro and how it had been specially ordered with pineapple for Hattie and pepperoni for Seth, and if they got going quickly, it would be just the right temperature to eat.

'Mum's got us fish and chips,' Seth told him with all the tact of a ten-year-old.

'No probs,' said Johnny, his real reaction hidden under a cardboard smile. 'The pizza will keep, we can have it for breakfast,' but then spoiled his effort by adding 'which is just as well because it cost a fortune.'

Katherine had jumped in as soon as the children left the room. 'Try and be a bit more consistent, will you? Apparently last time the fridge was full of beer and nothing else.'

Recognising the beginnings of a row, she had tried to change the subject and the first thing she had thought about was the car, and whether they ought to think about getting a second one to ease the hassle, but she'd scrapped that once she remembered how they'd come to be a one-car family in the first place.

It was then that Seth's first day at nursery school seven years ago had popped into her mind, triggered by the same brand of grim determination to see trauma through with a smile on one's face. All that three-year-old panic, the way she had prised his fat little fingers off the hem of her skirt as he hung on for his life, and her betrayal as she had accused him of playing to a crowd, had come straight back, this time with a double helping of guilt.

The mistake had been not in remembering it, but in sharing the memory with Johnny, because the moment she had ventured off their agreed path of pleasantry swapping, she'd found herself in a jungle of confused emotions, wanting him to stay, to share the wine, to send the children to bed together. The sudden and rather over-zealous sermon on the wisdom of putting on an act for the children that had followed had been a gut reaction to feeling sad, that was all.

Bang went her format so successfully laid down over the past few weeks of absent father arriving, children leaving, and abandoned mother staying put – all executed in one seamless logical manoeuvre – and instead, just when she should have been double checking that Hattie and Seth had their homework with them, she, still in full memory flow over the nursery story, had said dramatically, 'He was screaming for me. I regret to this day not going back to him, but that bitch of a house-mother had the palm of her hand on my back and was practically pushing me out the door, singing, 'Firm and controlled, Mrs Bates, firm and controlled . . .'

Both of them heard something else in the poignant delivery of her words – 'come back, this is all wrong' – but as neither of them knew how to amplify it, the echo died away.

Johnny's forte never was subtlety and he'd hardly known how to react to his estranged wife now that she was actually showing something of herself after so long, so he'd moved forward in a deliberate sort of way and pressed his hand on her shoulder, propelling her away from the bottle of wine she was just about to open.

'Firm and controlled, Mrs Bates, firm and controlled . . .'

It had been meant as a joke, his way of venturing off that same agreed path too, but when Katherine had turned round to face him, he saw that he too was in jungle territory. She'd barely recognised her own voice in the venomous little rasp that she let out.

'Is it funny? *Is it?* Listen hard enough, Johnny, and it won't be the cries of a three-year-old asking a parent to return you'll hear, it'll be the collective sobbing of two grown children.'

'And their mother?' The question had been out before he could rein it back in.

'You must be joking. Now move out the way, please, and take your hand off my back.'

'Oh. Right. Fine. Firm, but not controlled then,' he said, more sarcastically than he intended, just as Hattie re-entered the room, then adding 'Shall we go back to being polite? Perhaps it's the best approach in the circumstances.'

'Don't worry about me,' Hattie had said as confidently as she could. 'You don't fool us.'

'Don't we?' Johnny smiled. He was getting good at arranging his expression to mask his emotions.

'No,' Hattie had replied, sounding exactly like her mother. 'Listen, I've decided to stay here this weekend.' For a twelve-year-old, she said it well and might just have been able to carry it off but for the arrival of Seth.

Her younger brother, who saw the prospect of a weekend with Johnny as the next best thing to being allowed to camp out in the garden, and was obviously indulged in this judging by the number of crisps that fell out of his sleeping bag every

Sunday night, was in there like a shot. Before anyone older had time to reply, he told her to shut up and grow up, which made Hattie cry in front of them all for the first time since Johnny had left.

That was more than an hour ago now, and the memory of it was no less awful than the original scene. Katherine wanted to pick it to pieces before she filed it away, to make sure it wouldn't leap out at her and catch her unawares when they returned in forty-six hours' time, not that she was counting.

Should have stuck with a flavourless discussion on the weather, she thought miserably, pouring herself more wine and collapsing back into the heap of velvet cushions, shutting her eyes. She opened them again seconds later when the phone rang. If it was Hattie asking to come home, then Johnny would just have to swallow his pride and bring her back, right away. She hoped it would be. Hattie managed to be a huge comfort without even knowing it.

'Hello?' Katherine's voice sounded unfamiliar, as if she hadn't spoken to another soul for days. The background noise suggested a call box and something tightened inside her stomach. The car has crashed, Johnny has managed to crawl out and limp to the nearest phone, leaving the children trapped inside. They need me.

'Hello, Katherine? It's Patrick.'

The relief and surprise made her legs wobble and she sat down. A small, much less personal panic rose again when she realised Patrick sounded too close to be calling from America.

'Patrick? What's the matter?'

There was a strange clicking on the line which she took to be him lighting his customary Marlboro but he didn't reply.

'Where are you?'

She could hear him taking his first lungful.

'Plymouth. I left the States last night – bit of a spur of the moment decision.'

To hear him was to see him, all tousled and preoccupied, like an embryonic mad professor with the added advantage of bone structure and curls. He only ever wore four colours – black, grey, navy and white – and whilst there was nothing chirpy about him like there was with Johnny, he still knew exactly which button to press to make her laugh, which she did now, partly out of shock and partly out of the sheer pleasure of hearing his voice again – deep, lazy, absent-minded and entirely familiar. She was hit by a rush of excitement. Excitement and Patrick went together. Sometimes, in the distant past, it had been dangerous excitement, and he'd taken her on adventures for which she was far from ready. Now that she had grown out of such experimenting, he offered a more palatable kind of challenge, sporadically calling from crazy corners of the world with persistent attempts to persuade her and Johnny and Beth to join him on his far-flung assignments. What would be on offer this time? she wondered, as the troubled first half of her evening evaporated into thin air.

'Katherine? Speak to me.'

Three years since they'd last seen each other, and probably at least three months since they'd last exchanged letters. She suddenly realised how much water had gone under the bridge.

'Did you say *Plymouth*? As in our Plymouth? You're having me on,' she said, hoping he was not.

'Would I do that? No, I am really. Listen – I'll read a train timetable out. Penzance to London, 10.20, calling at Plymouth, Exeter St Davids, Taunton, Castle Cary . . .'

'Good grief, you really are here. Why? I mean, what are you doing back now? I wasn't expecting to see you until December, for you-know-what.'

He ignored her question.

'This is an awful thing to do to a woman with a husband and two children to support, but I don't suppose I could ask you or Johnny to come and pick me up, could I? There's some sort of delay on the line from Truro and the next train isn't for three hours.'

'You're coming here *now*? But Johnny's got the car.'

'*The* car? Times are hard are they? When will he be back?'

This time it was Katherine who failed to reply.

'Hello?' Patrick tried stuffing another coin into the slot and found himself in credit by another pound.

'Hello.' She couldn't think what to say. He had been top of her list of people to write to since Johnny had left, but she just hadn't been able to find the energy or the words. Besides, Johnny could equally have done it, Patrick was his best friend too, although she would put a bet on the fact that Johnny felt as she did, that they were letting the side down, breaking up much more than a marriage, ruining a whole adulthood of memories, giving up on friendship – the same shame she'd felt when telling Beth. They all understood each other too well to justify anything, or they used to. There had been a time not so long ago when they had all known even the tiniest detail of each other's lives and she hadn't even noticed its passing.

'Oh, I thought you'd gone,' Patrick said. 'Is it a problem? No worries. I'll wait for the train.'

Katherine toyed with the idea of leaving it at that until she saw him, and then she said clumsily, as if she was referring to a new kitten or a change of car, 'Oh, we haven't told you, have we?'

'Told me what?'

'Johnny doesn't actually come back any more, apart from to drop the children off. We're living apart.'

'What do you mean? You've separated?' He said it half as a joke.

'Yep.'

'Did you really say "Yep" then?'

'Yep,' she replied, trying to be funny. 'Don't worry, listen, I'll come and get you. Loveday's in, I can hear her playing the piano through the wall, she might be able to help. Ring again in an hour and a half if I'm not with you by then.'

'Katherine, I'll wait for the train.'

'No, please, I can't wait another four hours before seeing you now I know you're so close. Anyway, I go to bed at ten nowadays. No, I'll be there.'

'I've still got ninety pence worth.'

But Katherine had put the phone down. He could wait for the full version of events until they were face to face, but she was already regretting saying what she had. Of all the people in all the world who should have been told properly, it was Patrick, but he hadn't even been consulted, not once in the whole sorry saga. Why hadn't she sought his advice when Johnny first started behaving oddly? Patrick might just have been the one to put them back on track. Then she remembered her vague feeling of fear that he would take Johnny's side, or that he might console her in a way she wouldn't be able to resist, and how, all in all, it had been easier to assume Johnny would tell him.

Once she had stopped feeling ashamed of herself, she realised how uncharacteristic it was for Patrick to ask for a lift. Arriving out of the blue was nothing new, but asking for a lift? He would normally hitch, surely. Patrick hitched everywhere. He was the one who'd first introduced them all to the concept of free travel back in 1985, by claiming they could reach the Edinburgh festival in two days from Plymouth. Five hundred miles without spending more than a fiver, he'd promised, *and* they'd done it. Perhaps he's feeling his age along with the rest of us, Katherine thought. Thirty-five is no joke, especially when it coincides with the last year of the century – make that millennium, she corrected herself, and multiply our angst by ten.

Plymouth station was chaos. Patrick found no comfort in the apologetic announcements that kept coming, falteringly, over the tannoy. A collective groan murmured round him at each one and he slugged back a can of warm beer for want of something better. Families argued, businessmen sighed, and pensioners worried. I remain unaffected by it all, he thought. It doesn't matter to me, because I have no deadline. I could walk it if I needed to.

One ample mother parked her screaming baby by a bench next to him and waddled self-consciously across the platform to retrieve an escaped toddler who kicked her repeatedly and noisily in the stomach. The woman was obviously embarrassed, in pain and exhausted but Patrick viewed the whole scene without pity. Any sympathy he had, he kept to himself, *for* himself.

The air on Plymouth station always used to smell of train diesel and sea, and the platforms had always buzzed with sailors on leave and students on railcards. He had hoped that being there again would feel like coming home. After all, when was the last time he had travelled as lightly as this – one holdall, a few changes of clothes, money, passport, wash bag? When he was a student himself, and nothing really mattered. Fleetingly, painfully, he conceded that things had actually mattered more then, not less. Surely, he would have found some compassion for that ample mother in those days; he would probably even have helped her.

Now he was actually here, any idea of a 'homecoming' had vanished. A tiled reception area, a shop selling CD-Roms and portable fax machines? He thought of an article he'd read on the train claiming that a weekday edition of a national newspaper contained more information than the average person was likely to come across in a lifetime during seventeenth century England, but the irony was lost on him as he headed for a newsagents stand and started to scan the wire stacks for an American paper. They were all so old he'd read them once already, at his kitchen table in Washington Street, Hoboken, New Jersey.

The image of his table, heaped with all sorts of vital clutter that needed his attention, drew him up sharply. For the first time since he'd left the day before, he wondered what the hell he was doing. He had at least two outstanding magazine articles to write, there was a party at The Shore this weekend, he'd arranged an interview with Chelsea Clinton for tomorrow, and more than any of this, Dido was there, in his flat, in his bed, wanting to share more than just the duvet.

He shook his head, trying to dislodge the picture of her in bed. There was little point in physically removing himself from the situation if he couldn't mentally remove himself too. The phone call to Katherine had just given him the perfect excuse to stop questioning his own choices and concentrate on someone else's, and he tried to stick with that. Introspection was bad news, and it was much easier to dissect the lives of others as an alternative. No wonder his work as a heavyweight profile journalist had started to fizz in the last eight months. Perhaps his unexplained absence from the New York press scene would be noted, maybe even making the news itself.

The opportunity of evaluating the Katherine and Johnny thing while he waited for her to arrive was strangely unappealing. There were all sorts of questions to be asked, like who would he stay with, were they talking to each other, who had been unfaithful to whom, what did Beth make of it – but he could hardly be bothered with the answers. What he *did* want to know was why none of them had told him. They were his best friends, all three of them; their lives had been shared since the day they all met at University, and they always told each other everything. It didn't occur to him how far from the truth this had become, that there was one brutal subject he *hadn't* shared with them, hadn't shared with anybody, nor did it occur to Patrick to ask himself why he should expect them to talk things over with him, when he had just left Dido to wake up alone in a flat in New Jersey where she would be expecting him to make her coffee or at the very least come home for dinner?

The thought of it terrified him all over again. He pushed up the sleeve of his creased blue jacket and looked at his watch, still showing New Jersey time, five hours earlier. Digging deep into the equally crumpled pocket of his baggy black linen trousers, he scrabbled around for change. He could buy a phone card, call her, try and explain his absence, or at least apologise for it – and if he managed to do none of those things, at least he'd hear her voice again.

'You're a dysfunctional bastard,' he said to himself as he pulled the drawer on the cigarette machine for another packet of Marlboro. 'You've got a stack of duty free in your bag, you're desperate to talk to her, and you spend your only ready cash on a packet of fags you don't need just to remove the temptation.'

He returned to the same red metal bench in the waiting area, sat as far away from a cosy looking woman with a shopping trolley as he could as if her self-satisfaction might be catching, and he lit up, dragging noisily and unselfconsciously on a cigarette he not only didn't need, but didn't even want. The woman's happy little expression annoyed him, as if she had something he didn't, and it prompted a recollection of someone who hadn't crossed his mind for seventeen years – a student at University called Paul. He dredged his memory for more information and came up with a surname. Grogan, Paul Grogan, that was it.

In the very first term, as freshers, Patrick and Johnny had been in neighbouring rooms in one of the Halls of Residence, sharing a corridor with what they called 'The God Squad' (had the phrase really seemed so funny at the time?) Initially, Patrick had decided the group must be a Canadian student exchange because they were all so obviously missing the essential hint of Oxfam required for survival in hip 1980s Britain, but then Johnny had stumbled upon them saying grace before a plate of bread and cheese in the communal kitchen.

'Jesus, just our luck,' Patrick had said too loudly as Johnny had opened a can of baked beans and flicked one at him. 'Born Again Christians.'

Afterwards, the neat desert-booted boy – Paul Grogan – had cornered him by the fridge. 'You may not know it,' Paul had said, 'but there's a big empty space inside you waiting to be filled by the truth.'

'I'm cool and you're not – is that it?'

'Well, that's one, but there's a higher one and I'm going to pray that you discover it one day.'

'Pray away, but I'm fine with the truth we've already identified, thanks,' Patrick had told him, thinking himself clever.

'You know the difference between you and me?' Paul had asked, still kindly. 'The difference is that I have the answers.'

Seventeen years later, and Patrick saw Paul's shiny fulfilment once more. How odd that he could remember something as insignificant as that in so much detail. He looked across at the cosy woman on the red bench and surreptitiously checked for a little silver fish brooch on her coat lapel. Surely this woman, who had just made herself considerably more uncomfortable by moving closer to him to make room for someone else, was one of *them*, promoting her faith by being happily selfless? No fish. No *Good News Bible* either. She caught his glance and smiled and it was enough to persuade him to leave the bench and find another hiding place.

In Loveday's faithful if sluggish car on the way to Plymouth, Patrick was being discussed more intimately than he would have liked. It often occurred to Katherine that she would never in a million years talk to her own mother in the same way she spoke to Beth's, but then it was almost impossible to accept that the two women belonged to the same generation. Margaret Jamieson talked about organza, Loveday Jago about orgasms; Margaret weeded nasturtiums, Loveday planted them. At Beth and Katherine's graduation in 1987, Loveday had sniffed the air and claimed she could smell cannabis. 'Ooh, lovely, I could do with a nibble,' Margaret had squeaked, mishearing. 'You never said there'd be canapés, Katherine. I packed us a picnic.'

The most personal detail Katherine had ever disclosed to

her mother was when her first period started, and even then, it had all been in some strange code. With Loveday, she felt she never had to qualify or edit anything. Even when Loveday said the wrong thing, it turned out to be the right thing after all, and at times, Katherine felt so confident about their friendship that she would take it for granted and behave more like a daughter with Loveday than she did with her own mother. Occasionally, Beth saw it and resented it, but if it wasn't Beth feeling usurped, it was Katherine feeling deprived and so sometimes, Loveday just couldn't win and on such occasions she would always think how fortunate it was that she had enough love to go round.

Between the two women now they had consumed the best part of a bottle of wine, albeit from different labels either side of the dividing wall that split their homes. Loveday was a naturally self-disciplined drinker and had only managed a single glass before Katherine, in the height of laziness and a slightly slurred voice, had telephoned to ask the favour. The telephone was possibly the only source of dispute between them and even that was light-hearted. If Loveday ever wanted to talk to Katherine, she refrained from the phone and preferred instead to walk the two steps out of her front door, turn to the right, and knock, and she could not, for the life of her, see why Katherine couldn't do the same.

Putting in a new front entrance had been the only structural change needed to make the larger cottage into two smaller ones when Katherine and Johnny had bought half of it eleven years ago. At the time, Katherine had been a little doubtful about the wisdom of moving next door to your best friend's mother, especially into a cottage that still had interconnecting doors and rooms that had Beth stamped all over them, but it could not have been a happier experience, to the point that dividing the large garden by planting a hedge down the middle had seemed an almost hostile gesture. The only time it ever seemed a strange turn-out for the books was when Beth said something like, 'What have you done to my old bedroom cupboard? I hope you checked the drawers before you ripped it out,' and she only did that when she was feeling dethroned. Anyway, she was married now and was mistress of another kingdom.

One of the more surprising advantages to the arrangement was that Loveday felt so entirely relaxed in Katherine's space that whenever she was in it and the occasion demanded it, she opened right up. Her honesty was infectious and she somehow managed to encourage others to do the same, without letting introspection run away with them at the same time. Many a winter evening had been passed pleasantly soul-baring in her company, and the best bit was that it always ended on an up.

She had always been public property as far as her daughter's friends were concerned, but she and Katherine now worked without reference to anyone else, and Loveday suspected they would probably have found each other somehow anyway, regardless.

The car chugged on, and Loveday caught a yawn out of the corner of her eye.

'Close your eyes if you want to. I'll poke you when we get there.'

'It's the windscreen wipers, they're having a hypnotic effect on me,' Katherine said, running her hands through her hair to wake herself up.

'No, it's not, it's the wine. Your lips are burgundy.'

'Are they?' asked Katherine, flipping down the sun-visor and grimacing into the mirror.

Loveday kept her eyes on the road but as she heard the

squeak squeak squeak of Katherine's finger being rubbed frantically across her teeth, she remembered that it was Beth who had the physical confidence, not Katherine, and she had been wrong to tease.

'They're not really, you look lovely,' she said.

'No I don't, I look awful.'

'You don't give yourself any credit, do you? But perhaps that's your attraction, that you're totally oblivious of it.'

'Come off it!' laughed Katherine, displaying the kind of basic realism that Beth certainly did not possess, the sort that allows you to laugh at yourself for wanting something so transparently useless as prettiness. And that *is* what makes her attractive, thought Loveday, taking a quick glance at her passenger and wishing Katherine could sometimes see herself through other people's eyes.

After fifteen minutes of silence, both of them spoke at once.

'You first,' said Loveday. They had been in the car for three-quarters of an hour already but the conversation had been bobbing around aimlessly.

'I was just going to say this is really good of you. I'm sure you'd much rather be holed up in Tremewan playing your lovely piano than driving in the drizzle up the A38, but I really appreciate it. I must speak to Johnny about this car arrangement.'

'Thank you. I applaud your manners. But that *isn't* what you were going to say.'

'Isn't it?' Katherine had a tendency, and she wasn't the only one, to assume that Loveday always spoke with the gift of insight. Beth claimed it was just a 'hippy pose' of her mother's, this wise sage bit she often did, but then Loveday would just say that daughters were allowed to cast aspersions.

'You think I haven't noticed, don't you?' Loveday laughed.

'Noticed what?' Katherine was playing the innocent.

'That those seriously under-used batteries of yours marked "sexual responses" have just received a medium-sized charge from the sound of Patrick's voice down the telephone.'

'Rubbish!'

'Not rubbish!'

'Oh God, is it that obvious?'

'Only to someone who knows you.'

'Oh well, that's okay then! Medium-sized, did you say?'

'Well, it *was* down the phone. Whether it will be anything more than that when you actually see him I can't say, but a wise man would put his money on—'

The rest of her sentence was consumed by an exaggerated wail from Katherine, but when Loveday took her hand, with its usual array of Celtic rings, off the wheel and quickly squeezed her passenger's knee, the knee withdrew noticeably. It was one thing to half admit to yourself that there may be some sexual mileage in an unexpected visit from a previous lover, but to have someone else spell it out for you was an altogether different matter. Conspiratorial encouragement to indulge in extra-marital sex was not something that sat comfortably with Katherine, not even when that encouragement came from Loveday.

Her driver was not to be so easily deterred. 'I don't envy you contemplating a possible sexual adventure with someone other than Johnny after so long, even if that someone is Patrick.'

'That's enough conjecture, thank you. Anyway, who said anything about sex?'

Katherine wanted the subject closed. She hadn't got round to discussing the intriguing possibilities of a life minus Johnny with herself yet, let alone with anyone else.

'What is Patrick doing back here now when he is due over in December for the party anyway? He only had to wait another few months,' Loveday persisted, with a sudden sense that it was her duty to sort out Katherine's mood before the girl unleashed herself on Patrick.

'I did ask, but I can't remember if he replied, in fact, I'm sure he didn't. I hope this trip isn't in place of the other one. I'm not going to the millennium party if he's not.'

'Oh yes you are. Trial separation or not, you owe it to Johnny to be there, more so than Patrick or Beth do.'

'No, I don't. I don't owe him anything. And the guest list was originally only supposed to have our names on it anyway. The four of us, and any partners and children we had picked up on the way, raising a glass to each other over a dinner table somewhere, that's what we said – not squashing ourselves into an unfamiliar hotel with two hundred strangers.'

'Really? That doesn't sound too gripping. Anyway, they won't be strangers. I've seen the guest list and if I know at least half, then you must know more – and Johnny has sold all the tickets word of mouth, hasn't he?'

'Johnny has a very big mouth.'

'Well, you can't kiss goodbye to the twentieth century at home over a plate of pasta now, can you?'

'Why not?'

'Well, because you can't. Because it's a milestone, a turning point, an Event.'

'I know,' Katherine sighed. 'It seems as if it's been hovering at the back of my mind my entire life. When I was young, I used to try and work out how old I would be in the year 2000. Thirty-five seemed *so* old. Did you ever do that?'

'I was born at the end of the war, remember – the wrong side of 1950. That kind of fantasy only belongs to people

your age and younger, to those who know for sure they
might stand a chance of doing something exciting – having
children, getting seriously promoted, travelling the world.
Me? What could I have fantasised about? Collecting an
early pension? Having my grandchildren for the weekend?
I'm old, Katherine, old . . .'

'You're fifty-five.'

'I'm teasing you, you sweet child. You're the one with
the hang-up about your age, not me.' Loveday said it
affectionately, but they fell into silence again, the older
woman thinking that perhaps she ought to make up her
mind just how she would spend the moment, to avoid
offending anyone at the last minute.

Katherine was off on a more introspective tangent altogether.
What man or woman of her age *hadn't* held the year
2000 up as a personal deadline for as long as they could
remember? She vowed that when she got home, she would go
up into the loft and find that sentimental and embarrassing
scrap of paper she'd written on as a thirteen-year-old, and
tear it up. *Life Plan*, it said on the sealed envelope. What
would a thirteen-year-old know about life? Katherine had
broken the seal only a few days ago, out of curiosity for
something long forgotten. The handwriting had been eerily
similar to Hattie's . . .

'*By the year 2000 I want to be happily married with two
children, a boy and a girl, and a cottage in the country.
I want to be a famous author, writing my third book. I
do NOT want to be like Mum and I do NOT want my
husband to be like Dad (well, just a bit maybe). Signed,
Katherine Jamieson, aged 13.*'

Her first book had yet to materialise, let alone her third,
the only printed words she sold lately being easy-to-read
articles for glossy home interior magazines about the cream

of Cornish houses. No book, no big deal, but no marriage? The happy family should have been the easiest fulfilment of all, and she hadn't even managed that.

'I loathe being thirty-five,' she told Loveday suddenly.

'Do you?'

'It's an awful age. Not young, not old. Too old to really change, too young to feel you don't have to. We're trapped in the middle of this millennium nightmare, us Thirty-somethings.'

'Pah! You'll have forgotten all about it by March.'

'You wish!' replied Katherine, and went back to her contemplation.

She and Johnny had taken to spending their New Year's Eves in the public bar of the Miners, Tremewan's only pub. Most had turned out to be better by far than the inescapable black tie dinner in someone's soulless dining room followed by a few weak rounds of charades, but for some reason last year, on the eve of 1999, the whole night had been deeply and curiously depressing, despite the fact that almost the entire adult population of the village had turned up at the pub in fancy dress. At the time, she had blamed it on the increasing strain of keeping a public face on a private disaster, the floundering of her marriage. Now though, with the year 2000 not exactly staring her in the face but more cramming itself up her nose, she could identify the problem more accurately. 1999 had been her own deep-rooted self-imposed deadline to get her life in order. Even a year ago she knew it was destined to fall way short of her expectations, and that was before one of her achievements – 'Happily married' – had been reclaimed.

'Do you know,' Loveday began, grating the gears as she changed down to keep pace with a lorry crawling up one of the last hills before Plymouth; her voice had just changed up a gear, 'I used to wonder when you all came to me at the weekends as fresh-faced nineteen-year-olds just who was sleeping with whom.'

She had been thinking, during the silence, of how her life had come to be so inexorably mixed up with her daughter's friends. How many other mothers became a surrogate parent for the children of complete strangers just because their daughter happened to bring all her friends with her every time she came home? She often thought how odd it was that Katherine and Johnny had in time become so much a part of her life, buying half her cottage, tucking their own children into bed in the same room that Beth used to sleep in, living in the space that she was so familiar with, making it their own. And Katherine was now her own friend, not just her daughter's friend, and sometimes, guiltily, she felt closer to Katherine than she did to Beth.

'Who was sleeping with whom? Even I don't know that for sure,' Katherine lied with a smile. She nearly said that since they were all constantly sleeping with each other, they had long since lost count, but then she remembered the often overlooked fact that Loveday was, after all, Beth's mother, and some things – your daughter's promiscuity being one of them – should be sacred. Joke about one's own sexual generosity by all means, but leave daughters out of it. If in the future anyone ever found it amusing to talk about Hattie like that . . .

'I especially wondered who Patrick was involved with,' said Loveday more seriously, still keen to keep him at the forefront of the conversation for Katherine's sake. The more she could demystify him in the last few miles, the better.

'Why do you say that?'

'Because he always seemed keen to try and promote such an intensely sexual presence, and I thought it might possibly have been felt by people who perhaps ought not to feel it.'

'Like who?'

'Well, not you for a start!' Loveday laughed in response to the alarm in Katherine's voice. 'I know both you and Beth have done more than merely feel it, you've told me that before, and that's not what I meant at all. No, it's just . . .'

'Just what?'

One of the down sides to being able to say anything to Loveday was that you also had to be prepared to hear anything too, and Katherine, just at this frail moment, wasn't sure she was.

'Just Dido,' said Loveday.

Katherine nodded but said nothing, so Loveday carried on.

'I know she's his step-sister, but they always seemed to have something much more than that between them.'

'Mmm . . .'

It was more an ambiguous noise than an answer, but it was enough to make Loveday leave the subject alone. It said: 'I'm not sure about this, but I do know I don't want to think about it,' and Loveday decided she didn't want to dwell on it either. It was hardly incest – Patrick and Dido shared no blood – but at the same time, they had been brought up together as brother and sister, they had called the same two people Mum and Dad, and they even looked alike, with their thick dark hair, long limbs and slightly exotic air. No, it was all too involved, even for her broad mind. It should have been a simple question of: Why shouldn't they? And yet for some reason, it wasn't simple at all. There was a big *Private – Keep Out* sign pinned to the whole thing, and that was what made it somehow more discomfiting.

She forced her mind away from Dido and back to Katherine, and then inevitably to Beth, and of course Johnny and Patrick. Not so long ago it used to seem to her as if the four of them barely existed without each other.

'Quite what the landlord thought of you all I can't imagine.'

'Uh?'

'Can you remember the first time Beth brought you all home from University? Hallowe'en in your first term, October 1982 – you can't have known each other much longer than a few weeks. We went to the Miners. You only had enough money between you for three pints, but instead of ordering enough halves to go round, you bought a single pint, and sat there sharing it until it was empty, and then when that was gone, you all had another, and then another. Patrick was rolling little cigarettes for you all, in twos, and you were passing them round like joints. I was mesmerised. I was thinking, who are these people that are so like my daughter?'

Katherine jumped at the chance to talk about University. 'It was as if we'd always known each other, right from the start. When I first saw Patrick, sitting on the floor at the back of a lecture theatre, with his legs stretching across the carpet, I looked at him and thought, I know you. It was the same with Beth. We just immediately realised we had found something special. Fantastic, uncanny.'

'Good times?'

'Untouchable. I'd give anything for those years back again.'

'Even Hattie and Seth?' If there was one thing Loveday found repellent with the four of them, her own daughter included, it was their tendency to cling to the past the moment the present became difficult.

Katherine let out an okay-you-win snort.

'Well then,' said Loveday 'you can't have everything.' And, pulling up with a lurch alongside the taxis outside Plymouth station and practically yanking the handbrake out of its socket, she added with an intuition that was entirely lost on her passenger: 'I wonder if anyone has ever told Patrick that?'

But Katherine was already halfway out the car, racing towards the wet but unmistakable hunched figure.

'God, it's good to see you,' said Patrick into her hair which smelt of shampoo and rain. They held on to their hug as he repeated the same words. 'God, it really is good to see you.'

'Not half as good as it is to see you,' replied Katherine. 'Or feel you, come to that,' she laughed as his squeeze pressed her chin even further into his shoulderblade and the shudder of his relief reverberated through her coat.

Chapter 2

Patrick Seal slept for the first time in twenty-four hours, comatose under Seth Bates' duvet in a bedroom of the cottage he had known since his teens, his consolation at reaching Cornwall, and Katherine in particular, washing through him like some kind of unconscious therapy. When Loveday had finally said her traditionally lengthy goodnights, he had been alone with Katherine barely fifteen minutes before exhaustion overcame him, but they had been enormously gratifying minutes in which he felt no pressure to explain his surprise presence, nor any flicker of that stilted effort that usually comes with reunion. He was too far gone for his exhaustion to translate itself into immediate sleep and so he had spent the night staring at the luminous stars on Seth's ceiling and, for once, not thinking of anything very much.

Now, in the middle of the following afternoon, that serenity had left him and he was dreaming of his dead father throwing a stone into the centre of a stagnant pond. In the dream, his father was on the safe side, having crossed the water before the bridge collapsed, and a disconnected mix of family and friends were stranded on the other, trying to figure out if and how they should do it themselves.

Beth Ross, who as yet had no idea that Patrick was back in Cornwall but was feeling unusually buoyant all the same, pulled into her own drive six miles away and parked haphazardly behind her husband's car instead of pulling up to the left of it like she usually did. Just once, about five years ago, Evan Ross had found himself blocked in by her which had sent him into a disproportionate frenzy. Their marriage then was in its infancy, young enough for his pompous mini-lecture to be amusing, and she still naive enough to come home later and chalk parking lots on the shiny black tarmac, a joke he hadn't entirely shared. Since then, the seemingly insignificant matter of where she left her car could tip the balance between marital harmony and discord.

It had been a long and trying day and she wanted to be inside. As Evan had reminded her before she left, organising the raffle at the school's Autumn Fayre wasn't exactly in her contract of employment as deputy head teacher, but as she had then reminded him, she had done the honours for the last seven years as a mere teacher so she could hardly sniff at it now she had been recognised for her dedication. 'Come with me,' she'd said when he began to complain, but he had just snorted.

As she swung open the car door it bashed against her newly placed collection of terracotta urns, purchased as part of her continuing fruitless efforts to try and stamp some personality on her home. How a few feeble tubs were going to compensate for the overall staggering lack of identity of 4, Lander Parc, she didn't know, but at least she was still trying. When they had been house-hunting six years ago, she'd initially refused to even view the place. '"A three-bedroomed executive residence on one of Truro's most sought-after private estates"?' she'd read out. 'No thanks!' But they'd bought it all the same, because Evan said it would be easier to sell on.

Her argument that since they were lucky enough to live in a county where they could choose to look out on to almost any view they could think of – yachts sailing up an estuary, majestic revolutions of state-of-the-art windmills, stupendous cliffs and immense seas, or even a simple field full of cows – they would be stupid to hole themselves up in a house that looked out on to more identical houses, all of which could have been anywhere in Britain, had fallen on utterly deaf ears.

As she stepped in and out of the pots to reach the front door she hoped he wasn't watching. It would be just the kind of thing to spark off another one of his sermons.

She was pleased to hear his voice on the phone, guessing that he would be standing by his desk in the sitting room looking out on to their sad excuse for a back garden, fiddling with one of his hideous executive toys while he spoke. It gave her a little hit to put her head round the door and find him doing exactly that. One of the good things about their marriage was Evan's inability to surprise. He hadn't done anything remotely impulsive since the first time they met, and having grown up with Loveday for a mother, whose ways were eccentric if not erratic, Beth found it made a nice change.

Seven and a half years ago, she had walked into his High Street office on a whim. The words EVAN ROSS – SOLICITOR painted neatly in the centre of the gleaming square window surrounded by the healthiest plants she'd ever seen had made her feel that inside would be a man who would see her right. Evan had viewed her from behind the plants and despite acknowledging that he hadn't yet managed to shake off the last woman who had turned up without appointment and that had been three years ago, he buzzed his receptionist to say that if the woman in the short denim culotte dress needed any advice, she could be shown straight to his office as he had no further appointments until noon. He'd then scurried behind his large oak desk in anticipation of an interesting consultation, and he hadn't been disappointed.

The very first words Beth had spoken to her husband were: 'I like your plants.' She hadn't meant to say anything half as absurd, but the sight of him, leaning casually back in his leather chair with his hands clamped behind his head had, for some reason, put into her mind the startling possibility of something more than a professional interest between them. Evan had felt it too, and it had been just as big a shock to him.

'Well, it's not often a woman tells me that,' he'd replied. 'I like them too now. I was thinking of getting rid of them so I could see out, but if they're going to attract beautiful strangers in off the street, then maybe I won't.'

Beth had smiled, looking young for her twenty-seven years, but she hadn't blushed, which threw him a little.

'Anyway, plants aside,' he went on, 'how can I help you?'

'Um, well, this might sound rather peculiar, but is there any way you could draw me up a will before this afternoon?' He told her afterwards it had been her soft apologetic laugh that had really done it.

'Oh, but dying would be so unfair when we've only just met.'

'I'm not planning to, but I'm doing a charity parachute jump at three, and I was just thinking of the possibility that it might go wrong when I passed your office and saw your plants.'

Looking at her, refusing to blend in with the muted apricot and grey mottled wallpaper of his office, Evan had been consumed with a familiar fear that he was missing out. He was only then in his mid-thirties, but his life was middle-aged, the devil-may-care attitude of the young having left him long ago. Even when he *had* possessed it, if indeed he ever had, it had taken a responsible shape involving investment gambles with his own money. He could possibly count the risk he was taking with his current mistress, but only in terms of the damage it could do him in the community if news of the affair ever got out. Messing around with the wife of a senior partner in Cornwall's biggest estate agency had become something of a liability, and the only thing that was stopping him wriggling away from her was the unlikelihood of sex coming from any other quarter.

Studying Beth, he felt he was being presented with a chance to connect with a world he should already know, and so he'd taken immediate action.

'There's one condition. If you do survive, would you consider celebrating by having dinner with me?'

'Okay,' she smiled. 'But don't bother about the will. I suddenly feel invincible.'

He hadn't been half as alluring since, except maybe during that first meal, but at least you knew where you were with him, and Beth certainly liked to know where she was. It was something he delighted in, her all-too-evident desire for stability, and he would bring it up with tedious regularity whenever he felt like having a go at Loveday.

'The problem with your mother,' he'd say, 'is that she has always failed to see how her hippy methods have forced you to be the exact opposite of a free spirit. A child has to rebel against the parent, and you have done it by joining the real world. The fact that your childhood has left you craving a secure and routine existence as an adult is now her problem, not yours. She can't bear to see you leading an ordinary life.'

'I don't crave security,' Beth would protest. 'Or routine.'
He might have been right but his words implied far too much
criticism and she would argue with him until he pulled her
tiny body towards him, wrapped her in his six foot four
frame and said, 'So exactly why *have* you married me then?'
and she'd say, 'Because I want your money,' and they would
invariably end up in bed, or on the stairs, or once – and she'd
been genuinely surprised when he hadn't told her to get off
– the kitchen table.

Her thoughts were interrupted by the sound of Evan
putting the phone down, but it rang again immediately, and
so she went back to them. She realised it had been some time
since any room, let alone the kitchen, had seen such wild sexual activity, although there was no need to search for reasons
why. The incessant ticking of her biological clock, which had
been getting louder and louder over the last two years, was
too intrusive for any kind of uninhibited lovemaking – it
seemed a waste to do it on a Monday or Tuesday if she was
going to ovulate on the Wednesday, and she didn't want to
satiate her man at the start of the month when she would
need him to be hungry a week or so later, or at least she
could see that is how Evan could view it if he wanted to.

As she clicked the kettle on and threw a peppermint tea
bag into her favourite mug, she resolved, not for the first
time, to try and somehow bring an element of abandonment,
of sex for sex's sake, back into their marriage. Lately, when
she remembered the early days and how they would make
love wherever and whenever the mood took them, she
would sometimes forget she was thinking about Evan and
assume she was remembering some other ex-boyfriend and
she would start feeling unfaithful until she realised it had
been with Evan after all, and then a different kind of guilt
would set in.

Not that their whole marriage was based on sexual compatibility. The initial interest for her had been the feeling that she had attracted the attention of a full-blown adult, someone who was on his second mortgage and whose friends had, in more than one case, already paid theirs off. Ironically, what Evan had fallen for in her was the complete opposite. He loved his little girl who forgot to fill in her cheque stubs and put oil in the car. A bit of a problem that, thought Beth, now that the little girl has grown up.

She knew the obstacles that stood in the way were altogether of her own making, and sprang entirely from her desire to be pregnant, and that Evan would be more than happy to give the whole idea of babies up in favour of more regular sex, but could they not have both?

They could at least try, she thought, dipping her tea bag in and out of the mug by its little paper tab and being soothed by the minty steam in her face. If only he would begin to discuss it. She wandered into the sitting room.

'Sorry about that,' he said into the phone, not sounding sorry in the slightest. He must be talking to one of his less lucrative clients who had just asked him to do a favour. It didn't look to her like a vital phone call. Perhaps she would slip her hand inside his shirt . . .

'No, Monday is out too,' he said flatly. It sounded as if he really didn't want anything to do with the person on the other end of the phone at all. Her other hand was on the waistband of his pristine jeans. When she had first moved in with him, she'd tried to coax him out of his habit of ironing them, but his addiction to creases was just too strong.

'Listen, I'll get her to phone you when she's got a moment, okay? But we're pretty much tied up this week.'

Beth was just beginning to undo one of his shirt buttons

when she suddenly clicked. *The phone call is for me. Who wants me? Why isn't he letting me speak?* She stopped fiddling – she could tell it wasn't going to lead anywhere anyway, he was feeling extremely tense, and to be honest, she was feeling silly – and she put her hand up to take the phone.

'Got to go, 'bye,' he said hurriedly, putting the receiver down before she got a chance to retrieve it.

'Was that for me?' Her peppy mood had evaporated.

'More you than me, that's for sure. It was Katherine.' He had never made any bones about the fact that her friends, or at least the ones she had made before she'd met him, didn't interest him.

'Katherine? I only spoke to her yesterday. What did she want?'

'To ask us over to supper tomorrow night because Patrick has taken it upon himself to turn up unannounced, and she thought you would like to see him.' He was trying hard to sound casually monotone but failed. They both knew Patrick left him feeling anything but casual and in the light of this, it might have been more useful if Beth had contained her excitement.

'Patrick? What's he doing back now? We were expecting him in December! Is he here, in Cornwall? Why didn't you hand the phone over?' Beth could hear the little voice at the back of her head telling her to cool down, but it was being drowned by a louder one shouting, 'Patrick is back, Patrick is back!'

'Would you like me to move the furniture back so you can perform a cartwheel? For goodness sake Beth, you've been spending too much time with your eleven-year-olds. We can't go anyway.'

'Why?'

'I've booked a table at La Tienda's, that new restaurant in Lemon Street, the one I pointed out to you last week.'

'Unbook it then.' Nowadays, she very rarely told him to do anything. She'd tried it a little at the start of their marriage, but his subtle moulding of her had flattened her spirit.

'I can't do that. I may well be using the place for client entertaining and I don't want to mess the new owners around before I've even stepped foot inside the place. Anyway, what's the big rush to see Patrick? You've managed without him for three years.'

It was interesting that Evan knew how long it had been since his last visit.

'Three years and two months actually.'

'I should go and live with him if I were you, then you wouldn't have to keep count.'

'For God's sake, Evan,' Beth shouted as contemptuously as she could. 'For a grown man, you can be so pubescent,' and she dumped her hot tea just where she knew it would annoy him on the mahogany surface of his gleaming desk, next to but purposefully not on, a little china coaster his mother had given them, and went upstairs to run a bath, freeing her hair from its one thick plait as she went.

In the bedroom, waiting for the reproduction Victorian free-standing white tub in their en suite bathroom to fill, Beth flumped across their quilted King Size throw and picked up the phone from Evan's side of the bed. Calling Katherine would be a fair interim compromise, especially if she rearranged things to suit them both.

'Apologies Chris, one moment,' she heard Evan's voice say from the other end. 'Darling, would you be an angel and keep the line free? Sorry about that, Chris, she has a weakness for phoning her friends while she's in the bath . . .'

She hoped the force with which she slammed the receiver back into its cradle was enough to tell 'Chris', whoever s/he was, that 'Darling' was not an appropriate term just at this moment.

The warmth of the bath water made it easier for her to be less cross somehow, even though she felt she had plenty of reason to be as cross as she liked. If there was one thing guaranteed to produce unpleasant behaviour from Evan it was the prospect of spending time with her University friends. He could have coped if the invitation had come from just Katherine and Johnny, or even, believe it or not, just Patrick, but the combination of all three was just too threatening. En masse, their friendship was just too impenetrable.

She'd realised it from the very start of their relationship, before they'd married and after she'd made the mistake of believing that Evan could happily join in one of their famous impromptu picnics at Landurgan Gardens. She'd lost count of the number of times she, Katherine, Johnny and Patrick had been there as a foursome and eaten pasties in the centre of the laurel maze before going down to the small beach to skim pebbles across the flat sea. It always had to be maze, picnic, beach, in that order, because that was the way they had done it the first time and it was tradition, and she had just assumed Evan would go along with all that. *Wrong.* He had been disgusted to learn that none of them had ever set foot inside Landurgan House itself, and even more outraged when they agreed in loud unison that they had no desire to. Instead of letting it drop, he had insisted on telling them all how 'architecturally significant' it was, how its entrance front was Palladian and how elegant the cantilever staircase in the Main Hall was, but they had all laughed at him and tried to lose him in the maze. The awful thing was that she had been the instigator.

Immerse yourself in these decadent bubbles and surface a more tolerant woman, she advised herself. That way, you can have your cake and eat it. Down she slid, holding her nose and closing her eyes, her long black hair that took an age to dry swirling around her pale face. Ah, sweet liberation from foul mood! Coming up, she shook her head like a spaniel and sent a corkscrew of vanilla scented bathwater hurling across the room, hitting him with it full on.

'So how did the Hallowe'en party go, pumpkin? Who made the best witch? I've heard you call the headmistress an old hag so many times, I would hardly consider it to be a fair competition.'

Evan's pale pink cotton shirt now sported a trail of wet patches. He was obviously choosing to ignore the argument. It wasn't often she was rude to him, but when she was, he invariably dealt with it in the way a parent would deal with a toddler tantrum, by disregarding it, not lending it credence. His other response was to get so angry Beth would be forced to apologise. She could never be sure whether she preferred to be irritated or frightened by him but accepted that it was usually the alternative to whatever was being delivered at the time.

'Hallowe'en isn't for another fortnight. It was an Autumn Fayre, and it was okay, thank you. The children enjoyed it anyway.'

'Excellent. And did their favourite deputy head support the worthy cause and buy up the entire contents of the cake stall?' His mother had weaned him on sugar, Beth was certain. Sometimes, it was the only thing he responded to.

'There was only a dead hedgehog left by the time I

got to it, but it was nicely iced, so I bought it anyway.' Oh, she thought, I've just made a joke. I must have forgiven him.

'Let me at this delicacy,' he said, his head full of row upon row of chocolate buttons set in a quagmire of butter cream. What she had actually managed to buy were four flat, hard and overdone muesli squares made by Year 4 as part of their Healthy Eating project. 'Where is it?'

'In the back of the car,' she mumbled, disappearing under the water again, just catching his parting words.

'Which reminds me, can you move it when you get out, please? You practically parked it right on top of those ridiculous pots which shouldn't be there anyway.'

It was at that moment that Beth decided she would be seeing Patrick the following evening after all, regardless of what Evan might or might not be doing.

In the other half of Loveday's cottage, in the room that was once Beth's playroom and Johnny's study but was now Hattie and Seth's den, Katherine put the phone down and made a face at Patrick. She had warned him before she'd even made the call that if Evan answered, the chances of actually getting to speak to Beth were minimal.

'He hasn't improved with age then?' he said.

'Sadly not. He seems to get worse. He came up with a bogus dinner-date this time.'

Patrick lit a cigarette and flopped on to the children's bean bags in an irritatingly adolescent way. 'Poor Beth,' he muttered.

'You don't sound as if you really mean that.'

'Oh, I do. It's just that everyone else's problems seem too far away to touch me, that's all.'

Katherine glanced at him, and he did indeed look far

away. It was six o'clock on Saturday evening, nearly twenty-four hours after their hug at Plymouth station, and she was having withdrawal symptoms. By the time they'd got home last night and downed the remnants of the wine, all either of them had wanted to do was to sleep. Katherine had gone out like a light, worn out by her own imagination, but Patrick had lain there in the next room, in his single bed under a duvet of bright blue boats, staring at the ceiling, too drained even to wonder what was possessing him. Consequently, this morning, just as Katherine had woken with a suppressed expectancy, so Patrick had fallen into a jet-lagged hibernation which had lasted the entire day, a day in which Katherine felt she had been on a considerable personal journey.

Her realisation, which had come in the car on the way to Plymouth, that she would actually rather like an interlude with Patrick for old time's sake, had been something of a revelation and she had been wishing ever since that it had never even entered her mind because now it was refusing to make room for anything else.

Patrick's day-long sleep-in had made matters worse, prolonging her agitation. She had tried willing him to get up and do something off-putting like spend hours in the loo, or cough into his cigarette, or smell or something, so that she could then have had a quiet laugh at herself and got on with behaving her age. But the longer he stayed upstairs, in bed, presumably naked, the more she found herself picturing her own body next to his.

Her day had verged on the obsessive. She had done the washing up, ironed the children's school clothes, then rewritten part of an article for a rural living magazine, all of which took her to eleven o'clock. She'd had a bath, washed her hair and played around with a few clothes trying to decide which old shirt looked the most effortless. She had made an even more exhausting effort to look busier than normal, as if being on her own on a Saturday was a god-given opportunity to catch up, nothing to worry about or sympathise over. At three o'clock, she had put her head round Seth's bedroom door and studied Patrick's dark curls motionless against the blue pillow, imagining herself crawling in beside him and sliding her arms around his warm body. At five past three, she had pulled the door quietly to again and gone downstairs.

Over a lonely coffee, the only noise punctuating the quiet of the cottage being a gentle snore coming from under the blue boat duvet, she had finally given in. She closed her eyes and just before sinking indulgently into a memory she knew would only make matters worse, she had the sense to remind herself of the difference between love and lust.

The first time she and Patrick had made love had been in the second year at Tamar University, 1984, in a typically dingy student dump in a cheap but green part of Plymouth. Where Johnny and Beth had been that weekend she couldn't remember, but it wouldn't have been significant then anyway since none of them had any claims on each other until halfway through their final year. At any rate, it was undoubtedly the absence of the other two that had triggered the mutual hunger she and Patrick had discovered.

There had been a growing suggestiveness during the day which had ended with the two of them, in yellow paint-spattered clothes from trying to cheer up a dismal kitchen, eating kebabs lying on her bed watching a Richard Gere film – or was it Harrison Ford? There was nothing provocative about being in her room – her television was the only one that worked and her bed was the only double in the flat so it had become something of a communal space for all four of them. But that night, there had been a new mood between them. At exactly the same time that she had been charged with a desire to touch him, he had suddenly and assuredly put his hand around the back of her neck and flicked her hair out from under the collar of her man's shirt to find and stroke the warm skin of her nape. The confidence with which he had done it was electrifying, like he'd known not only that she'd wanted him to seduce her, but also exactly how to go about it. And yet there had been none of the seducer about him either, nothing too smooth or too calculating.

With their eyes still fixed on the screen, she had responded to his touch by singlehandedly undoing her own buttons to reveal her naked breasts. The fumbling and embarrassment that comes with first-time inexperience just didn't happen. She'd found her buttons, and he'd found her breasts, he'd let his fingers explore her soft and then harder nipple and she'd let her fingers trace the seam of his pocket, his inner leg, and eventually, the hard line of his zip. Afraid they would break the spell if they looked at each other, they'd kept their eyes determinedly focused ahead, but eventually, when the desire to see what they were each touching became too much, they'd turned and kissed, and made love with the flicker of the film over their shoulders. Whether the actual deed was as perfect as the recollection she wasn't sure, but it had certainly been good enough to repeat a few memorable times over the course of the next year.

By the time Patrick did surface at half past five, dressed exactly as he had been the night before in clothes so wrinkled they made Katherine suspect that he had in fact not been naked after all, she had been verging on the jittery.

'What do you fancy for supper?' she asked him for the sake of something to say when his bleary-eyed and unshaven face had finally appeared. Johnny would have

51

said, 'Apart from you?' Please don't say that, she pleaded silently, please don't.

'Don't you mean breakfast?' Patrick screwed up his face as if the glow from Katherine's one table lamp was too much for him and she laughed nervously.

'Your body clock is out. It's practically dark out there. Wine then, or coffee – do you want coffee?' She felt quite ridiculous. *His* body clock? What about hers?

'What year is it?' he asked lazily, pulling out the carver's chair.

'1999, I should think. Are you properly awake?'

'I meant the wine. I was trying to be Evan. Sorry, I'm still too tired to try and make jokes.'

'Oh well, that's a 1996 Vin de Pays de L'Ardeche.'

'Chateau Spar?'

'Chateau Sainsbury's.'

'Great, I'll have some.'

'Anything else?'

'Yes, a proper conversation please.'

The speed with which fantasy had flown out the window to be replaced by a new set of realities marching in was quite something. He'd needed a chat. Not nostalgic sex, not even a naked but platonic hug, but a chat. Where was that famous sexual intensity Loveday had mentioned in the car last night? He was a lost soul with jet lag.

'Have some bread and cheese. You haven't eaten anything yet.'

'I'm not sure I can.'

'Well, you ought to.'

'I ought to do a lot of things.'

'Mmm. I suppose you could start the proper conversation by telling me why you're here.'

Patrick put on a helpless face. 'I'm not sure I can do that either.'

'Course you can, if you try.'

'Oh, you know what the States can be like sometimes – in your face, too frantic. I had some free time and I just suddenly decided I'd rather be in Cornwall.'

'Oh, yeah?' said Katherine, cutting him a chunk of brie and ripping the end off a French stick. 'As you do.'

Patrick just laughed.

'So, am I allowed to guess?' she asked.

'No. It really isn't a game.'

'But it *is* a woman? Yes?'

'Probably,' he said. 'But I'd really like you to accept the lamentably pathetic explanation I've just given, and leave it at that.'

'Would you? I mean, do you really want that? Because that's the sort of thing I say when I really want someone to keep at it.'

'I really want that.'

'Okay, sorry. I'll try not to quiz you further. I can wait.'

There was a small pause before Katherine spoke again, knowing that if she left it any longer, it could be ages before he opened up.

'Is it Dido?'

It was as if she had tapped the fragile framework that was keeping him together with too clumsy a hammer.

'What makes you say that?' he asked quickly and cautiously.

'I don't know. I just thought it might be. I know how she affects you.'

'What do you mean, affects me? She's my sister. Sisters don't affect you. They just irritate you.'

His defensive tone reminded her exactly why she and

Johnny were no longer under the same roof, and she nearly screamed something angry at him about bloody men and their bloody secrets.

'You're right. Let's leave it,' she sighed.

'Oh, okay. She came over, decided to move in with me, didn't even ask. I thought that was a bit much, that's all. So I've fucked off for a bit, to let her make her own life without relying on mine.'

It was Katherine's turn to wince. 'Oh.' Now what? she thought, because she knew there was more.

'So, I really don't want to think about Dido. She's far too complicated. I'm after a simple life.'

'Aren't we all? 'she asked softly, going over to him and taking his head in her hands thinking what a different kind of embrace it was to the one she'd imagined. He looked so weary as he leaned his forehead against her breast.

'If it helps any, we've all pretty much run aground lately,' she added.

'Thanks, but it doesn't,' he said, putting an end to any idea of soul-searching she might have had, and sending her in the direction of the telephone instead. What a pity Beth hadn't answered it instead of her bully of a husband.

Chapter 3

In Hoboken, New Jersey, on the third floor of a five-floor apartment block, Dido Seal was sweeping the debris from Patrick's steel-topped kitchen table. If she was going to be without him, then she was going to be without his junk too, and the force with which she pushed a pile of papers into a large trash-can liner before dumping it ceremoniously in one of the many empty cupboards summed up her resolve utterly.

His absence on Thursday night hadn't felt in the least bit significant. He could have been anywhere – chasing a story, seeing friends, at the office. By Friday evening, she'd suddenly had the presence of mind to check for his passport which he kept in his bedside table: it had gone. By lunchtime today, the phone had rung at least four times before it had finally been him, a string of cloned weekend editors all demanding urgent copy and then an indignant phone call from Chelsea Clinton's office. It was only after the third 'Where the hell is he?' that the bubble of fury began inside her.

By the time it really was him on the phone, she had lapped herself on the circuit of reactions – calm, panic, anger, calm, panic and then anger again.

'*Cornwall?*' she had repeated in disbelief, gripping the receiver with one hand and clutching the short fringe of her cropped dark hair with the other. 'To be with Katherine? She needs you because she's split up with Johnny?'

'Yes, sorry. Last-minute decision.' Using Katherine as an excuse for his departure had only just occurred to him.

'Patrick, what are you saying?'

'That I probably won't be back until after the party. I'll sort everything out from this end, like apartment payments and work. You won't have to worry about that.'

'The party as in millennium party? Come on, that's nearly three months away.'

'It's October already, it's hardly worth me coming back. I can do everything I need to do from here.'

'Including explaining to me what the hell is going on?'

There had been a silence, then a click and a deep breath. She could hear him lighting up, and she'd felt the pain of his absence for the first time.

'I will do, I promise. Just as soon as I sort it myself,' he replied quietly.

'Oh, great. Is that the only clarification I get? And what about work? I've already had three angry men barking at me down the phone asking where your copy is, and I don't know what to tell them.'

'Say that I'll e-mail them. I can write just as easily over here as I can over there, they won't even notice the difference. Listen, bear with me, yeah? I'll speak to you soon.'

'Don't you dare even think about putting the phone down. I gave up a good job to be with you. I've let my flat, I've changed my entire life—'

'That was your choice, Dido.'

'There was no choice, that's the whole point,' she remembered wailing. 'We have to spend some time together, you know that, if only to teach us that we can't be together for ever.'

'We don't have a choice, you're right about that. I will explain soon, I promise. I'm sorry.'

But sorry wasn't good enough for Dido just then and nothing short of a guarantee to return immediately would have been, so she had put the phone down in a temper.

Fired now by a combination of indignity and hurt, she moved systematically through each room, packing into drawers and shoving into bags anything that might suggest his imminent return. A crumpled shirt hanging on the back of a chair, a tiny tape recorder he used for interviewing, shoes, unwashed coffee cups, half a packet of Marlboro – had he left the place like this to make her believe he was coming back? If she was a detective, called to the premises by suspicious neighbours, what would she think she was dealing with here? A murder? A sudden death? A mystery disappearance? The truth – that the flat's owner had absconded to England on a whim – would undoubtedly be somewhere at the bottom of the list.

In the eight weeks since she'd moved in, the place had grown on her – probably because there was something about its dishevelled emptiness that said Patrick. Empty was absolutely not a word she would have used to describe her step-brother before she'd seen his life over here for herself, but now it had to be first choice. She totted up the highs they'd enjoyed together since she'd arrived – two reasonable restaurant meals, one silly shopping day, a party that was so bad it was actually good, a drive in the country and a movie. Hardly living life at breakneck speed. In the old days, that would have been the running total for eight days, not eight weeks. The gaps between had been filled with a kind of falseness, although she couldn't quite put her finger on what kind.

When they had been growing up in Oxford, Patrick's

goal from the age of fourteen was to become a foreign correspondent for the BBC. His drive for fame and fortune was infectious and Dido had certainly caught some of it. Whether the twins, Will and Agnes, were influenced by him or not was hard to tell because they had been that much younger, but they too were bent on success. Obviously, it had something to do with their parents who had always tested them with unconventional family holidays – a week's art history in Venice, a three-week trek in the Himalayas, a self-sufficiency test on a hostile little island off the west coast of Scotland – and persuaded them to take the more unusual choice of subjects at school and courses at college. Theirs had not been a run-of-the-mill upbringing, and so far, the approach of their parents to widen their children's horizons had worked. Patrick had discarded the BBC in favour of more money and was now operating a cushy little number in the States writing for magazines and newspapers of his choice with the added bonus of being used by American television as a friendly armchair critic of British life; Will was an actor with an innovative national touring theatre company and beginning to dabble in film-making; Agnes was designing children's clothes for a lively new mail-order company that had already had rave reviews from the Sunday supplements, and Dido herself was a food stylist.

'A food stylist?' the man at the passport control at Newark Airport in New Jersey had asked, looking at her travel-battered document on the day she had arrived. 'What's a food stylist?' He hadn't bothered to speak to any of the other travellers that particular shift, but Dido had looked good enough to eat.

'Someone who pretends mashed potato is ice cream for the sake of the camera,' she'd answered, used to being asked the question, and even more used to being spoken to by strange men. She'd enjoyed her answer and found its mildly pornographic overtones amusing but it wasn't the first time she'd used it. Men very often reacted on a purely sexual level with her, but it was superficial flirting. Only rarely did she get taken up.

During her late teens and early twenties, when having a sexual partner was the be-all and end-all, Patrick had been the one who could sit back and wait for it to happen, and Dido, despite her looks, had found herself single for huge chunks of the year. Patrick used to say that it was because she was 'sexually intimidating'. 'How do you know?' she'd asked him once, and he had replied, 'Well, you are to me anyway.'

So, all in all, it had been something of a shock to arrive on his doorstep in August and discover the extent of his solitude. Turning up unannounced is always the best way to see how someone really lives, but she wished now that she had given him some warning because try as she could, she couldn't shake that initial heart-sinking realisation that here was a man with nothing much going on.

For a space that had been occupied by the same person for the last three years, his flat had shown no signs of a settled existence. A hand whisk might not be an essential item for survival, but the fact that there wasn't one (nor a wooden spoon, a large saucepan, a garlic press, a cheese grater or any of the other gadgets that graced most people's drawers and cupboards) had spoken volumes. Equally revealing had been the paucity of bathroom towels and spare sheets, the picture-free walls, the way he kept his CDs in a cardboard box and – most incriminating of all – the hook on the back of the bedroom door as the only possible place to hang clothes. Within a day or two of her arrival, she had deduced that he was resolutely single.

Back in London, in her lovely Chiswick flat which, if you ignored the noise of the Tube and concentrated on the views of the Common could have you believe you were miles out of the city, there had been just one argument against her going out to join him. If Patrick had found, at long last, someone other than her to make him happy, then their pact had to be obsolete, and she had promised herself that she would turn straight back and come home. She'd taken that risk because no matter how many times she approached it, she'd reached the same conclusion – that she would never be given the remotest chance of uncomplicated fulfilment until she had properly explored the possibilities between herself and Patrick. If this plan of hers ended in humiliation, if it was obvious she was barging in on something good, then at least she would know.

When she'd discovered there was no such complication, she should have been pleased – triumphant even. After all, what else stood in their way? But she hadn't been. She'd been troubled, and still was.

Looking back, Patrick's gut reaction to her sudden arrival had been one closer to terror than joy.

'I'm holding you to our pact,' she'd said, after they had hugged.

'Pact,' he'd muttered. 'Pact. You're going to have to remind me,' although the two bulging suitcases had been a good enough clue.

'The one we made on my thirtieth birthday. If we are still lurching from one miserable relationship to the next by the time we are thirty-five, we said, then we will chuck it all in and sail into the twenty-first century together. That one. I've got it in writing. So here I am, ready to sail.'

Patrick had laughed. 'So what are you really doing here?'

'I've just told you. We both know we've already found what we're looking for. That's what you said.'

'Did I? Were we drunk?'

'In vino veritas,' she had replied, and given him a kiss. It hadn't been the kind of kiss she'd planned to give him, but the time wasn't right. She'd quickly come to realise that the time would never be right, but what did it matter? She loved him and she wanted to be with him. Who could say what was out there for them?

It still puzzled her that he was on his own. Surely sex without commitment still existed here, just like it did in London. It wasn't possible for a man with looks like Patrick's to escape unnoticed, and hadn't he always been involved somewhere? He'd always been central to things, and to people. If a party was happening, he'd know about it. If a new face appeared, he'd either have been responsible for its introduction, or he'd go home with it. His calendar used to be enviable for its illegibility – now she couldn't even find one.

Her new friend Joe Polledri had come up with the ridiculous idea that Patrick was celibate. She'd met Joe when she'd served him with clams on the half shell in the Cafe Madison where she had picked up a part-time bar job. It wasn't exactly the work she'd envisaged doing when she'd made her decision to leave London but she was actually having a lot of fun with it, including learning how to make chowders and prepare fresh Maine lobsters. Working with food that tasted better than it looked instead of the other way around made her feel a lot less fraudulent, and she had started to see her old life for what it was, a bit of a charade, too full of what you saw not necessarily being what you got. Her job had been frippery, her relationships were surface, her speech was even littered with harmless lies. Now she was here, she was being more honest – with herself and with Patrick in particular. In the past, men, and even women sometimes, had accused her of being daunting, but only a few recognised it as an act, a cover for the precariousness she felt in her life. Joe, who was probably the first new friend ever to be presented with the real Dido, thought she was great, not least because she'd been so up front with him about everything.

The money at the Cafe was hopeless, and she had been initially reluctant to give up her evenings, but the friendship she had forged with Joe, and the fact that he was a shrink made up for all that. It was just a pity that when he got off the bar stool, he was about three inches too short, but at least he made no efforts to compensate.

'I thought it was just a tired British joke that the States crawled with therapists,' she told him once she'd given up trying to persuade him to have what the in-house pastry chef called an 'erotic cake'. 'But I've met three already. That's one a week.'

'Oh, we get everywhere,' Joe had told her, with a touch of fake menace.

'That could be useful. How would you feel about getting inside my step-brother's head? He lives just around the corner. Or do you prefer not to work with really good messes?'

Like most professionals, the moment a friend or an acquaintance asked for free advice, Joe walked quickly in the other direction. It usually ended with ill-feeling on one side or the other, but there was something about Dido that made him think it was probably worth his while, and so hearing about Patrick, and her feelings for him, over the polished wooden bar became something of a regular consultation. Joe was a divorcé – 'hot on other people's problems, refrigerated on my own' – and he took to stopping at the Madison after work, before going home. Eventually, it got to the stage where home was somewhere to go to sleep. Dido suspected that if he didn't eat at the bar, then he didn't eat at all.

'You should eat more,' she told him.

'You can talk.'

'I've always been skinny. It's in my genes.'

'Or not, as the case may be,' Joe said, assuming she'd get it, which she didn't.

Dido curled her lip and said 'Uh?'

'Jeans, as in denim.'

'What?'

Joe leaned over the bar and put his arm on her shoulder to stage-whisper in her ear.

'Dido, you've got no butt.'

The joke finally sank in, and she laughed. Quick as a flash, she put her arm on his shoulder now, and whispered back in the same manner: 'But the question is, does it really matter?'

'Absolutely not.'

'So I'm okay then am I, butt or no butt?' she teased, wiping a glass.

'I would say so,' Joe smiled, making very sure his eyes were on her face and not scanning her body in that leery way he'd seen other men do.

'Phew!'

Show me a man who would say different.'

'Well, Patrick for a start.'

'He's your brother.'

'Step-brother.'

'And that small detail makes a difference, does it?'

'Why not?'

Her refusal to accept that it didn't, interested Joe greatly over the next few weeks. Most of his patients, affluent middle-class thirty and forty year-olds, he pigeonholed as the 'have-it-alls', the section of society responsible in the last quarter of a century for what he considered to be the obscene growth in consumerism. And now Dido seemed to be proving one of his own theories – that these 'have-it-alls' no longer just wanted every possible material experience available, they also wanted the whole gamut of emotional knowledge too. Philosophical arguments with a woman who could see nothing wrong in claiming her step-brother as her lover, despite the fact that he was obviously not happy with the idea himself, had a whole heap of intellectual mileage to them – and when that woman was intriguing in another more obvious way too, well, he just couldn't resist.

Joe considered himself on a learning curve as he spent his otherwise lonely evenings in her company, and the Cafe Madison, with its Jackson Pollack spattered walls and ten different beers on tap, became his second home. 'It beats running my Stress Busters for Parents Winter Course any day,' he told her, knowing not so deep down that what kept him coming back for more was nothing to do with any professional interest he might have in her story.

The more she thought about Joe's celibacy theory now that Patrick had put the distance of the Atlantic between them, the more it made sense. The Patrick she had been with over the last two months was not the same Patrick she was used to. His passion had gone. He was limp, she thought, excusing herself for the unfortunate choice of words. His hunger had gone. He was pared-down.

The flat now showed little sign of him and it was beginning to smell much more single woman than single man. He had bought Apartment 3L, 1016 Washington Street, because of what the real-estate girl had called its 'railroad' style. The front door opened into the kitchen, the kitchen led to the sitting room, the sitting room led to the bedroom, the bedroom led to the bathroom, each room perfectly aligned with the next. It did mean that any visitor needing the bathroom was also treated to the devastation of his sleeping quarters but that was something that embarrassed them more than him. If you opened all the doors, you could roll a tennis ball from front to back, which apparently, he frequently did. There had been a small collection of green balls collecting dust in the bathroom when she'd arrived.

'Do you roll these things for a pastime?' she'd asked him when she'd first seen them, nestling in the grimy little space between the sink and the lavatory.

'I used to,' he'd said and not bothered to explain further, which made Dido assume, with a little tinge of hope, that a woman was involved somewhere along the line. Perhaps they used to hold competitions to see whose ball could travel the furthest and then whoever won would get a free massage.

'So what was her name?'

'No, I said I used to, not we,' he'd replied curtly. 'It used to help me think.'

There was something about that memory that made Dido even more angry now than she had been just after putting the phone down. She went straight to where she knew she'd tidied the balls away, in a bag by his shoes in the wardrobe with no door, and took out as many as she could carry. Marching back through the empty flat, she shouted in anger, 'You bastard!' and turned round to throw each of the six balls as hard as she could back towards the bedroom, not remembering that it only worked if you rolled them. Consequently, the balls ricocheted off the walls, off the furniture and on to the floor, all of them ending up a few feet from where she stood in the kitchen.

It was strange, this bombardment of memory. The more she tried to switch off, the more it happened – snatches of conversations, an expression on Patrick's face, a succession of rapid action moments, getting on the plane at Gatwick, kissing her London neighbour goodbye, that first tense night in bed with him. She hesitated over a half packet of Marlboro he'd left lying on the sofa, looked at the time to see if she could justify having one and decided she could seeing as it was Saturday. She took one carefully out and lit it with the disposable lighter that lay next to the full ashtray and, as she dropped her leggy olive-skinned body into a large cream armchair, she realised how tired of it all she was.

As she stroked the worn fabric of the arm, she saw the image of her father doing the same, sitting in the corner of his Oxford cottage, looking into the fire. It used to be a habit of his, stroking. He would stroke anything – chairs, table surfaces, his children's hair, even the back of his own hand if there was nothing else more soothing available. What would he have made of all this, his daughter believing herself in love with his step-son? She shut her eyes and tried to invoke his face. In her head, she always saw him how he really was, a mobile, creased face that would break into a familiar expression without her even asking, sometimes a frown, or a look of pride, a smile or a look of concern. There was no conjuring on her behalf, he simply appeared, and it was the reason she never looked at his photograph. This time, she got an unfamiliar expression that looked almost guilty or ashamed, and it was puzzling enough to persuade her that Adam still lived on, somewhere, and that he probably understood more about all this than she did.

The chair offered another comfort too – tangible proof that Patrick had loved Adam just as much, enough to spend a small fortune dragging a worthless old chair halfway across the world just to sit in it and smell his tobacco for a few months. Could Patrick's decline be traced back to Adam's death? Had a part of Patrick died along with Adam, or had Adam taken it without asking?

It was the first time in Dido's life she had neither of them. Adam was dead, and the distance between her and Patrick had nothing to do with the thousands of miles of sea separating Cornwall from New Jersey. A new estrangement had settled between the two of them, disrupting the complicated symmetry of the lines they had followed for the previous thirty-three years.

Her favourite story as a child had been Hansel and Gretel; she used to pretend she was Gretel and Patrick was Hansel, and she would create an elaborate scene in her head where she rescued him from the witch's cage and he would be eternally grateful to her. Hansel and Gretel couldn't find their way home after the wood pigeons had eaten the crumbs they'd left as a trail, and she felt now as if Patrick had gobbled up his own crumbs on purpose, so he could lose her, once and for all.

'More like twins than the twins!' she'd heard her step-mother Jean say time and time again. Maybe that was the problem. The more your parents tell you things, the more you believe them.

When Jean Botsford, Patrick's mother, had wed Adam Seal, Dido's father, they each had one small child to bring to the marriage. People often assumed when they saw the four of them together that Patrick was the older by at least a year, a neat little nuclear family, boy first, then girl. In fact the gap was just three months and the children came from different wombs. At two years old, the age at which their lives were thrown together, Dido could neither talk nor walk – a reaction, Adam believed, from seeing her mother killed when she was still a baby. Jenny Seal had died the moment a spinning car driven by a drunk ploughed into her, although she had seen it coming in enough time to give Dido's pushchair a mighty shove in the direction of a hedge, so preventing a double tragedy. Not even the hawthorn had left a mark on Dido's perfect little body, but her father had always wondered what damage might have been done to her spirit.

When Will and Agnes were born five years later, Jean had taken one look at them lying entwined in their hospital crib and said to her husband, 'Patrick and Dido.' He'd known exactly what she meant. The twins shared the same olive colouring as their older siblings, and even then, it looked like they shared the same requited love and understanding. The notion that his eldest children were also twins, intrinsically linked in a way no one would ever truly understand, stayed with Adam all his life. Only when he was sure of his own imminent death could he find the courage to tell Patrick the truth, a truth that Dido had yet to learn.

That night, she went to bed with one of Patrick's sweaters. It smelt of him, of stale Marlboro and soft soapiness, and she ended up wearing it. When was the last time a man had given up the chance of being with her? Maybe that was it – maybe it was just because she had always been the rejecter and not the rejected.

'I'm going to find out what's eating you up,' she whispered into it. 'I am, I am, I am.' But sleep did not come. Instead, again and again, she trawled over the mess Patrick's truancy had caused. It was midnight now, and she tried to shut her mind down by mentally pressing the delete button. If she could only envisage a computer screen, open a new document, send all previous stuff to the recycle bin, then she might sleep. A fresh page.

As she wriggled further down the bed and pulled the duvet over her head, she remembered the warnings of a magazine editor in London.

'Take a break – no one will miss you for two months. You've got a great career, your name is known, you don't have to look for work, you'd be mad to give it up just because you want to follow a man. Any longer than two months and they'll assume you're dead and start using someone else. They won't chase you, they never do. They'll replace you. We are all replaceable.'

But Dido had been confident of two things – one, that she could pick up the same kind of work without difficulty in New York, and two, that Patrick would be as determined as she was to ride the storm of their new relationship, regardless of the opposition they met from family and friends. Wrong, and wrong.

She started weighing up the arguments for and against going home, but it was a half-hearted effort. What was there, really, to go back for? She had reached saturation point well before she'd left. Hers was an international life, with friends scattered across the globe and only a handful left in London. Her job had long lost its novelty, and any scope for finding that elusive long-term relationship had narrowed considerably. And anyway, she'd rented out her flat to an ex-boyfriend and his new wife, giving them the first month's rent as a wedding present, so she could hardly turf them out just because she'd changed her mind. Besides, she liked New York.

'Joe?' she said apologetically into the phone two hours

later, still not really sure if she found him attractive enough to be doing this. He was Dustin Hoffman or Al Pacino short, but then if Dustin Hoffman and Al Pacino weren't world famous film stars, she'd reasoned, then they would be just plain short.

'I think so,' he said blearily.

'I can't sleep.'

'That's too bad.' He was still only half awake.

'Patrick has done a bunk to the UK and he says he's staying there until January.'

'I told you your demands were unreasonable,' he mumbled in jest.

'I don't demand. I hint.'

'Too subtle a difference for us men.'

'I was hoping you might be able to suggest something to take my mind off it.'

Joe Polledri knew too much about the way a woman's mind worked to believe for one moment that it was him she really wanted.

'Do you have any brandy in the house?' he suggested, thinking he was probably missing his only chance. He'd been used before, by his ex-wife, and the fear that it would happen again was stronger than any desire he had to touch Dido's naked flesh, beautiful as he imagined it to be.

Chapter 4

It was one o'clock in the morning when Johnny Bates finally found the mettle to heave himself up and make a move to the door. He had missed the family sofa so much that to sit in it again was pure luxury, and during the course of the evening he had all but buried himself in the velvet familiarity of its ancient cushions, pretending he could stay there all night, prising off his legendary leather boots and drawing the throw around him just like a hundred nights before.

His haircut yesterday which, egged on by his children, turned out to be more of a head shave, rather suited him Katherine thought, but then he'd always had the air of a friendly thug. At a dinner party years ago, someone they'd never met before had been asked to guess Johnny's job. A bookmaker had been the running favourite, with bouncer coming a close second, neither speculation being wholly tongue-in-cheek. Civil servant had sounded such a let-down in the end that the guest had refused to believe him, and Johnny had eventually 'admitted' he was, in fact, a freelance minder for world leaders and visiting celebrities on incognito holidays in Cornwall, which had gone down a bomb.

Just as he was about to get up now, the cat jumped on to his lap, giving him the excuse to sit for a few minutes more. For the last half an hour, the conversation between the four of them had calmed down to an occasional lazy comment and reply. Between the spoken words they were lost in their own separate worlds. The fire was burning to a rhythm – flicker flicker, spit spit – and the same little orange flame kept dying and springing back into life at regular intervals, holding them all in focus on their own peculiar problems.

Johnny looked in turn at Patrick, whose dark deep-set eyes were even darker and deeper than he remembered, at Beth, whose tiny curled frame took up so little space at the other end of the sofa that he had stretched out as if he'd had it to himself, and then at his wife, whose expression was impossible to read. Gone were the days when the two of them knew what was in the other's head. At one time they could probably have spoken for each other on matters of huge importance and great sensitivity, but they inhabited independent worlds now, looking at the same crisis from different vantage points.

He surveyed his sitting room, if you could still call it his, which was furnished by chairs they had bought together and hung with pictures they had given to each other and he remembered how, not so long ago, he had seen it all with very different eyes. There were no obvious signs of material indulgence now, not to the extent he had suspected in those dark months before he'd left, when everywhere he had looked there had been evidence of wanton consumerism. He'd grown to despise the computer, the CD-player, the video, the dishwasher, the mountain bikes, the surf boards, the wet suits – everything that had once been deemed a necessity, and that he worked so relentlessly to provide. Now that they were no longer tripping him up in his daily struggle to get out of the house and to the office to earn the money to pay for more things to trip over, they didn't seem quite so dangerous.

Katherine had been right to recognise the motorbike as the

first tangible proof of his personal quagmire, although she had got it wrong by seeing it not as a tentative step towards moving down a gear, but as a bid for freedom. Okay, so he'd fallen at the first fence by buying a bike that was almost as expensive as the car and less practical to boot, but why she couldn't see the decision in less clear cut terms, as a bid to get shot of unnecessary burdens, to make their greed-driven lives simpler, he didn't know. He'd wondered for a time why she refused to discuss the concept of downscaling their lives, until he realised that he had never actually ventured it. If they spent less, he could earn less, and if he earned less, they would spend less. It was just a question of breaking the circle.

And yet how could he even speak of feeling ensnared in a Cornish rat-race? Cornwall, a land where children still had that instinct for spontaneous play, building elaborate dens from bending willows in the local woods without asking permission or advice, where families still walked along cliffs every Sunday afternoon come rain or shine, where old people still lived in the houses they were born in, where your neighbour was still probably related to your other neighbour in some distant complicated way, where buckets of daffodils were sold outside people's garden gates, where fields had names and everyone knew them. How could Cornwall have a rat-race? He could hear the mockery from here.

Dream on, Johnny Boy, he told himself before finally dragging his tired body on to its feet, you don't live here any more and it is time to go home. Katherine was waiting for him to make a move, he could tell. Maybe she was threatened by the cosiness, by the rekindling of the friendship they all still undoubtedly shared, not just because of the way Patrick and Beth lifted things above the usual humdrum, but because of the suggestion that Katherine and he still enjoyed something specific and that this new life they were leading was no better and possibly even worse than their old one. He comforted himself with a silent acknowledgment that the exhilaration of all being together again was almost tangible. The old spark had taken a frighteningly long time to get going tonight, but once it had, there'd been no looking back.

How the mood had changed so agreeably he didn't know, but it had. Certainly, the evening had not begun at all promisingly. It had been the shock of seeing Patrick, sitting in the cottage kitchen like a helpless little cuckoo waiting to be fed by some other chick's mother, that got it off to such a bad start.

When Johnny had walked through the door with Hattie and Seth at the prescribed time of seven o'clock as instructed only to be greeted by someone he believed to be the other side of the Atlantic, he had not been entirely delighted. Patrick had been sitting there in the carver's chair with his long legs and bare feet stretching across the slate floor like he'd lived there for years, drinking Johnny's beer out of Johnny's glass. Johnny being Johnny, of course, he had done his best to make it look like a welcome surprise.

'What the hell?' he'd smiled, crossing the room with his arm outstretched and at the same time betraying himself to Katherine with a hissed, 'Nice of you to let me know!'

His immediate reaction had been to assume it was all prearranged and that something had gone wrong with the finer detail which was why they were now trying to brazen it out as if it was all meant to be above board in the first place. If he hadn't had the excuse of returning his children to their mother, would he ever have discovered Patrick's arrival? There had been no mention of the man forty-eight hours earlier, and when you had to cross the Atlantic, you didn't just turn up unannounced. Katherine must have known he was coming and chosen not to mention it. Even as these conjectures flashed through his mind, he had been able to hear his wife saying, 'Do you really think I would keep something like that from you?' and himself replying, 'Well, yes, yes I do,' and the way she would look at him would make it his problem, not hers.

Mild paranoia was a particular affliction of his, something to do, much as he hated to admit it, with his parents, who were loving, demonstrative and devoted, but also seriously under-educated. It mattered not a jot, until sometimes, very rarely, he found himself totting up the reasons why he was as good as the company he kept. He was an unlikely victim of such conditioning, especially when he so deeply detested class divide, but the fact was that he *did* suffer these intermittent stirrings of inferiority and when he did, his behaviour became hesitant, less confident, and altogether different. It was made no easier by the knowledge that he was adopted by these good people, and that his birth mother had neither loved nor wanted him, a child given to her by an unsuspecting client whom she viewed in much the same way as if he had been a sexually transmitted disease.

As a teenager, he'd dealt with his insecurity by being aggressive but they had been unhappy years during which he'd disappointed not only his adoptive parents but himself, so he'd chosen to fight it since by achieving. The better his exam results, the more confidence he'd gained, and by the time he had graduated with a first-class degree in English and Politics, Johnny was happy to be just Johnny, warts and all. Most of the time, anyway. Just not earlier tonight.

'Does Beth know you're here?' he'd asked Patrick almost rudely. He'd thought at the time what a good test of the truth that would be, because if Beth didn't know either, then the situation really would stink, but Patrick hadn't even had time to reply. At that very moment, her face had peeped round the cottage kitchen door and cooed as she always did, 'Hi, guys!' in the kind of cheery soul voice that would resign most people to the sick bucket.

'Good timing!' Patrick had cheered.

It *was* indisputably good timing because as soon as Johnny had seen her, his traces of suspicion faded away. The fact that he chose to credit Beth rather than Katherine with his change of mood was in truth a little childish, since Katherine had taken him to one side a few moments earlier and told him to check his answer machine when he got back to his cottage.

'Why?'

'Because you'll hear two messages. One from me on Friday night telling you I was off to Plymouth with Loveday to pick up Patrick, and one from Patrick this morning telling you to bring the children home early and join us for lunch.'

'Oh,' he'd said sheepishly.

Somehow, though, it was still Beth who managed to make the awkward little gathering in the kitchen ease up. Instead of suspicious, Johnny had begun to feel ashamed, which was a doddle to deal with in comparison, as long as he pushed to the back of his mind a new truth – that tonight had been the only time he had ever felt anything remotely like jealousy towards either his wife or his best friend.

Not being a man accustomed to such quickfire emotional discovery, he'd slipped off for a while to be with the children in their den under the pretext of sorting out a problem with the computer. In all their thirteen years of marriage, Katherine had only seen Johnny wrong-footed twice, and never with his two closest friends. He hadn't batted an eyelash at going solo to a parents' evening at school since the split, or being seen in the supermarket with his basket of ready meals, but the scrutiny of close friends was obviously very different. The worst thing was, she couldn't think of one good reason why the two of them should be living apart either, except that somehow, it felt less wrong than being together, and how could she voice that?

Things had taken another awkward turn when Beth brought up the inevitable subject of the millennium.

'So, is everything sorted for the celebration of the century?' she'd asked Johnny, slipping her tiny little arms around his thinning waist, reminding him of the stone in weight he'd lost since the split. He'd forgotten how much of a toucher she was – her years with Evan hadn't knocked it out of her then. You're so sweet, you're only asking me because you can see me dying on my feet here, he'd thought. Out loud, he'd opted for something more perfunctory.

'Yep! All sorted!'

'We wish!' Katherine shouted from the cooking end of the kitchen, her back to them as she stirred a hasty cream sauce for the pasta. 'The Party. Ten minutes together, and we're talking about The Party.'

'So come on then,' Patrick had baited, 'tempt us. You still haven't explained precisely what we're going to get for our £500 investment. I could fly home on that and still have enough left to take someone out for supper.'

'Go on then,' Johnny said, encouraging himself with a boyish toss of a wine cork in Patrick's direction, hoping it would help things along a bit and wondering if the others could also sense that the old magic wasn't working as it used to. 'But then again, we are talking possibly the most historic moment of your life.'

'Historic moment?' Patrick snorted derisively. 'As Sigmund Freud once said, the only thing we can be sure of in the next century is that we're all going to die in it.'

'And a Happy New Year to you,' said Beth.

'So you might as well enjoy yourself before you do. A good groove, and then you croak,' Johnny said, with a little wiggle of the hips.

'Sorry,' Katherine sneered, 'but you looked just like my father then, trying to dance to Queen at our wedding.'

It was bitchy, and out of character, and if she and Johnny had still been together, someone would have told her off.

'Well, this *is* nice,' said Beth, after the awkward pause. God, that was nasty, she thought, deciding she would side with Johnny for the next round.

'Enjoy?' Patrick said, still keen on getting Johnny's back up for some reason. 'Did you say enjoy? Our enjoying days are over, mate – or soon will be. Haven't you realised we're not life's movers and shakers any more? That mantle has been wrested from us by the young.'

Johnny had laughed.

'No, really,' Patrick carried on, getting the bit between his teeth. 'We're not. That's right.'

'What is?'

'That we will become instantly old after midnight on the thirty-first of December. That we have a few months left in which to call ourselves young.'

'If only I'd been in New York for the last three years, taking part in discussions about the Millennium and The Ageing Process till it comes out of my ears like you have, I might see where you're coming from, but sadly, I've been in Cornwall, so instead the word crap springs to mind.'

It had been Patrick's turn to laugh.

'Is this just banter?' Beth asked, unfamiliar with the antagonism.

'*I* know what you mean, Patrick, 'Katherine interrupted, in a voice that was designed to make Johnny feel adolescent.

'It *is* a bridge to cross for us all, like it or not. If you take three score years and ten, then we are in the very middle of our lives, aren't we? And that dividing line between the twentieth and the twenty-first centuries will split us in two. Young and Old. Our lives will be in two halves forever afterwards – what we did before the year 2000 and what we did after.'

'Thank you, Katherine,' Patrick said professorially. 'And there'll always be that sense of what we did before being better than anything we could possibly achieve after, yes?'

Johnny had watched her nod slowly back at him, recognising the intimacy about it, or at least something mutually understood. In all the years he had known them both, the only time he ever thought Patrick knew Katherine better than *he* did was when they started getting philosophical. It made him react adolescently again.

'You do know that Christian academics have already persuaded the experts that Jesus was born no later than 4BC, which makes us approximately four years too late, do you? That the monk who divided the calendar into BC and AD in 664 made a fairly fundamental cock-up, and all this millennium mania is a creation of the media, do you?'

'Is that right? And what was his name, this monk?' asked Patrick, looking to score a point.

'Dionysus Exiguus,' Johnny fired back without hesitation.

'You should know better than to ask Johnny something like that!' shouted Beth, not really enjoying the joshing as much as she was pretending to. 'He's far too good at storing useless information to be caught out by a mere journalist. You ought to be a politician Johnny, especially since you're still shirking the question. What *are* we getting for our £500 investment?'

'Two bands – one jazz funk, one sixties retro – a casino, a downhill ski simulator, four-star accommodation on one of Britain's most picturesque islands, as much champagne as you can drink . . .'

'Oh, please,' Katherine interrupted, her brow unattractively furrowed. 'You sound like a bloody timeshare salesman.'

'That's no way to talk to your—' Patrick had suddenly realised, halfway through the sentence, that he didn't know what word to use but it was too late to cover up the hesitation. The silence was excruciating.

'Husband,' answered Beth with an admirable mix of humour and tact, making the first public acknowledgment of the new order between them.

'Well, okay, husband,' Patrick laughed nervously.

It's all so sad, thought Beth, knowing that if she didn't keep the conversation going, the evening would have fallen apart there and then. The party was probably not the best topic, but it had to do. 'Anyway, you were saying, Johnny, before you were so rudely interrupted. I want a complete rundown of the plans so far. Who's coming? Let's have a look at the guest list.'

'I think I have actually got one somewhere,' Johnny said. 'Katherine, are my papers still in the top drawer of the desk?'

'Well, I haven't moved them.'

He came back with a folded sheet of A4, covered in handwritten columns of names, some crossed out, some inserted.

'There you go. It's an old one, so there will be at least another fifty names to add to that, but you might recognise some.'

Beth grabbed it like a lifeline and immediately began

shouting. 'Caro and Adrian Woods? Not Caro as in Caro Harris? She didn't marry Adrian Woods, did she?'

'Last year,' said Katherine. 'They didn't tell anyone until they'd done it. Apparently, they grabbed a couple of people off the streets as witnesses.'

'I don't believe it! I thought he'd come out!'

'No, *you* decided he ought to come out, Beth, no one else did. He is *not* gay, despite his dress sense.'

'Are you sure?' Beth laughed. 'But I thought Caro married an Australian.'

'She did.'

'When did that all fall to pieces then?'

'Four or five years ago. He went off with her sister.'

Johnny hadn't been able to resist coming in, despite it being almost girl's talk. 'Both of them called Mel.'

They all took comfort in this ridiculous coincidence, and made much mockery of it, in support of Caro, aware at the same time that their famous equilibrium was gently returning.

'Hey, is Bill coming?'

'He was, until his wife left him last month,' said Johnny, pulling a face.

'Not another one,' said Patrick. 'Is anyone still together?'

'You didn't tell me that,' Katherine said accusingly but avoiding his eye.

'Yep, she just moved out one Saturday morning, taking the children, while he was still in bed. Apparently, she had it planned like a military operation. Bill told me he had absolutely no idea until he came downstairs at midday and found a note. She'd rented a house, changed the children's schools, packed everything up during the course of the last week . . . really nasty stuff.'

Beth gasped and Patrick exhaled, but Katherine reacted

exactly as Johnny thought she would, which was why he'd kept it from her in the first place.

'No, hold on,' said Katherine. 'You know as well as I do she's been carrying that marriage for years. Bill has never had a proper job.' She looked at Beth as if to say, 'What woman would put up with what I'm about to tell you?'

'He still plays in his beloved band, goes out every Friday and Saturday night to gigs, comes in pissed having earned less than it costs to keep all his equipment going, and then lies in bed all morning while Sue looks after the children. She gave him an ultimatum last year to either get a proper job or she'd leave and it looks like she's kept her word. Good for her, I say. She's been the only thing keeping the children fed and clothed since they had them. Bill's worse than useless. He's had it coming a long time.'

The atmosphere completely imbalanced once more, Beth had decided it might be politic to leave Bill where he was, and so she'd moved her finger further down the list to see who else she could find while Katherine's character assassination continued to ring in everyone's ears. As Johnny had listened to his wife's castigation of an old friend, his normally even-tempered face had slowly taken on the expression of a vegetarian in a butcher shop – lips curled down, nose screwed, eyes squinting. What she was saying, and how she was saying it had surely held an echo for their own marriage too. She knew how the idea of walking away from his job was becoming increasingly inviting for him, and he knew he was closer to doing it than he allowed himself to think. He'd thanked God it hadn't been an issue when they'd separated, and that they had split up *before* he resigned, and not because of, which meant no one could be entirely blamed for anything – not that he had decided one way or another about his job yet, he'd been forced to remind himself.

The name-spotting game had started to wear thin. There were too many divorces and other predicaments woven into the list, and it was taking its toll on the already agitated mood.

'What would we talk about if we didn't have the party?' Johnny had said eventually, knowing he had to say something.

'What indeed?' Katherine had whispered, thinking specifically of all those discouragingly silent summer evenings they had both barely tolerated. Her back still turned, and her sauce now stirred, she waited for him to begin.

It was a physical impossibility for Johnny to talk about the party without becoming animated. His commentary would be illustrated with elaborate gesticulations and his 'pitch' – the speech he saved for possible investors as he liked to call them, or ticket buyers as any normal person did – was so beguiling that he'd managed to sell every one of the 200 places within a few months. Katherine had grown to hate it, not because of its repetition but because it was the only time she ever caught a glimpse of the old Johnny. There was a time, not so long ago, when he'd been able to find the same enthusiasm for family projects – bonfire night, a weekend camping, Seth's tree-house – but that had all gone, along with the second car. And he had given so many hours so freely to the damn thing when in the same day he would complain about having no time to be with the children or talk to her.

'What are the numbers, did you say, Johnny?' asked Beth.

'Two hundred. Twenty-five pounds a quarter since 1995, standing order. I've had them queuing up to make back payments.'

Katherine had practically thrown the wooden spoon into

the sink from where she was standing. Had he forgotten the origins of this monster? Those nice simple origins?

'Mmm,' she murmured, grating the last of the cheese and nearly taking her fingers with it.

'Did you say something?' asked Patrick.

'More wine, please,' she said, holding up an empty glass.

While the others listened to Johnny, it suited Katherine to put herself somewhere else, and where better than New Year's Eve 1989, when the four of them had been in Brittany, France together, toasting the arrival of the 1990s in a freezing cottage with thick stone walls tucked away at the bottom of a grand garden attached to an old Abbey.

The Abbey, which had been a hotel for as long as any local could remember, was a shabby and rambling building that Katherine and Johnny had discovered during a wet week the previous summer. It was so easy to reach Brittany from Cornwall – a quick ferry trip across the water from Plymouth – that they had never holidayed anywhere else, often going back and forth two or three times a year.

When the four of them – five if you included the two-year-old Hattie – had docked in France on the evening of 27 December, they had all looked forward to a quick drive through a few Breton villages and then an even quicker collapse into bed at the Abbey. That would undoubtedly have happened if they hadn't a) forgotten the map, and b) been stupid enough to leave the booking to Patrick. The journey took two hours longer than it should have done, and hence, when they arrived at nearly midnight, the hotel staff hadn't a clue who they were. Somewhere along the way, a fax of confirmation hadn't arrived, or a deposit cheque had been lost, and Patrick could come up with no proof to the contrary. The day had been saved when the owner, Madame Brandivy – who still sent them all a joint Christmas Card – noticed that Katherine was hiding a growing bump under her baggy sweater and she had refused to let them leave, making them temporary beds in the cavernous wooden panelled library instead. The next morning at breakfast, she had double-checked departure dates with every available guest and eventually, she had exclaimed, 'La Petite Maison. C'est petite mais c'est jolie,' and taken them all off down the garden to their emergency accommodation.

'La Petite Maison' had certainly lived up to its name with only one room top and bottom and a huge stone fireplace as the only means of heating. Every morning Johnny and Patrick would take up the challenge to revive the embers by breakfast, the fires getting bigger and faster as the week progressed. There was a wrought-iron single bed in the far right corner next to the hearth with a lumpy mattress and three feather quilts of varying sizes, but as it was the only aired bed in the house, the four of them used to take it in turns to sleep there. Whoever that was also had to contend with Hattie, who snuggled into the downy heap like a dream at around seven every evening lulled by the quiet chatter of her parents and godparents, and then woke up later just long enough to wrap her layered little self round her nightly guardian as soon as whoever it was clambered in to join her. The three others then had to make do upstairs with a double bed of equal lumpiness and another iron bed that had apparently been made for a midget. Everyone had backache for weeks afterwards, but it had been such an extraordinary time, they had all been sentimental about the pain.

Even now, Katherine could remember in detail how they first came up with the idea of a millennium party. They had been waiting for midnight to strike in La Petite Maison –

or rather bleep to a travel alarm clock – and they had embarked on some rather drunken theorising. Patrick's pissed postulations were notorious, and as always, he had been the one to start.

'We are about to enter the last decade of the century. And yet, none of us really care, do we? After the swinging sixties, the glam rock seventies, and the greedy eighties, the nineties are hardly worth thinking about. What we want is the third millennium,' he'd proclaimed. 'But instead, we've all got to hang around for the next decade, getting older and grumpier, when really, we are at our prime now. We've peaked too early. Bloody typical.'

'You should never wish your life away like that,' Beth said; she had a tendency to get appallingly sentimental when under the influence of alcohol. 'Who knows what riches lie before us in the next ten years?'

'Here's to the age of the family – the caring sharing nineties!' Johnny saluted. 'Although how we're supposed to get that off the ground when we've still got Maggie making our decisions for us, I don't know. No, sod the age of the family. Here's to the death of Thatcherism!'

The discussion that followed, a great long list of ambitions and prophesies, had eaten well into the early hours, and Katherine could still hear clearly her own contribution. As a twenty-five-year-old, pregnant with her second child, had she really been naive enough to think a career in television journalism might still be in front of her? Had she truly believed that by getting the baby thing out of the way early on, she might then have had the freedom to return to work whilst she was still young enough to count? At that time, she'd been working on the local BBC radio station, and everyone knew what a springboard that was meant to be. Spot the bellyflop, she thought.

Patrick had been similarly career-struck. They had both been on the same post-graduate journalism course a few years earlier, and whilst she had been told she would 'bubble in the provinces', Patrick had been earmarked for greater things.

'Foreign correspondent for BBC TV news,' he'd forecast confidently, and he hadn't done too badly, really. Well, at least he was living abroad, and still in work. Neither Johnny or Beth had been in the least bit interested in discussing their jobs, but Beth had persevered in making specific references to the fact that New Zealand sheep farmers were a lucrative bet on the marriage front, something which had more to do with her latest relationship than any serious social observation. She'd already been teaching for three years by then and it didn't need to be said that she'd chosen the right path. The first twelve months in an inner city primary school in London had been touch and go, but once she'd made the big decision to return to Cornwall, her doubts had dissolved. The deprivation and the despair of London she'd been able to cope with, likewise the widespread lack of interest from both parents and teachers; it was just she hadn't been able to breathe the air.

Johnny had said memorably, 'I'd like to see a Labour government,' which had brought on much cheering, although his next comment, 'I want to be Hattie's best mate, her role model for a good decent bloke, I want to be loved by my wife, adored by my kids, liked by my friends. I want to be as happy then as I am now,' had brought on just as much jeering. Admittedly, he had been the most drunk, and his words had come out in a saccharine slur, but everyone had forgiven him all the same because of the tears in his eyes.

Katherine had quickly forced herself to steer her mind

in another direction because the pain she felt when she remembered his meltingly lovely little speech had stung at her heart like TCP on a fresh cut. Was it Johnny or Beth who'd thought of the party? She could check anyway, because the chastening thing was, they had taped their conversation for a laugh and the little C60 cassette lay somewhere in the muddle of their music collection, in the bottom drawer of a desk in the den. Katherine wondered if she was the only one who could remember its existence.

She could recall Beth's misgivings about the year 2000, all based on a preoccupation with the way people would write it on their chequebooks.

'But it still sounds like it belongs to science fiction,' Beth had wailed in La Petite Maison. 'What will we write on our cheques? Will it be abbreviated to zero zero? It sounds as if nothing has happened, as if we're at the very beginning, and I don't like it.'

'We won't be writing cheques by then,' Johnny said. 'It'll be all credit card.'

'But zero zero?' repeated Beth. 'Will it be zero zero, do you think?'

'Who cares? Nothing is going to change, is it? And anyway, it's ten whole years away.'

'Ten years can go just like that,' Katherine had said, clicking her fingers.

'Then we should all make a pact now to spend it together.'

Yes, that had been Johnny, Katherine was sure.

And so the idea of the party had been born. She couldn't now remember how or when it had eventually come to be the Isles of Scilly, although at one time, they had contemplated a week's skiing in Scotland, and wasn't Fiji mentioned once too? For the last decade, they had each been religiously putting £12 a quarter into a joint account which now stood at more than £2,000 including interest. It had been Johnny's enthusiasm and insistence that had carried them through – left to any of the others, she was sure they would never have reached the first bank statement.

It had hit her then, standing in her kitchen listening to the ramblings of her estranged husband, how cocksure they all used to be, happy just to respond to life's easier, multiple choice questions.

She'd picked up a photograph Johnny must have pulled out from the desk drawer along with his guest list and looked at it. As usual, it was an awful one of her, but good of Beth. Katherine always managed to look frumpy in photos somehow and yet she persisted in believing them to be a true likeness. Johnny had once kindly tried to say that her face was too 'mobile' to capture on film, which had made her feel as if she was made of rubber.

'How bizarre,' she'd said, turning at last to the others, and cutting Johnny off in his prime. 'Look at this. Johnny must have picked it up with the guest list. It's Brittany, isn't it?'

'That's it,' Johnny had replied crankily. 'Let's talk about the past. It is so much less challenging.'

'There's nothing wrong with seeking refuge in nostalgia,' Beth said, jumping to Katherine's defence in just the same way she had jumped to Johnny's earlier. 'Old people do it all the time. It's a recognised form of therapy, peeling away all those complicated layers that life lays down over the years. You go back to your own point in history, when you were last . . .' her voice trailed off.

'Last what?' asked Johnny.

'Last truly happy,' Katherine told him.

'Oh, you're right, this *is* Brittany,' he had said quickly. 'Look, there's our old car.'

And so Brittany had saved the day. The mollifying babble

that followed turned out to be a sorting office of emotions, a repository, a filter, or a place to dump irritation. Slowly, the present began to take on the patina of the past, and they moved unselfconsciously away from Brittany, from the party, and from the past, on to any other topic that took their fancy, controversial or otherwise. The rest of the evening had been as warm as the start had been cold, perhaps even warmer, since they couldn't help but appreciate the cheer all the more for the contrast.

With the clock now threatening one-thirty, half an hour after he'd first intended to leave, Johnny was discovering he had a capacity for self-pity. Feeling sorry for oneself was much more Patrick's line, and much as he loved the man, he didn't want to be him. Patrick's complicated approach to life was the last one he wanted to adopt. But not once in all the seventeen years they'd known each other had one of them been morally obliged to leave at the end of an evening, and he was about to break with tradition.

At University of course they'd all shared a home anyway which meant that as soon as anyone became too tired or bored to keep going, all they had to do was to crawl away to their unmade beds, with or without each other. When he and Katherine had married, the natural solution was for the others to come to them. On the rare occasion that a get-together *had* happened elsewhere, there was always his wife to hold in the cold night air, to talk to and laugh with until sleep came. It was as much as he could do now not to suggest they do the same, not that there had been much talking and laughing in the last few months, but propriety told him he had to get up and go out into the night, back to an empty, damp, strange cottage that was supposed to, but never would, feel like home.

As he stood up and took his leather jacket from the old

church pew that ran the length of one wall, he seemed to dominate the space and no one knew quite where to look.

'Okay, you intoxicated layabouts, you just lie there and fall asleep. I'll see you all later in the week.' And he bent to kiss Beth, waved at Katherine, and left the room, biting the inside of his mouth to stop any unwanted facial movement betraying how he felt.

Katherine's eyebrows were raised, her thin lips were pursed and her astute hazel eyes had that startled rabbit look they got when words failed her. Beth had her fingers to her mouth and she began stroking her upper lip nervously, also trying to think of something to say. Patrick, who felt suddenly as if he'd spent hours mindlessly staring at the blank screen of a television that had just burst back into broadcast, jumped up from the floor. Holy shit, he thought, Johnny is leaving his own home, his wife and his two sleeping children to return to God knows where, and I don't know why because I haven't bothered to ask.

'Hey!' he shouted far louder than he needed to towards the door. 'Don't leave me on my own with these two!' Then, turning back in a blind panic towards the girls. 'I'll go with him Kate, if that's okay.'

'Yes,' cried Katherine and Beth together. 'Yes!'

As Johnny cornered his Triumph Daytona round one of the narrowest lanes in Cornwall and felt Patrick's grip on the edge of his jacket tighten, he let out a blast of raw exhilaration.

'YAAAAAHHHH!!' he screamed into the night, the freezing wind biting his face and devouring his noise. What he meant was, 'I thought I was going to have to leave the three of them there, but Patrick, my friend, my "brother", my best mate, saw it, and he came with me! So now, the two girls are together back there, the kids are asleep, we're here on this crazy bike and everything is going to be alright!' He took the next corner even faster, and felt Patrick grip even tighter.

Back in Tremewan, Katherine spoke first.

'Can you stay?' She wasn't sure if she wanted Beth to say yes or no. It had been such a roller coaster of a weekend she could have done with some time off.

'Well, Evan was so cross with me for coming in the first place, I can't see how I could annoy him further,' Beth replied. 'And I don't have it in me to listen to another lecture just yet.'

'Is that what you'd get?'

'Oh, undoubtedly, but it can wait till tomorrow. It'll give him the chance to practice his lines a bit more, make them really polished. He prides himself on his delivery, you know.'

'I've never heard you speak about him so . . .' Katherine scrabbled for a word.

'So what?'

'So . . . irreverently.'

'What do you think he is, a vicar or something?'

A shared vision of Evan in a cassock danced fleetingly across the sitting room and they fell into convulsions. Much to the annoyance of others, Katherine and Beth sometimes had the capacity to adopt the same brand of humour favoured by sixth-formers on buses, the sort triggered by an unsuspecting victim in a funny hat that causes tears to stream relentlessly down even the most sophisticated of faces rendering useless all powers of speech.

'I needed that,' puffed Katherine after the five-minute outburst, wiping her eyes and making a bad job of removing her smudged mascara.

'Not as much as me. I needed it more than you.'

'Well, for someone who walked out in defiance of their husband earlier tonight in favour of the company of old friends, I think you did a fantastic job of holding it together.'

'Holding what together?' Beth always pretended to be what Loveday referred to as 'a scat behind'. She liked things spelled out to her, just in case she had got it wrong which made some people, including her husband, doubt her quick brain.

'The entire evening. If you hadn't been here, then it would most probably have been a disaster. You were brilliant with Johnny, teasing him, building him up, making him feel as special as Patrick.'

'He is.'

'I know, I didn't mean that, but . . .'

'But what?'

'But Patrick arrives out of the blue and he's the novelty, isn't he? And I haven't asked Johnny about the party arrangements for months, which is mean of me because I know he wants to talk about them. It's just I got so sick of hearing them when we hit the crunch. He hung on to this bloody party for dear life when we were splitting up. We would be in the middle of a crucial talk about our future and the phone would go and it would be some band or other, or maybe another guest, asking who to make the cheque payable to or something, and our talk would go down the pan, and I would seethe with anger while he burbled on the phone for hours. Did you see the way he came alive the moment you asked him how things were going?'

'I did actually,' said Beth, managing to sound as if the idea had only just occurred to her when in fact the truth was so much more flattering to her sense of perception. She had wanted to cry for Johnny earlier. Seeing him so displaced and bewildered in his own home had diffused any excitement she'd experienced over seeing Patrick again, and her one purpose was to make him feel better. She had been hit full on with the realisation that they had now known each other for almost as long as they hadn't, that they had passed not only the student stage, but the one after that, and even the one after that again, and that any rock any of them hit now would have at least two or three different seams running through it.

'He's been so miserable,' continued Katherine, pouring them both another glass, 'fighting to get away from something all year. I thought it might have been his job rather than me, but he's still working in the same depressing office, dealing presumably with the same depressing rows, and yet I have to accept the fact that he's happier. I must have just been that one extra irritation he was unwilling to bear.'

'Well, that's rubbish and you know it. For a start, you asked him to go.'

'I didn't exactly ask him, I gave him the choice, but I expected him to stay. Anyway, he had made it more or less impossible for me to do anything else. He was *so* hard to live with. I felt I was a burden to him, because I wasn't really earning enough to warrant the childcare costs, and because I'd got pregnant twice, and provided him with two more burdens and—'

'I know you don't really think that. Anyway, he *did* say he'd stay, didn't he? Or that's what you told me, if you remember correctly.'

Katherine did suddenly remember correctly. Both of them at regular intervals over the summer had suggested a time apart, and the final decision had been, without any doubt at all, a joint decision, taken late one night after a horrid row which had left them both emotionally exhausted, and one they had both felt better for making the next day.

'I know. It's just that when he left tonight and took Patrick with him, I wasn't sure which one of them it was that I wanted to stay,' she said.

'I didn't want either of them to. It's ages since we had a night on our own and I need a chat.'

'Not you as well. That's what Patrick keeps telling me!'

'We'll all be celebrating the millennium in a hospital for the mentally deranged if we're not careful!' said Beth, back on her favourite mission of trying to lighten things up.

'Oh, God, don't,' said Katherine. 'It's not funny, don't.'

'You'd have laughed out of politeness at that earlier. You were appallingly tense.'

'It was Johnny. He was winding me up. I could tell he thought I'd deliberately kept Patrick's visit a secret. He kept giving me hostile little looks.'

'I didn't see that. I thought it was you winding *him* up.'

'This was before you arrived,' said Katherine, starting on a blow-by-blow account of the first half hour.

But Beth was no longer listening because she had just had another inkling. It was Sunday night, and her period was now a day and a half late.

Chapter 5

It always amused Johnny that Truro called itself a city. 'So it has a cathedral,' he would say to Loveday, who could get amazingly uppity about it, 'but I can walk from one edge to the other in half an hour and anyway, where's the inner? Truro is a relatively affluent market town, and much as you would love to slap the socially impoverished label on it, I'm not going to let you.'

'But that's exactly what Cornwall is,' Loveday would come back at him, smacking her pewter-ringed hands down on the nearest surface with a clap with relish for the verbal battle that was about to commence. 'Our communities have been battered shockingly over the years and the response from central government has been nothing short of complacent.'

'Order, order!' he'd tease. 'Would the right honourable lady kindly refrain from physical abuse of the furniture.'

'Shut up! The extraction of tin has been the main activity in Cornwall for the last two thousand years and now we're down to just one working mine, and even that is constantly threatened with closure. Our fishing industry is under enormous pressure to meet all the new EC regulations on conservation of fish stocks and health and hygiene. Even our china clay quarries which should have a future well into the next century, have laid off two thousand men in the last ten years because of competition from alternative sources.'

'Yes, but Loveday the fact is—'

'No, it's still my turn. Look at the level of suicide among farmers, and the evidence that up to half our farmers will not be succeeded by their sons, and then tell me we're not socially impoverished. Our unemployment level is higher than the national average, and our gross domestic product has fallen by ten per cent in fifteen years.'

'Sure, but you've still got the edge over places like—'

'No, we haven't.' Loveday knew that if she gave him time to form an argument, he'd nail her. 'Tourism so very conveniently distorts the economic facts that if it wasn't for people like me continually banging the drum, things might be a lot worse.'

'I'll give you that.'

'Aaaaah,' she would sigh with a satisfied smirk. 'I just love shutting you up. Did I shut you up? I think I did shut you up, didn't I?'

'Loveday, I said Truro, not the whole of Cornwall. Anyway, you forget, we're fighting the same war. You're talking to Cornwall's Deputy Economic Grants Director. I know exactly how scarce resources are because I spend my whole working life trying to promote business growth, don't I?'

'Not *the* Deputy Economic Grants Director? Not Mr Johnnie Bates? Oh my, I'm so thrilled to meet you at last!'

'Away with you, you irritating old woman! But if you think Truro really is deprived, then why don't you come with me the next time I visit my parents and I'll show you where I grew up?'

'Show me a real city, and I'll show you a ghetto,' Loveday would mock, vintage John Wayne, and there the discussion would end. Johnny was always tempted to take it a stage further but if he did, he ran the risk of becoming not only emotional but political too which would be a shame, since it would deprive him of his right to tease Loveday. That was how the two of them worked best – him teasing, her rising to it, her teasing, him rising. She revelled in a fight, especially when it was about Cornwall, and although she and Johnny never really got to each other in the way that some members of the county council got to Loveday, or drivers of Range Rovers got to Johnny, they loved the spat all the same.

He admired her work on behalf of her beloved Cornwall, and thanked her for it often, but she was such a tempting target. All her arguments sprang from one ardently held belief – that everyone ultimately responds to their origins, regardless of the distance they have travelled from them subsequently. Barely a debate went by without her mentioning the word 'birthplace' and a surefire way of heating up a debate was to point this out, especially if you hinted that her 'birthplace' was hugely advantaged. Calling her 'a woolly liberal' was good fun too, especially as she favoured ethnic jumpers and chunky handmade sandals, but she could give as good as she got, and she often had a poke at his more extreme left-wing views, so all in all they were more or less quits. The fact was, she had such an enormous air of contentment about her, based on who she loved and how she lived, that he happily appreciated he wasn't even chipping at the surface.

When Johnny felt the need to refer to his roots, he did it quietly. The sprawling crime-ridden South London housing estate on which he had spent his entire pre-University life was so far removed both socially and geographically from where he was now that he struggled to remember the reality of it. Twenty-four members of his family still lived there, brothers, wives, sisters, husbands, nephews, nieces and his Mum and Dad, occupying seven separate flats and clocking up hundreds of years residency between them. He told Katherine once that he saw his life in Cornwall as one of those soft-focus portraits you see in High Street photographers' windows – Johnny Bates with a makeover. Periodically, when the urge to wipe some of the Vaseline off the lens came over him, he would take Hattie or Seth back to his parents for a weekend and for a while afterwards, Katherine would notice he had an extra edge, harder and more seasoned, like a soldier who had seen active service standing alongside colleagues who had yet to leave the training field.

Phyllis and Stan Bates were not his natural parents and Katherine believed this was why he held them in such reverential esteem. He, on the other hand, found it almost impossible to accept that she felt barely a scrap of gratitude towards her mother and father, and so when he tried to instill into his own children a little appreciation of the sacrifices parents make, even though they owed him nothing or maybe even less than that lately, a certain annoyance would creep across his wife's face.

Johnny had been the only one of five brothers and two sisters to fly the nest to further education, and although no one had ever actually voiced it, they all secretly believed it was down to some genetic advantage in the brain department.

Phyllis, his adoptive mother, would often mull it over in her mind. Sylvie, Johnny's true mother and Phyllis' own first cousin, had certainly not been blessed with intellect – she hadn't even had the sense to take precautions against pregnancy in her chosen high-risk profession – but who's to say his father wasn't? Sylvie used to boast around the estate that she would only work with 'gentlemen who come word of mouth', and she considered herself different to the other prostitutes on the estate who would ply their trade openly on the nearby streets. At least those girls did it to feed their families, Phyllis would say, not like Sylvie, who did it to wrap herself in fur.

When she had arrived on Phyllis and Stan's doorstep on 22 December, 1964 and told them she was going to dump her baby where the police would find him, Phyllis had felt like calling her bluff. But then she'd seen Johnny's raw little cheeks all chapped from wind and a lack of love, and she'd said, 'You'd better dump him here then.' Sylvie hadn't wasted a moment and what had happened to her after that no one really cared. There was gossip every now and again that she'd been seen in some expensive car in some rich London street, but she was more or less forgotten.

'I wasn't given you by Sylvie, I was given you by God,' Phyllis would tell Johnny when he was growing up.

'So am I adopted?'

'I don't need a piece of paper to tell me you're mine. Nor does your Dad. We've got this feeling here,' she would say, thumping her heart. 'It says Phyllis and Stan Bates, you have seven children, and the second from youngest is a bright little button who's going to make something of his life.'

Making something of his life was a phrase that had

come back to haunt him over the last twelve months. His job, second-in-command in a local government department that concentrated on renewal and growth for the Cornish economy, was – as civil servants' posts go – a good one. Not only did it come with a free moral passport to live in a safe and beautiful corner of Britain, but it gave him the opportunity to help sustain that corner too. Cornwall may be rich in landscape, he was keen to tell Phyllis and Stan, but – and he always gave a mental salute to Loveday at this point – it is on the breadline where jobs are concerned. Sure, it has a magnificent coastline and picturesque harbours, and that is the image most tourists take home with them, but for those who live and try to work here, the reality is different, he would remind them at every visit. He needed them to know that, just in case the comparison with their own stomping ground sometimes felt too cruel to bear.

'You ought to be proud of yourself,' Phyllis told him once when he found the courage to hint at his private stagnation. 'You're not like one of those outsiders your lovely neighbour talks about who go down there and use it like some great big holiday park. You're trying to get a better deal for the people it really belongs to.'

'Loveday said that? To you?'

'I always want to call her Lovejoy,' Phyllis had said, raising her eyebrows in exasperation at her daft old brain. 'I asked her once if it got on her nerves, having all these visitors down, clogging up the roads and the shops, and she said she liked it as long as they went home again. So I said, "Johnny didn't go home, did he?" And she said you were different. She said you cared like a Cornishman.'

Loveday was right. The responsibility to improve Cornwall's lot had kept Johnny's interest for nearly ten years. But lately, much as he continued to strive for economic growth for the county, he couldn't shake the feeling that his own growth had stopped, and more and more, he was asking himself the question 'Do I want to be doing this for the rest of my working life?' The answer was always a resounding no. He had tried to talk to Katherine about it before they split, but she had simply confirmed what he himself believed – that he was more or less trapped. He had a mortgage to pay, he had two children to clothe and feed and he had a wife who only earned enough to keep the pets. What answer was there, other than to stick with it like everybody else out there does? He even tried talking to Patrick about it, pretending that he was really talking about Patrick's career, not his own.

'How come you're so laid back about what's happening to your job prospects back in the States then? Surely, the longer you mooch around here, the more damage you'll do to your career over there. Doesn't it worry you that you might go back to square one?'

'Not really. I'm drip-feeding a few pieces here and there, just so they don't forget my name. I've just been paid a handsome sum to write a few words on some missing transatlantic sailor who pitched up in Falmouth last week. Old news, re-hashed. Easy money.'

'I know, Katherine told me. It really winds her up you know, the way you pick up commissions without even trying.'

'British titles wouldn't order anything from me because they don't know me, which is why I'm trying to keep a presence in the States, but if they forget me, they forget me. I'll just have to remind them once I get back.'

'Things would be different if you had kids.'

'But I don't.'

'As far as you know ... God, what it is to have no responsibilities. Here am I, working too many hours to earn the money to spend on too many things, and going mad into the bargain. If I could just break the circuit somewhere, things might get better.'

'Isn't that what you've done by leaving your wife and children?'

'I've still got to work the hours to earn the money though, haven't I? All I have done is increase the burden by having to find extra rent money. That's hardly a solution, is it?'

Patrick had actually been closer to the truth than Johnny let him believe. Leaving Katherine *had* been a step towards breaking the circuit, although in practice, it had just bent it out of shape a little. There was no room for manoeuvre in his job, so he had looked for space at home. He hadn't meant it to happen, but the more he shut down, the more she did, until they'd barely been operating as a couple any more.

'If I could find a job that brought me the same buzz that planning this party does,' he told Patrick, 'I'd take it like a shot. The one thing I've noticed is that most people are genuinely hopeful about the millennium – like it offers them an opportunity for a fresh start. The idea of seeing it in with a bang just sets them alight. Encouraging people to feel good about the future – that's the kind of job I want.'

'Er, forgive me for depriving you of a goal, Johnny, but isn't that the job you've already got?' Johnny might have done better to talk to Beth. She had heard Katherine say more than once that she thought Johnny was in the wrong job.

No one understood, just no one. He looked as if he had it all, and was hell-bent on chucking it away. Now, if he could chuck *half* of it away, and still persuade the other half to stick with him . . . but that was just a non-starter. What would they live on, and what would they live *in*? Money makes the world go round, and in his family, he made the money. End of story.

Walking out from the cavern-like atmosphere of Truro's bustling undercover market into the autumn sun, Johnny's mind wandered back to Loveday's insistence that here was a city with all the sufferings of one ten times larger. What a joke. It had taken him twice as long as necessary to get from the travel agency to his motorbike because he had crossed the paths of at least three people he knew well, including his landlord and friend, Nick Shepherd. Nick had thankfully not been in a mood to chat and they knew each other well enough to just hit each other intentionally with their shoulders and offer exaggerated apologies. When Johnny had phoned him that awful Sunday after he and Katherine had eventually reached the grim conclusion that their marriage was over, Nick had immediately offered the cottage at a low rent, followed up by an invitation to supper. And when Johnny had torn himself away from a sleeping Hattie and Seth five days later, and opened the door on his new home with a face full of tears, the whole place had been filled with flowers. How could Katherine accuse him of drawing up a guest-list of strangers when most of the people going were the Nick and Penny Shepherds of this world?

Out of the corner of his eye, he caught sight of Beth. Forget city, he thought, some days it's more like an extension of the village pump.

'Why aren't you at school?' he shouted, stupidly excited about seeing her on the off-chance. He hadn't spoken to her since leaving the cottage on Sunday night and he wanted some reassurance that she saw it as he did – an evening that started badly but ended well, in the way that only evenings with proper friends can. He waved the helicopter flight tickets he had just bought, but she didn't look up. It was only going to be a quick recce to the Isles of Scilly, but Patrick had agreed to go with him, and there were some important cogs to turn next weekend, not least the catering arrangements.

He was just about to hop across the road to catch her by surprise when it registered that her eyes were hidden by sunglasses and her cheeks looked unusually puffy. For a moment, he hesitated, and then his feet started towards her again with the renewed intention of checking to see if she needed him. She looked unhappy, and it troubled him. As if to confirm his judgment, she disappeared into the open door of a doctor's surgery and he knew instinctively that she was not ill and some other reason must be taking her there. He walked the short distance to his parked bike and stood there for a while, trying to decide whether or not he should follow her in. Katherine would have done, he thought, but then she's a woman. And if there was something really wrong, Evan would be with her, wouldn't he?

He checked his watch and decided there was just enough time to pop round to Tremewan, using the excuse of the tickets, before getting back to work. He shuddered at the thought of needing a reason to arrive uninvited at his own home, but then some might say he had made his bed and he now had to lie in it. If only he could invite his wife to join him, he wished fleetingly.

Taking longer than necessary to put on his helmet in case Beth re-emerged, he suddenly felt unusually lonely, and to make up for it, he started the bike just a little aggressively. An elderly woman on her way to the bus station shook her head in annoyance and he shook his rudely back. The journey, up the wide hill out of Truro past the family-run furniture store that Loveday once told him marked the city limits, and on to the winding country lanes that took him home blew most of his cobwebs away.

Everyone should travel this way, he thought, as he took in the smell of autumn and saw how the vegetation in the hedgerows was already receding into its wintry role. He passed his favourite tree – a bent-double hawthorn growing up through part of a broken wall, lashed over the years by the wild south-westerly wind that often came howling across the land without warning. Of course the comparison with a South East London housing estate was too cruel on the South East Londoners. How could he pretend otherwise?

The following weekend was on his mind now – three days on the island of St Mary's in which he had to turn the first few wheels of phase four.

One hundred and twenty entertainingly printed invitations were sitting in a fat bundle locked safely in the black courier's box behind him. As soon as the decision of what the guests should eat had been made, the menus could also be designed and printed, and then it would simply be a question of licking the stamps. It was a happy prospect, not least because it would mean he could stop thinking about it for a while, and if he stopped thinking about it, he might stop talking about it, and that would please Katherine.

Food was not something close to Johnny's heart, as the contents of his fridge told anyone who chose to look in. He ate because it stopped him feeling hungry, and he enjoyed meals around the table only because of the opportunity they offered for communication, but other than that, the pleasures of food were a mystery. The party menu was the one area he had no interest in. He had toyed more than once with the idea of asking Katherine to help out, but her blatant irritation had stopped him each time.

No doubt Patrick will come up with something, he

thought, opening up the throttle, and if he doesn't, then I'll pick the brains of the hotel chef. Whatever happens, I'll make sure I get it right. A surge of confidence ran through him as it often did when he was on his bike – something to do with the way he felt in control and keen for a challenge. He wondered, not for the first time, where his newly discovered appetite and talent for organisation came from. Acquired or inherited? Inherited, he suspected. All his life he had given full credit to Phyllis and Stan for his good points – how to show affection, keep a sense of humour, put others first – and he laid the blame squarely on Sylvie for his bad ones – his tendency to give in if something wasn't going his way, his small streak of violence (never against women or children) when he got angry, and his mistaken belief that everyone would always understand his motives.

His new organisational skills could hardly be a trait picked up from Phyllis and Stan. Between them, they couldn't arrange a train trip from Paddington to Plymouth without a diversion to Preston. As for Sylvie, she couldn't even organise herself not to get pregnant. That left the bloke who got her like that in the first place, he concluded, as he drew up outside the cottage. By the time he walked up his short front path, he'd stopped caring. What did it matter? All this inherited genes stuff was nonsense – he'd never been able to understand men who put so much store in producing a son and 'continuing the line'. He was who he was, regardless, just as he hoped Hattie was Hattie and Seth was Seth.

Katherine's car wasn't parked on the kerb like he'd expected and both halves of the cottage were empty, so he couldn't even have a coffee with Loveday. A note would do. If he'd known Beth would see it before the others, he might have scribbled a message to her as well – something like: *Saw you at the doctor's today Beth – Truro is too small for secrets*. He didn't realise it, but he had a knack of only just avoiding offence.

The moment a woman of a certain age entered the room, Beth's eyes, swollen from five days of crying, would zoom in on the stomach, and then upwards to the face. She couldn't help it, even though the last thing she wanted to encourage was any kind of interaction with a stranger. It was as if she had to torture herself just a tiny bit more to prove that she could not possibly feel any more tormented than she already did, and as each smiling face was one more twist of the knife, it was also one more opportunity to pity herself.

Beth still believed, despite plenty of evidence to the contrary, that all pregnant women bloomed, and there they all were to prove it, sitting smugly on the standard and consistently uncomfortable yellow and green seats of the doctor's waiting room, showing off their shiny hair and clear skin as if to say to their audience: 'I'm only here because something good is happening to me. Illness cannot touch the fertile.'

She had been told often enough that she only ever saw what she wanted to see, and was often criticised by Evan for her ostrich-like tendencies but she had never taken any notice before. Today, there was no refuge to be had from head-burying anyway. Even if she had closed her eyes and shut herself in a dark room, she would still feel everyone else's happiness apart from her own. She was so full of self-pity that she was even resenting the receptionist for not reminding her that Fridays were also ante-natal days, and now, being forced to look upon bump after bump after bump, she interpreted the unhappy coincidence as life's way of jeering at her.

The girl in the corner chewing her nails couldn't have been a day over fifteen yet it was odds on she was attending the clinic too, and Beth was oddly desperate for her not to be. She wanted the girl to start coughing uncontrollably, or for her mother to walk in and start fussing about her headache. If the girl *was* pregnant, Beth had been watching long enough to know she would be called by either the sweet-looking middle-aged nurse or the bald doctor with trendy glasses.

'What difference does it make to me if she is pregnant or not? It has absolutely no bearing on my own life at all. It shouldn't, doesn't, matter one way or the other,' Beth argued silently, knowing that it did matter, a lot, just for that moment.

'Lisa Rowe?' called the bald doctor with the trendy glasses, poking his head around the reinforced glass door, and sure enough, the girl got up and slopped towards the consultation room as if the whole process was boring her to tears.

With each lazy step the girl took, something began to stir in Beth and make sense of her excessive interest. The girl could have been anybody, and that was the point. If she could have been anybody, then she could also be somebody – somebody's daughter, and soon maybe, somebody's mother. It made Beth want to join in whatever drama was about to unfold, to follow the girl, hold her hand, help her talk things through. 'Don't ask for an abortion!' she wanted to shout. 'Hang on to the life inside you, it needs you and you don't yet know how much you will need it too one day. Anyway, I'll have it if you don't want it.'

By the time the girl's round shoulders and scuffed boots had disappeared into the bowels of the surgery, Beth had already filed Lisa Rowe away, and her mind had made the leap to another young mother, one who thirty-five years ago had had to fight prejudice and disgust, and one who suddenly seemed like the most optimistic, least selfish woman who ever lived.

They had talked about it many times, Loveday and Beth, but for reasons not even known to herself, Beth had always preferred to stop short of hearing the whole story. She knew that when the nineteen-year-old Loveday had realised she was pregnant, the sixties were not yet as swinging as they were going to be, not even in London, and that Loveday had been forced to give up her art course to return to Cornwall and her elderly parents. Beth knew that her father had been called Mick, and although he had never been given a second name, she did know a few other details about him – that he had been a third year English student who had called the relationship to a halt just before Loveday had decided to do the same, that the one thing Loveday would always remember about him was his frail face, that he had not been her mother's first lover and that he had never been told about his baby.

Mick, if he was still alive, would probably be married with other grown children by now, oblivious to the fact that a thirty-five-year-old woman was carrying fifty per cent of his genes around with her, and that was the way Beth liked it. Loveday had made it quite clear that if her daughter ever felt otherwise, all she had to do was ask and the search would begin, although where they would begin, neither of them had a clue. During a happy childhood and adolescence, little reference had been made to the matter, and now, with Beth a grown woman and Loveday well settled into middle age, the existence of Mick was not only not mentioned, it didn't even cross their minds. Even now, when Beth's whole perspective was full of the two halves of a whole, he didn't count.

It was odd that she should be so hell-bent on the nuclear

family thing. As long as she could remember she had nurtured dreams of a husband and children, and yet her own upbringing was living proof that convention is not the only way to do it, that a child does not necessarily need a father nor a woman a husband. Loveday was adamant about this, and she had more than demonstrated her case, but Beth still believed that her mother's refusal to share her home with a man, however much she loved or trusted him, was the reason she was alone today. For Beth, that was a source of regret, but for Loveday, it remained something to celebrate.

As a child, Beth had shared in both the great loves of Loveday's life. Bill had been an intermittent but much cherished male presence during her primary school years and was now running the same pub in Ireland that, having failed to persuade them to come with him, he'd left Cornwall for in 1975. Peter had also failed to hook them five years later, despite the fact that he only wanted to take them as far as the next village, and whenever Loveday struck up a friendship with a man nowadays, Beth knew it would only ever be just that.

As far as the rest of the early years were concerned, Beth understood that the attitude in Cornwall towards an unmarried pregnant teenager had been far more accommodating than the one Loveday had met in the capital, and that it was this experience alone, the feeling that she was among friends, that had made Loveday determined never to live anywhere else. Mother and daughter were not very much alike but the one thing Loveday had actually given Beth was a fervent sense of identity and a pride in being Cornish.

What Loveday hadn't given Beth though, and she wished increasingly lately that she had, was the absolute conviction that happiness does not come through other people, or good fortune, or security, or popularity, or any of the other places she suspected Beth was looking, but that it only comes once you've been thrown into the bear pit, had a wrestle and come out knowing yourself to be the victor. At eighteen, role-playing as an adult with her first lover, Loveday hadn't known she could win anything. At nineteen and pregnant, she had thought for a while that the bear would win, or that, if she was lucky, she might be rescued by someone before the match was over. At twenty, as a mother, holding her baby and nursing her wounds, Loveday had claimed victory, and really, she had been celebrating ever since, pausing every now and again to try and find a way of passing that self-belief on. The mistake she had made was in thinking she could be Beth's everything, and then Beth had made her mistake by swapping one everything for another, called Evan. Too many ready-made meals in the fridge and not enough delving into the cupboards to see what you can rustle up.

Beth's lower tummy was still dragging heavily, an unnecessary reminder that her period had started three days later than expected. She instinctively rubbed along the line of her stomach between her hips, withdrawing her hand in horror as she realised she was echoing the movements of a hugely pregnant woman opposite. For all the terrible things she and Evan had said and done to each other since Sunday, none of them had come near to hurting her as much as the unmistakable sight of her own menstrual blood against the white porcelain of the staff lavatory on Tuesday lunchtime. Once she had let in the theory that it might not be just the redundant lining of an empty womb but something more essential, the very early loss of life perhaps, snatched away by the selfish anger of its parents, she couldn't let it drop. Perhaps the minute dividing cells had sensed the hostile atmosphere out there and decided that life wasn't worth the struggle. Maybe she had missed her one chance of motherhood because she had been too busy tormenting herself and punishing Evan. Considering the dreadful possibility of it all over again brought the events of the whole ghastly week crashing down around her.

She accepted that she just might have started it by not bothering to go home on Sunday night. That decision, born out of drunken bravado and a revived sense of mischief had been the most defiant of her marriage so far. Evan had made it more than clear when she left the house that he was not happy about her going. In fact, there had almost been a threat to his voice.

'You know my feelings on the matter. You are old enough to make a choice without me having to spell it out to you, but I hope you are also wise enough to accept whatever consequences your decision might bring,' he'd said as she'd taken her cashmere donkey jacket from its peg on Sunday night.

'And you are old enough to go to the restaurant on your own, just this once,' she'd replied. 'I am not going to commit adultery, I am going to supper with my three best friends, a supper to which you have also been invited. I don't quite know what you mean by the consequences of my decision, but I'll take the risk and assume that, yes, I am wise enough to accept them.' She'd been careful then to wait a moment longer to give him one last opportunity to change his mind and come with her.

'Well, go on then. Get out if you're going,' he'd barked unpleasantly, and she'd fled, feeling just a tiny bit scared but rather a lot triumphant.

All day at school on Monday she had fought the temptation to phone his office. Whether she would have apologised she didn't know, but at both breaks and at lunchtime, she'd found herself hovering outside Dan Carver's office, like an unruly child waiting to be taken in and dealt with. Hovering was about as far as she got, because from within, she heard the deep murmuring of Dan's voice on the phone himself. She could hardly have kicked the headmaster out of his own office just to patch up a marital tiff, and as there was no other telephone private enough for the job, she had decided to leave any reconciliatory work until the evening.

When midnight had been and gone and there had still been no sign of Evan – no note, no phone call, no car – she realised she was in trouble.

'I did it last night, he's doing it tonight,' she had reassured herself. 'Good luck to him.' But the empty house had seemed sinister in his absence, as if it had been busy inventing a new slightly malevolent personality for itself while she had been away, one that suggested it did not want her there. When Evan had eventually returned twenty-four hours later satisfied with his demonstration, the malevolence had been replaced by a growing feeling that *she* no longer wanted to be there. By that time, her hopes had been dashed anyway, and she was feeling less like making up.

The tension had still been there between them this morning, before she'd left for the doctor's, when Evan had announced over a tense breakfast that he would be away the following weekend at a Law Society dinner.

'Oh, you know I'm ovulating then, do you? There's no need to go all the way to London just because I'm entering a fertile period, Evan. Buy me a handbell and I'll ring "Unclean, unclean" if you like. It'll save on the train fare.'

'Goodbye Beth, have a nice day,' he'd said, leaving half a piece of toast and a freshly brewed coffee. Her cycle was the last thing he could be bothered with, and he only really noticed she had one when the box of Tampax was left out in the bathroom and he had to keep putting them away. That, and the fact that sex was off the menu every now and again.

'Beth Ross?' came the amiable voice of her own doctor from a different glass door to the one that led to the ante-natal clinic, dragging her back to the present. She could feel the sets of female eyes following her across the floor as they all digested the new information with glee. 'Oh, so she's not one of us then. Bet she'd like to be.' What they were really wondering was whether they would ever have a waistline like that again, but Beth was blind to her physical advantages at the moment, dwelling instead on her disadvantages, which were all on the inside.

'Okay?' asked her doctor who was so similar in age to herself that she always wanted to call him by his first name, Jeremy. As he sat down, she could see the ripped inner lining to his tweed jacket. It was always the most peculiar things that made her like people. He smiled and could see she'd been crying. 'What's up?' he said, so kindly she almost cried again.

'Well, I've come really, against my husband's wishes, to discuss our difficulty in conceiving.' She was blushing, not out of any prudishness, but because she was finding it hard to choose the right facial expression. How do you begin to talk openly about the one thing that is eating you up when the only other exchange of words you have had is to say, 'Hello.'

'Sure,' replied Dr Jeremy Shaw, looking at her and nodding, but waiting for more. He spoke sensitively but without that brand of off-the-shelf compassion many of his colleagues in the medical profession chose to adopt. 'Remind me, how long have you been trying?'

'I came off the pill three years ago and we've been using nothing since.'

'Right. Okay. Well, are you acquainted with your own cycle? Do you know when you ovulate, for example?'

'I do, Evan doesn't. Or at least, I think I do.'

And Beth felt herself letting out a long sigh as the conversation turned to menstrual charts, temperature taking, progesterone tests and sperm counts. It was the first time she had ever properly discussed anything like pregnancy with anyone else, including Evan and it felt wonderfully liberating, an entirely new experience for her. From time to time she asked Evan if he thought they would ever have children. He would reply with something like 'I've already got my baby,' but that kind of thing just wasn't enough any more.

A few months ago, her period had been no more than a day late, and in her excitement, she had phoned Dr Shaw from the headmaster's office during a lunch-hour at school. Only after going through a lengthy and excruciating 'I could be pregnant' preamble was she stopped dead in her tracks by a question: 'Have you done a test?' She hadn't, of course, and when she did one the following morning, it showed negative, which was further confirmed by the onset of bleeding two hours later. Even in those few hopeful moments, she had known underneath that it was all just a matter of time before disappointment came, but now, sitting here and talking about it properly for the first time, she could sense real potential.

'I know we have made love at least three times around ovulation over the last six months because I've been using an ovulation predictor kit, but he doesn't know. I hide it, I make sure I do the tests when he's not around.' Now, the words were coming freely.

'Do you mind me asking why you don't want him to know?' Dr Shaw said, trying to establish the nature of Evan's reluctance.

'Only because he has this thing about not wanting to make

love to order. I wouldn't want him to believe that the only reason I was – well – initiating sex was to get pregnant. I want him to feel that I still desire him just for him, and not for a baby.'

Jeremy wanted to ask 'And do you?' but it was none of his business, so instead, he asked another question.

'How would he feel if he saw you taking your temperature every morning before you got up? We should really start by drawing up an accurate picture of your monthly cycle.'

'Would I have to do it in front of him?'

'It's best done before you move around too much, just to get an accurate reading.'

'So exactly how does that work then?'

It was a routine conversation, one that Jeremy Shaw had delivered many times before, and he did it almost on auto-pilot. There was something else on his mind about this couple's infertility. He would have to check, but if he was right, it could be tricky – patient confidentiality was an issue to which he was firmly committed. He doodled a memo to himself on the corner of his notes, hoping it looked more like a meaningless scribble than a pressing reminder to do further research.

'Make an appointment to see me in just over a fortnight,' he said, smiling and raising his sandy eyebrows encouragingly. 'You should have ovulated by then, and we'll be able to work out your cycle in a little more detail.'

'I might even be pregnant,' Beth replied, only half meaning it.

'That's it – positive thinking!' Jeremy said, thinking how young she seemed for her age, and how much the antithesis of a pregnant woman she looked, with her high pert breasts and ironing-board stomach. He put a warm firm hand on her shaking shoulder. 'And try to stop crying. It's an exhausting business, tear production.'

The gentle gesture brought another three or four more tears to the surface and she began to say sorry.

'Never apologise to a doctor,' he smiled, and when he thought she was safely out of earshot, he phoned reception.

'Before you send the next patient in, could you possibly bring me Evan Ross' notes? Four, Lander Parc. Thanks, Val.'

Chapter 6

The fifteen minutes or so Beth had spent with Dr Jeremy Shaw had been like an escape into another world, a world in which she was able to imagine herself, somewhere in the far and distant future, as a mother. It was the only view of herself that made life worth living, and for the duration of her appointment, it felt real. As soon as she had left the almost conspiratorial air of his surgery however, the image had disappeared and walking back past the rows of women with their full to bursting wombs, she succumbed to the old representation of herself – beautiful, barren and thirty-five.

The prospect of a day at home staring at the carefully chosen curtains, designer sofas and stain-free carpets made her think she should perhaps go into school after all, but then she found her MG turning right instead of left, going up the hill towards the village of Tremewan and, she hoped, Loveday. Every conceivable space in her mother's cottage was filled by junk. She pictured the kitchen with the wonky shelf as you walked in groaning under the weight of the candlestick, and the antique perfume bottle, the empty silver photo frame, the wooden cat, and the assortment of pebbles and shells Loveday had a habit of picking up every time she walked on the beach. Even the beams on the ceiling were graced with every plausible hanging object there ever was – china jugs, poppy seed heads, salt dough shapes, a string of papier-mâché beads Beth had made as a ten-year-old – and each thing with its own story to tell. It was exactly where she wanted to be, amid jumble and disarray – so much more comforting than order and arrangement.

Dido Seal rarely thought about Beth Ross so when she did, the moment lasted. Of all three of Patrick's closest friends, Beth was the one Dido utterly failed to bond with. Katherine she liked, and Johnny could be devilish in a way Patrick never was, but Beth and she had never really gelled. The most appropriate adjective people normally came up with for Beth was 'sweet', which in Dido's book was condemning indeed. Once, in one of her more vehement moods after she had spent an evening with the four of them, she voiced her theory to Patrick, which had ended in her hearing some memorably painful truths about herself.

'You're all too heavily influenced by the fact that she is Loveday's daughter and therefore ought to possess some of her mother's uniqueness,' she'd told Patrick after hearing one too many of Beth's virtues extolled.

'Non-starter,' Patrick said. 'You forget that we met Beth before we met Loveday.'

'Only because she shared a room next to Katherine in the Halls of Residence for the first term.'

'Oh yes? And you've stayed as close to your next-door neighbour at Cambridge, have you?'

'I might have done if she'd had a mother like Loveday.'

'I believe I'm seeing a little jealousy here. Is it because she is just as effortlessly beautiful as you are? She's kind, she's innocent . . .' Patrick had begun counting Beth's qualities on his hands, intending to use all ten fingers.

'She's simple, Patrick,' Dido had intervened.

'I know how fond you are of sticking to initial impressions, but in this case Dido, really, you're wrong. Beth might not be Loveday, but she doesn't need to be.'

'I bet she wishes she was,' Dido had said bitchily and then immediately regretted it.

'I wish you wouldn't do this,' Patrick had said wearily. 'It puts you in such an unfavourable light.'

'Why do I do it then?'

'Because you're jealous. Because underneath, you're more like Beth than anyone would ever guess. Because you've built up such a hard persona for yourself over the years that you can't shake that, because you're angry with Beth for being able to live with herself the way she is, or rather, the way you yourself could quite easily be. Because you're sick of your own success as a superbitch.'

'Clever you,' she'd said, not haughtily enough. If anyone other than Patrick had had the gall to tell her that, she would have fought to the bitter end to prove them wrong, but because it was him, and he knew her too well, she'd left it at that. Strangely, she even loved him all the more for his perception.

Even so, Dido had still never been convinced enough to make an effort with Beth, which was why now, as she picked up the phone in Hoboken to dial her number, she felt quite disgraceful. Her yearning to hear news about Patrick – any news, what he was wearing, what mood he was in, what he'd been talking about – was so strong, her methods were becoming despicable. She had tried Johnny at work three times already this week, but he had been out. Katherine she wasn't sure could be trusted to tell the truth at the moment – she had already detected a certain protectiveness – and Beth was the only other option.

'Hi, I'm afraid neither Beth nor Evan Ross can answer

the phone right now, so please leave your message after the tone and we'll get back to you.'

'Hi Beth,' said Dido, trying to hide her disappointment and irritation at the answermachine. 'Just phoning to try and catch up with Patrick. No worries, I'll contact him later. See you at the millennium!'

She might have been more generous if she had known that Beth was not in fact out, but sitting on the floor of her bedroom, hugging her knees, and crying. Loveday had not been in, and the key hadn't even been under the stone. Then, when she had gone next door to seek out the company of Katherine or Patrick, she had seen a note on the door from Johnny: *Next time I call round with some important travel documents ready to whisk you off for a weekend of fun and excitement, don't be out, okay?*

Beth had sobbed all the way home. No one needs me, her heart had cried. I need someone to need me, I need my baby. Please, if there is a God, let me have a baby. She had continued to cry for the rest of the day.

In New Jersey, dropping the phone in frustration, Dido was helping herself to a large portion of the same kind of misery. Everyone else had a life apart from her. There she was, a woman of energy and brains with a consummate conviction that she and Patrick should be together, wasting her days doing part-time work in a bar on The Shore and waiting patiently for him to ride his own personal storm. She pondered a little over the consummate conviction bit. Did she still feel so convinced they should be together? Her whole future had been based on that one premise, and now, she wasn't so sure. Well, she damn well had to be sure, because there was too much riding on it now.

Why was no one in Cornwall talking to her? She knew

they didn't like her very much, or at least they weren't sure of her, and it bothered her much more than she would ever let on, but as Patrick pointed out, she only had herself to blame. At home, or when she was with close family, she was more or less ordinary in a sleek sort of way, and she was at her nicest when she dropped her guard, but away from that security, she relied on the two assets that always make a woman unpopular with her peers – extreme beauty and aggressive wit. It went down even more uncomfortably in Cornwall than it did elsewhere. No one down there looked the way she did – modern, lean, and invariably leathered – and that used to give her a boost, even make her laugh a little, until she felt a need to be loved, like she did now.

As instinctively as Beth's MG had turned towards Tremewan an hour earlier to seek the company of her mother, so Dido's smooth hand moved towards the telephone again, dialling a number she had been taught by rote as a five-year-old.

'Hello Mum?' she wavered transatlantically. 'Can I come home? Patrick and I have hit a major problem.'

'Of course,' Jean croaked down the phone in a grip of fear. Adam had spoken just before his death of the problem he thought Dido and Patrick were about to hit, and if it was the same one, then there was trouble ahead.

'What weekend of fun and excitement is this?' asked Katherine, ripping the note off the door with a flourish.

Patrick could tell by the way she shouldered the door open and dumped her shopping bags on the table that she wasn't going to endorse the proposal. Not that it was up to her anyway, he reminded himself.

'Your errant husband has invited me to join him on a jaunt to the Isles of Scilly under the pretext that I know something about party fodder.'

'Since when have you been a gastronome?' she snapped.
'Johnny's misconception, not mine.'

'Or is it just a convenient excuse for a boys' weekend?'

'Oh, I didn't think Johnny needed excuses any more.'

'No, but *you* do,' she said. 'You're accountable to me, even if he isn't.' The look of total horror on his face made her add, 'Joke, Patrick, joke.'

Even so, it was the wrong thing to say. Their conversations over the last week had certainly revealed enough about his tangled web in Hoboken for her to know that jokes about having to make excuses to women were not really on, even though, despite valiant efforts on her part, she still had no firm grasp of what his problem was.

'It's the way you tell them,' Patrick mumbled, pulling out a Marlboro from a fresh packet of cigarettes. 'Want one?'

'You know I don't smoke.' Katherine had a habit of maintaining this untruth.

'So what were you doing last night then? And the night before?'

'Making you feel better. I know how you hate to indulge alone.'

'Only because I've heard it makes you go blind.'

'The old ones are always the best.'

'Ha. So just think, while Johnny and I have our lads' only mini-break on St Mary's, singing rugby songs, picking up women and having a few late-night vindaloos, you can look forward to a nice healthy nicotine-free weekend here.'

'Oh, happy me,' she said, thinking she could add all sorts of other deprivations to that description as well. Even the children would be away. It was half-term and as tradition had it, Hattie and Seth would be with her parents in Somerset. 'Anyway, there aren't any curry houses on Scilly,' she added with mock petulance.

'What is it exactly about this party that you can't cope with then?' asked Patrick with an alarming switch of tone.

'Ooh, a probing personal question from Patrick Seal. Is your tape recorder switched on?'

'Oh, this interview is for my own personal gratification, I promise not to publish. Anyway, I shouldn't think anyone else really cares, except Johnny maybe.'

'You do have a way with women,' Katherine laughed. 'Have you been talking about me then?'

'Not much. But you don't exactly need a degree in psychology to see you're not happy about it.'

'Are *you*?' she asked, busying herself with putting a load of tins in the cupboard.

'I asked first. You know what a New York therapist would tell you? Verbalise your anxiety, Mrs Bates, and we'll take it from there.'

'I don't have any anxiety about it. It's just one more second in the relentless march of the human race. It's not going to make any difference to me if I have to think twice before writing a double zero on my cheques.'

'Oh, so it's the actual millennium thing you're uptight about, not the party. Is that right?'

'I'm fine with it all.'

'I don't believe you, but it's okay, I'll get it out of you eventually.'

'Like I'll get the reason you're here out of you, you mean?'

Patrick's expression changed from flippant to cagey. Katherine was frustratingly good at batting back.

'Is it okay if I give Johnny a call?' he asked, moving their conversation swiftly on.

'Of course,' she said, suddenly not wanting to be anywhere near a conversation between the two of them and making a bid for the garden, plumping up already plumped cushions in the sitting room on her way. How dare Johnny just whisk him off like that without asking when he knows the children won't be here. He's done it on purpose. What is he, jealous or something? Is he threatened by the thought of me here with Patrick on my own? How dare he! How scheming! She was trying hard to ignore a shock reappearance of the sexual undercurrent she had felt so strongly on the first day of Patrick's stay. Have I been anticipating a fling while the children are away? Is that why I'm cross, because Johnny is depriving me of a bit of excitement? A velvet cushion spat a few tiny feathers at her and she whacked it against the back of the sofa to see if any more wanted to escape.

The French windows needed a swift kick at the bottom before they would open but as soon as Katherine walked out and on to the granite circle, she felt immediately better. It was almost hot in the autumnal sun if you stood in the right place, and the view of fields and woodland was, as always, wonderfully therapeutic. Seth's favourite old sweatshirt was hanging from a branch by the stream and although when she'd noticed it a few days ago she'd decided on a cunning strategy to leave it there until it got so disgusting even *he* would agree to it going in the bin, she now thought she would retrieve it after all. That way, if Patrick saw her, he'd assume she had gone out there with a purpose and not just to get way from him.

On the way back up the gentle sloping lawn, holding Seth's sopping top at arm's length and wondering whether the grass would be dry enough to give it one last cut before winter, she thought she heard Loveday calling for Patrick.

'Loveday?' she called, going to the only gap in the hedge. The grass had worn to nothing around it where the children had used it as a thoroughfare and the two women had convened so many times. 'Are you all right?'

There was a pause, a laugh, the unexpected arrival of a dog and then Loveday.

'Oh Katherine, I'm sorry!'said Loveday, still laughing and grabbing the dog by the scruff. 'He just turned up late last night at my back door, whimpering, so I took him in.'

The dog, a scrawny black mongrel probably only just out of the puppy stage, kept his tail firmly between his legs. Katherine looked at him with pity and reservation.

'You're like a bloody magnet, Loveday! All life's waifs and strays somehow find their way.'

'You can talk!'

'He's a bit manky, isn't he? Are you going to keep him?'

Loveday laughed really loudly this time, an explosion of a laugh, as if there were a great joke going on behind Katherine's back that was all the more hilarious for Katherine's ignorance.

'What's so funny?' asked Katherine.

'I've been calling him Patrick all morning, virtue of the fact that he turned up out of the blue and keeps looking at me with sad eyes, whining for affection, so when you said he was a bit manky and was I going to keep him, it struck a chord!'

Katherine laughed too now. 'Well, if you are, watch your wine supply and your telephone bill. That's the only advice I have!'

'I've got to take him to the RSPCA this afternoon.'

'What a fantastic idea. Do they take stray men too?'

'I can always ask.'

'Loveday, you are the perfect panacea.'

The women continued to cackle until Loveday's telephone rang. The silly interlude had made Katherine feel much less irascible and she went back inside. Underneath, she knew her irritation had undoubtedly been triggered by Patrick's comments. He had been right to accuse her of an unease towards the millennium, but what did he expect? Bloody timing. Broken marriage, end of century, middle-age . . .

Patrick's languorous voice drifted in from the kitchen. 'Yeah, sure, pop round anytime, Johnny. I'm not going anywhere,' and an exasperation overtook her which sent her marching in, her intention of armistice gone. Before she could stop herself, she was ranting angrily.

'That's Johnny as in my estranged husband, is it? Not that I'd want you to trouble yourself with the insignificant details of a marital separation or anything. I shouldn't think Hattie and Seth will mind when they discover their father has turned up mid-week to see an old mate, and that he's taking the same old mate off for a piss-up on an island that Seth is currently doing a school project on and has been begging his Dad to take him to all term—'

'Hey, hey, hold on a second,' said Patrick gently.

'No,' she shouted, 'why should I hold on a second? You arrive out of the blue, and start buggering things up just when they were beginning to feel normal.' She had intended to rage for as long as the words kept coming but she ran out of steam embarrassingly quickly and allowed him to pull out a chair and guide her into it. She rubbed her hands through her hair and laid her head on the table. He sat down too, very close, then he put his hand under her chin and raised it to look into her face.

'Why don't you come with us?'

'Because Johnny won't want me to,' she mumbled into the heap of ironing on the table, 'and stop looking so closely at me. All you'll see are my wrinkles.'

'That's where you're wrong,' said Patrick, pulling a strand of hair away from the corner of her mouth and tucking it behind her ear.

Her smile was both apologetic and grateful, and because she didn't know what else to do after that, she got up and put the kettle on.

When Johnny turned up half an hour later, Katherine made herself scarce. He found her in the bedroom pretending to change the sheets and he realised it was the first time he had been upstairs since he'd moved out.

'Hi,' he said, standing in the doorway. She had changed the furniture round and he could no longer tell which side of the bed used to be his.

'I'll be down in a minute.'

'Do you want a hand?'

'No, thanks.'

'It looks different in here.'

'It is.'

Johnny breathed out audibly. 'Patrick said you'd like to come to St Mary's.'

'He didn't, did he?' said Katherine, cross for being mono-syllabic and embarrassed at the fuss she had made. 'I don't really. It's just that the children won't be here, and I was half thinking of suggesting we all go out somewhere, maybe with Beth, so I was a bit peeved when I saw your note, that's all.' Stop smoothing the sheet, she told herself. Stop it, it looks nervous.

'I'd really like you to,' Johnny said quickly, before she had even finished speaking.

'No, it's crazy, you wouldn't.'

'Why not?'

'It's a daft idea. We're living apart – couples who have

only just decided to split up don't go away for the weekend together, it's silly . . .'

'No it's not. Why don't they? Who says?'

'Well, anyway, it didn't naturally occur to you to ask me, and now you're only doing it because Patrick has suggested it. Really, it doesn't matter.'

'Actually, it did occur to me, but I was almost sure you'd say no. I need your help. I've got to decide the menu next weekend, and you know me where fiddly bits of food are concerned.' He suddenly had a vision of them both in bed, talking about the merits of prawns over chicken.

'Stop inventing reasons,' she said, shaking out the duvet, and thinking of the first few days after Hattie's birth and how Johnny had bought her a rubber ring to sit on. What did you do with such intimate knowledge once you were no longer sharing lives?

'You know I'd love you to be more involved.'

'I'll come if Beth will,' said Katherine impulsively. She wanted to get back down to the safety of the kitchen and a third party – the sexual undercurrent wasn't only tugging her Patrick's way.

'Done,' Johnny smiled, taking the stairs back down two at a time. In the kitchen, Patrick was just putting the phone down.

'She's coming?'

'Yep. If Beth will. Who were you calling?'

'Dido, but the phone is constantly engaged. I don't know how women manage to talk for so long.'

Johnny prickled, as if Patrick was taking a liberty, but whether it was because of the distance involved or because it was Dido, he wasn't sure. He liked her even less lately, and only because he suspected she was the sole cause of Patrick's darkness.

'Maybe she's discussing you. It would take more than a quick chat to do justice to that subject, wouldn't it?'

'Did you say Dido?' asked Katherine, appearing in the room. 'As in New York? In the middle of the day? Go ahead, call the speaking clock in Australia while you're at it.'

Forty-eight hours later, in Oxford, Jean Seal sat in her favourite armchair resting her feet on a stool and listened to the bathwater being run upstairs. The extra burden on the cottage's ancient plumbing system made the whole house croak and clatter as if it was about to be reduced to a pile of rubble, but to Jean, it was all rather comforting.

She shut her eyes and pretended for a moment that it was not Dido up there, but Adam, preparing for his legendary evening bath. One of the floorboards between the bathroom and his dressing room, the room in which Dido had touchingly asked to sleep when she had arrived last night, had been loose for years, and Jean used to use its creak as a cue for opening their nightly bottle of wine, knowing he would be down, in cords and mules, to take the first glass of the evening together. Its familiar groan under Dido's bare foot tonight made her heart cry out.

Her step-daughter was usually one for making light of disaster so when she had said over the phone, 'Patrick and I have hit a major problem,' Jean had known instinctively the game was up. After putting the receiver down in a stupor, she had shouted angrily to Adam's memory, 'You said I'd never have to deal with this!' And then, feeling betrayed and frightened, she had accused him of breaking a thirty-five-year-old promise. Two days later and her poise restored, she realised the onus to sort it out lay with her and no one else.

It had been her decision to keep the truth locked away,

although when she first turned the key, she never meant the door to stay so tightly shut for so long. It was 1964, and middle-class married women just didn't have affairs, especially when their husbands were terminally ill. Both she and her first husband Don knew he wouldn't live to see the baby Patrick's first birthday and she could not bear to deny him and his parents their only consolation that he had produced a son. She knew it wasn't his, and maybe he did too, but neither of them were prepared to say and so it remained unvoiced.

When the doctors had suggested to Don that if he and Jean wanted a family they should waste no time before chemotherapy treatment started, his desire to be a father had become all consuming. In that frighteningly awful two months, between the visits to the consultant, the X-rays, the diagnosis and prognosis and the hopeless scrabble to find a way out of advanced cancer, they had successfully made love just twice. Wonderful desperate moments.

Adam Seal, Don's schoolfriend and best man, became part of the furniture during those harrowing weeks, something Don thanked him for on a daily basis.

'Don't,' Adam kept saying, and he meant it. The guilt he felt about starting a relationship with Jean before her husband, his friend, was even dead stayed with him for ever.

The week Don's chemotherapy ended was the week that Adam and Jean first kissed. Patrick was born ten months later, six weeks before Don Botsford died. Adam, accompanied by his own very pregnant wife Jenny, had held the tiny Patrick in his arms at the funeral and had known without being told that he was looking at his own child.

He wasn't to see the two of them – mother and son – for another twenty-two months and when he did, his own grief was such that he barely noticed them. As he walked behind the coffin which carried the crushed body of his wife, he didn't register Jean in the pews, even though she was holding his own precious daughter Dido while the two-year-old Patrick stood closely by, hanging on to the younger child's dangling foot.

It was only after the burial that he had recalled seeing Dido in Jean's arms.

'It looked so right,' he said. 'I didn't even think to question the fact that she'd never even seen you before.'

Dido and Jean's first encounter had by now passed into family legend and Adam would repeat it proudly whenever the opportunity arose. The tiny bereaved Dido had been crying uncontrollably under the charge of Adam's sister, and Jean had instinctively picked her up to give her a cuddle. The screaming had stopped almost immediately and Jean was trying hard to suppress a victorious beam when she looked down to see that Patrick, in his two-year-old wisdom, had reached up and grabbed hold of Dido's little foot. When Patrick took his hand away, Dido started crying again, but as long as he kept hold and looked up at her, she was quiet. So there the three of them stayed, a little linked unit, all hanging on to each other for what seemed an age until Adam arrived, at which point in the story Patrick always claimed he recognised a superior male and let go.

Jean and Adam and Patrick and Dido had been inseparable from then on, from that sunny June afternoon in 1967 to the foggy February morning eight months ago when Adam's immense spirit had finally parted company from his body.

Adam had always backed Jean in their secret over Patrick's parentage and he used to promise that if it ever needed to be told, he would do the telling. How it had become such a hugely classified piece of information she didn't know, but it had, and that was all there was to it. When Adam had been alive, she'd been confident that when push came to shove, the bewildering truth would somehow be revealed in a way that wouldn't hurt. Now he was dead, that truth felt dangerous enough to blow all their lives apart.

Dido was sloshing about in the tub upstairs. Adam never did that. Once he was in, he would lie there motionless, eyes shut, for an almost exact ten minutes, barely disturbing the surface of the water even when he got out. All four of their children were the complete opposite, leaving great puddles all over the floor, and bubbles sliding down the bath to collect in the plughole. The twins were the worst culprits.

Patrick was the only one who shared his father's need for peace and occasional solitude. As a child he would sometimes ask if he could eat his meal in the garden shed, or switch off the television. Jean used to be thankful that he had inherited that, and not his father's lean face or lanky build – as a child Patrick had been round – but it had been a strange comfort to her at Adam's funeral to see her husband staring back at her through Patrick's deep brown sad eyes.

'Mum?' asked Dido, standing in a towel at the bottom of the stairs. Her hair was so short it was almost dry already. 'You look so pale, are you okay?'

'I'm fine. I've been thinking about Daddy. Perhaps I've just seen his ghost.'

Dido smiled, relieved to discover Jean still had her sense of play. 'It does feel as if he is still here, doesn't it?'

'I wish he was. Maybe he is. Who knows?'

Dido came over, kissed Jean on the top of her soft grey hair and sat on the rug by the fire massaging moisturiser into her own long legs. When she discovered she'd used far too much, she pulled Jean's hands from her lap and rubbed the excess into the tight skin, running her fingers round and round her step-mother's wedding band buried deep among the swollen joints. In terms of physical advantage, Jean was as commonplace as her children were unforgettable. She had always preferred to let the ageing process do what it wanted to her moony face and fleshy body, an approach that had paid more dividends than any face-lift ever could. After years of stress-free ripening, it was her inner beauty that people noticed, and it was what Dido caught now. She kept her eyes down as she spoke.

'Mummy, I don't want you to be shocked by what I am about to tell you.'

It was not the opening Jean, who thought she was the one who had to do the telling, was expecting.

'Well, I'm very good at not being shocked. I've had a lot of practice.'

'Mainly thanks to me?' Dido ventured.

'You've all had your moments,' Jean smiled, 'but fore-warned is forearmed.'

Dido stopped moisturising and held tight.

'This is really difficult to say, because I know it's just going to hang in the air and neither of us will know how to bring it back down.'

'Yes, we will. Go on.' Jean encouraged her with warm eyes and a lingering squeeze of the hands. Dido whispered her next utterance. 'Um, I'm in love.'

The warm eyes continued to look right into her, inviting her to finish.

'With Patrick,' she eventually managed to add.

'I thought you might be,' said Jean softly, even though she *was* shocked, to the core, just from hearing it spoken. Adam had noticed it a long time ago, when the two children were in their teens and she had refused to discuss it then, other than to keep reminding him that they were brother and sister. 'But *they* don't know that, do they?' Adam had said.

'So you're not shocked?' asked Dido, her gaze fixed on her mother's face.

'Dido . . .' Jean started, only to be interrupted immediately.

'But I *am*. Please don't try and tell me I'm not. I know I am, I have been for years, maybe for ever. And he loves me, I know that too, except that he's in denial. I want to be with him, properly, not like we have been, but as we should be, or would be, if we hadn't been thrown together by the marriage of our parents.'

'But there's a problem with that.' Jean spoke slowly and carefully, not wanting to burst what could have been such a lovely bubble.

'Only if other people make it one,' Dido leapt in again with purpose. 'We can ride the wave of astonishment together, all of us, the whole family. Will and Agnes could cope with it, they half know anyway, and if you think you can . . . it's not so shocking, is it, to love the son of the woman my father loved?'

'Listen to me, darling. Before you go any further you need to know what the problem is.'

Dido suddenly felt an ice-cold grip on her stomach. The towel she had wrapped herself in was now damp and the room seemed bigger, or she smaller.

'What kind of problem?'

'One that doesn't have an answer, I'm afraid. One that I wish your daddy was here to tell you about because I don't think I have the heart.'

'You're frightening me,' said Dido. She had thought it was going to be her who would do the shocking, and Jean who would do the crying. She'd rehearsed that role so often in the last few days that she hadn't even contemplated anything else.

'Come here,' Jean said, holding out her warm puffy hands.

'No. What are you going to say?'

Jean took a deep breath. 'I'm going to tell you something I should have told you long ago. You know how much Daddy and I loved each other, don't you?'

'Yes.'

'Well, it was a love that started long before we were married, before you and Patrick were even born. He was always there for me, when Don got ill, when he died, when I was alone. He made me brave, he made me who I am. He's in me, even now.'

Dido's imagination was already running amok. What did she mean, he was there for her? Did he make her unfaithful as well as brave? She began picking the tufts of the rug frantically and piling them up on the slate hearth as she plucked up the courage to speak.

'Mum, are you saying that you and Dad had an affair before Don and my mother died?'

'Yes,' Jean whispered, realising the enormity of the moment. 'I am. We did.'

Dido let out a long breathy whistle and the pile of tufts blew away behind the coal-bucket. They both sat in silence for a minute, staring at each other.

'But I thought you only realised your feelings for each other when you were both alone, after Mum—'

'No. We'd known for more than two years by then. We couldn't be together, not with Don's death and you so tiny, so we carried each other around in our hearts all that time, not speaking, just remembering.'

'Remembering what? How long was the affair?'

'Two crazy months. Don was dying, and I was falling in love. I was terribly sad and terribly happy at the same time. And then I got pregnant.' Jean said the last few words so tentatively that Dido wasn't sure she'd heard correctly.

'Pregnant?'

Jean nodded.

'Did you have the baby?' Dido was still trying to write an ending that didn't link Patrick with Adam even though the truth had already landed, like a lead balloon, in her heart.

'Yes, I did.'

'And is that baby Patrick?'

'Yes.'

Dido waited for the pain of knowledge to hit. She wished she could feel sick or faint, or burst into tears, or scream, or hit out, but she couldn't. All she felt was an awful numbness making her limbs too heavy to move, pinned down by helplessness.

'But you don't know for sure that Patrick is Daddy's child. I mean, you've never had tests, have you?'

'Don was having enormous amounts of chemotherapy to beat his cancer. We were told it would make him sterile. That's all.'

'Oh,' said Dido, and she stayed sitting exactly where she was for a long time, thinking about how completely that changed things, not noticing her damp towel or the direct angry heat on her back from the fire. Jean sat there too, not thinking anything, but just holding Adam's face in her head, gradually feeling the supportive spiritual embrace of him in her heart. Eventually, Dido spoke.

'Patrick knows, doesn't he?'

'It has occurred to me,' Jean replied, thinking hard. 'I think Adam may have told him, but if he did, it was one of the last things he said.'

'Wouldn't Dad have told you if he had?'

'How could he, darling? He was unconscious. Don't you remember? Patrick was with him at teatime, and then when Patrick came down, I went up. Daddy didn't speak from then on.'

'No,' said Dido, remembering those last few hours. 'He didn't. He told me he loved me at lunchtime.' She suddenly looked twelve again.

'He adored you, darling, like no man has ever adored a daughter before.'

It made Dido cry at last, great big tears plopping from her beautiful eyes, falling on to her bare legs and staying there, sitting on the layer of moisturiser and then trickling down the curve of her thigh. She didn't know and didn't care if she was crying for Adam, Patrick, herself, Jean, or even her own betrayed mother Jenny, crushed by a car before she could be crushed by infidelity. She only knew that the tears had been a long time in coming. Jean comforted herself by imagining each one washing away a little more of the hard veneer with which her step-daughter had so frantically coated her adult self, hoping the shell would be thin enough to expose a little of that soft centre that no one but her family believed existed.

Jean was on the rug too now, crouching uncomfortably, oblivious to a gritty piece of clinker burrowing into her arthritic knee, holding her girl and crying with her. *Don't worry*, she told Adam's memory, *these are cathartic tears. Just pray that Patrick cries them too one day.*

Dido stopped first and Jean, still weeping, said, 'Don't you think Patrick would have told you though, if he knew? You've never had any secrets from each other, have you?'

'I don't know. I thought he *did* have a secret, still does have one, I'm sure, but what it is, I'm too frightened to find out. Maybe he does know and he didn't tell me because he was afraid he'd lose me.'

'But he can't spend his whole life running away from you.'

'When have you ever known him to confront anything?'

Jean put her forefinger to her lips and bowed her head as her eyes dried. 'He knows,' she said, 'he knows. And we had better let him know we know he knows too. It's time to stop the deception.'

Dido sat and thought just how dreadful a deception it really was. 'Mum?'

'Mmm?'

'I don't feel like forgiving you.'

'Nor do I, but that's not going to be very helpful, is it? Think of what Daddy would say.'

'He'd say it's Patrick who has to forgive first.'

'And I suppose he'd be right,' said Jean, running her hand over Dido's cheek. 'I'm sorry, my angel, I really am.'

Chapter 7

TWO AND A HALF MONTHS TO GO

The Times, 15 October, 1999: The world's stock markets continue to soar as speculators feed on the bubble of New Age optimism. Investment opportunities are being snapped up across the globe despite warnings from City analysts that the rises have no economic foundations and are a spin-off from the hype surrounding the turn of the millennium. Meanwhile, unemployment in Britain has fallen to a ten-year low as regions across the country benefit from a pick-up in manufacturing activity and everything from cars to coins roll off the commemorative conveyor belt.

'Sorry, I wasn't listening.' said Katherine, raising her voice over the scrape of the windscreen wipers. 'What did you say?'

Her face was contorted with concentration as she drove in the pouring rain towards Penzance heliport but her mind wasn't entirely on the road ahead, preoccupied instead with a dream she'd woken from in which a giant egg-timer kept spilling its sand on the heads of ordinary people as its glass began to crack. Men, women and children were all running around like headless chickens, shaking the sand – a golden glitter – out of their hair and then trying to catch it before it hit the ground. Katherine had scooped some off her own head but it had quickly fallen through her fingers and was taken away by the wind. Johnny was there, telling her it didn't matter, but she was sure it did, and she went chasing after it, leaving him shouting after her to stop. She never had caught it, or at least she couldn't remember catching it if she did.

'Don't worry,' answered Johnny, from the back of the car, echoing the words he'd kept saying in her dream. 'Keep your eyes on the road. I can ask you later.'

'No, go on.' They had already had a little skirmish and she was keen not to sound withdrawn, but Johnny was no longer listening. She looked at him in her driver's mirror, crouched and overgrown in the back seat of their battered Volvo estate, and she wondered if it was the first time he'd ever actually sat there. When they'd bought it ten years ago, their first and only brand new car, the front had belonged to a baby Seth and his carry seat. Even then, Katherine couldn't remember a time when Johnny had taken the back with Hattie and she had driven. Here the roles were reversed, and she guessed it probably made him feel awkward. She drove, he entertained – not that Patrick or Beth exactly needed babysitting – or was there room for argument in that?

Any tension in the car was down to her. She had made such a pig's ear of the first few minutes of the weekend that it shamed her to remember, especially her reaction to the way Johnny had automatically made for the driver's side just before they'd left Tremewan.

'What are you doing?' she'd asked, watching him try the locked driver's door.

'Oh. Do you want to drive then?'

'Well, I thought we'd agreed that it was my car unless you had the children.'

'Or did we agree simply that you had the use of it unless I had the children?'

'There's no reason why you *should* drive, is there? I mean, you're not one of these people who get travel sick unless you're at the wheel, are you? Although you probably can't answer that, not having been a passenger for so long.'

Patrick and Beth had stood on the pavement wondering if this weekend was a good idea after all.

'Male pride,' Johnny had apologised with his knees up to his chin once they'd all packed themselves in. 'It's something I need to work on.'

If she hadn't been so pedantic, *he* could now be at the wheel and *she* could be asleep, and there wouldn't be that awkwardness in the air. She hoped they all understood that going away for the weekend with him was bizarre enough, without reverting to cosy stereotypes. Was she the only one who realised what a God-given opportunity they suddenly had, to strip fifteen years off their lives if they wanted to? The structures – or did she mean strictures – that had helped form their post-University relationships were no longer in place. She and Johnny were effectively single again, she felt sure that Evan's absence had a hidden message along the same lines for Beth, and then there was Patrick, in this country and without Dido, which was a novelty in itself.

If these few days were going to work, then she would have to drop a few grievances. It had been a long slog getting the children ready for a holiday with their grandparents. Once she'd packed all three cases, she'd then had to turn round and blitz the cottage in readiness for the arrival of her critical parents, although Johnny had disputed the need for that, forecasting that they would only stay long enough to use the loo and re-fill their Thermos and they wouldn't have time to check the accuracy of the dusting. But she knew better – vaguely habitable wasn't good enough for Margaret Jamieson, she demanded precision cleaning, and since Katherine was all too aware of the gulf between them as women, she used any method she could to bridge the gap, even if it was temporary.

The flicker of her jealousy was towards Beth in particular, but she was annoyed with all three of them, for the lazy selfish way they had all ambled towards this trip. No wonder they all looked younger than she did, none of them had to think of anyone other than themselves. She though would have to ask for an iron at the hotel before she dressed for dinner – that's if she'd even packed her dress at all, and she had a horrible feeling it was still on the bed, waiting to go in last of all. Her eyes were stinging from the strain of peering through the rain and she had a headache. Why not just pull over, hand the keys to Johnny and climb in the back with Beth for a few minutes of shut-eye? Female pride, she conceded, glancing again in her mirror and seeing Beth lean her head momentarily on Johnny's shoulder in response to some sweet thing he'd just said. He always said sweet things to Beth.

Beth was at the other end of the mood spectrum, swimming not drowning, contemplating the possibility that she might be two hours' pregnant, not having learned a single lesson from her last experience or the one before that. Hope sprang eternal in the fortnight between ovulation and menstruation, the only time nowadays that she was even bordering on happy. It made the depression at the end of it all the more crushing but at least it fed her in some small way. She was running over in her mind the last hour she had spent with Evan before they had each gone their separate ways, marvelling over the way sex healed rifts and wondering briefly if Katherine and Johnny would seek its benefits this weekend.

She had been quite stunned by the tenor of her husband's kiss. After a fortnight of such controlled anger, the last thing she had expected was any kind of eleventh-hour sexual reunion. Only moments before they had found themselves hungrily entwined in each other's legs, she'd thought they'd reached an irretrievable breakdown. How could that changeabout have happened? Anger and near violence one minute, passion and intimacy the next.

Evan had come in from work at lunchtime with the same frosty expression he'd been wearing for days, taking refuge in his post and avoiding her eye. One envelope had been a mail-shot from the RSPCA.

'There you are,' he'd said, throwing down a picture of a wide-eyed puppy on the table. 'That's what you need – a child-substitute.'

Unkind wasn't the word for it, nor was vicious, or spiteful or cruel. She had lifted her hand with the intention of giving him an almighty slap across the face but he had grabbed her by the wrist, and held her arm outstretched, breathing into her face. There had been a split second when she'd thought he might be about to hit her, but instead, astonishingly, he had pulled her towards him and put his hands on both her cheeks before kissing her with unbelievable intensity. She'd never been turned on by intimidation before, but of course there was the knowledge that she was ovulating to take into account too, and she'd groaned with the pleasure of it.

'Sweetheart?' he'd asked her as he lay satiated and half-naked on the soft carpet of the sitting-room floor twenty minutes later. Preparing herself to accept an apology for his recent behaviour with good grace, she whispered, 'That's me.'

'Don't you ever walk out on me like that again, do you hear?'

Instead of saying what she thought, she had smiled sweetly at a surprising image of Dr Jeremy Shaw, with his ripped jacket and sandy eyebrows, beaming with pride at her having negotiated sex against all the odds at such an optimum time.

Three hours' pregnant, she mused as she looked at the back of Patrick's dark curls in the front passenger's seat. Why should I be? I've done it at peak times before to no avail, and yet this time, it feels different. Was it her body gently introducing her to the idea of motherhood, she wondered, or her mind playing tricks? She felt a sudden thrill for being in the car at all, away from Evan, with her friends, *and* she hadn't missed her monthly opportunity. All manner of possibilities suddenly seemed there for the taking, and she traced a tentative circle on her stomach before letting her hand retreat to her lap again.

Johnny noticed her do it. He'd seen Katherine do the same thing at least twice before, and impulsively, he put his arm round her and gave her a small squeeze, remembering how awful she had looked outside the doctor's.

'Are you still awake up there?' he asked in the general direction of the front. When the two girls had agreed against all the odds to join him and Patrick for the weekend, he'd basked in memories of the Students' Union. So far, the atmosphere in the car had been more reminiscent of the Mothers' Union.

'Only just,' said Patrick apathetically. 'What time will we get there?'

'By five.'

'But it's four already.'

'I know. Easy, isn't it? Twelve minutes from the mainland by chopper and no passport control or baggage points to hold you up once you're there.'

No one replied and Johnny felt stupid, eventually breaking the silence with a poignant little speech. 'Look, I'm not stupid. I can tell none of you are particularly excited by this party. Maybe you should just forget it and do your own thing, and then I won't feel the need to apologise to you when you don't enjoy it. There are more than enough guests coming who are actually looking forward to it for the thing to work, so your presence isn't entirely necessary.'

'We *do* want to come to your party,' assured Beth.

'It's not *my* party, it's supposed to be *our* party.'

'It doesn't feel like our party though, does it?' said Patrick. 'I mean, it isn't exactly what we set out to do, is it? It has sort of rolled away from us – well, from me anyway.'

'Sure, but that is the way it is,' Johnny said. 'We just happened to hit on an idea that everyone wanted a part of. That's not my fault, or anyone else's. This millennium bandwagon is crazy. Everyone is on it. At least this way none of us will be out of pocket.'

'Let's not talk about what it should or should not be,' said Beth. 'Let's just try and have some fun.' Johnny found her gloved hand and put it to his lips, kissing the warm wool which was already wet – she'd been drawing on the inside of her window.

'Who can remember Brittany?' she asked cajolingly. Katherine cringed. It sounded like a question she might put to her class.

'The Abbey, Madame Brandivy, La Petite Maison, roaring fires, damp beds, crêpes until they were coming out of our ears,' Beth carried on.

'Bloody freezing, wasn't it?' said Patrick.

'And thank you, Mr Happy,' Beth applauded.

'Was that the last time we were all together, without extras?' Katherine asked.

Without Evan, she means, thought Beth, but she said, 'I think it was. Are we all sharing beds this time too then?'

149

There was a pause.

'Only if you want to,' said Johnny as a different silence hung in the air.

Oh God, thought Katherine, I do.

'Now you're talking!' said Patrick to everyone's relief as he thought how easy to say that kind of thing but how difficult it was to carry it through nowadays.

In Somerset, Seth was bagging the top bunk.

'Mum says I get asthma if I sleep on the bottom,' he told his grandmother who was trying to sort out the dispute.

'Is that true, Hattie?' Margaret Jamieson asked, her voice sounding sharp but her face looking flustered. 'Is it the dust?'

'No, it's complete rubbish. He always uses his asthma to get what he wants.'

Hattie didn't want to cry, not within half an hour of arriving anyway, and she concentrated instead on trying to count how many lemon ribbon bows there were poking out of the hideous silk flower arrangement on the windowsill. She hated herself for still being so easily turned to tears at her age and lately, it had been worse than ever.

When she had discovered that her parents were going away together for the weekend, she'd been filled with an almost overwhelming hope, until she realised that Patrick had been going too. He was always there lately, right next to Mum, as though he belonged there. Leaving them alone together at weekends made it worse, as if she was encouraging them, and sometimes, when she couldn't sleep, she worried that Johnny might think she was in on it too. Anyway, why couldn't Patrick find a bed and breakfast like anyone else? It made her feel guilty, this new animosity towards him – he was her godfather and she used to love him, but she had lost respect for him. He was too glum, too weak. Couldn't he see that Mum needed some support too? No, of course he couldn't, because he had decided his need for Katherine was greater than Johnny's, and worse than that, he thought he had a right to think that. Well, he didn't and she had to let him know somehow.

'Eleven,' Hattie said out loud without thinking, having counted the bows twice to make sure. Seth was beginning to sulk. 'He can have it, I don't care,' she added, not wanting to let her mother down and cause a scene.

'You can swap tomorrow night. How about that?' suggested Margaret, making an attempt at being a granny by patting Hattie's head, but as she left the room, her mind caught at the edge of a twenty-year-old memory and she too could have cried.

The whole of Katherine's teenage years had been wrapped, for Margaret, in a growing sense of failure. She had since worked out that the distance in their adult relationship had started specifically with her reluctance to tackle head-on the problems that had come with adolescence – the moods, the desire to rebel or explore, the sexual confusion. Even now, she didn't know how to help. She hadn't been able to find one right word of comfort or advice since Johnny had moved out, and it wasn't that she hadn't felt the pain, or been able to see it coming, it was just that her love always seemed to stay on the inside. And there it stayed, even now, after seeing Hattie's quivering bottom lip.

'Children?' she called from the other side of the bedroom door, where it was safer.

'Yes, Granny?' shouted Seth.

'It's lovely to have you here at last.'

It was all she could manage, but at least it was a start.

Hattie felt tears coming again, and this time, she started counting the floral sprigs on the wallpaper.

'Is there a mini-bar or are we talking room service?' asked Beth.

The two women were prowling around their new space, opening drawers, assessing the bathroom, pulling open the desk. They had already been through each other's clothes and suggested a temporary swap of sweaters.

'This looks as if it could be a pretty spectacular view if it wasn't dark and raining,' Katherine said, peering out of the window.

'If, if, if . . . always an if,' Beth sighed theatrically.

'What?'

'Well, *if* it wasn't raining, we'd have a view. *If* I wasn't married, I might leap into bed with Patrick. *if* you and Johnny weren't both such idealists, you'd still be together.'

'*If* I didn't like you as much as I do, I'd punch you in the face.'

'What for? The sleeping with Patrick bit?'

They both laughed and stretched out on the neat quilts of their matching single beds.

'So, do you still fancy him then?' Katherine asked, keen on the idea of a chat about Patrick and sex.

'That was going to be my question to you.'

'I got there first.'

'Okay, well, is that the same thing as wanting him to still fancy me?'

'Um, no, I think that's just because you're a woman.'

'So you still want him to fancy you then?'

'Um . . .'

There was another explosion of laughter.

'*How* old are we?' Beth squealed. 'Are we really asking

152

each other if we fancy Patrick? Please tell me we're not! Please tell me we're actually discussing devolution, or the concept of eternity or something!'

Katherine threw a complimentary chocolate at her and unwrapped one herself.

'Are the boys sharing a room too?' she asked, trying not to expose the question's hidden agenda.

'How should I know?' said Beth. 'I've only been invited to make up the numbers.'

'Well, someone had to come along to sleep with Patrick.'

'Ha! I'm married. You're separated. You go first.'

'That's really kind of you, but I'm afraid, on this occasion, I shall have to decline.'

'Oh, shame. What about with your estranged husband then?'

'I'd rather you didn't,' Katherine teased.

'No, not me, you.'

'How did we get on to this? I'm not ready to discuss it!' Katherine pretended to wail dramatically.

'But would you? If the opportunity arose?' Beth knew she was pushing her luck but she decided to ask all the same, on the grounds that once she had, she wouldn't feel the need to again.

'No, I wouldn't. I don't want this to be any big deal for me and Johnny, you know? I'm sure neither of us have any intention of using it as a means of getting back together – we've only just made the decision to part. Anyway, we've had it, we're finished. So no more innuendo, okay?'

'Nerves,' Beth smiled. 'I'm not used to the new order yet. I don't think I've ever actually shared a room with you before, have I?'

'That's because one of us has always been with a man.'

'What a pair of strumpets!'

'Hold on, don't the various flats at University count? What about in Mannamead Road?' said Katherine.

'We didn't even share then,' Beth answered with conviction.

'We did. We had the back room with the window leading out on to the flat roof. Can't you remember we used to sunbathe out there until the landlord caught us one day and told us we'd have to re-felt it?'

'Yes, but can't *you* remember how you and Johnny ended up in his bed together the very same night we all moved in? And how you never actually spent one night in your own bed from then on?'

Katherine paused and then turned a very slight pink.

'Oh, is that when it happened?'

'You mean you don't know?'

'Well, the bit between me and Johnny being friends and then becoming lovers is all a bit hazy. I can't quite get it into sequence. Are you sure it was then?' Katherine felt a passing wave of sadness in recollecting their beginning now that they were at their end, but then she was puzzled by a stronger buzz of optimism. She was on St Mary's with the three of them when she could have been at home alone, and anyway, whatever happened, they would always have the children.

'Absolutely sure,' said Beth. 'I know because I used to sleep in one bed one night, and the other bed the next, just to make use of the space. But you still kept all your stuff in our room, your clothes, your hair dryer, your books. In fact, you did everything in our room apart from sleep in it.'

'You weren't cross with me, were you?'

'No, it's just that . . .'

'What?' asked Katherine, worrying in case Beth revealed a concealed hurt.

'If you should feel the urge to decamp again this weekend, could you please leave the hair dryer?' Beth had to finish the sentence from under a flying pillow, emerging in time to pick up the ringing phone.

'Oh, we were just talking about you,' she shouted into the receiver.

'No, we weren't,' shouted Katherine even louder.

From the hotel breakfast room which overlooked the harbour, the four of them watched some of the island's fishermen bring in the few remaining inkwell pots for the winter while others chalked up blackboards advertising boat trips to the off-islands, Tresco, St Agnes, St Martin's and Bryher. The sky looked more early September than mid-October, people were in shirt sleeves, and the thrice-weekly boat bringing provisions from the mainland had just arrived. A three-piece suite was being carried up the quay, followed by crates of fresh fruit, vegetables and dog food.

'Well, how else do you think everything arrives?' Johnny asked, as Beth pointed out a garden bench wrapped in cellophane being carted up the hill.

'I know, I know. I'm just showing Patrick. He's never been here before.'

'What are we, vying for Head Guide?'

'You're supposed to be working,' Katherine reminded her husband, reverting to her group role as the responsible one.

'I'm seeing the chef at three. Look at it out there, it's perfect.'

'So how about a boat to one of the off-islands, Tresco maybe. We could do the Abbey's tropical gardens, have a pub lunch in that little place with the stone-walled garden, and get back here for Johnny to keep his appointment?

Then us three can hire bikes and explore St Mary's,' Beth suggested.

'Or Bryher? Feel like some time-travel do you, Patrick?' asked Johnny. It was *his* treat, bringing them here. The helicopter firm had paid for two free tickets and one of the hotel rooms was also complimentary – a thank-you for sending so much business its way. The rest of the bill was being picked up by party funds. None of it would have been possible without him.

'You're right,' said Beth. 'Bryher makes St Mary's look positively cosmopolitan. What do you think, Katherine?'

'I think,' said Katherine, 'that we all ought to chuck in our jobs, sell our homes and come and live here.' She looked at Johnny. 'But, yes,' she added, 'Bryher. I vote for Bryher. It's just out of this world.'

And so Bryher it was. They wavered momentarily about taking a boat to see the seals but were finally persuaded by the gappy smile on the boatman's face.

'You twitchers?' he asked them, helping the girls on board.

'Do we look like twitchers?' Beth smiled back.

'Well, you're a rare breed today then. Sit up here with me. I've heard enough about the bloody red-crested grebe of 1997 to last me a lifetime.'

'What are twitchers?' Patrick hissed to Beth.

'God, Patrick, keep your voice down. They'll throw us off. Birdwatchers.'

As the boat reached the pretty little island quay and disgorged its passengers, the boatman stopped Patrick in his tracks.

'You want to know a bit more about twitchers?' he asked, laughing.

Ever the journalist, Patrick nodded.

'My mate's a farmer on St Agnes, and he got so fed up with them all leaning on his dry stone wall trying to catch a glimpse of the lesser-spotted dandybird that he asked them all to move. "We can't, we're watching a bird," they said. "Which bird's that?" my mate asked. "That one," they said, making their fatal mistake by pointing at it, so off he goes, comes back with his shotgun and crack, he shoots the bloody thing out of the tree. Then he goes through his own gate, picks up the dead bird, and hands it to the bloke who'd refused to move and says, "There you are, you can take it home, nail it to a nearby telegraph pole and lean on your own bloody wall now".'

The boatman was laughing too much to say goodbye as he motioned them off the boat. 'It's true, all true,' he coughed, trying to cover his mouth with one hand and point at something with the other. 'If it rains, you use the boathouse now. It's always open, but don't tell everyone.'

The weather stayed with them as they walked round Samson Hill, down to Droppy Nose Point, up to Gweal Hill, past Hell Bay and back round for a lunch at Fraggle Rock Cafe. The four of them lay on their backs in a row on Rushy Bay beach, watching the migratory birds stop on their way to warmer climes.

'I can't think why they want to leave,' Beth murmured into the air, sandwiched between the two men. There had been a minute or two of self-conscious hesitation before they had all stretched out, but now that they had, it seemed completely normal to be lying on a damp beach in mid-October. She'd taken hold of both Patrick and Johnny's hands, and Johnny had risked taking Katherine's too; his wife had put up no opposition, enjoying its familiar warmth and knowing that he was also holding Beth's which made it a less important gesture somehow. Then they had all raised their linked arms in a kind of salute to togetherness, and lowered them again, continuing to watch the clouds in silence as they turned to grey and began to send rain in quick bursts down on them.

'Quick, the boathouse,' Johnny shouted when it got too wet, and they all started to run up a rough path after him.

It was obviously a refuge, perhaps used by fishermen who got stuck on the island when the weather turned, brewing tea and playing cards until it was safe enough to put out again. There was a corner with a couple of armchairs and some oilskins, and a kettle on the windowsill next to a plug, a few filthy mugs and a sink, but the room was dominated by the huge space left for a boat.

'Would that be for a lifeboat?' asked Beth.

'Well, if it is, there must be a rescue going on. No, it's probably owned by the islanders, or a fishing co-operative. It'll be maintained by everyone who uses it. There's probably a small fee,' said Johnny.

'You're so full of bullshit!' Katherine laughed. 'You have no more idea than the rest of us.'

'It sounded good though, didn't it?'

'You'd make a lovely tour guide.'

'And in here,' said Johnny, playing the part, 'more than a few dangerous liaisons have gone on over the years, with vicars' daughters stealing out at night to meet their fishermen, headmasters leaving school early to fulfil the wishes of farmers' wives . . .'

'Oh yeah? And where's the bed?'

'Bed? You don't need a bed! Since when have you been such a traditionalist, Katherine?'

Katherine couldn't believe she was blushing at the comment. He had no right to say things like that any more, even if she had quite enjoyed hearing it.

'Did that boatman mean it, do you think? That we could use it?' asked Beth, suddenly feeling like a trespasser.

'He must have known it was going to rain,' Johnny said.

Katherine had started thinking about her egg-timer dream again. 'I've just worked out we've got seventy-five days left before the second millennium comes to an end.'

'I don't need a reminder, thank you. What the hell are we going to feed them on?' Johnny said.

'Forget the party for a minute,' Katherine told him without the usual edge to her voice. 'I want to hear if anyone else feels they're not quite done with it.'

'With what?'

'With this century – you know, the best years of our life and all that.'

Beth thought about her own deadline, how she'd vowed that if she wasn't pregnant by the year 2000 then she would accept it wasn't going to happen and get on with other aspects of her life, and how funny it was that goalposts get further apart the closer you get, but as it wasn't the sort of thing you could just say in passing, she picked up an old yachting magazine and pretended to look through it.

Patrick said, 'My life is screwed regardless of which millennium it happens to be,' but he delivered it in such a droll voice everyone thought he was joking, and anyway, they didn't hear the rest of it, about his future being a featureless landscape, and how he broke out in a cold sweat when he tried to think about it, because he made sure he kept that bit to himself.

Johnny contemplated that now might be the time to ask his wife how she would feel if he packed in his job and went back to college, but instead, he just laughed mildly.

'Oh well, that was a fascinating insight,' Katherine grumbled sarcastically. 'Thank you. It's good to know I'm not alone. That's what I like about having such close friends. You can all talk things through with such honesty.'

'The boat!' Beth called from the door, waving at the boatman who was shouting to them to hurry up. 'It's already there.'

All four of them fled from the house as if they'd just seen a ghost. In reality, it was the conversation that haunted them, and they had escaped its spectre by the skin of their teeth.

'Come with me to meet the chef, Kath?' Johnny proposed in the launch as they watched Bryher become an outline. 'I need someone to translate for me. I won't know what he's going on about.'

'Okay,' she agreed, 'but I wish you'd answered me.'

'Answered me what?'

'Are you done with the twentieth century?'

He looked right at her. 'I know I'm not done with you.'

'How about a fish theme?' she said laughing, but looking deliberately away and out to sea in case he heard her heart beating and saw the blush to her cheeks come back for the second time that afternoon.

'Another farmer,' the boatman was saying to Patrick, 'my mate's brother, he got so fed up with people leaning on *his* gate that he got up extra early one morning and creosoted the top of it. Hundreds of twitchers went home that year with stripes up the arms of their jackets. Can't beat it, can you?'

Johnny made good progress with the chef who said he would work on a Thai fish menu and get back to him. Katherine hardly needed to open her mouth, other than to run her tongue over a stainless steel spoon to taste a few sauces. It was quite apparent Johnny hadn't really needed her at all and that he was well in control of everything, or everything to do with the party anyway, but she had enjoyed being consulted, and it had been the first time they'd been on their own with something pleasant to discuss for a long time. The meeting was over by four o'clock and by five, they had met up with the other two in the hotel bar where they sank pleasurably into the sofas and read newspapers until changing for dinner.

Something in the way the waiter headed so purposefully towards their table later that evening told Katherine that he wasn't going to enquire if everything was all right.

'Oh my God, the children,' she said, turning white, as he bent over and quietly told Johnny: 'There is a phone call for you, Mr Bates. A Margaret Jamieson.'

A thousand terrifying images rushed through her head. Something so terrible must have happened that Mum cannot bear to tell me, she thought. Dad has told her she must speak to Johnny first, and he'll have to break the news to me. In her moment of inner hysteria, Katherine shot to her feet, knocking her wine glass across the table as she did so. Her napkin fell to the floor and her chair tipped backwards against a wall.

'Don't panic,' Johnny said, putting his hand on her bare arm but not looking so easy himself. 'It won't be anything serious. Sit down, I'll be back in a minute.'

He thinks it is serious, she thought, watching him race across the room behind the waiter. I can tell. Johnny always knows when something is wrong, he's got an intuition. Please, do not let this be the start of my nightmare. My children, please God, let them be okay. She pulled back her chair and sat down again with her hand over her mouth, the sound of her heart pumping away inside her head.

'Come on, don't panic,' said Beth, repeating Johnny's

reassuring tone, although her face hardly looked the picture of complacency either. 'If it was anything to worry about, you'd both have been called to the phone.'

Patrick nodded, thinking the exact opposite and already wondering how the hell they would all deal with it, if it was bad news. Katherine stayed perfectly still, too scared to eat, as the other two pushed food around their plates, pretending not to worry. Come back with a smile on your face, please Johnny, please, they all willed.

As Johnny approached the phone in reception, he swallowed and then coughed. What am I about to hear? Something that will blast our lives apart? He could see the receiver lying upwards on the desk and tried to ignore the forceful image of a tear-stained, shaking and shocked Margaret on the other end. Was she phoning from a hospital? A police station? If it was really awful, wouldn't Derek have phoned? Unless it was him who had—

'Hello, Margaret,' he said as confidently as he could. 'Is everything okay?'

'I'm sorry to drag you away from dinner,' she started apologetically as Johnny instinctively let his fear go. 'I thought I'd better ask for you because I knew they'd know you, but it's actually Katherine I need. We can't find Seth's inhaler anywhere and he's getting uncomfortably wheezy.'

'Oh, sure, right,' answered Johnny, out of breath. 'God, Margaret, I thought for one minute you were going to tell me something awful.'

Margaret, who couldn't feel Johnny's clammy palms or see her daughter's deathly pallor, suddenly felt as if her decision to phone was being questioned, and she didn't like her decisions being questioned, especially not by a man who had just walked out on his children. A rash bloomed from the crew neck of her leisure suit.

'Well, I'm sorry to disappoint you,' she said sarcastically. 'Now, if I could speak to my daughter?'

'What?' asked Johnny, a little stunned. It was only the second time they had spoken since the split. 'Disappoint me? Margaret, I thought something might have happened – oh, never mind.'

'Johnny, Seth is ill. He needs his medication. Now, would you have preferred it if I had left it until morning before bothering you, by which time he would probably need hospitalisation?'

'No, of course not, it's just that for one moment – let me speak to him.'

'He's in the bathroom. We're steaming him.'

Johnny remembered Katherine telling him once it felt as if her entire childhood had been spent being steamed in the bathroom, and he felt such a colossal relief he let out a little laugh.

'Well, tell him to breathe as deeply as he can, and slowly and—'

'Can you get Katherine, please?'

Johnny tried to look as composed as he could as he laid the receiver back on the desk and walked towards the restaurant. Relief had turned to resentment. What a witch that woman could be. Was she blaming him for Seth's attack? Maybe she thought that as an absent father, he was no longer entitled to be concerned, or indeed had anything useful to offer his children at all. Would she have been so offensive if he'd still been living at home?

In his fury, he'd forgotten Katherine's panic, but as soon as he saw her ashen face staring back at him, he remembered, and hated himself for not smiling at it as he walked towards her. Somehow, his indignation found a target.

'You've forgotten to pack Seth's inhaler,' he said, not

looking at her as he sat back down. 'And you can tell your mother from me that she's only their grandmother, I'm their father, and I count more than she does.'

'What? Oh, thank God. Is he okay?'

She might have overlooked her husband's unpleasantness if she hadn't caught his opening words to the others as she hurried away.

'How can you forget to pack your son's daily medication? Of all the things . . .'

Katherine felt a white rage simmering inside her as she headed towards the phone but for now she needed to sort Seth out. It was an easy task. Hattie was able to put the whole thing into perspective quite brilliantly by saying that if they were at home and it was a weekday, Katherine would probably make him go to school, and that he was enjoying all the fuss, especially as he was now getting a second night on the top bunk like he wanted. Katherine then suggested calling a doctor who would be sure to have emergency supplies of Ventolin, and Margaret said she would do that if things got any worse, and that was the end of that. Having spoken to Seth herself, she was satisfied that the root of the problem lay more or less where Hattie had hinted, and she was able to say her goodnights without any misgivings.

On the way back to the table, she tried to put Johnny's comment at the back of her mind, but it wasn't easy. The nerves had set in and the equilibrium they had found since yesterday had been tipped.

'Next time, I'll do the packing,' he tried to joke.

'There won't bloody well be a next time,' Katherine snapped back.

Beth could smell the touch paper being lit. 'Leave it, you two. Seth's okay, that's all that matters.'

'No,' said Katherine, 'I'd like an apology, please. When

it is you, Johnny, who has to bring the children up single-handed, to organise the school run, the weekly shop, the cleaning of the house, the washing of clothes, the paying of the bills, when it is you who has to decide when to call the doctor in the middle of the night, to comfort or discipline a twelve-year-old girl, to say no to your son who wants to join another after-school club because of the extra workload it would put on you, when it is you who has to catch an hour here and an hour there in the day to write an article to pay for a school trip, then you can criticise, but while you sit there, in your empty little cottage—'

'Hold it.' Johnny's face was taut, but it was hard to tell if it was with anger or alarm.

'In your empty little cottage, doing little else but planning the breakfast menus of two hundred complete strangers, then you have absolutely no right to cast judgment on my ability to look after my children.'

'*Our* children.'

The couple at the next table were beginning to look on in amazement. The waiter hovered, trying to decide what to do should the argument become any more heated. Beth took the matter into her own hands.

'You two had better continue this elsewhere, unless of course you want to forget it and carry on with your meal.'

Katherine took the cue and threw her napkin into the centre of the table. 'Come on then,' she said to Johnny. 'You said you weren't done with me yet.'

'I am staying here,' he said quietly and slowly, his normal rhythm having left him. 'You take your temper outside for a bit and come back and join us when it has had some fresh air.'

'If you don't come with me now,' she threatened, already

standing up, 'then I'm telling you, our marriage really is over and done with.'

'Fine.'

'Fine.'

Beth looked at her with sit-down eyes. It worked on her eleven-year-olds, but this situation was rather less innocent, and Katherine walked out.

Patrick spoke first. 'Johnny, for God's sake go after her.'

'No.'

Then Beth. 'Johnny, if you don't, you'll have one hell of a job to patch this thing up later.'

'I really don't care.'

'Then if you don't mind,' said Beth, 'I shall go.'

'No, I will,' said Patrick.

It was the thought of Patrick finding her, perhaps crying on the harbour wall, cold and shaking, and the two of them walking off somewhere together to dissect the row in Katherine's favour that made Johnny throw in his towel too and follow his wife out the door.

Chapter 8

The rather public dining-room row between Katherine and Johnny sent shock-waves through many more hearts than they could ever have known. It was as if their mutually unpleasant words had started an echo in other people's minds of a time when they too had spoken to each other in such a way. Some guests heard a distant echo, one which faded quickly enough for them to get on with their puddings with a lightheartedness, others heard a far nearer ring, one that had either just passed or was just about to arrive. One couple, who had barely spoken since they sat down anyway, actually left mid-course, as though the very food had been contaminated by the altercation. The waitress saw it all and adopted the disposition of a doctor's receptionist, one privy to personal details but trained to keep her distance.

Try as they did, Patrick and Beth could not rescue the rest of their meal, at least not under the spotlight. They had been sitting diagonally from each other and neither of them had moved since the other two places had become vacant and so the empty chairs glared at them, saying, 'We have failed to pull this weekend off. The magic formula no longer works. Our present is a different creature from our past.'

Patrick was talking about Christmas for want of something better.

'When someone dies, everyone tries to do the first Christmas the same as it has always been done in an effort to close the gap, and of course, it doesn't work. What they should do is break with tradition.'

'It'll be the first one you'll do without Adam, won't it?' said Beth, not sure what he was getting at.

'Oh, I'm not talking about Adam, I'm talking about us four. Three-quarters of a whole and all that.'

'Maths isn't my strong point,' she said, 'but don't you mean four quarters?'

'No, because then we'd be complete, wouldn't we?'

'So, which one of us is missing?'

'Maybe it's a part of all of us.'

'Maybe it is,' Beth said, knowing there was no maybe about it.

'What do you think we were all trying to prove by coming away together this weekend?' Patrick asked. 'That we've all still got what it takes? Johnny was really keen for Katherine to come, and she would only come if you came, and if Katherine was coming, I wanted you to come too and so did Johnny. All four quarters, correct and present. But are we all now secretly thinking that even the whole isn't enough any more?'

'I don't think we're trying to prove anything, are we? There are bound to be times when it's hard to have a good time. Katherine's only here because you and Johnny twisted her arm, and I'm only here because Evan happened to be in London all weekend.'

'Are you?' he asked sceptically.

'What do you mean? Yes, I am.'

'I don't believe you. I think you're here because you couldn't bear the three of us doing something without you.'

Patrick was trying to drag Beth down with him into his dark little pit, his deep black hole from which there was no point in trying to climb out because there wasn't an awful lot at the top to climb out for. The row between Johnny and Katherine had sapped the last bit of social energy he had and Beth's optimism made him fear it might be just him who could see the end of it all. The shadow lurking at the back of his disarmingly blue eyes started to cast shadows elsewhere.

'Come on, let's go to bed,' said Beth, not wanting to be stifled by a blanket of unnecessary gloom. A flash of panic crossed Patrick's face as he thought for a moment she meant the same bed. 'I didn't mean . . .' she added.

'I know you didn't,' he laughed nervously, although now, worryingly for both of them, the prospect was suddenly a lot closer.

As she followed him up the wide carpeted stairs, along a silent corridor and past the door to her own room, she wondered if she was still in control of her marriage vows. It wasn't that she was feeling in any way excited by him, nor even inexplicably aroused like she could sometimes be, but it was more a desire to erase the last few hours. How easily they used to fall into bed through boredom or loneliness, she remembered. Would it be as easy to do the same through sadness?

Patrick was wondering too. Did she mean to come to bed with him, despite what she'd said? Did he want to? Was he ready to find out how he would perform? Better not to. Certainly easier not to. He wasn't in the mood to confront his self-imposed abstinence, nor to finally discover his own suspected impotence.

The single bed which dominated the room in just the same way they dominate all students' rooms in Halls of Residence up and down the country gave Beth an uncomfortable sense of déjà-vu; she knew they had been in precisely the same situation before. Would she ever have guessed at nineteen that she would be presented with the same kind of opportunity at thirty-five? They were both heading towards middle age – well, they *were* middle-aged if Katherine's sums were fair – and here they were, same bodies, same spirits, a little wiser, a little less supple, still unencumbered, or not tied in the way Katherine and Johnny were. By that, she supposed she meant children. Please let me be encumbered, she thought.

Not knowing quite where to sit, they both stood, attempting to behave normally, as if nothing other than being vertical had occurred to them.

'Ssshh,' Beth said, even though Patrick wasn't speaking. 'I can hear them.'

Katherine and Johnny were talking in low voices next door. She and Patrick had done more than enough dissecting of the Bates marriage for one night, but even so, the subject was a safe lifebelt in a potentially dangerous sea, so she grabbed hold.

'Is that a post-coital murmur, or an end-of-argument kind of voice, would you say?' she asked.

'I've forgotten what post-coital murmuring sounds like,' Patrick replied.

'It's kind of like this,' and she half-spoke, half-whispered. The way her voice cracked reminded him of how much she used to talk when they made love. Curious how he could recall the smallest details of his sexual moments with both Beth and Katherine, and could retain almost nothing of any other woman he'd ever been with. For the first time in ten months, he felt a slight pull of desire.

'I still can't quite remember. Do some more.' See if it has an effect, he willed. Bury my reluctance, make me like I once was.

'I shouldn't really be here,' Beth suddenly said, finding herself up against a barrier of awkwardness.

'Why not? We're not breaking any rules. Don't go. I want to talk to you.'

'It's the bed. It's putting me off,' she laughed nervously.

'Let's get in it then. That way, we won't have to look at it.'

They had every reason in the world not to make love, so he wouldn't need an excuse if he couldn't manage it, yet if the mood took them, then maybe he might let it carry him off and bury once and for all his self-portrait of an inhibited man, unable to request or respond to a woman's touch.

Not once in Beth's seven-year marriage had she been even remotely unfaithful. Now she had the chance to share a bed with an ex-lover just when she was after some reassurance and no one need ever know. But it was something other than marital fidelity that was holding her back. How dangerous was it to make love during the first few days after conception? The fear of dislodging a microscopic nugget of hope was a far stronger deterrent than the knowledge that she would be betraying Evan. She looked at Patrick.

'We'll find it much easier to talk,' he said, feeling the tiny spark of passion threatening to leave him and wanting to fan its flames before it went out altogether.

'Was that a joke?'

'No. Really. We needn't do anything else.'

Beth could see he was genuine in his suggestion as soon as they were next to each other under the sheets. Both of them kept their underwear on – him grey jersey fly-front boxers, her, cami-knickers and a white vest. She had taken care in choosing her underwear, even buying the vest the afternoon they left. There had to be some advantage in being childless, even if it was just to flaunt, a tiny bit, her remarkably toned and lissome body in front of one that carried the marks of childbirth and contentment. She would swap her flat tummy for Katherine's stretchmarks any day of the week if it meant having a baby, but rather than being pitied for her childlessness, she preferred envy – or at least she imagined she did. From Katherine, she had never experienced either.

Even though the natural shape of her breasts and bottom was within easy reach of Patrick's own body, she could tell through the soft fabric of his shorts that he was not in any hurry, and it surprised her. It also, if she was honest, wounded her ego a little.

'I've changed,' said Patrick, knowing he could hardly pretend otherwise.

'I don't think so,' she lied. She was on her left side with her elbow on the pillow. He was on his back staring at the ceiling. You have, she said to herself, but that's not what you want to hear, is it?

'So you think I would have passed up an opportunity like this a few years ago, do you?'

'Well, I wouldn't let you anyway.'

'You might. You wouldn't be in bed with me now if you found the idea totally abhorrent.'

'If you really think that, then you lied to me,' Beth said. 'You said it would be easier to talk in bed.'

'And is it?' he asked.

'I don't know yet. We haven't really tried.'

'Does it change your view of me?'

'What, that you lied?'

'No, that I'm lifeless.'

She heard his desperation and shame and confusion and

a myriad of other feelings she was so well acquainted with herself.

'You're not lifeless. People always see themselves differently from the way others do.'

'I don't see myself as anything. I've lost myself. I can't not just raise an interest in you, I can't raise an interest in anything. Not even myself.'

'Patrick.' Beth pushed his hair away from his face and ran her fingers down his cheek to check if it was wet, which it wasn't. 'Will you tell me why?'

'I think you'd prefer not to know. I don't want to burden you with it.'

'It's a heavier burden to see you like this.'

The murmuring through the wall had stopped and there was the sound of a door opening and closing. Beth recognised Katherine's footsteps and she sat up, her loyalties momentarily split.

'Don't go,' he said, pulling her gently back down by her plait. 'They'll be okay. Katherine's fine. She just thinks she needs to get a life.'

'She's already got one. 'What are they doing, those two? Do they know what they're throwing away?'

'They don't think they're throwing away anything. They think they're simply shifting stuff around to make room for other things.'

'Like what?'

'Don't ask me.'

'I thought we were talking about you.'

'Okay,' he said.

Beth could detect through the silence his struggle to verbalise whatever it was that was causing his life to career out of control, like a juggernaut with brakes failure on the first bend of a steep hill. But it was less sudden than that, a build-up of some months, more like a fault with the engine itself than a mere broken brake cable.

Eventually he said, 'I wish I could just make love to you like we used to, but I can't, not even if you wanted me to. I avoid it like the plague nowadays. I haven't sought a woman's company for nearly a year, not since Adam died. I do everything I can to circumvent it. The whole idea of it scares me to death.'

Beth didn't know what to say so she just asked the obvious. 'Why?'

After a long sigh, he said, 'It's a reaction to something very complicated. I'm not sure I even really know myself.'

'Talk to me, Patrick. It's quite obvious you need to talk to *someone* and it might as well be me, now that I'm here, practically naked, next to you. What do you think I am going to do? Walk out?' she replied. 'Please.'

'It's not clear-cut, you'll get the wrong idea.'

'Try me.'

'I'd really appreciate this being between you and me. I don't want it up for public discussion. I find it easier to deal with if it's just my problem.'

'Of course.'

'Not that I think you would.'

'I won't, I promise.'

'Okay, well, Dido turned up on my doorstep in August and said she was moving in with me. No, no, that's wrong – well, it's not wrong, but it's the wrong place to start.' He'd never tried to verbalise it before since he'd never intended to share it with anyone. 'I should go back to Adam's death really.'

Beth lay there, trying to unravel his words as he carried on.

'But it's more complicated than that, it begins even earlier than that.' After a pause, he asked a direct question. 'Did you know that Dido and I have always been sexually attracted to each other?'

'Is the Pope a Catholic?' Beth answered, attempting levity.

'We've never done anything about it though,' he said quickly. 'We were fairly drunk on her birthday a few years ago, and we nearly kissed, which is the only time we've ever come near to any kind of real physical expression of our love, and we ended up making a pact. We even wrote it down. We said that if we still felt the same way about each other by the time we hit thirty-five – that is, if she was still comparing every boyfriend she ever had with me and I was still vainly searching for a girlfriend who could even touch her – then we'd give up the hunt and go for it together. Which was why she turned up in August.'

'Sounds reasonable,' said Beth, dredging her soul for every scrap of moral tolerance.

'Well, it isn't, but I still let us share a bed, like this, for six weeks before I left. Cohabiting in every sense but one.'

'Like this as in underpants on?'

'They might as well have been.'

'But you wish they weren't?'

'No, I'm really glad they were.'

Beth tried to work out what he was saying. 'I might be momentarily shocked if you told me you'd gone the whole hog, but what you're saying seems reasonable – unconventional, but reasonable too. If you love each other,' she said.

'We haven't even gone half the hog.'

'Quarter?'

'No, not even a quarter.'

'You wouldn't be the first step-siblings to fall in love.'

'We're not step-siblings.'

'What?' she asked, putting her fingers lightly on his chest and picking up the pump of his heart mingled with the vibration of his voice which faltered over his next few words.

'Dido and I share the same father. I'm her brother. Adam was my father.'

'What do you mean? Say that again.'

'Dido and I are from the same sperm bank. Adam told me before he died that he's my real father, not Don as I'd been brought up to believe, but him. He told me the same day he died, saved it till the very last, depriving me of the right to reply.'

'Adam is your real father?'

'Yes.'

'God, Patrick,' said Beth, her head spinning. 'And you haven't told Dido, which is why she still thinks you two could . . . ?'

'Yes.'

'You've been sharing a bed with her for six weeks and you haven't told her? Patrick, for goodness sake!'

'I know. That's why I came here – I didn't know what else to do. She'd given up her life to join me. I should never have let her do that, knowing what I did. I should have told her before she made that decision, but I didn't and, well, it's been fucking impossible ever since.'

'Quite.'

'Yeah, right, bad choice of words.'

'Why didn't you tell her?'

'Lots of reasons. I was scared of losing her, Adam told me not to, it was easier to deal with on my own. Anyway, why should it be me who tells her something like that? Adam should have done it years ago, or Mum.'

'Adam told you not to?' Beth gasped incredulously. 'Is that the main reason you haven't told her?'

'No. Honest to God, Beth, when she turned up in August out of the blue, my life actually picked up. Not much, I grant you, but at least there was a point in getting up in the mornings, if only to get away from lying next to her. I'd had six months of terrifying bleak confusion since Adam died, and then Dido – the source of all my panic – arrived on my doorstep, uninvited, to call in the pact. It should have been the worst thing that could possibly happen, but I was comforted by it – appalled as well, but comforted mainly. And I kept trying to tell her, honestly I did, but every time I got close to it, I imagined life without her, and I backed out. Then it got to the point where she was pursuing this complete relationship thing so much that my excuses were getting implausible.'

'So you left.'

'So I left.'

'And do you still feel the same passion for her that you used to?'

'No, the desire has turned into an almost pathological fear of getting too close to her. After Adam died, and I was back in the States, everything I ever felt for any member of my family just went, and I was totally cold, especially towards Dido. Even all the normal feelings one should have went, but then she turned up, and . . . I can't help but love her, you know? And because I love her, and I want her to be happy, I can't bring myself to tell her she can't have me.'

'Have you spoken to your mother about this?' Beth asked, going up on one elbow. The room was too dark to see him properly.

'No. She doesn't know I know, unless Adam told her he was going to tell me, but I doubt it. The way he said it, the way it just came out, unplanned, I can't think that he did. There was no preparation in it, it wasn't a rehearsed speech, it was a death-bed confession. He died six hours later. I don't think Mum knows I know. If she does, she's even more emotionally bankrupt than I think.'

Patrick stopped, not wanting to talk about the ocean of resentment he felt towards Jean now, how angry he was when he recalled how he'd been marched off to put flowers on Don's grave every year, how he'd been given an album of carefully captioned photographs of the two of them together, how he'd been encouraged to keep in touch with Don's parents and accept their gifts of money at birthdays and Christmas. They'd even left him a couple of thousand on each of their deaths. He let the intensity pass and then he carried on.

'And Adam, who never ever asked me to call him Dad like Dido and Will and Agnes did, let me grow up feeling the odd one out because I believed my male genes came from an uncelebrated source, and yet he changed my name by deed poll to his the week after he married my mother. I grew up feeling like a fraud, a boy who carried the name of a good man, but not the name of his father. And then this good man tells me, on his death-bed, that he *is* my father, with the express wish that it was to be between him and me, that Dido need never know, and that Mum should be allowed the privilege of telling me when she felt she could. I mean, for God's sake!'

'But Dido could say the same, couldn't she? That she is the only one of the four not to have Jean as a mother. That's just the way your family is – a complicated patchwork.' She wanted to feel his cheek again to check for tears but she stopped herself. What proof did she need?

'I do really love her,' Patrick said quietly, almost to himself. 'You know?'

Beth spoke slowly, because she suddenly felt her own misery again. 'No, I don't. I don't know about real love.'

He didn't answer and then she said, not knowing where the words came from, 'My pond is stagnant.' Her voice disturbed her, it sounded so dead, so lacking.

'You have Loveday,' he said eventually.

'That's a love you're born with. I'm talking about a love you find.'

'And you haven't found it with Evan?'

'You know I haven't.'

But Patrick's ears were closed to any other noise than his own. He wished he *could* comfort her, say the right thing, give her a platform to bare her soul, but he just didn't have it in him.

'Oh, God,' he groaned. 'I want this thing wrapped up. I want to put it all away. I'm not carrying this thing any longer. I can't.'

Beth felt foolish for trying to claim for herself some of the sympathy flying around, and she pushed herself back into Patrick's agenda.

'Then do it properly, with counselling. Have you had any help?'

'What do you think?'

'Then you must. There are some things that are too heavy to carry on your own. You'll crumple under the weight.' He didn't answer, and she carried on. 'We all carry stuff around that we needn't. I'm crumpling under the weight of something too, but I'm going to do something about it.' She felt sure he would respond now, ask her what. That's what friends were for.

'Beth.'

'Yes?'

'Kiss me.'

'I'd rather talk to you.'

'Talk to me and kiss me afterwards then.' He tried not to but he had already switched off and Beth knew it. I'll just use this as a cleansing experience for myself, she decided. I'll blurt it all out, he can pretend to listen, and I'll feel better. He is about as useful to me as I am to him, which is hardly at all. She spoke as if to herself.

'I want a child, really badly, more than anything else in the world, but time is running out on me. I don't think I love Evan any more, he's way down on my list of priorities, and he's not what I want any more, but he's my best chance. He refuses to talk about our childlessness, so I am having infertility tests. If I can't have a baby, I don't see the point. I thought it would have happened by now. Perhaps it has – we made love before I came away, it was a good time and—'

'Doesn't Evan want children?'

Beth was surprised he was even listening. 'He's never actually admitted it, but I don't think he does.'

'Ah,' said Patrick.

'So where does that leave me?'

'More or less in the same place as me, I should think.'

Up shit creek, thought Beth. Although maybe not quite as far up.

They lay together saying nothing for a long time, both recognising that Patrick was caring for Patrick, and Beth was caring for Beth, or for the child she believed to be in her womb. Finally, the kiss that Patrick had thought he wanted came as a peck on the cheek as Beth clambered over him, put on her clothes and went back to her own room.

That night she dreamed of four empty ponds, cracked by

drought. Two of the ponds were joined by a rickety bridge and still held some water, enough to muddy their bottoms. Another pond had a sign stuck in the middle which read *Under Renovation* and the last one had a crevasse running through its middle, a ravine so deep that one instinctively knew that there was no end to it. Beth felt herself being drawn into the abyss, not because she wanted to, but because she felt she ought to, like she'd be hurting someone more if she didn't than if she did. She saved herself by waking, in a state of hyper-ventilation. It was 5.30 a.m. and Katherine was sitting up.

'Good morning.' Katherine sounded as if she had been awake for ages. There was apology and embarrassment in her voice.

'Uh? Oh God, I've just had the most peculiar dream.'

'It wasn't about a giant egg-timer, was it?'

'No, ponds.'

'Ponds? Very sexual.' Katherine's eyes looked puffy, but not as puffy as Beth had expected.

'How are you? Did you and Johnny patch it up?'

'Not exactly. The word divorce was mentioned, I seem to remember.'

'In anger?' Beth asked, more shocked than she thought she'd be.

'No, with scary calm. I'm sorry about storming out last night. I had actually been responding to Johnny's suggestion that I go outside for some fresh air and return when I'd cooled down, but he doesn't believe me. He thinks I did the "our marriage is over" thing in front of you and Patrick so I couldn't back out – like I wanted to prove to myself that is what I wanted.'

'And is it?'

'More so now than it was yesterday, that's for sure.

Anyway, we went back to his room to see if we could talk things through, and he just wouldn't let go of this imagined desire of mine to end it all in front of you two. He kept on and on about it, and then we heard your voices next door, and Johnny said, "Why don't we ask them in and see what they think we should do?"'

Beth hit her head back on her pillow and gripped her duvet closely around her neck as Katherine carried on. 'I suddenly thought, we either go backwards here, over the same old ground and still reach no conclusion, or we go forward, and if we go forward, then that means change. We've done marriage, so now maybe we should do divorce.'

'Is that what you said to him?' Beth was horrified, although she could believe it of her. Katherine could sometimes be so cold. It was the only time she ever seemed her mother's daughter.

'Yes.'

'And what did he think?'

'He said that was fine by him. He was annoying me so much by then that I just said I thought we should set things rolling before the millennium and that I thought that was what we both wanted, and then he just looked at me and said okay, fine, new century, new life, why not?'

'And do you still feel that is the way to go, now that you've slept on it?'

'I haven't slept.'

Beth knew that wasn't true. When she had crept into their room three and a half hours earlier, at least two hours after hearing Katherine leave Johnny's room, her friend had been sleep-talking, mumbling something about a bunk bed and she'd thought then how basically secure Katherine must be – to be able not only to sleep after a row, but to dream of something completely unconnected.

182

'Well,' said Beth. 'That all sounds like a bad idea to me. Are you sure you want that?'

'I don't know what I want. I do know I want things to be sorted, but I don't know what to do to achieve that.'

'If you're not sure, you had better not do anything.'

'I'm sick of not doing anything. That's how we got into this mess in the first place. Anyway, I'm bored of talking about it. What about you? What did you two do after we left?'

'Not much. We've got to face each other this morning in the knowledge that neither of us could raise even a passing interest in each other last night.'

'What do you mean? When I heard you in Patrick's room, I assumed you were getting on famously, not wanting the evening to end and all that. Did you . . . I mean, did he . . . ?'

'No. God knows why, but we decided that it would be easier to talk if we got into bed together, which in a funny way it was, except there was a complete and utter lack of anything sexual about it. We both thought, no thanks.'

'That's got to be a first.'

'Yes.' Beth promised herself not to talk about Patrick's situation. 'We heard you and Johnny talking though – well, we didn't hear the words, we weren't listening – but I was tempted to come and get you both. I was relieved to hear you still together.'

'I'm glad you didn't.'

'You weren't in bed as well, were you?'

'Yes. Is that stupid or is that stupid? It didn't help any.'

'Was it lovely though? Did you feel you loved him still?'

'For a moment. Until the argument resumed.'

'So you were in bed with Johnny on one side of the

wall, and I was in bed with Patrick on the other. What symmetry!'

'Except that we were doing it and you weren't. You must be lying! I can't believe you didn't. Why didn't you?'

'I wasn't sure if it might harm the baby.' Why did I say that? Beth screamed to herself. Why? Why?

'*What?*' Katherine demanded, her previously listless murmur becoming a shout. 'No! Beth! How far gone are you?'

'I don't know,' Beth said quickly, realising how stupid it would sound to say any missed period was still a fortnight away, and beginning to twist her loose hair round her forefinger. 'Only just, I should think.'

'But are your breasts tingling? Do you keep needing the loo? Are you feeling sick, or tired?'

'Definitely tired, but then I've only had about three hours' sleep.' She felt her breasts, and they were not tingling, nor did she want a pee.

'I can't believe this! I didn't think you were that keen.'

'God, Katherine, where have we been for each other lately? I'm not just keen, I'm obsessed.'

It was the very first time she had voiced it. She'd heard it said to her of course, from Evan, but never from her own mouth.

'Are you?' Katherine asked with a mix of astonishment and pity.

'Mmm, completely.'

'But you've never said.'

'No, but you never asked.'

'So this is great! Exactly how late are you?'

Beth felt something go at the back of her throat. How good it would feel to say something like 'three months'. 'I'm not. It's just a feeling.'

Katherine had a feeling too, that Beth was about to be

devastated in a couple of weeks, but that was not what she said.

'Woman's intuition, you never know.'

'It would be nice, wouldn't it? Hattie could babysit.'

'You wouldn't be able to keep her away!'

'This is crazy. I'm probably not even pregnant.'

'But it's fun to think you might be.'

As they both sank back into their beds, Beth wondered how Katherine could possibly use the word 'fun' and mean it. Therein lies the difference between a woman who's already a mother and a woman who fears she never will be, she thought, feeling the passing of another special bond.

Beth woke again at half past nine. Katherine's bed was empty and her suitcase had gone. On her quilt was a little note saying she had decided to get back to the children. *Don't worry*, the message read. *I'm not upset, I just thought it would be better all round if I wasn't here.*

Outside the hotel, Patrick looked up at the sky and watched a plane leave the most perfect vapour trail he'd ever seen. It didn't occur to him that the plane might be bound for Newark Airport, New Jersey, or that Dido might be on it, returning to his Hoboken flat with her mind a little more in order than when she had left it only a week earlier. If he had known she had been in the UK for seven whole days without making any attempt to see him, he might have guessed her discovery. Dido liked to sort her own feelings out before she began rummaging around anyone else's, and he wouldn't hear from her again until she had.

Watching the vapour trail disperse and disguise itself as a series of little clouds, he cursed himself for failing to take the perfect opportunity with Beth last night to put an end to his self-imposed abstinence. And he remembered how, just before falling asleep, he'd thought of Katherine and wondered if things might have been different had it been her in bed with him partially unclothed. It had been his first thought on waking up too.

Chapter 9

TWO MONTHS TO GO

The Times, 29 October, 1999: After 1,999 years of preparation for the next millennium, it appears the majority of Britain has left it until the last minute before deciding how to spend it. FHA – one of the country's main travel agencies – ran aground yesterday when its central computer overheated. A company spokesman blamed the 'absurd' number of bookings for late December. Meanwhile, the price of a bottle of champagne has doubled since July, and Banner Fireworks are to take on two hundred extra workers from Monday to cope with demand. A recent MORI poll has revealed that fifty-one per cent of the population still have no concrete plans for their own millennium celebrations.

The weekend on St Mary's was not mentioned again, not even in idle chat. If any one time had to go down in history as the moment they nearly fell apart, it would be that Saturday night, and they all knew it.

Johnny cursed himself for trying to make something of the opportunity in the first place and spent the first few days back home wishing he'd had the foresight to go alone. At her parents', Katherine silently appointed herself as the weekend's chief fly in the ointment, one who had buzzed angrily around Johnny's head until she had got her invitation, and then who'd spoilt it all by spreading disease when she got there. Beth, out of all of them, saw the truth – that their friendship was no longer invincible,

187

that they were no longer able to claim immunity from life's complexities. She was also the only one who saw that the core was still intact.

Patrick was having trouble shifting the thought of Katherine from his mind. He knew it should have been Beth he was thinking of, wondering how she was interpreting what had gone between them, whether she was regretting the way it had been, or what they had told each other, but it wasn't. A comment Katherine had made a few weeks ago kept coming back to him – 'Our lives will be in two halves for ever once we cross the divide – what we did before and what we did after'. Was it possible she hadn't just meant the shift of time, but also the shift of friendship, and that he might belong more to her 'after' life than he did to her 'before'?

He was floored to discover that he liked the idea of belonging to her life at all. He'd always believed that the no-strings policy he shared with her was what gave their bond its force, that the love between them was releasingly different from the complicated mix of obligation and responsibility one has towards one's family, or the convoluted negotiations involved in keeping a girlfriend happy. Since striking the treasure of a physical rapport all those years ago, they had also found a meeting of the minds but they had never wanted or needed to be together, which was what he'd always believed made it such a rare alliance. The fact that he was playing around with that now disturbed but also intrigued him. If he'd dived deep down into his conscience, he'd have discovered that all he was trying to do was raise the wreck and dredge up a bit of that treasure again.

He caught himself looking sideways at Johnny, checking to see if Johnny was in turn looking at him, and he felt guilty for even thinking about it. Women didn't belong to men, but if they did, she belonged to Johnny. And anyway, in reality, he knew he didn't love her in the way he loved Dido, or *had* loved Dido. Maybe that was it. His life would be in two halves because of his relationship with Dido – the before and the after. Before truth, and after truth.

Johnny was in one of the two brown corduroy foam filled single chairs of Nick and Penny Shepherd's rented cottage, while Patrick sat on something even less relaxing – a chair from the kitchen with a broken wicker seat. It suited him to sit uncomfortably; he wouldn't have known what to do with solace, the mood he was in.

Katherine had, quite rightly, taken her own house keys with her when she took flight from St Mary's and the two men had taken her hint. 'Don't let yourselves in. It is my territory.' So there they were at Johnny's. He had his own keys, of course, but it would have felt like trespassing without the children there.

'Why are you looking at me like that?' Johnny asked, amused by Patrick's scrutiny.

'Like what?'

'Like you've done something you don't want me to find out about, or you're waiting for me to say something profound.'

'I thought you said something.'

'Oh, right,' said Johnny, wondering if Patrick really expected him to believe that.

They continued to watch the football, a mid-season match between two unsung European teams and pretended to care one way or the other who won. The more they watched, the more they found they *did* care. It occurred to Patrick how funny it was that you could whip allegiance out of nothing, for the colour of a shirt, or the name of a player, and yet you couldn't always find it for the people you loved.

* * *

In Somerset, Katherine made her excuses and headed up the immaculately hoovered stairs to bed, leaving her parents sitting in silence below. Her father had wanted to watch the football and her mother hadn't, so they had compromised by having the television on but the sound down. She had stuck it out for as long as possible, watching her father talk to them both with one side of his face while the other side flinched and fell to the action on the screen in the corner, but as soon as ten o'clock came – a reasonable if not expected time for bed in the Jamieson household – she was up and out of there like a shot.

Her mother's grieved expression, as if to say, 'Can't you show just a little more interest, dear?' had almost been the last straw and Katherine had felt herself regressing twenty years as she shut the sitting-room door noisily and took the stairs two at a time.

'Ssh!' her mother rasped after her. 'You'll wake the children.'

The bed had been turned down and a pink towel with a silk motif sat neatly folded at the end. She wondered if it was usually her father's bedroom and whether he had been kicked out of it for the occasion of their only child paying them a visit. Bring out the warm white wine. Maybe they did still sleep together, but Katherine doubted it. She must have been about Hattie's age when the thought of her parents actually making love had occurred to her. 'Yes, but they've only done it once,' her friend Emily had said. 'Mine have done it three times, think of that!' and Katherine had suddenly been jealous that Emily's mum and dad were obviously racier than hers.

She thought about the particular pressure attached to being an only child. Of all her close friends, she was the only one with a full complement of parents. Beth had never

190

known the conventional structure of a family, Patrick had his mother (and although Adam had done his best, Patrick had always complained that the knowledge of being another man's son set him apart from the rest of the family), and Johnny had a mother and father who were really his aunt and uncle. It was a very definite late twentieth century thing, this disintegration of the nuclear family. Historians would have a field day in later years. But for now, it felt as if only she lived with the burden of being the undeniable sum of two parts, both present and correct.

Too correct sometimes, she conceded, looking at the pink candlewick spread and the spotless pink rag doll sitting pertly on the pillow in just the same way it had sat all those years of her childhood. Even if she did get between the uninviting pink sheets and lay her head on the pressed pink and white floral pillowcase, she knew she wouldn't sleep, despite her exhaustion. A fleeting vision of herself in pyjamas, shinning down the drainpipe outside the bedroom window and running to meet Colin Pepper flashed through her mind. Those were the days, sixteen and reckless, she thought, wishing she had even a quarter of that boldness now.

'Mum?' It was Hattie in an oversized brushed cotton nightshirt.

'Hello you. Not asleep yet?'

'I've been waiting for you to come up. Can I sleep with you? Seth's snoring.'

Hattie was one of those children who hadn't left the parental bed until she started school. In her very early days, when night and day had little to define them, Katherine and Johnny had slept better if she had been with them. As she progressed from a cot to a bed, which coincided more or less with the arrival of Seth, she would patter into her parents' room without fail every time she heard the baby wake. He was in a crib by Katherine's side and for some reason – possibly because Hattie still staked her claim on it – he had never been taken into the double bed, and she would climb over both that and her mother and brother and find the warmth of her sleeping father's back which is where she would stay until morning. Seth had never done it, not even when he was ill. In fact, the only time Katherine had tried to encourage him to fall asleep alongside her, on a cross-Channel ferry where the cabin bunks were so narrow she was afraid he'd roll off on his own, he had screamed blue murder.

'Come on then. I bet it's freezing in there. Have you got any socks?' Katherine said, feeling a little glow of comfort at the prospect of having her baby with her again.

Hattie disappeared for a moment and returned with her feet cosily ensconced in chunky grey wool.

'They're nice. Did Granny buy them for you?'

'Dad sent them. They were here when we arrived. He sent Seth a vile T-shirt.'

'Did Seth think it was vile too?'

'No, course not, it's got a computer generated football on it.'

'That was nice of Daddy.'

Hattie felt pleased when her Mum said things like that, even if she was still using the embarrassingly babyish 'Daddy'. It meant she didn't hate Dad and as long as she didn't hate him, there was a chance she might still love him. At twelve, Hattie was just a little too young to understand how thin the dividing line was between the two, and that it was the word 'like' and not 'hate' that was the true enemy of love. She snuggled down next to Katherine.

'You can play with my hair if you like,' she said, more request than invitation.

Katherine took a small handful and began to plait it. It was hardly long enough to do anything with, but that had never made any difference to Hattie who, as a wispy-haired three-year-old, used to refuse to leave the house until Katherine had given her bunches.

'That's nice,' Hattie murmured. 'Granny tried to do it for me one night but she was hopeless. I didn't say anything but it made me miss you. I didn't like it when you were away.'

'Never mind, I'm back now. Actually, I didn't like it much either.'

'Why? Did you and Dad have another row?'

Katherine loosened the tiny plait and started to twirl the hair instead. 'Does it seem as if that's all we do?'

'Not really,' said Hattie. 'I know you try hard not to in front of us, but that makes me worry that you just do it more when me and Seth aren't around.'

'We don't. I love Daddy, really I do, and I know he loves me; it's just that our love for each other has changed and we get on better apart.'

'That's what you always say. If you still love each other, then why don't you get back together?'

'I'm sorry, squidge. I know it's hard for you, and you've been so brilliant, like my best friend.'

Katherine continued to twiddle the soft hair of her daughter and as Hattie started to fall asleep, she decided it would be a good time to talk to her mother about Patrick before they got home.

'Can we go somewhere on our own tomorrow, without Seth?'

'Why? Is he being a pain?'

'Well, yes, but it's not that. I just want to talk to you on your own.'

'Or we could talk now,' said Katherine, trying not to let the anxiety show in her voice.

'I don't want to go to sleep thinking about it.'

'What is it about? Give me a clue.' Hattie was at the age when it could have been anything. Boys. Periods. A new pair of jeans.

'It's Patrick.' She spoke his name with scorn.

'Patrick?' said Katherine, letting Hattie's hair go. 'Patrick what?'

'I don't want to hurt your feelings, but I don't like him living with us,' Hattie said forcefully.

Katherine very nearly asked, 'Why not?' but that was such a big question and there could be so many answers that she didn't feel quite brave enough. Anyway, she didn't like him living with them much herself if she was being honest, and why *should* the children take him on board as well as everything else. Now, if Hattie was me, and I was my mother, I would tell her to get some sleep. That was enough to persuade her to at least say something.

'Nor do I much,' she said. 'It's just sort of happened, hasn't it?'

'Can't we make it un-happen?' asked Hattie.

'What is it about him being there that you don't like the most?'

'Everything. He's always *there*.'

'And Daddy isn't?'

'Yes.'

'He's only with us because he needed somewhere to stay and I couldn't see a reason to say no, but if you find it difficult, then that's different. There are plenty of other places he could go.'

'Including back to America,' Hattie said mischievously, making her mother laugh.

'I'll talk to him about it,' Katherine promised.

'Can we still go out tomorrow, without Seth?'

'Why not? We can pretend I've got to get your feet measured or something.'

'Actually, I really do need my feet measured,' Hattie said seriously.

Katherine smiled and very gently began to plait again, watching as her daughter's skinny little frame, which in the last month had begun to show signs of shedding the child and assuming the woman, sank into the mattress and fell into relaxed breathing. Hattie no longer actually sucked her thumb, but Katherine noticed she had her 'huggie' with her – a little square of striped flannelette sheet that, at the age of three, she had been inseparable from. When she had started primary school, huggie had been told to stay at home, and it had become a night-time thing. Around the age of eight, it had been relegated from the bed to sitting on a chair with her dolls and Katherine had nearly collapsed under the strain of it all when she'd realised the long-forgotten huggie had re-entered the frame. She hoped she had heard all there was to hear about Hattie's desire to have Patrick removed. Surely there couldn't be more to it, could there?

Downstairs, Margaret Jamieson heard the footsteps across the landing and the soft voices of her daughter and grand-daughter. She popped the last few cups into the dishwasher, switched it on to take advantage of economy time, took off the apron and rubber gloves she had only put on five minutes ago, and walked up the stairs. As she passed the spare bedroom and saw the light on through the slightly open door, she found the courage to push it open a little and peep inside. There they were, mother and daughter, curled in on each other, their hair mixed up in each other's, making a string go twang somewhere inside her.

'Can't you sleep?' Derek asked her in bed after an hour of her twisting and turning.

'Sorry,' she said. 'And I can't even escape into the spare room to give you some peace.'

'Good,' he said, and turned to give the top of her freckled arm a small peck. 'I'll get you a brandy.'

So I don't have a successful relationship with my daughter like Katherine does with hers, but at least I have one with my husband – and you can't have everything, she told herself, wrapping herself up in the thought.

Once, a long time ago before she was married, her Mini had run out of petrol late at night, and rather than risk flagging down a passing motorist or walking in the dark and rain to find help, she had locked herself in and tried to sleep on the back seats. Just as it got really cold, she'd remembered the two velvet curtains her mother had packed up ready for dry cleaning earlier that day and which she had been told to drop off at the launderette after work. If she hadn't wasted so much time dreaming of her handsome new boyfriend and how she would say yes when he asked, she would have remembered to carry out the errand, and then what might have become of her? As she'd pulled one curtain around her and rolled the other up for a pillow, suddenly warm and comfortable, she'd had a conviction that Derek would always bring her contentment, security, and peace of mind. Tonight, she had reason to believe it all over again. How wrong was it to love your husband more than your daughter?

Katherine was awake too, feeling guilty about not turning to say goodnight to her mother and worrying about the

Hattie-Patrick thing. She had detected a certain coolness emanating from her daughter towards their house guest for a while, but she had naively assumed it was because Patrick was hogging the computer. The way Hattie had all but spat his name out tonight suggested something altogether more complex. Whatever she heard tomorrow, Katherine promised herself that she would listen first and talk afterwards because in her passionate attempt not to emulate her own mother, she often did the exact opposite, putting great emphasis on the importance of communication to such an extent that she sometimes did all the talking.

In a split second of immeasurable fear, she turned on the bedside light and tilted the shade to Hattie's face. The sight of her smooth unfurrowed brow, the upward curl of her slightly chapped lips and the discarded huggie amongst the candlewick was as soothing to Katherine as any velvet curtain, and she too found sleep.

Evan phoned from London on the Sunday to say he was staying an extra day, and when Monday arrived, Beth wished she was more excited at the prospect of seeing him again. She made more effort with supper than usual, in the hope that an enticing menu might mask her own lack of enthusiasm, but it was an uphill struggle. The house was stuffy and dry – he must have re-programmed the central heating in preparation for winter – and it was all in all rather stifling.

'Katherine went home early,' she told him. 'She and Johnny had an almighty row.'

'What?' said Evan, failing to disguise his pleasure at the thought of the foursome beginning to fracture. 'Not the reunion of the century then?'

Beth nearly said something to stop him in his tracks, like

197

the fact that she and Patrick had shared a single bed almost naked, but then she thought of the baby.

'It's nice to be home,' she said, putting her arms around his thickening waist and imagining herself vastly pregnant. Tomorrow I can go and see Dr Jeremy Shaw, she thought, and use words like ovulation and conception, and maybe even iron tablets, morning sickness. 'What about you? Did you have a good weekend?'

'Boring. You wouldn't have liked it. All work, no play,' he said, removing her.

She wondered whether he had gone the whole hog, or half, or maybe just the quarter, and although she found she didn't care too much either way, she did seem to bring the knife down on the celery just a little harder than was necessary. The first time she'd suspected his infidelity, she had cried for a month. The second time, she'd cried for a week, and the third a day. Was this the fourth or the fifth time? And how awful was it that it didn't really matter?

At last, ten months later than he should have done, Patrick telephoned his mother Jean. He hadn't quite decided what he was going to say to her, but he'd had a sudden urge to speak to Dido and Jean had been a last-minute safer option.

'Hello, Mum. It's Patrick.'

'Patrick, son, at last, thank goodness. I was hoping you'd call me eventually.'

'I'm in Cornwall.'

'I know you are. Dido told me. She came home for a few days last week. It was lovely to see her.'

'She came back to the UK?'

'Yes, last week. She's gone back to Hoboken now, to look after your flat. Darling, are you all right?'

'I'm okay.'

'Patrick, I want to talk to you.'

'I'm not ready,' he found himself saying quickly.

'Please. Can't you force yourself?' she pleaded. 'I know there's something wrong.'

'No, I can't. Look, this is why I don't phone.'

'Could we meet up,' she asked, 'so you don't have to hike all the way up here? I could hop on a train.'

'I'm really tied up for the next few weeks,' he replied quickly, 'but sure, we could think about it. I'll phone you.'

'Darling . . .'

The way she said it made him want to slam the phone down and run.

'I'm going now. I'll call again when I can.' And he cut himself off, all of a minute after picking it up. So Dido had been back to England. Why didn't they contact him? What was he – contagious or something? Why all the subterfuge? It was then that Patrick made the conscious decision that if they wanted him, they would have to come and find him – because he sure as hell wasn't going to seek *them*.

'We have to talk,' Katherine said to Johnny over the phone from her mother's three days later.

She means divorce, thought Johnny, and as a joke to deflect the awfulness, he said, 'Neither of us is having Evan, okay?'

'Actually, it wasn't divorce I was wanting to discuss, although you're right, we must get round to it. It's Hattie. She doesn't want Patrick in the house.'

'Why not?'

Katherine still hadn't forgiven him for the hotel restaurant episode and how he had walked back to their table without giving away a single clue that their children were all right, so that she had thought, for one unforgettably terrible moment, that her life was over. It was this lingering anger that made her voice deliberately veiled. She was confident she had got to the bottom of Hattie's resentment, and it was nothing more than an understandable reaction to another man apparently stepping into the shoes of her father, but she could tell Johnnie that when she saw him. What he chose to think in the meantime was his problem.

'It's not something I particularly want to talk about over the phone, especially with you at work.'

'Why, what do you mean?'

'I've told you, we'll talk about it later. Would tonight be okay? We're leaving in a minute.'

'Of course. Ring me when you want me. I'd like to see the children before they're in bed though.' He suddenly missed them terribly.

She hung up with a mumbled goodbye, not feeling at all guilty about her intended ambiguity.

It took Beth two attempts to secure an appointment with Dr Shaw, in which time her self-induced certainty that she was pregnant had grown to irrational levels. By the time she was with him, in his small square co-ordinated surgery with its wooden rocking horse and coloured abacus, she could almost see the beginnings of a bump.

'Do you have children?' she asked.

'Not that I know of,' he laughed. 'Why?'

'This surgery seems geared up to cope with them.'

'My partners decided on my behalf that I would take on all new young families. They said I had the kind of face that wouldn't scare babies.'

'So I'm with the right man then?' Beth joked.

I would say no, Dr Jeremy Shaw said silently. You are with entirely the wrong man. But to her he just laughed again and said, 'Did we say we'd do an ovulation test today?'

Johnny took a corner so quickly he frightened himself. What had Katherine been hinting at? That Patrick had done something to upset Hattie? It was ludicrous. But why had she phoned him at work, in the middle of the day to make a formal request for his time? Somewhere in the very centre of him, a gremlin sniggered. Maybe this was the end of the road for them all. Not the end of a decade, or a century, or even a bloody millennium, but the end of everything that was ever good.

Chunks of life on the South London estate came hurtling back to him. There had been a girl called Sammy whose father was jailed when she was just thirteen, and neighbours had thrown bricks through his window during the trial. Johnny could remember asking his mother why.

'He's not a kind man. Sammy will be pleased to get him out of the house.'

'Has he been hurting her?'

'Yes,' Phyllis had said, and given Johnny too tight a hug. He'd been about eight, and even then he could tell she was talking about a different kind of hurt than the one his other friend Mark got from his Dad, who beat him up if he caught him stealing.

Johnny slowed right down as he entered Tremewan. There were far too many free-range children and deaf pensioners to drive at anything other than snail's pace down the main hill, but he also had to stop his mind racing before he got home. The phone call had thrown him completely. It couldn't have come through at a worse time. His boss – Richard Lyons, Cornwall's Chief Economic Grants Director – had just shocked the entire office by announcing his retirement on grounds of ill-health, and then followed it straight up by a request to see Johnny privately in his office where he had suggested he apply for the position himself. Before Johnny had even had time to babble out the niceties – 'Well, I'm very flattered, Richard, and I shall obviously give it some thought, but . . .' – Katherine's phone call had come through. Richard had simply said, 'Think about it. Let me know,' and that had been it.

What was he supposed to think, for God's sake? If Katherine hadn't wanted him to get the wrong end of the stick then she would have been less ambiguous, and he thought he'd detected a dark hint in her clipped tones. She had meant him to panic, he was sure.

As he drew his bike up alongside the stone wall of his damp rented cottage, he took a few even breaths and tried to steady himself. We are talking about Patrick here, the man you would trust beyond all others, your closest friend, the godfather of your daughter. It just isn't possible. But Katherine's voice . . . those strangled words.

Patrick was in the sparsely furnished kitchen, reading a newspaper.

'What are you doing back at this time?' he asked in mild surprise, getting up and moving to the small fridge in the corner. 'Beer? I was just going to have one.'

'No, thanks.'

'What are you, working a half day?'

'No.'

Patrick opened the fridge and took a can, scanning the shelves for a possible lunch. 'Have you eaten?'

'No.'

'Are you okay? Has something happened?'

'You tell me.' It felt wrong, challenging him.

Patrick noticed the skin above Johnny's top lip was white and taut. 'You're a bit aggressive, aren't you?'

'I just want to hear what you've got to say about Hattie,' Johnny said in a rush. I'll fucking thump him so hard his brains will spill, he promised – the sort of thing he used to say almost daily as a fourteen-year-old.

'What do you mean? What's wrong?'

'I mean Hattie. You know, my daughter, your god-daughter. Why is she upset?'

'Hold on, John. I'm lost. Why should I know? She's at Katherine's mother's, isn't she?'

Johnny found the control to study Patrick's face. He tried to check his breathing and when he braced himself to look into Patrick's eyes, he saw bewilderment, not betrayal.

'She thinks you're taking my place,' he said in a flash of understanding. 'That's it. Hattie loses one father, and then thinks she has gained another.' He thought for one moment he was going to be sick and he put his hand to his mouth, then he said, 'I've left the keys in the bike,' and rushed back out the door.

Patrick found him sitting on a grass verge in the lane with his head between his knees.

'Come inside,' Patrick said, pulling his friend up. 'What's going on? Come on, come inside.'

Now hold on, Johnny kept saying to himself, hold on. Either I come clean about what I thought, or I let Patrick think I'm cracking up.

Patrick still had hold of him by the arm. 'Did you say Hattie thinks I am taking your place?'

Johnny decided he would let Patrick think he was cracking up.

'Sorry, yes, sure, look, let's go inside. I will have that beer. It's been a hell of a day.'

'Are you going to tell me what the fuck all this is about?'

'Yes, well no, I mean . . .'

'Johnny, are you all right?'

'I am now. Sorry. It's been a bad day. First my boss tells me I'm in line for the chief officer's job, then Katherine phones to say we need to talk about divorce, and that Hattie doesn't like you being in the house – it all just got to me back there.'

'Hattie doesn't like me being in the house?'

'That is what I gathered.'

'God, how embarrassing. She thinks I've got my feet under the table, doesn't she? I hadn't realised. Does Katherine think that too?'

'I've no idea. She wouldn't discuss it, she just said she had to talk to me about you and Hattie.'

'What the hell does she mean by that?'

'She's just doing her best, mate. Look, this is my fault, forget it. We'll talk about it when she gets back, when we know a bit more.' He started to walk up the path.

'Listen, let's nip back to Tremewan now, before they all get home, and collect my stuff. I'll move in here,' Patrick said, standing by the gate.

'Oh, will you?' said Johnny with a hint of hostility. If Patrick wasn't – he couldn't even put it into words, but if he wasn't in any way intentionally hurting Hattie – then what was he doing to, or with, Katherine? What had given a twelve-year-old girl reason to want a good friend out of the house?

'Look, I don't want to be in the way. I have a comfortable apartment in New Jersey. Maybe I should go back there instead.'

Johnny thought that if it wasn't for the increasing delirium surrounding them, that is exactly where Patrick should go. But they had their pact. They had their party.

'Sorry,' he apologised, offering a hand. 'It's been a bad week, not just a bad day. Okay, let's do that – fetch your stuff now before they get back. They'll have already left Somerset by now. I'll go over there tonight and find out what Hattie is worried about. Whatever it is, I'm sure it is nothing you've done.'

'I'm pleased to hear you say that,' said Patrick, his stomach churning.

'Listen, I've got a lot on my plate. Ignore me, yeah?'

I wish I bloody could, thought Patrick.

Chapter 10

SEVEN WEEKS TO GO

The Times, 10 November, 1999: 'Children of Enlightenment', the religious cult headed by self-styled guru Steven Haitink, has just announced its latest member – Oscar-winning actor Jacques J. Mahon. Mahon, a Canadian, is now reported to be with the other 209 cult members in self-imposed exile in a former military hospital outside Ontario where Haitink says they will stay until midnight on 31 December has passed. Mahon was due to start filming the sequel to *Whistler* – the film which won him Best Actor at last year's Oscar ceremony – this week. A cult spokesman refused to disclose the reason for their voluntary imprisonment but Haitink has been quoted as saying, 'We choose not to talk in terms of suicide and prefer the term divine sacrifice.'

On Beth's bedside table were two clay figures – one a small woman sitting and hugging her knees and the other a taller woman, also naked, but standing upright with her arms outstretched and her head thrown back, beseeching something or someone, and this second one had a perfectly round hole where her belly should have been. When Beth had brought them home from her pottery evening class a year ago, Evan had pretended to admire them but only until she had placed them on the coffee table in the sitting room.

'You can't put those there,' he'd said.

'Why not?' she'd answered back.

'Because they're personal.'

'How do you know?'

'Well, they must be. Nobody makes things like that for no reason. Take them upstairs, will you?'

Beth had carried out his instructions like the dutiful wife she tried hard to be, and the little women had been crying her to sleep ever since.

As she sat on the edge of her bed now, she picked up the one with the hole where her baby should be, and pushed her finger through. I know I'm pregnant, I don't care about the result of this test, I know I am, she repeated to herself over and over again. Pride in being Cornish was one gift Loveday had passed on to her daughter, and being instinctive was the other. The first one had diminished sadly, eroded by seven years of superior attitude emanating from the man she lay next to every night, but Beth's power of instinct was still on full charge, and she hung on to that now, her eyes still staring blankly into space. And when, after a while, her protestations began to sound petulant, she started instead to try and recapture the certainty she had just lost.

A blue line, distinct, strong and definitely there, had appeared in the first window. That just means the tester is working, Beth told herself, it just means the tester is working. It is the second window you have to concentrate on. Ignore the first. Look at the second. Her head was almost on her knees as she held the white wand out in front of her. One wave and my wish is granted? She had done home pregnancy tests before and been disappointed, so why did this time feel so hopeful? Was it that she could feel the flutterings of something inside her? That this time she wasn't a day late, but a week? Was that a blue line in the second window? Oh, God, there it was . . . the beginnings, a tinge . . . was it? It *seemed* bluer, or was that the light? And was that a line? Beth scrabbled frantically in the tester box for the instructions. Where was the bit about the blue line? How blue did it have to be?

'If you ARE pregnant, a distinct blue line will appear in the second larger window. If you are NOT pregnant, no line will appear in the second window.'

That wasn't good enough. What about a bluey tinge in the second window? A *possible* line? What did that mean?

Beth felt herself starting to swim against the tide, suddenly needing stronger strokes to get to the place she thought she had already reached. She had been living towards this moment for three weeks, ever since she and Evan had made love on the sitting-room floor of 4, Lander Parc before the disastrous weekend on St Mary's. She'd promised herself she wouldn't do one until she was a week late. Four days to go, she'd insisted. Three. Two. Tomorrow. And now here she was, and the deed had been done.

A heavy numbness began to sink in. It isn't a line, is it? Maybe she had done the test too early and there weren't enough of the right kind of hormones yet. But there was definitely a bit of blue in the window. The helpline number, where's the helpline number? She read the instruction leaflet again, and found it.

'If you are in any doubt about your result, call the helpline on 0800 969000.'

'I'll go and make a cup of camomile tea,' she said out loud, as if there were someone else in the room who had just had a bad shock. She got as far as the bedroom door and then came straight back in, picked up the tester, pulled off its protective lid, and stared again. I'm not, am I? I'm not.

She lay down on the bed and stared for a long time at the ceiling, waiting to cry, knowing actually that there was nothing inside to come out, not even a whimper. All week, her tummy had seemed full, compact. When she had pressed it, it had resisted a little and then sprung back, and she'd had a feeling that could have been pre-menstrual but wasn't. Now, from nowhere, just because there was no blue line in the second window, she could sense a gap, a vacuum, or a big bag of wind. She pressed her tummy again and there was no hardness to it this time.

But I actually *felt* pregnant, she reminded herself, a thread of hope still keeping her hanging. My breasts ached, I was walking around with something inside me, I felt grown-up. Is that instinct? And where have all those feelings gone now? Do my breasts still ache? What is in there? Anything at all?

She got up and walked into the en suite bathroom. The pregnancy test box with one un-used stick still inside lay on the floor, but instead of picking it up, she walked over it and turned on the taps to fill a bath and then jumped as she heard, 'No school today?'

His voice came from behind, but she hadn't heard his steps.

'Oh Evan, you frightened me,' she said, putting her bare foot on the box.

'I've come home to change my suit. I put this one on thinking I had a day in the office, but I'm doing lunch with John Bartlett and his architect and I don't think this one gives off quite the right message, off-the-peg and all that. No school?'

'Going in late,' she mumbled.

He walked back into the bedroom. The completed pregnancy test was still on the cabinet on her side of the bed next to the two clay figures. The instructions were on the quilt.

Beth sidled back in, still in her cream vest and shorts that she had worn to bed the night before, and as her husband took off his jacket and hung it carefully in his side of the walk-through wardrobe, she tried to think sensibly. She wondered if she seemed normal. How could she just suddenly drop into the conversation the fact that she had done a pregnancy test that seemed to be showing negative but could possibly be positive. What would she be telling him? That they might be having a baby or might not? And he would ask why she hadn't told him before. Well, that was a good point. Why *hadn't* she told him before?

She lay on the bed, covering the crisp paper instructions which crackled beneath her.

'Is that an invitation to join you?' Evan asked, trousers off, socks on.

The very idea of sex with him at that moment almost had her retching and she got up quickly, diving back into the bathroom and slamming the door shut. As she knelt in front of the lavatory, knowing damn well that if she stared at the bowl long enough she probably would display a classic Pavlovian reaction and start to retch, she tried to think again. I'm not really going to throw up. Why do I need to be away from him?

Just as she grabbed the pregnancy test box and threw it into an open empty wash bag, Evan walked in. She was still kneeling in front of the loo.

'Oh sorry,' he said, sounding sheepish. 'I thought you had slammed the door in temper. Are you okay?'

'I thought for a moment I was going to be sick. That paella last night. Do you feel okay?'

'Fine.'

She sloshed some water over her face and patted it dry. Then she stepped out of her cream shorts, flicking them with her foot into the linen basket, and stretched upwards to take off her lacy vest. With her arms in the air, her head tipped back and her long hair brushing against the small of

211

her back, she was the exact echo for a moment of the little clay figure with the hole in her belly. The skin across her flat stomach was so tightly pulled it might have been the skin covering a drum. A hollow drum. If Evan hadn't been there, she would have let out a wail, a deep loud moan full of anguish and self-pity and she would have let it go on for ever and ever.

Patrick had seen Beth's little clay figures the day before, when he had turned up unexpectedly and she had given him the guided tour. Her home had disarmed him considerably, despite having heard all her own protestations about how awful it was. It wasn't the position that was so dreadful, although living in the middle of an executive housing development that had been designed to create the atmosphere of a smart spa town crescent was hardly where he'd put her if he'd been asked to guess seventeen years ago. It was much more the inside that he found disturbing. Everything matched and nothing was scratched. The sofa was too large and the mahogany desk was too shiny. There was a profusion of glass, some of it even smoked. It was about as far removed from the kind of climate she'd been brought up in as you could get.

'Don't say it,' Beth laughed. 'It's Evan, not me. He can't live with my taste so I have to live with his.'

'Right.'

'You must see the guest bathroom. It is hideous!' and she took him upstairs, pointing out the offensive wallpaper on the way.

'If you don't like it, why don't you say?' he'd asked.

'Oh, I've learned with Evan that you weigh up what you can put up with and what you can't, and you only complain about what you can't.'

'So what *do* you complain about then?'

Beth looked at him. He hadn't been listening to her that night in the hotel bedroom on St Mary's or he wouldn't have been asking that question.

'Not much,' she smiled. Why bother letting him in? He wouldn't be able to help, even if he wanted to.

'What are these?' The little clay figures in her bedroom were the only interesting objects he'd seen so far and he'd picked up the one with the hole.

'I made them. Evan wouldn't let me have them downstairs. He said they were too intimate.'

'Are they you?'

'Maybe,' she replied. Of course he hadn't been listening in the hotel.

He'd almost dropped it, as if it had suddenly caught fire or he'd just noticed it crawling with maggots. The little figure hadn't reminded him of one woman's desperation to have a child like he knew it was meant to, but of other things – Paul Grogan, the awkward Christian at University who had spoken about the big empty space inside everyone, and who had told Patrick he would pray for him, and then, from the back of his memory, an American news show he had appeared on five years previously. Because the current hot issue at that time had been the imminent collapse of the British monarchy as a result of the Royal divorce, Patrick had been called in his capacity as an Englishman. The Americans had absolutely no concept of how stupid that was, but they were paying him well so he went in, expecting to gain little from it. During the show, part of a television interview with Prince Charles was played, and something Charles said had stayed with Patrick ever since.

'For all the advances of science, there remains deep in the

soul a persistent and unconscious anxiety that something is missing, some ingredient that makes life worth living.'

When Beth looked at her little clay woman, she knew it was a baby that was missing, but when Patrick looked, all he saw was the hole.

After Evan had changed his suit and gone again, Beth managed to get through the rest of the day somehow, going into school and burying that part of her mind in water displacement experiments and nativity play auditions, but the moment she got home, she went straight to her bedroom to check the test again. It now showed no sign of a blue line in the second window, not even the tinge she was so sure she had seen earlier. She knew she really ought to let go, but for the last three weeks her mind as well as her body had been pregnant and it was intolerable. I'll phone the helpline, she decided. They'll just tell me to do another one, I'm sure, but at least I'll be able to talk to someone about it.

She had no recollection of tidying away the debris of the test that morning, but the instructions were neatly folded back in the box with the second 'wand', and the box itself was in her underwear drawer where she had presumably put it. She picked up the phone and dialled the first two digits of the 0800 number, and then had to put it down again as Evan walked in through the front door, an hour earlier than usual.

'Shit,' she huffed in panic to herself. Look normal. What would I be doing in real life? Walking downstairs maybe.

'Feeling better?' he asked, keeping his distance and foregoing the customary mechanical kiss. The last thing he wanted was a gastric bug, especially if it originated from schoolchildren.

'Yes, thanks. I'm sure it was that paella.'

In the kitchen, she reached into the fridge and scraped what was going to be leftovers supper into the bin, just to confirm her lie. Now what are we going to have? she wondered, thinking she might be taking things a little too far. She had been so preoccupied with herself in the last few days that she hadn't thought about food shopping, and if there was one thing that got Evan going . . .

'You'll have to take that bin liner out now and put it in the garage. I don't want to be catching the smell of old prawns all week,' he said, watching her struggle to retrieve the dish that had fallen in with its contents.

There was an ache behind her eyes and a nervousness in her stomach as he walked up the stairs to the bedroom where he would leave his work shirt on but swap his suit and tie for the clean jeans he would find folded on his chair. The knot inside her suggested there was trouble ahead and she didn't think she had the stamina for it.

'Beth?' Evan called from upstairs. 'Could you come here a minute, please?'

It was a summons. He was standing by her side of the bed holding the test.

'What is this?'

'What do you think it is?'

'I would say it was a pregnancy tester.'

'And then you would be right.' How odd that he hadn't yet asked if it was negative or positive. He looked affronted or something. She had forgotten how she had dashed to the loo that morning in a sudden bolt of nausea.

'And how long have you suspected that you might be pregnant?'

Perhaps he doesn't want to know the result yet, she thought. Perhaps he needs time to prepare himself one way or the other. He might be discovering a hitherto hidden desire for a child after all and be too nervous to ask. Or he might simply be scared.

'Three weeks, although—'

'Three weeks? Let's see . . .' Oh, but I detected sarcasm then, surely, thought Beth as he continued. 'Three weeks would take us back to mid-October. would it not? Oh, goodness me, look at that.' He had his slimline diary out. 'Would we be talking that abortive weekend of yours on the Isles of Scilly, by any chance?'

'I'm sorry, Evan, what are you saying?' Was he attempting to draw some conclusion or other between her weekend away and the pregnancy test, before even asking the result? Surely not. Perhaps he didn't care.

Evan almost shouted. 'How late is your period?'

She decided quickly that she was damned if she was going to let him off the hook by telling him it has all been a false alarm. There was going to be a row, that much was clear.

'Over a week.'

'So was it Johnny or Patrick then? Was Johnny's tongue hanging too far out for you to ignore his needs? It must be hard going without it when it's been so easily available for so long. Or was it Patrick – for old time's sake?'

'How dare you,' was all Beth managed to say.

'What do you mean, how dare I? I tell you how I dare. You and Patrick, left alone while Katherine and Johnny patch up their sad little marriage? Not been together like that for years? Husband conveniently away? I'm not stupid, Beth. I know damn well you ended up in bed with him. I saw it in your eyes the moment I walked back through the door on the Monday.'

He hadn't seen anything of the kind because he had been too busy trying to hide his own discrepancies, but Beth wasn't listening to the undercurrent. It was all she could do to keep up with the main gist.

'I did not sleep with him. I slept with you, if you remember, before I left.'

'Oh, I remember that. I thought at the time you were doing it for a reason, now I see why.'

'I don't know what you are talking about.'

Evan threw the pregnancy test on to the bed in disgust and Beth looked at him. There was a redness to his eyes which wasn't fear or hope as she had half imagined – it was anger. Whether or not he thought she was pregnant seemed to be the last thing on his mind. Well, she would keep it going then, let him believe whatever he liked. The tester was too old to read anything from it now anyway.

'I want to know who has made a fool of me, Johnny or Patrick,' he carried on.

'You're doing a fairly good job of it yourself. I don't think you really need any help.'

'Tell me,' he shouted. 'Tell me!'

Beth suddenly felt scared. He was irrational, almost out of control. Listen, she told herself. He is still your best bet. You are thirty-five and you want a baby. Stick with it. She used a soft voice as she said, 'There isn't anything to tell. Patrick was in a state that weekend and I comforted him as any good friend would.'

'By letting him fuck you?'

'No, Evan. Listen to me, you're not listening. What's wrong with you?'

'What other sort of comfort is there?'

'I have never been unfaithful to you, never. Can you honestly say that to me? Can you? I bet you can't.'

'Stop twisting it round and tell me.'

'Look, Evan, I know what I've done, you can think what you like.'

He gave an incredulous laugh, and Beth could see their life together was hanging on by a thread. Thirty-five. Baby. Hang on in there. She made a subtle attempt to reverse the conversation. 'Listen, Patrick is having a bad time. He's just discovered something that has changed his whole life. He's deeply screwed-up—'

'I don't wish to know about the sad little workings of Patrick's puny mind, I just want to know who you slept with.'

'Stop it, Evan. I didn't sleep with anyone, least of all Patrick.'

'I don't believe you. His brains have always been in his boxers.'

'Not any more they're not. He hasn't slept with anyone for a year. The man he has always believed to be his step-father has turned out to be his father. That means the woman he's always believed to be his step-sister has turned out to be his real sister.'

'What's that got to do with anything?' asked Evan sarcastically.

'Everything, as a matter of fact. Dido is his real sister. He didn't know that.'

'Oh, how shocking. No wonder he needed you.'

'It is shocking if you know what kind of relationship Patrick and Dido have.'

'What, you mean he's been knocking her off?'

'No, but there is a closeness there that . . . I don't know why I should tell you this, it's nothing to do with you. All you need to know is that Patrick is not up for casual sex any more than I am.'

'What, he can't get it up? Is that it? You tried, but

218

he couldn't And I am meant to find some sympathy for him, am I?'

'That is enough. I mean it, Evan. You're being disgusting.'

'I couldn't care less,' Evan spat. 'Patrick's a loser, and I'm sure his sexy little sister knows that.'

'She doesn't know anything,' said Beth. 'Patrick has been sworn to secrecy, so I don't want this conversation to go any further. It's nothing to do with you. I shouldn't have told you.'

'What? Patrick hasn't told her she's his real sister? Still snogging, are they?'

'You're really quite pathetic, aren't you? Now, would you like to ask if the pregnancy test is positive?'

'I have absolutely no desire to know,' he said, and walked out of the bedroom, slamming the door, bringing three years of frustration and disappointment crashing down around her.

At the very beginning of their marriage, she used to comfort herself with the thought that men can react very strangely faced with the thought of fatherhood. Later, when the very mention of babies became a no go area, she assumed he must be worried about losing her to someone else, even if that someone else was a baby. After eighteen months or so, the pain kicked in, and two and a half years after that, she had thought it was a control thing, that he refused to discuss their infertility because that way he coped with it better than she did and that would keep him on top, where he liked to be. But it was seven years now, and she'd had it. He cared about the pregnancy test for one reason – that it might suggest her infidelity. Now why was that? Slowly, Beth became aware that a cog was not moving somewhere in the workings of her brain, or maybe it was even missing.

Suddenly, the frustration and disappointment turned to a searing anger. She opened the door and ran down the stairs after him, catching him just as he reached the bottom.

'I want a baby!' she screamed, thumping his back and yanking his head by the hair as he tried to turn the corner. 'I want a baby and I'm going to do all I can to have one. I've already been to the doctor's. He's doing tests. You're going to have to go too. I don't care what you say, you've got to listen to me now because I have had enough.'

He didn't even turn round.

'Are you going mad?' he asked coldly.

'Yes, probably. God! I just want a baby, Evan, please. You know I do.' She flumped to the floor and lay at the foot of the stairs, sobbing.

He stood over her, detached. Nothing in him wanted to pick her up or comfort her. She repulsed him, this heap of emotional disaster, and he wanted her to go away, to leave him in his sane house with its clean windows and nice neighbours. Her friends could pick up the pieces. He'd had his fun. Seven years was a fair enough run. He knew the way out.

'Get up. I've got something to tell you.'

'Whatever it is, I can hear it from down here,' she cried, not moving.

'Very well. Are you listening?'

'Yes.'

'You aren't going to get a baby from me, no matter how many tests you have. I am not father material. I can't do it.'

'Yes, you can. You can, there's nothing to be afraid—'

'Shut up. I mean I can't do it physically. I had a vasectomy, a year before I met you. There's a knot in it.'

220

At first Beth just lay there with her wet face in her tangled hair. Then she remembered how to speak.

'Liar.'

'I'm afraid not. That's the truth. Now if you want any more details, I'll be in the sitting room.'

Chapter 11

Loveday enjoyed chairing meetings, taking a certain pleasure in calling for 'organic debate rather than stifled argument', and allowing raised voices and friendly disagreement instead of the usual council rigmarole. All sorts of people came up with all sorts of ideas, when she felt sure they would not have done if they had been obliged to go through 'Madam Chairman' every time they wanted to speak. Tonight had been a case in point. Even the councillors who had initially felt alienated when she first took the chair three years ago now jumped to their feet or thumped the table with the best of them. At the very least, they now had concrete proof of how well her approach worked.

Thirty-five thousand pounds had seemed an impossible amount of money to find at first and yet the extension to the village hall had already been built and the equipment was on its way. All that remained for her Tremewan Millennium Project Committee to do now was finalise arrangements for the opening ceremony and come up with a better name than the Information Technology Centre – or 'computer room' as everyone preferred to call it.

Loveday had been the mover of the project from the word go, securing a National Lottery grant of fifteen thousand pounds, matching it with a sum raised by the village, the district council and the Rural Development Commission.

The hardware had been bought using a grant from a regeneration project with a title so long and full of capital letters that she had never bothered to pay it any attention but the fact was they had the money, and soon, anyone in Tremewan would be able to surf the Net when they felt like it. Children could swap CD-Roms and DVDs, the church congregation could raise money for a digital video camera . . . the entire community could ride the waves of technology all the way into the twenty-first century.

It was exactly the kind of thing that made her tick, realising that she could make a difference. Her sense of belonging was immense, and it was why she had finally decided to spend the approaching New Year at the village party and not at any number of the other smarter gatherings to which she had been invited. The idea of being among faces she had grown up with, some who had even known her as a child, seemed entirely appropriate, and as soon as she had committed herself by buying a ticket, the thought of anything else – a glitzy gala or a gourmet dinner – left her cold.

As she walked home, Loveday felt childishly proud. She imagined knocking on cottage doors which would then be answered by people her own age whom she knew and loved, and she could say to them, 'There's an e-mail waiting for you in the computer room.'

She could become almost evangelical about the freedom that comes with not being scared of the future, and in this case, new technology. '*Trapped in the twentieth century? Here's the key to get out!*' she had written in the parish magazine.

Loveday was fifty-five, and still had her finger on the pulse – or should that be mouse? She wanted every other woman of her age in Tremewan to be as relaxed with the word 'modem' as she was.

When she had been asked back in 1996 if she had any ideas how Tremewan should mark the close of the second millennium and celebrate the start of the third, she had initially suggested the refurbishment of the clock-tower. What a dull meeting that had been, in the freezing parish rooms with the same old faces trying to raise enthusiasm for an age they had no desire to enter. 'Third millennium? Sounds like science fiction. Don't want to know, thank you, I'll stick with the second. Give me a date that begins with 19 and I'm happy. Me? I'm too old to worry about all that.'

At the time, Loveday had almost subscribed to their reluctance, and it was only after watching a *Where Are They Now?* television programme about what had become of the hot new talent of the 1960s that she fluttered with a rare panic. Every one of those people on the screen – men and women she had admired in her youth – had moved on. None of them thankfully wore flowers in their hair any more, or fell into the trap of advocating peace and love, but what *was* frightening was how they had spoken in a language she barely understood. Multimedia PC's, microprocessors, CD-Rom drives, Windows, Program Managers, Click, Icon, Systems. She could spell the words but not translate them, and it was quite clear there was a life going on out there that she knew nothing about, that she was about to enter a new age not having learned any new tricks.

'We must equip ourselves for the third millennium!' she had proclaimed at one of the very first meetings, starting up all sorts of fuss.

'With respect, Loveday,' Frank Pascoe had said, 'what you must appreciate is that people our age simply do not feel good around computers, and as it is people our age who are going to have to get this project off the ground, I think we'd be better off with the clock tower.'

'In the same way that our parents didn't feel good around decimalisation, is that what you mean?' she had retorted. 'Didn't we used to laugh at them? Couldn't quite shake the habit of talking in shillings, could they? And the way they cursed those shiny new coins – wasn't it sad? Is that what you want?'

There had been an embarrassed mumbling and Loveday seized her chance.

'How many of you have received a Christmas card that plays *Jingle Bells* when you open it? Did you know that each one of those cards represents more computer power than existed in the entire world when we were born? That's how much everything has changed. And anyway, was it not our generation who revolutionised the twentieth century with our new ideas and our inventive approach? Hands up who can effectively use a modem?'

And her case was made. Since then, she had taken a beginner's course in Knowing Your Computer, then an intermediate one, and now, an advanced. Loveday knew her way round a keyboard all right, and it had made her feel so much less feeble. Soon, the whole village would have the chance.

'Not that I'm actually terribly interested in computers,' she confessed to Mouser, the cat that shared itself between herself and next door. 'But I do like what they do for people.'

That's one thing I suppose you can say about me, she thought, as she passed the Miners and waved through the window at the same few regulars at the bar, I have always lived in the present. She was on a high, and indulged her ego further by coming up with other examples of how she had made things happen in her life. When she got pregnant with Beth, she could have had the child adopted and she could even have risked abortion but she didn't. She threw herself into motherhood with the same energy and commitment she had intended to put towards her art course, and it had worked. She had been both challenged and fulfilled by Beth and anyway, she had created something far more beautiful than a portfolio. When money became an issue, she had decided to put her talents to material use and market herself as the only female painter and decorator in Cornwall. It was amusing to think that the name she'd come up with – *Gilding Lily* – had stuck. It sounded very early 1970s to her, but people still phoned on the strength of her *Yellow Pages* advertisement and asked to speak to Lily!

So it was a smug Loveday who unlocked her front door that night, thinking she would try and come down from her ego-trip by playing the piano for a while. As soon as she was inside, however, she was immediately aware of an extra presence in the house – it was perfectly quiet but the air was fuller – and all traces of conceit drained away. Her famous instinct told her it was Beth.

Every maternal heartstring that had ever been pulled was pulled again as she walked into the sitting room and saw her child – for she looked exactly like a child just then – curled in the armchair. Beth had made a fire but it was the sort of fire that made the room look even colder somehow, and it was also exactly the sort of fire that Loveday would expect her to make – a firelighter, a few carefully arranged lumps of coal and a neat little wigwam of sticks. It was what Loveday used to call a 'a maid's fire', meaning it looked like the work of a child. The last time Beth had made a fire in Loveday's cottage, she *had* been a child. It didn't seem so strange to find her there either, despite the fact that she no longer lived there and the time was pushing eleven o'clock. It looked as if she had come home.

Suddenly, the excitement of the meeting seemed entirely sterile, and Loveday's sense of fulfilment, her self-built edifice of activity, things to think about and do, shrank to a negligible corner of her mind. She could see the rawness of Beth's eyes as they looked apologetically at her.

'Bethie, you've been crying,' she said in alarm, unwrapping herself from a large blanket stitched shawl and bundling it on the piano stool, before going over and kneeling down.

Beth had no energy left to answer, and she let her head hit the arm of the chair. As she felt the loving grip of maternal concern on her arm, she began to cry all over again.

'I can't . . . it's just so . . .'

Loveday moved to hold her as best she could. The armchair was in the way, and Beth was much bigger than she used to be, but echoing times from twenty and thirty years ago, Loveday pushed back her daughter's hair and said, 'Tell me, darling.' The hair felt the same, but the tears were different. Children's tears just dry into nothing with the brush of an adult hand; there is no residue with the tears of an infant, no visible trace, just a smoother skin and a peachier cheek. In these tears, Loveday could taste the spike of someone else's poison and see the scars of a yawning hurt.

She had known on Beth's wedding day that Evan was never going to make her daughter happy, but what do you say? She also knew it would be his disloyalty that would eventually bring the whole thing down, but when Beth began to talk, she realised she hadn't seen the half of it. What disloyalty! What brutality! She had not known wickedness like it, not ever.

'Just tell me this again,' she repeated in bewilderment after hearing a story she could hardly believe, combing her hands through her short peppery hair. 'Evan had a vasectomy a year *before* he met you. And he has only just told you?'

'Yes.' What Beth proceeded to paint, with manic attention to detail, was an ugly picture indeed. Loveday hated that house, but she had always assumed, or at least hoped, that what you saw was not necessarily what you got. Now she could see that even that had been a more sympathetic version of the truth. The low ceilings and brooding shades of the cottage seemed friendlier than ever.

'He just left me there at the foot of the stairs, and I thought for a moment that I had gone mad, that I was watching a play and putting myself in it. I wasn't even sure if I could get up. It felt as if someone had cut the top of my head off and my thoughts were all escaping up into the centrally-heated air and I couldn't get them back.'

The fire was no longer a 'maid's fire' but belting out a proper heat now, one that actually warmed you. It was the only comfort. Her daughter, her lovely kind sweet and innocent daughter, was speaking with the voice of experience. Loveday thought about Blake's poetry, his *Voices of Innocence and Experience*, and how trite she had found them when she had first read them, and how appalling the transition is when it comes.

'And then after a while, I began to feel more stable, and I followed him into the sitting room. I was half expecting him to tell me it was a joke, that is the kind of thing he does, but he said, "Do you want the rest?" and I said I did, so he told me. It took him about twenty seconds.'

'Oh darling, my angel, my baby,' Loveday almost sang as she hugged her sobbing daughter, 'it's over, it's over, it's over.' She rocked Beth softly backwards and forwards, letting the ancient rhythm of mother and child lap over them both.

229

When the sobs became sniffles, she said, 'What would you like me to do? Phone him and get him over here, for you to have your say now? Would you like me to speak to him?'

'No. I want him out of me, just out of me and away from me and forgotten.'

'You don't want to confront him? Show him how angry you are, and let him see what he's done to you?'

Beth shook her head.

'Good girl, you're right, good girl,' said Loveday, muttering with no structure to her words.

'I'm okay,' Beth whispered. 'I'm okay.'

'You married a bastard,' Loveday blurted, not at all sure once it was out that it was the right sort of thing to say, but she'd heard a flicker of spirit dance across Beth's words, and she had been encouraged. 'Right, I'm going upstairs to run you a bath and make your bed up. You stay here by the fire and switch off,' she said, handing Beth a tumbler of whisky. 'You've done the right thing darling, really, I'm sure you have.'

As Loveday walked up the stairs, she felt a little like she did after she had fitted the last piece of a jigsaw, or finished a book. Beth was back with her. Now that should not be important to me, she argued as she turned on the taps, but it is. Just for the moment anyway. Or at least until the next century. Oh God, she prayed as she watched the bubbles grow, guide us through the next few weeks. And if You could also punish Evan for ever . . .

There was too much to pick over, too many remembered words and expressions and actions, to allow Beth to sleep when she eventually got to bed. How Evan had accused her of infidelity, his puzzling lack of interest over the test result,

230

and his eventual revelation. The dénouement. What a twist. Should she have seen it coming, months ago?

He had delivered his explanation in the voice she assumed he must save for clients who didn't matter. I'll explain this once and once only. Any further questions, please ask my secretary. I'm a very busy man.

'Do you want the rest?' he'd said when she had appeared before him. He was watching television, for God's sake.

'Yes,' she'd said, vowing she would never speak another unnecessary word to him, ever. All he'll get from me from now on is clipped questions and perfunctory replies, she promised herself.

'Fine. Listen then, because I'm not going over it again. I had a long affair with the wife of a prominent businessman in Truro. You don't need to know who. It suited me, it suited her and as we were intending to continue with the relationship for as long as it still suited us both, I took the decision to have a vasectomy. She was older than me, highly fertile, had four children already and was allergic to the pill, so as I was – always have been – keen to avoid having any kids of my own, it was a good option. Then I met you and I thought I'd rather have you than her, so we finished. And that is more or less it.'

Beth stared at him for a while, repulsed, and he stared back.

'Why did you not tell me?'

'I just have.'

'Why did you not tell me before we were married?'

'What, you married me so you could have kids, is that it?'

'Why did you not tell me?'

'It's not a very good chat-up line is it? Hello, I'm Evan, I've had a vasectomy.'

'Are you going to tell me why you have lied over these past few years?'

'I haven't lied. I have been very careful not to lie. That you cannot accuse me of.'

'By omission you have most definitely lied.'

'Really? Oh, well . . .' and he had actually turned the television back on.

She had walked upstairs, hardly knowing how to put one foot in front of the other, and she had packed. Clothes, shoes, jewellery. Downstairs, books and coats. Just as she was about to open the front door, she stopped, turned and walked back upstairs. She took the two clay figures from her side of the bed and popped the one with the hole into her pocket. Then she threw her pillow on the floor, put his in the centre, and placed the other huddled tortured female clay figure on top of it, where he would be sure to see it. He would have to decide what to do with it himself, but she knew he wouldn't be able just to pop it on the bedside table where it would stare at him all night.

He heard her go and wondered how long it would be before she came back and how much she would make him suffer for his lie. It never occurred to him that she might not do either.

'That is the last time I set foot inside the place,' she said as she climbed into her MG. 'The last time.'

Loveday was not asleep either. She had thought, at fifty-five, that she had experienced most of what life had to offer, that she was better equipped than, say, Katherine, to deal with a crisis, that she could see the wood for the trees simply because she had clambered through so many forests and that when something like this was thrown her way, she could catch it. A rich tapestry rather than a cotton print, that was the way she had always secretly seen herself, not that she loved herself too much or anything, rather that she just knew she was made up of more parts than most. Not so, it seemed that night. The church clock rang two, and she shook her head. More parts maybe, but only one that really counts. An anger boiled inside her. How dare Evan live such a lie? Is it for Beth to resolve alone? How I want to confront him! Would he ever have realised, when Beth was post-menopausal, childless and empty, that it was his fault, his selfishness, that he had denied her a huge and significant part of what her life had to offer?

It was a long time since Loveday had been in turmoil. Her life was fertile, yes, and there was plenty to think about, but it suddenly felt as if it had all been spun from nothing. Beth had been Evan's, and during that time, Loveday had bolstered herself by acting up the role she played in other people's lives. Now, in the quiet early hours with her child lying in the next room, she realised how bereft it had also been.

'Mum?' Beth's head appeared round the door.

'Hello.'

'Can I sleep with you?'

'Of course. Shall I nip down and make a cup of tea?'

'No, you go back to sleep. I can't switch off, but I might be able to if I'm with you.'

'Come on in then, you'll get cold. I wasn't asleep either. How could we expect to? I can't believe anyone could ever live with such a lie.'

'No. It takes some beating, doesn't it?' Beth got in and lay down under the threadbare patchwork quilt feigning sleep but the tick tick tick of her mind was so loud, Loveday could hear it.

'Beth?'

'Mmm?'

'I've been trying to imagine how difficult it must be, facing a future without a child and what I can say to you to make it better. The opposite happened to me. You came along before I'd even realised I wanted you, and then when I had you, I couldn't believe I'd ever survived without you.'

'Yes.'

'You're the best thing that ever happened to me. Even now.'

'Yes.'

'Which makes it hard for me to think of anything comforting. But something will happen to sort all this out, I promise.'

'Hope so.'

'It'll even seem easier by the morning, once you've slept.'

'Yes.'

'My poor little monosyllabic Beth,' said Loveday, curling up to her. 'But he's released you now, hasn't he? It's terrible that he kept you captive for so long, but at least you got out before it was too late.'

'You make it sound like prison,' Beth said. 'Which it was.'

'But you're free, that's the important thing. None of us knows what the future may bring, do we? I didn't know when I found myself pregnant with you that I was carrying the reason for my being around with me, did I? I didn't know, in the few fleeting moments that I contemplated abortion or adoption, quite what a happiness you'd be to me, how you'd shape my life and make me whole. We never know what's out there for us, do we?'

A baby please, maybe even a man and a baby, thought Beth. Loveday's voice was getting heavier with sleep.

'When you were little, I could sort out every little problem

234

you had, usually with a cuddle. If that didn't work, we'd get to the bottom of it by talking. I wish I could give you what you need now. I can't bear to see you wanting something so much and not being able to give it you.'

'Oh Mum, you've never wanted anything really badly, have you? It's awful, bloody awful. I want something so much.'

'Then you go out there and get it,' said her mother. 'You go out there and you get it. The reason you haven't got it yet is because you trusted your life to someone not worthy of you. And now he's gone, he can take his wretched infertility with him, because it's not yours, is it? It's his.'

'If only it was that easy,' Beth said, feeling more comforted by the thought than she sounded. 'Babies don't grow on trees you know.'

'Really? You did. All I had to do was pluck.'

'Did you say pluck then?'

The two women allowed themselves a little laugh and then they were quiet. Loveday's breathing became deep and regular and Beth lay there, focusing her thoughts on the gap that used to be so well-defined inside her and that no longer seemed necessarily quite so permanent. A few hours ago, her life had collapsed, along with her body, in a heap at the foot of her carpeted stairs at 4, Lander Parc. Now, it was already picking itself up and dusting itself down. Her mother was right. Evan *had* released her. He had been her captor, no doubt about that, but she was now free to do exactly what she wanted to do – spend time with her friends when she felt like it, leave her boxes of Tampax out on the bathroom windowsill, and – it was almost too intoxicating to say – maybe even find someone who could give her a baby.

She wanted to confirm the moment, to give recognition to the fact that from this day on she stood a greater chance of being whole, so she crept out from under the blankets and went back downstairs where she started looking in the dark for her coat.

She found it by the side of the tapestry chair she'd curled up in, and from the pocket she pulled out the little clay woman with the hole in her belly. Then she went into the kitchen and turned on the light to look at the display of miscellany hanging from the beams – jugs, hats, dried flowers, ancient saucepans – bits and pieces from hundreds of times over the years. Rummaging in the junk drawer for a ribbon or a piece of string – Loveday never threw anything away – she found a long narrow strip of lace, the edging to an old linen handkerchief, and she started to thread it through her little clay figure. She got up on a stool, letting the yellowy glow from the overhead light shine through the little woman's hole, and just as she was choosing a sturdy hook from which to suspend her new curiosity, she heard her mother's soft voice behind her.

'What are you doing up there?'

'Giving myself a rite of passage,' Beth replied. 'Giving my little clay woman a purpose for her hole.'

'Let's see.'

Beth dangled the tiny piece of pottery on the end of the lace ribbon and passed it to her mother. 'I made it, a year ago. It's me. The hole was my unhappiness.'

Loveday looked at the swinging figure and the tears welled. 'Oh Beth, it's beautiful, but it's so sad.'

'Not any more, it's not. It's just another one of our eccentric kitchen curios now.'

Loveday looked at the beams and saw the mouldy salt dough star Beth had made when she was five, and a strange little straw thing, and a painted blown egg.

'Go on then,' Beth said. 'Hang it up.'

'No,' said Loveday, handing it back. 'I think you should. It's your passage, not mine.'

'I don't feel she's me any more.'

'No. She doesn't look like you any more either.'

'If I'd shown her to you when I made her last year, would she have looked like me then?'

'I would like to think I might have recognised the hole.'

'I didn't think you'd understand, not about holes. I didn't think you had a gap to fill – you've always been so complete. I thought you'd think it was a failing, to need something so much it ruined the rest of your life.'

'Beth, Beth, Beth. I do know, believe me, I do know. I was just tested much earlier in my life than most, that's all. We all need that bottom line, only I didn't know yours was a child. And I thought maybe Evan was enough, maybe he was all you wanted or needed to feel complete.'

'You knew he wasn't. I could see it in your eyes every time we spoke.'

'I've never liked him, that's true, but maybe that is because he *doesn't* have a hole, and because even if he ever discovered one, he wouldn't know how to go about filling it. He'll never find out what it is that makes life worth living, not now that he's lost the only good thing about him,' Loveday said with a certain amount of pleasure.

'Let's not talk about him,' Beth replied. 'Tell me what makes life worth living for you?'

'I do, and you do.'

'That just makes me want a child even more.'

'Come on, hang your woman and come back to bed. You'll exhaust yourself if you try to think much more.'

So Beth chose a hook in the middle of a beam where everyone would notice it, and she popped her unhappy little charm over it. It twirled a few times and then settled in a sort of flying position, arms outstretched.

'She looks like a mini version of Superwoman!' Beth laughed.

'And so she is,' said Loveday. 'So she is.'

Chapter 12

ONE MONTH TO GO

The Times, 3 December, 1999: Stock markets crashed across the world yesterday as speculators called in their profits, triggering mass automatic share sales. After months of 'New Age optimism' came the realism, with scenes in New York, Tokyo and London reminiscent of the Black Monday crash of October 1987. The US Dow Jones index plunged to a hazardous low as did Japan's Nikkei Dow and Britain's FTSE – an inevitability foreseen by this newspaper three months ago in a *Business Pages* special when we predicted that world stock markets would fall before the new millennium.

When Seth came shrieking into Katherine's room and told her it was snowing, her first impulse was to stay in bed with her head under the duvet all day. She thought how clichéd it was that it should snow now, just when she was at her lowest ebb. How dare it? How depressing.

The sight of virgin snow had always had the capacity to make her feel wistful (or since having the children anyway) in the same way that Christmas carols did, the magic ever so slightly tinged with the burden of experience, the promise dappled with a wish that the world really was that innocent. It was never a lasting affliction though, and in normal times, she would have been out there before anyone else, breathing in as much of the serenity as she could before the children destroyed it, letting it singe her lungs before blowing it back out to watch it disappear in the frosty morning air.

This morning, even with the unbridled excitement of Seth hanging over her, the wish outweighed the promise by a very long way.

'Mum, I said it's snowing!' he repeated. He already had a sweater on over his pyjamas.

'Ooh, enough to settle?' she asked, trying to muster some enthusiasm in her voice, although the whiteness and the stillness of the light coming through her curtains told her it was a winter wonderland out there.

Seth's laugh was the same one Johnny used when the children said something endearing. It happened more and more lately, this momentary glimpse of Seth as a grown man, and although she told herself it was only because Johnny wasn't around to make the comparison unfavourable, it was enough to stir her into action. Seth had only seen deep snow in Cornwall once before, and she had the sudden thought that by the time it snowed again, the magic might be tinged by the burden of experience for him too.

She dragged on her ancient towelling robe and went over to the window. 'Oh, wow!' she shouted, despite herself. 'Where's Hattie?'

Get me Hattie, she'll deflect the attention, she thought. They can go out in it, pick it up, toss it in the air, feel its nothingness – then I can feel my nothingness too, and it won't matter, because they won't see me.

'That *is* incredible,' she whistled, saying all the right things.

'I know,' Seth whispered back.

In the kitchen, Katherine tuned into the local radio station. Villages near Lands End were cut off, parts of Truro were without power, lists of schools closed because

240

of inaccessible roads or burst pipes were being read out. Up came Tremewan County Primary. Katherine imagined the head teacher Stephen Rook looking out on to his own garden and his own children playing in it and thinking, What the hell! I'm sure we can muster a frozen water supply or something. Academically inspired he was not, but a good man, undoubtedly. Hattie's school – Penmount Comprehensive – was a different kettle of fish. If any of them would stay open against all the odds, it would be Penmount. 'Things must be bad,' she mumbled as, sure enough, the Truro school joined the growing list.

In true local radio tradition, the school closures were top of the news, followed by something altogether more global. 'Snow and ice in Europe has been matched with cyclones in Australia and freak storms in California and Asia. The extreme weather wreaking havoc around the world shows little sign of letting up,' read the hesitant female voice. 'At least twenty-two people have been killed in a mudslide in Los Angeles with States of Emergency being declared in twenty-four Californian counties. Residents in Darwin, Northern Australia, are being told to prepare for a storm reminiscent of one at the turn of the last century, which killed eighty-two people and flattened ninety per cent of the city. In Borneo, rescuers are still finding bodies from the tropical storm which hit two days ago killing at least two hundred people. The cold weather has killed at least fifty in Poland, thirty-five in Germany, twenty-nine in France, nineteen in Hungary, and ten in Moscow. More than twelve thousand travellers have been stranded in the Rhone Valley in France by ice up to four inches thick on railway lines. The Loire has frozen over and ice building up between the North and the Baltic Seas has closed many harbours.'

'No school today!' Katherine shouted, opening the French

windows which usually led on to the granite circle and a gentle step down to the lawn. The world was freezing over, and the children had the day off school. Which fact would they find the more interesting?

'Yo!' shouted Seth. Hattie smiled and carried on building.

The garden was already ransacked. Great roads of exposed grass criss-crossed the white where Hattie had rolled her ever-increasing snowball. The lawn sloped slightly towards the field and river beyond, and Katherine watched as daughter and ball gained momentum, thinking what a metaphysically perfect example of life the little scene was – a small but flawless snowball, pure and new, being steered in random direction and all the while losing its perfection. It had picked up bits of stone, clumps of grass and lumps of mud, and Katherine fought the urge to run to it and check for hidden dangers – a shard of glass or a knot of barbed wire that could present itself at just the wrong moment. Would the ball, now at least half Hattie's size, collapse in a heap before it reached the hedge and become just another pile of dirty snow?

She waited for the inevitable disappointment, but instead, her daughter negotiated a tidy little U-turn and began to push the snowball back up the hill, collecting a fresh track of white. By the time she was near enough for her mother to see she was not wearing gloves, the ball was somehow less unsightly than Katherine had imagined.

'Would you say that was big enough for his body?' Hattie asked through her scarf, beginning to smooth down its sides.

'I should think so,' Katherine laughed. 'Look at you, you need gloves, your hands are going blue.'

'I'm not cold,' said her daughter, shaking her head and

looking amazed that anyone should think she might be. 'I need my fingers to be free for the sculpting bits. I'm going to carve arms and legs on him.'

'It won't take two seconds to put on a pair of gloves. Come in and have some breakfast, wrap up a bit warmer, and then you can stay out there as long as you like.'

'I'm not hungry either. I love it, it's such good fun!' Hattie shouted, running off, her nose dripping and her cheeks a wintry red. 'Come out with us.'

'I will after breakfast. I'm going to make some porridge. Ten minutes, okay? Then you can have the rest of the day out there.'

Katherine shouted this last bit, and Seth, way down the garden reconstructing the Leaning Tower of Pisa, stuck up his thumbs. Not cold and not hungry. My wonderful, resilient children. If I could only get there myself, she thought.

Inside, the phone rang.

'Hello, fairyland,' she said, expecting it to be Penny Shepherd asking about school.

'Could I speak to the chief goblin, please?'

It was Johnny.

'Speaking.'

'Kath, we're frozen up here. No water. I thought I'd better let you know in case you'd made plans for a child-free weekend, only it looks like you might be stuck with them.'

'What did you think I might be planning? A snow orgy?'

He laughed. 'I don't have any plans.'

'It's too cold.'

'How about an indoor snow orgy?'

'What's wrong with you today? It can't be something in the water because you haven't got any.'

He nearly admitted that he'd been propositioned by a girl

243

at work and that he'd almost taken her up on her offer, and that ever since she'd made it, he'd been thinking about it. Instead, he said, 'No, funny you should mention that . . .'

'Ye-es?' Katherine asked with deliberation, knowing what was coming next.

'Well, Patrick and I are now effectively homeless. It's no fun here without water. It's no fun here anyway, but it's even less fun here without water.'

'And?'

'God, you're tough sometimes. You want me to beg, don't you?'

'And can you come and stay for the weekend? I'd say yes, but I don't think Hattie would appreciate it, do you? We've only just worked things out to suit her.'

'She is twelve. She might just have to lump it,' said Johnny with control. It was a touchy subject. He was still disgusted with himself for entertaining, even if it was only for a few minutes, the idea that Patrick would do anything to harm Hattie, and he was still angry with Katherine for allowing that suspicion to seep in. She'd dispelled it the moment they'd begun to discuss it of course, but the damage had already been done. He was also flabbergasted at the credence Katherine gave to Hattie's demands. His daughter's main argument against Patrick seemed to be that he kept hijacking the computer. Obviously, she'd prefer her father to be living there instead, but that just wasn't the way of the world at the moment, and he couldn't see why a twelve-year-old child shouldn't be told that.

Katherine's reluctance to offer the obvious was actually nothing to do with Hattie. She would have been with Johnny on this one – that if push came to shove, Hattie would just have to put up with Patrick's presence, however difficult she found the situation. But as the prospect of a weekend cooped up with all five of them was so deeply unappealing, she decided to make it as problematic as she could. Anyway, she felt like a silly day at home with the children. Johnny could pick them up tonight, as arranged.

'What about Nick and Penny?'

'What about them?'

'I bet they'd have you for the weekend.'

'Oh, come on, Katherine. What am I? You make us sound like a pair of abandoned puppies.'

'Sorry.' She was laughing now. 'I didn't mean you and Patrick, I meant you and the children. Let me call Penny. I'm sure Luke would love to have Hattie.'

'I don't want to deposit myself on people like that, it's not good for the morale. It's okay, Patrick and I will stay here. I was just trying to find a more pleasant way out of the crisis.'

'Crisis,' Katherine snorted. 'You wouldn't know a crisis if one came up and smacked you in the mouth.'

'Apart from a broken-marriage-split-family kind of crisis, do you mean?' Johnny replied, suddenly irritated by her levity. He was living in a freezing cottage with no water and he'd been looking forward to having the children for the weekend. Still, she'd say it was his choice, wouldn't she?

'Yes, apart from that,' she replied quickly, trying to sound amused. 'I'll phone Penny and call you back. The chances are the children would want to get together this weekend anyway.'

On the phone to her friend, Penny tried hard to argue a case for Katherine, Johnny and the children all coming to the farm together and leaving Patrick back at the cottage.

'Neutral territory,' she reasoned, in the clipped way she often spoke. 'It would give you an ideal opportunity to spend

245

some time together without having the freedom to row, and Nick or I could leap in when the conversation got too heavy. Go on, we miss having dinner with you two.'

'I had dinner with you last week,' Katherine protested.

'It's not the same,' said Penny tactlessly.

'Thanks.'

'Sorry, that came out wrongly. Yes, of course we'll have them, the children have already been asking. I just wish you'd come too, I miss you.'

'I might saunter up, if I run out of food or drink. It would only take me a day or two to cross the fields. I've never been off-piste before.'

'You've been piste-off though, loads of times.'

'Ha! Which is why I'm not joining you all this weekend.'

'Okay, you win. I'll go and make up some beds, and talk to you some time over the weekend. Tell Johnny to go carefully down our lane. We've cleared most of it, but there is some sheet ice to look out for.'

'Thanks Pen,' Katherine replied, suddenly feeling a little bit left out.

It wasn't until much later on, once she had returned from dropping the children off at the farm, that Katherine realised exactly what she had let herself in for. In her eagerness not to end up with both men in the cottage, she had overlooked something else. Either one of them on their own would have been fine, Johnny maybe even more so than Patrick – that way, there might just have been a few intimate moments. It wasn't sex exactly that seemed to belong to other people's worlds, it was more the carefully chosen words and the light touches, the shared truths – but all of that could only ever happen if the children were there too, like latterday chaperones, running in and out of rooms, offering the permanent threat of interruption. It seemed a little perilous now that it was just her and Patrick, and he was upstairs, having a bath. There had been other weekends in the last few months when they'd been left on their own, of course, but for some reason, a bit of snow made all the difference.

The radio was still on, re-tuned to BBC Radio Four. The local station had painted a picture of utter chaos in Cornwall throughout the day and she was exhausted just listening to it. The Royal Naval Air Station forty miles away had been sending out its air sea rescue helicopters like buses, taking nebulisers to stranded bronchitic pensioners and ferrying labouring women to the maternity unit in Truro. One child had already been air-born, so to speak, the presenter had joked. But the national network was hardly easy listening either. A debate discussing the concept of predestined disasters was going on and an impressive panel of academics, archbishops and authors – impressive if you didn't include the frivolous addition of a self-styled spiritualist – were making much of the simultaneity between the freak weather conditions and the approach of what they were all calling 'the Third Age'.

'Are you saying there is a link between the extraordinarily high number of accidental deaths that have occurred in the last week and the end of the millennium?' the presenter asked the spiritualist.

'I am and I do,' replied the spiritualist. 'But I would argue with the word "accidental" and use the phrase "preordained".'

'Preordained by whom?' asked an archbishop.

'By whoever or whatever you choose to recognise as your Higher Power,' said the spiritualist.

247

'Oh God in heaven,' interjected an author, trying to be funny.

Katherine wished she had the peace of mind to switch back to the less sinister list of cancelled Christmas bazaars, but then the discussion moved on to the recent rash of religious cults that claimed to be preparing for self-destruction and she couldn't help but want to listen.

'There will undoubtedly be a few mass suicides,' said an American University professor nonchalantly.

'And many more individual ones,' offered a counsellor.

'Many more than the mass ones, or many more than you would normally expect at this time of year?' asked the presenter.

'What do you think?' asked the counsellor.

'Well, precisely,' Katherine replied and, detecting a drawn-out discussion on the individual right to take one's own life coming up, she found the courage to turn the thing off. Halfway up the stairs, going up them for no particular reason other than to shout something to Patrick through the bathroom door and have the silence of the cottage broken with his reply, she looked out of the deepset window on to the garden, putting her hand on the freezing slate sill. It all seemed very still, if not ghostly out there.

'No! Damn it!' Patrick was shouting from inside.

She ran up the rest of the stairs and called through the door. 'What?'

'The bloody radio. It's fallen in the bath. I was just getting into it.'

Katherine laughed. She could hear him fishing it out and shaking it. 'Is it still working?'

'Amazingly, yes. There's a debate going on about predestination and the spiritualist is such a prick, it's worth listening to just for him.'

248

'Isn't he just? I've just turned it off, it was getting predictable.'

'Is killing yourself predictable?'

'It would be if you did it.'

'Oh, I won't then,' he said, wondering if he had passed the test. 'Listen, I'd invite you in, but . . .'

She laughed again. 'I think I'll put it on in the sitting room. The fire's going. I might enjoy it more now I know you're listening to it too,' she said.

As the words came out of her mouth, their identity changed. She had meant them to be companionable, but somewhere round about the mention of 'fire', they took on a surprise intimacy. When he didn't reply, she imagined him in there trying to work out if he had picked up the right signal – or was it the wrong one? What *did* she mean?

At Tregollan Farm, Hattie was trying to explain to Luke why she was there and not at home.

'Dad's pipes are frozen. He hasn't got any water.'

'That happened to us once when we were there too. It's a hell-hole, that place.'

'I think it's quite sweet.'

'You haven't lived there.'

'I have. Sort of.'

'Every other weekend is not living there, it's dossing there. Just like you're dossing here. You wouldn't say you lived here, would you?'

Luke Shepherd and Hattie Bates had been friends from birth, or at least their mothers had been friends from that moment anyway, and so the two children – with a couple of months to separate their birthdays – were thrown together in the way that first children are. They went to the same playgroup, the same primary school, and now, the same comprehensive. Luke was more a brother than a boyfriend and that gave her the right, or so she felt, to treat him lightly.

'Why not make me feel like we're imposing? I would.'

'You're not.' Luke was less inclined to think of her in a brotherly way. Other boys in his class had already properly kissed girls. He just pretended he had. 'I don't mean that. I just wondered why your Mum didn't just tell your Dad to come home.'

'Are you a bit thick or something?' said Hattie.

'Yeah, a bit,' Luke replied, and gave her a smile that in a few years' time she would go considerably out of her way for.

'Okay, I'll explain. Get comfy. I'll go nice and slowly for you.'

Luke lay back on his bed and put his legs across Hattie's lap.

'You'll cut off my blood supply,' she giggled. It was the first time a boy had done anything like that to her. Usually, he twisted her arm back until she submitted.

'Carry on,' he said. 'Tell me everything.'

'Okay. Mum and Dad love each other, I'm sure they do. But they're having a panic about something or other at the moment, and Dad has gone off to your hell-hole just to get his head together for a bit. That's what they told me anyway. And then Patrick turns up, which is supposed to be a complete surprise, but I'm wondering if it wasn't planned by Mum or something because he lives in America and we haven't seen him for years and it seems a bit suspicious that the moment Dad goes, he arrives, and that Mum is a lot nicer to Patrick than she is to Dad. And then Patrick starts doing things like wearing Dad's shirts and using the computer without asking, and I go into the den and he's on it, and he just turns round and says, "Oh, hi Hattie. Good day?" and goes back to it.

'Okay? So you've got the picture? Dad not at home, Patrick at home. Dad freezing in hell-hole, Patrick warm as toast with us. Anyway, one day, Mum told me Patrick would be picking me up from school because she had to do an interview, and I tried to tell her that I didn't want him to, but she wasn't listening. I don't want my friends asking me who that man picking me up from school was. What do I say? "Oh, he's the one that is living with us now that my Dad isn't." So instead of meeting him where I was supposed to, I got a lift home with Helen. When I got back, Mum shouted at me, and Patrick tried to have a go too. Then Dad tells me he is taking Mum to the Isles of Scilly for the weekend.' Hattie paused. 'Is it boring?'

Luke shook his head. 'No, go on. Is there any sex in it?'

'Be patient. But you *are* cutting off my blood supply. Your legs are really heavy.'

'Lie down with me then.'

'What if Dad sees us?'

'Well, we're not doing anything wrong, are we? We're just talking.'

'Okay.'

Hattie lay down and with their arms pinned firmly to their sides, the two of them stared at the cobalt blue and gold ceiling of Luke's incredibly cool bedroom.

'Go on,' said Luke. 'Your Dad says he's taking your Mum off for a dirty weekend.'

'I didn't say that. Anyway, so I think maybe they are going to get back together, and then I discover that Patrick is going with them and I tried to be brave enough to tell him that he should stop being a gooseberry, but he's my godfather.'

'What's that got to do with anything?'

'I'm supposed to love him.'

'No, you're not. I don't even know who my godfather is. Mum and Dad fell out with him ages ago. Trevor someone. Who cares?'

'But actually, I did used to love Patrick. Not now though. He's a pain. Anyway, I told Mum when we were at Granny's that I didn't want him in the house any more.'

'What did your Mum say? It's not up to you?'

'No, I thought that was what she was going to say, but she went all soft and said she was pleased to think I was able to express my feelings and of course Patrick could go and stay with Dad.'

'What, so you've got Patrick running between the two houses just to avoid you?'

'Yes,' she smiled proudly. 'And then I asked Mum something really risky.'

'What?'

'I asked her if she was sleeping with Patrick.'

'You didn't!'

'I did.'

'Is she?'

'No, definitely not. She said she didn't want anything like that from anyone other than Dad.'

Luke was laughing. 'I'm going to ask my Mum who she's sleeping with!' he shouted. 'It's a classic, Hattie.'

'Luke,' she said, turning her face to his. 'You really are a bit thick, aren't you?'

And with that, he grabbed her arm and began twisting it behind her, calling for submission.

If anyone should have felt an icy remoteness, it ought to have been the Shepherds. Their farmhouse was down a long pot-holed lane at least a mile away from any other dwelling, but thanks to their unexpected visitors, the walls were vibrating to the noise of snow-induced excitement.

Katherine, whose cottage was not only joined to another, but on the main road of a large village, felt much more cut off. People were crunching past the front door on their way to the shop for emergency provisions but Katherine had no urge to go out and join them in their animated chatter. Loveday was predictably busy running hot meals up and down the street for anyone she could think of, and Beth was at school helping to lag the pipes. She had trudged round earlier, her small face framed by a fluffy sheepskin halo and her eyes sparkling with the cold and Seth had told her she looked like an angel. 'I'd much rather be a little devil!' she'd laughed, winking. Once Seth had left the room, she'd gone on to elaborate, but Katherine hadn't been in the mood to talk about such things, and Beth had given up, going outside to play with the children instead.

The garden was now annihilated by snow fights and the thought cheered Katherine as she looked out into the dark. Thank goodness they'd been at home on a day like this, running in and out, warming their soaking woollen gloves on the Aga and drinking hot chocolate, not off with Johnny as they were now, leaving her to rattle again.

Life's stage had shrunk to just one room. The fire was throwing out an extraordinary heat, it was pitch black out there despite the white, and the curtains were drawn. There was no need even to go as far as the kitchen because she had carried through enough bread, cheese and wine to see them to midnight if needs be. Patrick was reading, and Katherine was trying to. She knew if she switched the television on, she would see evidence of a global emergency and she decided she would rather not.

She studied the side of his face and tried to imagine what it would be like to spend the very last few moments with him. He wouldn't be enough, of course, she would be screaming for her children. If she *did* turn the television on, and heard, along with the rest of the universe, that it was all about to end, and that everyone had half an hour to brace themselves, she would just have to get to the farm, somehow. She didn't have the car. Maybe Johnny would drive down here, and they could all be together. But that wouldn't work, not with Patrick and Hattie. No, Patrick would have to try and get a line out to New Jersey and spend it on the phone to Dido, and leave them to it in the sitting room. Everyone would die together, wouldn't they? There wouldn't be a child left, waiting, would there?

Patrick looked up to see her staring into the fire. His voice broke the air.

'What are you thinking about?'

'Uh? Oh, nothing, being stupid,' she said through an embarrassed laugh. She couldn't tell him – he'd think she'd gone mad. She tried to think of something inconsequential to say but the way he was considering her was not inconsequential at all.

'You look really lovely.'

'You're joking! I look like a dog.'

'You should stop doing that you know. You never used to.'

'What?'

'Put yourself down.'

She held his gaze. And now where do we go? I suppose we just hold the look longer until we find an answer. He got slowly up and came to crouch in front of her, his hands on her knees. They both knew what was coming next.

'Can I kiss you?' he asked after a moment.

She nodded, which seemed a barely adequate response,

but it would have to do. He put his hands either side of her face and looked into her eyes. She knew what kind of kiss she wanted, but she wasn't at all sure what kind of kiss it *would* be. Please not a sympathetic one. His lips were on hers, his fingers on her neck, and then a split-second thrill shot through her as he pulled his mouth a centimetre away and brought it back again a little harder. That was when she made the kiss what she wanted it to be, bringing her own hands up to grip the top of his arms and then to join each other at the nape of his neck, heady with the forgotten sensation of wanting, needing, to be laid.

They pulled away, gave each other a smile, and kissed again. Patrick was more hesitant but as he felt an urgent little grip of her teeth on his bottom lip and the tip of her tongue run around his, a confidence came to him, one that he had not had for a long time, and one that he had been too scared to hope for.

'Kate,' he murmured into her hair, pulling her gently off the sofa so that she too was kneeling. 'Kate, Kate, Kate.'

He seemed lost in the moment, and hungry as she was, she had to make a conscious effort to get to that same place too. All the physical signs were there – she wanted him to find her breasts, and she could feel a distant pulse just where it mattered – but she was also aware of other things, that they were in the sitting room, that he wasn't Johnny, that she had told Hattie no way, that she wanted very much to make love, but that she knew that was *all* she wanted. Patrick though was truly lost.

He forced himself to be immersed in the lust, clinging to the memory of their beginnings and anticipating the sight of her, the feel of her again. He'd never forgotten the way she moved, the way her hips would rise and her buttocks tighten, how she could slide from underneath to on top with an agility he'd experienced nowhere else. And if he could keep hold of that, and get to the undressed moment, and the ones after that, he'd be there.

Not the sitting room but not my bedroom either, Katherine wavered, wishing she could do it without thinking. Now is my chance, if I must be doing this deliberating, to back out. But my body is too far gone, even if my mind is not. How damaging is this? Is it going to change things for ever? Not between him and me, because all that has gone before, but my marriage? Do I want infidelity in it, even if it is already a broken mess?

He found her breasts and her nipples hardened under his tongue, her back began to arch and she stopped thinking. The sitting room could have been any room.

'We ought to use something,' he murmured.

She had been out of the casual game for so long that she didn't stop to catch his meaning.

'Katherine, I don't have any . . .' he said through kisses '. . . any . . .'

'No, nor do I.' She followed him to the den where the sofa bed was out and his clothes were heaped on the floor. Her sweater was off, her linen shirt unbuttoned and her bra undone.

'Do we need to?' she asked, 'There's no risk is there?'

'No risk, I'm clean,' he said, quietly enough for it still to be somehow seductive.

'And I'm okay,' she replied as she had so many times before with Johnny when he'd look at her just before things got out of control, as if to say, should I, is it a safe time?

'You're more than okay,' he said, turning to her and taking her down to the mattress. 'Are you sure?'

'Yes,' she whispered, and turned her face away from a bead necklace that hung on a leather thong from the wall light. H-A-T-T-I-E spelt the beads, swinging to the movement of the air.

CHAPTER 9

Chapter 13

TWO AND A HALF WEEKS TO GO

The Times, 15 December, 1999: The global cost of the so-called 'millennium bug' – the time bomb ticking away inside some of the world's computers – has been put at $600 billion dollars according to new research. Although most systems are now 'millennium compliant' and designed to cope with the date switch from '99 to '00, some will still fail to recognise the double zero and shut down. Media hype over the problem ranges from claims that aircraft will fall from the skies and missiles will self-launch to the rather less dramatic worry that your gas bill may appear to arrive 99 years too late.

In New Jersey, Joe Polledri's children built a snowman so big it got in the paper – a front page picture of the three of them staring up at their unfeasibly tall creation. It had been a perfect exercise to test the old adage of necessity being the mother of invention. Once the pile of snow had reached a certain height, they had started taking buckets up the stairs to jettison through a second-floor window, and by the time they were using a third-floor window with spades attached to broom handles, quite a crowd had gathered, including the *Tribune* photographer. They'd been so proud of it, they'd telephoned Joe at his surgery a few blocks away and begged him to come and see it before it melted. It had made him laugh to think that the reception he'd got from his ex-wife, who hadn't been expecting him, had been far frostier than anything his children had built.

Laughing came easily to Joe. Dido liked the way he managed to keep happy without resorting to relentless jokes, and the fact that what he found funny never survived a second telling to someone after the event. You had to *be* there to get it. He was an awesome observer of people, and yet he never fell into the trap of derision.

For everyone else, 'Mr Cool' – as the snowman was coined by the paper – became the only frivolous topic of conversation to be had, because as Joe and Dido had both noted, the rest of the world around them seemed to be both closing in and closing down at the same time, like there was going to be no third millennium after all. Not that either of them were taking any notice of the current trend among ordinary people to subscribe to the view that the end of the world was in sight – or at least that is what they kept telling each other.

Twelve inches of snow were enough to bring New York City to a halt. The mayor declared the centre an emergency area and all vehicles were stopped from going in. A few show-offs were skiing to work but most of the city's population was at a loss.

Dido trudged along the sidewalk in the chunky walking boots she'd bought specifically for the purpose of winter survival, a whole head in height above Joe as he offered his insight into the psyche of a snowbound workaholic.

'I've had people in a queuing system on the phone, calling me on their mobiles because the main lines are all down, and they're literally demanding to see me,' he said in his fast New York accent. 'One guy even called me from his bathroom and said he wasn't coming out until I told him how to get through another day at home with his wife and kids.'

'You're joking!'

'No, this is for real, but you know, his life is normally cushioned with structure – out of the house by eight, meeting at ten, business lunch at one – even his weekends are organised along the lines of jogging in the park at nine, taking the kids to the movies at two, drinks party at seven. Then suddenly, it's the middle of the week and his secretary isn't available to tell him what to do.'

'You've got a theory for everything!' she laughed.

'Not everything,' he said, giving her a sideways look and a quick smile.

'Oh, you'll never find one for that. You'd be better off concentrating on your "big freeze phobia". Maybe you could write a book.'

'Maybe I will,' he carried on, taking her teasing lightly. 'There's plenty of material. Career nuts all presented with an unexpected chance of spending time at home without intrusion and they are stir-crazy. Their domestic phone lines are down, the car is stuck in the garage, and everywhere is closed. Fantastic, I say. Make the most of it. But of course, they don't know how to. The human race has lost its instinct for lazing around.'

'Sometimes Joe, you come out with a real gem. Most of what you say is bollocks, of course, but sometimes . . .'

'You're too kind, Miss Seal.'

'It's nothing. I wonder how Patrick is coping? He used to be so good at doing nothing. I heard a weather report for the UK and it's as bad there as it is here.'

'It's bad everywhere. The whole world is up for it. We're not going out with a bang exactly, more like a great silent whoosh, an avalanche of mud and snow and water that will bury us all.' Joe's voice got louder and his arms began to fling wildly around as he warmed to the role of psychic fruitcake.

'Apart from China, and India, and all the Jewish communities, of course,' Dido butted in, ducking to avoid a flailing hand. 'You know, the guys who don't live by the Gregorian calendar and for whom next year is just another twelve months. They'll all survive the mud slides, will they? Because to them, this religious milestone means nothing.'

'Ah, that depends on how sincerely they believe they will.'

'Are you *sure* you're in the right job? Wouldn't Prophesy be more your thing? You could make a fortune just now. Look, we could set you up right here, on this corner, in a little wooden booth, with a big sign saying *The Future Is Nigh*.'

'Get on to my secretary and have her arrange it,' he laughed, steering her into a subway station. The Path Train – the underground line that runs from Hoboken to New York City – was operating against all the odds. Dido expected it to be quiet, or at least to have an air of Sunday about it, but the first thing she saw was a snaking queue of ticket buyers.

'Is the city open again?' she asked someone in front of her.

'Who cares?' said the woman. 'I just want to go someplace.'

Dido made a face at Joe who did one back before kissing her on the cheek and saying goodbye.

'Aren't you coming?' she said, suddenly alarmed.

'Dido, I'm a psychotherapist. Psychotherapists don't go and see other psychotherapists – at least not when it is snowing they don't.'

'But you've come this far.'

'Out of chivalry. I couldn't let you walk all two streets from the bar to the station alone in broad daylight. What kind of man do you think I am?'

'Thanks for brunch,' she smiled. 'It was a good idea.'

'I've got the children tonight. We're cooking something out of the *Roald Dahl Revolting Recipe* book you gave Lara for her birthday, so I think it's only fair you should come and share the result.'

'Okay, but come with me now, I need you to hold my hand.'

'No, you don't. You've got gloves on. Besides, I have an appointment in twenty minutes. Mrs Riccardi. Thinks she's being pursued by the Children of Enlightenment.'

'Oh, go on,' Dido persisted, really wanting him with her. 'It'll be fun. The city will look really weird.'

'Send me a postcard. See you later.'

Dido watched him thrust his hands into the pockets of his bright yellow jacket and set off home. As he got further and further away from her, the impression that she knew him, properly, intimately, got closer and closer. She cringed momentarily when she remembered how she had invited him into her bed a week or so ago and he had declined on the grounds of her ambivalence. It had been a straightforward offer, unlike the tentative hints she'd made once or twice previously.

'I only like sleeping with women who are one hundred per cent behind the idea,' he'd told her, which was amazingly perceptive of him, since she was still only maybe seventy-five per cent there. Or possibly eighty now, she decided, her eyes still on the disappearing yellow jacket.

He was a tiny speck but she could still see his face in her head, the movement of his lips when he talked, the slightly greying curly hair around his temple, and his voice which could jump from sad to happy, contemplative to flippant all in the same sentence. She'd decided a while ago that his awareness and his sensitivity more than made up for the fact that he was short, but it was only this morning that she'd realised she had probably never put on an act for him, and that in his company, her famous guard was well and truly dropped.

Her mind flipped back to Patrick. I wonder if I repulsed him with that doorstep kiss, that indecision between full-blown snog and platonic peck, I wonder why he didn't tell me the truth, I wonder if he ever will, she thought.

'World Trade Centre please,' she said, sounding suddenly very British.

'It's closed.'

'What, the station?'

'No, the Centre. No trading today. Sorry.'

'I'm going to Chinatown. Mott Street.'

'Then you'll need to walk from the station. No cabs running, lady.'

'Thank you.'

She was herded on to the train, thinking this final trip – the fifth of five – to Dr Michael Lemmerman of Mott Street, Chinatown, should just about do it. Getting counselling was a sensible thing to do, she knew that, and she was grateful to Joe for nudging her into it. Nudging her into it was perhaps too kind a choice of words, and elbowing might do better, she conceded, remembering the impressive way Joe had taken her in hand when she'd returned from England in October, in possession of the truth at last.

She hadn't thought she'd been especially traumatised by it, and was almost conceited about the way she was handling it, until Joe said the reason she was sleeping badly was because she was in shock. And anyway, he told her, whilst he was waiting for Dr Lemmerman to come to the phone five weeks ago, it's much easier to unravel a few knots now than to wait until it gets so tangled you can't even find the ends. That way, you lose the thread completely.

Michael Lemmerman was a friend of Joe's, he was experienced, and he wasn't charging his full rate, which was all excellent. But Dido also knew she really *had* come to terms with it, under her own steam, a while ago. She knew now that her wish for a sexual liaison with Patrick was down to insecurity and not desire, that the muddied confusion of their recent history could be easily explained by the ambiguity of their relationship, and that they had lost nothing terribly serious in the process. All this had been prompted by plenty of talking to Joe and Dr Lemmerman, but the conclusions had been drawn by herself, alone in Patrick's flat, usually at night. The love she felt for him now was reminiscent of the love she'd had for him as a child, one that allowed her to feel cross with him, or even despise him for a while, and one that had no end.

What she possibly *did* need help with was a growing feeling of guilt for not suffering more. The truth should have thrown her into complete turmoil, so why hadn't it? Were a few sleepless nights and a disturbed dream or two enough? Maybe she would mention that to Michael Lemmerman today, come clean about her real state of mind, tell him she was worried about not being worried.

She looked around her at the faces sharing her train. They all looked eaten up by some anxiety or another. America – who'd have it?

The temperature outside was sub-zero. Fellow passengers were wrapped in layers of thermal fleece and fake fur, and their warm breath mingled together in the cramped compartment, making condensation form on the grimy windows. A few people were talking in subdued secret voices, and Dido started to want the journey to end, wondering how long it would take if she tried to walk. Two hours of slow plod through the snow would be better than ten minutes on this. She had hated the London tube too, but somehow, this was worse. Maybe it was the people. They all seemed so het up.

The train stopped with a jolt and Dido looked to see where they were, but they weren't anywhere. All she could see through the dribbles of watery breath on the glass was the vague outline of brickwork and wires. They were still in the tunnel. These things happened. All you had to do was sit and wait, and the train would start up again. The main thing was not to panic, to avoid other people's faces so as not to catch their concern as well. It had been one hell of a jolt though, obviously an unscheduled stop. Perhaps it was caused by the weather. Maybe the stop and go lights took longer to change because of the cold. She took a deep breath and held it before exhaling slowly, remembering the advice given her when she was in her twenties and suffering the classic 1980s syndrome of panic attacks, brought on by the stress of a new job on one of Britain's leading glossy magazines. Her doctor had taught her how to breathe through them, telling her they were brought on by a lack of oxygen, a hypertension which prevented you taking as big a breath as you would normally do.

The train was very still. Ten minutes or so passed and then the vibration of the engine stopped and the train was even stiller. They were obviously not going to be moving again for a while. If I wanted to get out, could I? she wondered, deciding she had better not ask herself that one. Anyway, there wouldn't be enough room between the train and the wall of the tunnel for me to . . . she took another deep breath, then another, and fumbled in her bag for a mint. All she could find was an indigestion tablet, so she ate one of those, for something to do, to experience another sensation, concentrate on the taste of something other than fear.

The crackle of the internal radio filled the train, then a dismembered male voice spoke through it. 'Apologies for the delay. There has been an accident on the line.' He sounded as if he was going to go on, but then he breathed in sharply and cut himself off.

Dido swallowed her tablet. What kind of accident? Is there a fire going on up there, heading our way? How many people are lying dead? Exactly how long are we going to be in this thing? She could see the think bubbles fusing in the air with all the hot uneasy breath.

The next inhalation she took didn't seem so deep, so she tried another, and that fell short too. Is there enough air in here to go round? She looked up and straight into the face of a woman her age sitting opposite whose foundation was shining eerily. A young man was pressing the door button.

'How long are we going to be in here?' the woman with the make-up asked the general crowd.

'Not long,' someone replied reassuringly.

Another ten minutes passed and the lights flickered. Dido unzipped her padded silver jacket and then zipped it up again. She was too hot and too cold at the same time.

'Can I get out?' a different woman asked a different stranger.

'Not just now.'

Dido could hear her heart pounding and she began to feel dizzy. Her vision was becoming less stable and she made mental arrangements for passing out as she tried to re-focus her eyes. Would anyone noticed if I fainted in the seat or should I stand? Should I talk to anyone? I really need to get out.

She wasn't the only one. One young man had a snow

shovel and, backed up by an unlikely-looking vandal in a city suit, he rammed it between the automatic doors and tried to force them open.

The crackle came again, and then the voice, a different one than before, more authoritative this time.

'We apologise for the delay. Please stay calm. The journey will resume as soon as possible.'

Dido stared through the window at the wires and the bricks. We can't be far from the next stop, she told herself. If those two men manage to open that door, I'm going with them. And if I ever get out of here, I'm going straight home. Home home, not Hoboken home. I'm going back to Mum, and I'll find Patrick and I'll tell him I know, and that'll be fine. What's the big problem? It's nothing really, just a complicated weave in the fabric of family life. It doesn't need to be unravelled and rewoven, not at all. Let's just have a look at it, talk about how weird it is, and move on to the next knot.

The train crunched forward, and then jolted to a stop again. At last, someone screamed. It must have been half an hour since they'd stopped. Dido checked her watch. Actually not even twenty minutes. Hardly an emergency.

Suddenly, the doors opened with a release of pressure and the men with the shovel looked heroic and embarrassed. A surge of people moved towards the gap and then stopped. Outside was unexplored territory, a dark tunnel leading where? And how far? These people really have been programmed, Dido thought suddenly. Why don't they just jump out and run for it? It's because they don't know what they'll find. Whilst they're in this hot, cramped, familiar environment, they are still in control, but once they cross the threshold, and step out into that unknown darkness, they will have to give themselves over. Me, I'm all for giving myself over, if it means I'll see daylight again soon.

'We have an unscheduled delay causing demobilisation,' said the intercom again. 'The doors have been opened for your comfort and the lights in the tunnel will illuminate shortly. Please stay in your seats or where you are standing, and we ask you again to stay calm. There is no need for alarm.'

The men with the spade hopped down, and grabbing her black leather rucksack, Dido took three large steps and joined them.

'Hi, I'm coming too,' she panted, trying to hide her fear.

The one in the pin stripe replied incoherently and the other said quite indifferently, 'Follow the line of the train.'

The three of them picked their way down the line with only the cold metal of the train's sleeve to guide them and the sense of a thick filthy oil underfoot. Faces stared out at them from inside the lit train, and yet not one of them jumped out too, despite the gaping hole of the doors inviting them to take their chance.

It was no more than two minutes before a more relaxed air floated around her, in her face and up her nostrils – the smell of normal human activity again. Seconds after that and she was out of Hades and back in the real world.

'Thank you,' she muttered to a man on the platform helping her up. 'Thank you.' There was no fire, no dead bodies, not even any official commotion. The tunnel was still in darkness and she looked back, thinking how she could still be inside, staring at the face of the woman with the shiny foundation.

'Well, that's me sorted,' she smiled to her younger companion on the journey from hell before walking briskly up and out of the city's bowels.

*   *   *

'I'm sorted,' she repeated to Dr Michael Lemmerman with a boldness. 'I was worrying on the way here that I wasn't worrying enough, but then the Path Train stopped in the tunnel and then I really *was* worrying, but I jumped out when the doors opened and walked along the line in the pitch black with two strange men, and now I'm not worried about not worrying at all. Nothing has to be a crisis, does it? There's always a way out, I know that now.'

'You were worrying about not worrying?' said Dr Lemmerman.

'Yes.'

'I think it's time you got back to England.'

Katherine felt as if she was in a dark tunnel that day too, with the lights flickering on and off, offering her glimpses of discernment followed by longer periods of confusion. Life had been a bit like that anyway lately, particularly since she and Patrick had added one more dollop of disorder to the already befuddling mess around them by sleeping together. That decision had certainly given momentum to the build-up of havoc and she wished now she hadn't done it but even so, it wasn't top of the list when it came to thinking time. Surprisingly, her reaction to Evan's disgusting deception was.

Her anger had almost been more ferocious than Beth's, and it was still there, burning inside her. She kept remembering all the times she had tried to like him, how she had gone out of her way to make him feel a part of things, laughing out of politeness at his crass jokes. And all the time, he had been poor Beth's puppeteer. Inevitably of course, every time she thought about his evil control and his repulsive perverted abhorrent little secret, her own marriage seemed near-perfect in comparison, which only put even more pace into the escalating chaos. Now though, she was thinking about her mother, prompted by a surprising conversation she'd had that afternoon with Loveday.

Loveday had always seemed – still did seem really, despite what she had just revealed – entirely comfortable with the cards life had dealt her. She'd made the best hand she could without complaint. She'd sailed through single motherhood proclaiming it to be a privilege; she'd used the knowledge gained during the one year of her aborted art degree to give her and Beth an income by painting murals on people's interior walls in the sixties, painting over those same walls with magnolia in the seventies, duck egg blue in the eighties and colourwash in the nineties; when her business had been on the brink of collapse during the recession ten years ago, she'd put it back on a solid footing by selling half her cottage to Katherine and Johnny; and when her role as a mother had finally diminished with Beth's marriage, she'd re-invented herself as a tireless political campaigner for Cornwall and agony aunt for most of its residents. It was hardly surprising people put her on something of a pedestal. Every time Katherine had whinged since Johnny had left, she'd thought of Loveday and been instantly chastened. It was just a question of being strong and true, she had told herself, like Loveday, a woman who dispelled the myth of the menopausal female and her empty life if ever there was one. So to hear her acknowledge an insecurity just made Katherine fonder of her than ever.

Beth had been living next door with her mother for five weeks now, during which time Katherine had noticed Loveday's permanently make-up free face looking younger and younger. The busy expression in her Celtic green eyes had been replaced by a softer lazier one, reminiscent of the days fifteen years ago when she would put them all up on one of their student weekend breaks.

'Have you had your hair cut?' Katherine had asked when Loveday bustled in one day with a huge bunch of holly from the woods.

'No. I do it myself anyway, you know that.'

'There's something about you. You look all . . . glowing. How do you manage that then, in the middle of a crisis? I wish I knew.'

'We are now post-crisis, thank God,' Loveday had replied, finding some newspaper to lay on the table before she put the holly down, not that she was ever as fastidious in her own home.

'I wish *I* was,' said Katherine, 'although I wouldn't suggest to Beth you think she's post-crisis if I were you. It sounds a bit like the "pull yourself together" sort of advice my mother would give, and in fact, *did* give when she first learned about *my* broken marriage.'

'Your marriage isn't broken, it's cracked. Beth's is already dust. Actually, the crisis ended when she walked out of that door last month. We all know she's spent the last I don't know how many years like an original painting hanging in a mass-produced frame, hiding her loveliness, and at last, she saw it for herself and left. Crisis, post . . . see?'

'She only saw it once Evan decided to shove it up her nose. She didn't choose this, did she? She *had* no choice.'

'Well, she could have stayed. Some women would have.'

'True. But Beth's her mother's daughter.'

'And hooray for that!' beamed Loveday.

'Try not to sound so excited. Just because you think it's a good thing she's left him, Beth might not.' Conversations with Loveday always went like this – straight in, no pussy-footing around.

'And has she given you any cause to believe that?' asked Loveday, not in the slightest bit ruffled.

'No.'

'But you've talked to her about it, more than once?'

'Loveday! We've been living next door to each other for five weeks. What do you think we've been talking about? The weather?'

'Well then. I rest my case.' Loveday was pulling the holly apart, trying to share the berries equally. 'I got this from the woods. Jack Rowe told me to take as much as I liked. Have you bought a tree yet, because if you haven't, Jack says we can uproot a holly bush or two. I think they look much better, and the children are old enough not to touch.'

'Listen to you! Your daughter is coming to terms with a seven-year betrayal and you are talking about my Christmas tree! It's like all the newsrooms I've ever worked in – a major air crash becomes an adrenalin hit, an evil husband becomes an idle topic of conversation.'

Johnny had the children again – he had picked them up from school and taken them to the cinema – and she had been on her own all day. Perhaps that was why she was on the attack. Loveday stopped playing with the holly and looked at Katherine with a very straight face.

'Life goes on you know.'

'I know, but—'

'Shall I tell you something? Not for Beth's ears?'

'What?'

'I *am* excited at the prospect of her leaving Evan. I'm not proud of myself for feeling this way, but her heart and soul seemed so far away with him that I often thought I'd lost her. I just somehow feel safer with her at home, more complete.'

273

'Do you mean you didn't feel safe before?'

'No, no, I've always made sure my life was anchored, so I couldn't just drift away, and the world I inhabit feels entirely safe. I'm surrounded by years of friendship, and the landscape I can paint with my eyes shut, my parents are buried in the churchyard and my initials are, I'm ashamed to say, carved on a church pew. I love my life. It is all I want. But you know, living and working alone, you tend to tie yourself down with obligations and deadlines and projects. I make myself a little bit indispensable, so I have a purpose. Of course I do, what else is there? I made myself feel safe, but I feel safer now.'

'I thought the reason you threw yourself into the things you do was because you had a genuine belief in them.'

'I do, of course I do, but they serve another minor purpose too, don't they? What else would you expect me to do?'

'And now Beth's back you're fulfilled?'

'No, Katherine, stop simplifying things!' Loveday laughed in mild frustration. 'I'm just trying to explain what it feels like to have your child back with you again, needing you. It feels great, for the moment. However passionately I feel about getting a computer room for the village, it doesn't beat taking a cup of tea to your daughter in the morning. You've got to have a bottom line, haven't you?'

'What are you going to do when she goes again? She won't be with you for ever.'

'I know that. It's not her physical presence I'm talking about, it's the return of her *spirit*. It was heartbreaking, watching her decline. Think what he took from her. Think of the girl she was when you first met her, and then remember her as she was, say, in the summer. Not the same girl, was she? But you must have seen the change in her already. She's getting her strength back. She's my Beth again.'

'Oh Loveday, I feel awful. I wish you could have talked about it.'

'Hey, come on! I don't need *that*! I'm just saying it is a good time rather than a bad time for me at the moment.' Loveday glanced at Katherine to see if she understood and realised how pale she looked. 'Are you all right? You don't seem your usual healthy self.'

'I'm just incredibly tired, that's all. It's probably accumulative. You know. Being on my own, juggling the Hattie Patrick thing, Christmas . . .'

'The party,' added Loveday.

'That is the last thing on my mind. Absolutely the last.'

When Loveday left, Katherine picked up the phone and called her mother, a straightforward need to hear her voice. Loveday had spoken about Beth so intensely and the link between mother and daughter had seemed so vital that Katherine suddenly wanted a part of it for herself, to see if there was any of it present between her and Margaret, and then to go on and dream about her future with Hattie.

The last time she and her mother had been together two months ago, after Katherine had abandoned the appalling weekend on St Mary's and run home to her children, something happened between the two of them that showed a glimmer of hope.

They had gone shopping together without the children, and on the way home in Margaret's economical little Japanese run-around car, Katherine had, for some reason, asked her mother if she was happy. Instead of replying, Margaret had gripped the washable cover of the steering wheel a little tighter and pursed her lips, and when Katherine reached out and touched her mother's shoulder, Margaret had let out an uncharacteristic little giggle which lacked the necessary control to stop it ending in a choke. She had pulled the car over on the hard shoulder of a dual carriageway and started to cry, the quiet howl that came from somewhere deep inside her reminding Katherine of the noise women make in labour, or at least the noise she had made when she was having Seth, a primitive release of effort and agony. Although Margaret's was barely audible, it had every bit as much strength to it and the two women, identical in profile if not in personality, had sat there, staring out at the passing traffic in silence. Eventually, Katherine had asked, 'Why are you unhappy?' and Margaret wanted to reply, 'Because *you* are,' but all she'd come out with was, 'It's the menopause,' which they both knew was long gone.

Still, it had been a start, and Katherine hoped to build on it now as she dialled the number.

'Hello, Mum. It's me.'

'Katherine? Is there anything wrong?'

'No, why should there be?'

'I just wondered why you were phoning.'

'Do I need a reason?'

'Of course not, but this is the most expensive time of the day. How are the children?'

'Fine. How are you?'

'Fine.'

It was not a successful call and it certainly did nothing to make Katherine believe she and her mother had reached any kind of turning point. Maybe sometimes, having a child makes no difference to a woman's fulfilment whatsoever. When Johnny arrived back with the children shortly afterwards, she hugged them both too hard.

'Are you okay?' Johnny asked.

'I wish people would stop asking me that.'

'You look tired, that's all.'

'Oh, really? Well, maybe I am. It's possible I suppose, looking after two children, trying to organise Christmas, keep up with my freelance work . . .'

'See you, kids!' Johnny called towards the den, not wanting an argument.

'Oh, I'm sorry,' Katherine said, flinging a tea towel on the table. 'I shouldn't go on like that, it's not like it's even that hard. I've had a strange day, and the end of term always drives me mad, you know that.'

'Well, let me help then. I keep offering, but you keep turning me down.'

'You can't, you're at work. It's all the ferrying around that gets to me.'

'I can be a few minutes late or leave early every now and again.'

'Okay, well, I'll shout.'

Johnny made to go, and then he turned and said, 'So why have you had a strange day then?'

'Just some of the conversations I've had.'

'Like?'

'Tell me, do you think Hattie and I will be more like Loveday and Beth or more like me and Mum when she grows up?'

Johnny gave her such an affectionate look it almost made her go weak at the knees. 'You'll be like you and Hattie, which is all anyone could ever ask.'

'Aaah!' she said gratefully. 'You say all the right things.'

'Sometimes,' smiled Johnny. 'See you.'

'Yes, see you,' she replied, suddenly feeling as if she were on a boat with the deck rocking beneath her. He noticed her hold the side of the kitchen table.

'Are you sure you're okay?'

And she just nodded, knowing that speaking would only make things worse.

Chapter 14

TWO WEEKS TO GO

The Times, 18 December, 1999: Britain's oldest woman, Mrs Josephine Peters, who will celebrate her 110th birthday on 1 January, 2000, looks set to enter the new millennium a rich lady. Five years ago, she bet an entire pools win of £10,000 on her surviving until the year 2000. Speaking from her nursing-home bed yesterday, she told journalists, 'I hope my bookmakers have got the money to pay for it. If I don't die in the next ten days, and I'm not planning to, then they owe me half a million pounds.' When asked how she might spend her winnings, she said 'My grand-daughter needs a hip replacement.'

Katherine didn't know how she'd got there, but she was in a kind of heaven. Gossamer clouds wafted past her as she drifted through a blueness where sparkling cobwebs hung from nothing and feathers floated around her; she was soaring up and out of a radiance and into peaceful flickering shafts of sunlight then above the diaphanous blue, where she began to fly fast and free into brilliance before swooping down . . . and down . . . to the ground.

The light changed from azure to powder, from powder to primrose and from primrose to leaf, and she landed in a woodland, sifting the soft lush petals through her fingers. The bark of the trees was knobbly and intriguing, the curve of their trunks led her round corners, into an open copse where the same blissful sunlight lit up the blossom falling around her and blew it gently towards a stream where the water gurgled and rushed. She became immersed in it, under its surface, floating first then sinking but happy, letting the riverbed take her along, washing her, long fingers of green weed brushing past her and then the sensation of the water draining away, leaving her in a peaceful empty space.

As the colours faded around her and she felt a compelling urgency to hang on to them, she wondered if this was what death was like. Before she had a chance to take one last wonderful look around her, the darkness came like a battery torch on the blink. Everything was silent and black. Then the words GAME OVER flashed before her, and a computerised voice told her to remove her headset and gloves.

Penny was already out, saying, 'Hell's bells,' and blinking her eyes. 'That was incredible,' Katherine heard as she emerged from virtual space.

'Wasn't it? Talk about put on, plug in, and forget about the real world.'

'I feel as if I've been on some kind of trip. They could market that as a drug to distract people from the conditions of their own lives.'

'I think that's what they're doing, isn't it?'

The children were taking their headsets off now too, talking in an excited rush to each other as if they had travelled the universe and been away for lifetimes.

'There was this really weird little troll who kept leading me into caves.'

'Did you get the space monster? The explosion?'

'The galactic battle, did you get the galactic battle? I got away!'

'Where have *they* been?' Katherine asked, looking at Penny. 'I got clouds and flowers . . .'

'Me too – well, a meadow, and a sort of heaven.'

'Life is what you make it, I suppose.'

'Or do you think they saw us from the control room and decided to give us the old persons' tour?'

The Virtual Space Exhibition was in Truro's old ten-pin bowling hall, not that you would recognise it as such. A huge screen across one wall, showing a video of what looked like a 3D subterranean earth, with roots and rocks, tunnels, worms, and hundreds of tiny glittering green globules of light, greeted you as you came in; on the facing wall, you were offered another world, underwater, full of tangled weeds, bubbles, and more rocks. What had struck Katherine most of all had been the quiet. Row upon row of silent twitching bodies all experiencing their own private interaction.

The chairs, in lines like a spacious cinema, were black. The headsets, sitting on purpose-built tables next to the chairs, were black and silver, so were the matching gloves. The assistants who positioned you and plugged you in, were dressed in black. The posters for the exhibition plastered all around Cornwall were black. Peculiar, when the computer-generated environment within your own head turned out to be so colourful.

'I feel like I'm in some sort of torture chamber,' she'd whispered, just before catching sight of Seth who was already fitted up and about to be switched on. She'd had a sudden crisis of confidence that she had given him permission to go somewhere dangerous on his own and she'd grabbed the male assistant by his forearm and said, 'There's nothing really unpleasant in these virtual worlds, is there? Only my children aren't used to being on their own.'

The assistant, a youth with an American accent, laughed. 'That's parenting for you! No, every habitat has a "U" certificate – they can choose where they go and get out of it at any time. You might like to go for a calming habitat. You'll feel like you've had a massage once you come outside,' and that was it, the last thing she heard before she entered virtual space, all of it actually only half an hour ago but it felt like a fortnight.

'I'm not sure it sounds all that healthy,' Johnny said when they got back to the Shepherds' farmhouse. 'An attempt to replace real nature with an artificial one? If it was that good, you could be in danger of wanting to stay in virtual space for ever.'

'Well, I can see the appeal,' replied Katherine, smiling.

'Hell!' laughed Johnny. 'Am I that bad?'

'Not really,'she said in a voice only he could hear, and then, louder, 'Must go. Beth's nipping round for a gossip and I've got a fish pie to cook.'

Tregollan – the Shepherds' lovely old farmhouse – had become something of a second home to the Bates refugees, but whilst the children accepted the hospitality unconditionally, Johnny intermittently offered to pay extra rent on the cottage or to help on the farm.

'If we can't invite you to supper without you asking for the bill, what kind of friends are we?' Penny insisted when he suggested for the third time that weekend that he should write a cheque.

'No, but this is the fourth overnight stay we've had in a fortnight. I don't want to impose, that's all.'

'Look, you forget, we lived in that horrid little cottage for a while too, and it nearly drove us mad. It's a pleasure to have you here.'

'Thanks. You're a star.'

'The one thing that bothers me is that I would hate Katherine to think we are taking sides.'

'It's not like that,' Johnny said quickly. 'We don't have sides.'

'Of course you don't,' Penny replied, 'but I know how divorce affects people. She might come to think of us as more your friends than hers, which would be awful. She was surprised to find you here when we got back this afternoon, I could see it in her face.'

'I don't think she goes out of her way to avoid me. And divorce is too strong a word for our situation anyway.'

'Is it? I'm glad to hear it. It's just I've seen it happen to other friends and—'

'Sure. I know what you're saying. Well, I could clear off and you could ask her over.'

'What about tonight, and you stay? Or is that pushing the point?'

'Push away,' said Johnny. 'Give her a ring. She looked incredibly tired, didn't you think? Patrick is hard work as a house-guest. He's okay with me, but when he's with her, I get the impression he wears her out with his introspection.'

'How's all that to-ing and fro-ing going? Is Hattie happier now?'

'Yes, but I'm not sure Patrick is. Whatever he wants is always at the other house. He's also had to buy a computer for my place just so he can carry on working.'

'I'm surprised he didn't just go back to the States for a bit. It would have been cheaper than a new computer, surely?'

'No, he's anti-States at the moment. I can't get the whole truth out of him, but it's definitely tied up with his step-father's death, that and the fact that his step-sister Dido turned up and moved in, which drove him round the bend apparently. I've tried to get him to open up, but you know what men are like at talking.'

'Dad?' shouted Seth, skidding across the slate floor of the kitchen in his socks. 'We've just found a voucher in the paper for "The Virtual Space Exhibition" – half price next week. Can we go again?'

A mile down the road, Katherine picked up the phone almost immediately.

'Tonight?' she said in response to Penny's rather peculiar and very speedily delivered invitation. She had earmarked tonight for putting the record straight with Patrick. He'd been with his mother in Plymouth all day and when he got home, she thought it would be a good time to tell him what she should have said straight off.

'No?' asked Penny.

'It's just that I'm seriously behind with an article, and—'

'Don't worry. It was just an idea.'

'Thanks, Penny. Maybe another time?'

'I'll hold you to it,' said Penny. 'Before the party.'

'How about instead of?'

Johnny, who was listening to Penny's half of it, tried to brush off the refusal by changing the subject, but it came as more of a blow than he'd thought. Between the time that Penny had suggested asking Katherine over, and the time she had put the phone down, shaking her head and saying, 'Well, it was a good try,' he had planned an entire dinner-table discussion. There they would all be, relaxed and replete after a good meal, and he would be able to find the courage to tell them all – but particularly Katherine – what he knew they ought to know. However it came out, it would certainly take his relationship with Katherine one step further either way and he suspected it would be towards court rather than bed. At least if Nick and Penny were there when he did it, there wouldn't be a row – well, not a big one anyway.

'It's probably for the best,' he said to Penny who was looking sorry for him. 'She probably wouldn't want to hear what I've got to say in any case.'

'Oh yes? What's that then?' Penny rushed in. Her habit of speaking quickly was something she developed early in her marriage to Nick, when she suspected her plummy accent pigeon-holed her, and made people assume she would find living in Cornwall with her new farmer husband a bit of a shock. As it happened, her fast delivery just made her sound even more like a fully paid up member of the chattering classes. She couldn't completely discard the upper-middle twang but she still tried to disguise it as best she could.

'I'll tell you later,' Johnny replied.

'No you won't, you'll tell me now.'

'No, honestly Pen . . .'

'You've done it, haven't you?' she asked, stopping her chopping and turning to him.

'Done what?' he replied, all innocence.

'Resigned.'

'Yes. Good guess.'

'Johnny, you haven't!'

'Yes, I have. I did it on the first of the month.'

'But that was three weeks ago. Why didn't you say?'

'Because you both did such a good job of trying to persuade me otherwise. I know I kept you up a few nights over it and I'm sorry. I really appreciated your advice and concern and I heard everything you said, but in the end, it just wasn't the right thing for me. The whole prospect just made me want to run.'

'Oh, my goodness. I hope you don't really feel the need to apologise for not taking our advice, Johnny. It's your life, and you lead it how you want. So what are you going to do now?'

'Well, I've thought about that long and hard too.'

'And?'

'I want to go back to college.'

'To do what?' Penny was completely lost.

'Politics.'

'A student? Johnny, are you sure that isn't just a reaction? It won't be the same. Mature students are isolated creatures, all work and no play. And how will you live? Where's the money going to come from?'

'Hold on, Penny, hold on. My resignation is being seen as a voluntary redundancy. The department is being shaken up, and my job is going, that's why I was asked to apply for the top one.'

'Yes, I know all that, you told us, but you said the package was too tight to be of any real help.'

'That's true, it is, but it's enough to pay off some of the mortgage and see me through college for a year.'

'And enough to keep Katherine and the children happy?'

'We weren't happy when I was earning £40,000 a year, so I can't see that it will make much difference,' he said. 'Do you think Nick will write me off? He was really against this, wasn't he?'

'Of course he won't,' said Penny. 'It's not something he'd want to do himself, but he won't disown you.' Katherine might though, she thought.

'I have thought about it all very hard and I know what I want.'

'Yes, but are you still going to be able to have it?' she asked, and felt so cross with him for picking up and putting down responsibility when it suited him, that she made an excuse to leave the room.

*   *   *

Katherine tried to persuade Beth to stay for supper, but failed. The assembling of the fish pie was far from appetising. Discarded haddock skin sat on a heap of bouncy egg white which was now being garnished with a few dangerous-looking bones Katherine kept finding in her good pile. 'Please. You can go to the cinema any night,' she said, pulling a bone the size of an upholstery needle from a lump of yellow flesh.

'No I can't, I only arranged it this afternoon. Anyway, why do you need me? It's only Patrick. It's not like a blind date or anything.'

Katherine picked over the contents of the oven dish again and tried not to look penitent.

'What's wrong?' Beth asked, feeling sure they couldn't be sleeping together – she had living proof of Patrick's disinterest. She steeled herself against discussing his secret, tempting as it was. The fact she'd told Evan haunted her on a daily basis, and if she told Katherine too, that would be a double betrayal.

Katherine was momentarily tempted to reveal *her* secret, but if the idea that she and Patrick might have made love hadn't even occurred to Beth of all people, then it was more of an aberration than she thought, so she deftly changed the subject.

'Nothing really, I just thought Patrick might enjoy the exclusive company of two gorgeous women. What film are you going to see?'

'One about a wife who decides not to leave her husband but manages to subtly ruin his life instead. There's a kind of appeal about it, I don't know why . . .' Beth was smiling.

'You wouldn't go back, would you? Even if it was just to ruin him?'

'What? Never! I can bug him quite satisfactorily from a distance. The house is already on the market, and I'm going to take every penny I'm entitled to, buy the loveliest cottage I can find and then tell him that none of it would have been possible without him. You can't hurt Evan any other way than through his pocket.'

'Attagirl!' said Katherine, forking the last of the mashed potato on to the pie. 'Sure you won't stay?'

But Beth wouldn't, and on her way out, she passed Patrick in the doorway, giving him a quick kiss and telling him Katherine had been trying all afternoon to get her to stay on his behalf. Not the most helpful thing she could have said, Katherine thought, but she's not to know. Patrick did though, she could tell by his face.

Katherine hid in her virtual reality experience for a considerable part of the evening, or at least, hid behind it. Rather than talk to Patrick about their future or lack of it as she had promised she would, she ended up talking about her virtual heaven and her virtual forest, her virtual anything. At one point, she was even making it up.

'I'm beginning to get the picture,' Patrick said finally. 'It sounds more or less like the celebrity space age exposition I covered in Manhattan a year or so ago.'

'What's a celebrity space age exposition, for goodness sake?' Not that I care, she thought, but at least it's a topic of conversation.

'A few famous people and a virtual reality bodysuit.'

'Did you wear it?'

'Of course. Just after Robin Williams. My sweat has touched his sweat.'

'Oh, you're so glamorous. Who else was there?'

'I can't remember.'

Damn, thought Katherine. That could have kept us going

for another few minutes. The fish pie and the chocolate mousse had been eaten – or at least Patrick had eaten his, and Katherine had pushed hers around her plate – the wine bottle was empty, and there was nothing left to do but talk.

'So, how was your Mum?' she ventured, still skirting round the subject she really had to deal with.

'Oh, I didn't actually get to see her after all.'

'I thought it was all arranged.'

'So did I, but she wasn't where she said she would be. Or maybe I wasn't where I said I'd be. One way or another, we didn't meet. It doesn't matter. It wasn't important.'

'You missed her on purpose, didn't you? Have you called her yet? She'll be worrying herself stupid.'

'No she won't, she's used to it. We never manage to keep appointments in our family,' Patrick replied, thinking how ironic it was therefore that Dido chose to keep the one she did.

'Well, you should,' she said, leaning back, picking up the phone and handing it to him.

'Maybe later,' he said.

She could tell he was more interested in keeping the appointment he felt he had with her rather than the one he had with his mother. She'd said and done nothing to suggest it, but somehow, she knew he thought they were on some sort of a promise that night, the first time they had been on their own since making love fourteen days ago. The timescale was mainly due to her considerable contrivances to avoid the issue that long – the children had invited friends to stay, Loveday and Beth had been to supper, Penny had kept popping in on her instructions, and she had invented all sorts of fictitious deadlines, but tonight she had run out of ideas. Her mistake had been not so much in their coming together in the first place, but rather in spending the whole night and most of the next morning doing the same. His appetite had been more than just hungry, like he seemed to be after some kind of reassurance each time, and she had been so voracious herself for a different kind of love that she had stayed with him, reading the morning papers and behaving as if it was all completely normal. No wonder he was sitting there now, wondering whether she would take him, or let him take her.

The after-effect of the whole episode was a creeping disquiet – not that she had shared something with Patrick, but that she had lost something with Johnny – that maybe she had just kissed goodbye to the one thing she had going for her. She had to give Patrick credit for broaching the subject first, even if he did do it rather abruptly.

'So, are we going to be sharing a bed tonight?'

'Um . . .' She fumbled and blushed. Quick, say something, just say no, like that, but nothing came out.

'I just thought I'd ask – you know, get rid of this tension between us.'

'Quite.' She smiled, and started to stack the dirty plates.

'Katherine?'

'I am going to answer, just as soon as I can.'

'It's okay. I think you already have. It doesn't feel right anyway, betraying Johnny and all that. Although I did enjoy it.' He sounded sad.

'So did I.'

'We could watch that film?'

'I was just thinking I might call it a day. I'm wiped out,' she said. The early nights she'd been sticking to had improved things a little, but the crushing exhaustion she felt sometimes was beginning to play on her mind.

'Sure,' he said, trying to keep the desperation out of his voice.

'You don't mind?'

'Of course not. I understand if it was a one-off. That makes it even more special.'

'Yes,' she said, kissing him on the cheek and walking upstairs feeling mean. Nine-thirty was making too much of a point. Still, she knew she could sleep – she could sleep on a clothes-line lately.

Patrick on the other hand knew he couldn't, and wouldn't, and so he took his coat from the back of the chair and let himself out. Walking had become his therapy. He thought more clearly when he was on the move. As he headed for the playing field, he tried to find a decent reason for either staying in Cornwall or going back to the States by the time he reached there, but he couldn't manage either. So Katherine didn't want him. He wasn't surprised – the list of reasons why she wouldn't was ridiculously long, and started with the names of her husband and children – but he was disheartened. To get that far, to have buried his hang-up so beautifully only to have to leave it alone, made him almost as nervous for the future as he had been before.

Inside the cottage, the phone was ringing. Katherine was already asleep, so the answermachine took the message.

'Hi, it's Dido here. Message for Patrick. I'm coming back to the UK tomorrow and I intend coming straight to Cornwall. I will phone you again en route. We need to talk. Don't worry. I've spoken to Mum. I think I understand everything. See you soon.'

Five minutes later it rang again. 'Hello. Sorry to phone so late. It is Jean Seal here. Patrick, do let me know if you are all right. I waited for you for an hour and a half and then took a train home. I do worry about you, you know. Please call.

Katherine, if he isn't with you, could you possibly call and let me know. I am rather concerned. My number is . . .'

Patrick came back through the door to hear the last few digits of his mother's number. She can wait, he thought. She ought to be more than 'rather concerned' after what she has done. He walked past the flashing answering machine with purpose, not knowing that there was another message waiting for his attention too.

Sarah Stokes, former wife of Robin Stokes (Estate Agent), current mistress of Geoffrey Baker (Accountant) and former mistress of Evan Ross (Solicitor), shut her front door firmly and waited a minute before allowing herself a robust laugh. If Evan had asked her seven years ago what he had just asked her tonight, she might have considered it, but how he had the gall – or naivety – to suggest a reconciliation now was beyond her. And the timing as Geoffrey had come down the stairs in his bathrobe had been perfect – she couldn't have asked for a better snub. How pathetic Evan had sounded as he'd tried to turn his doorstep proposition round and make it sound as if he had come about something entirely different – a request for an address he could have found in the phone book, for goodness sake!

She hadn't left the pause until she laughed quite long enough, and Evan had got back into his car with the sound of a scorned woman's derision ringing in his ears. What made them really burn with indignity was the knowledge that he had made a fool of himself in front of Geoffrey Baker. How could he have let that happen so soon after the gossip circulating that Beth had left him and gone home to her mother's because he couldn't give her a baby? Now where would he stand in the business community? On the platform formerly occupied by Robin Stokes – Public Idiot Number One. Bloody women.

Chapter 15

Dido's phone call to Katherine's cottage from Plymouth station the next day was just as much a shock as Patrick's had been twelve weeks previously.

'You're where?' asked Katherine, who hadn't bothered to listen to the answering machine either.

'Plymouth station.'

'Really?'

'Yes, listen . . . Penzance to London Paddington, ten-twenty, calling at Exeter St Davids, Taunton, Castle Cary . . .'

Sometimes the similarities between Patrick and Dido verged on the spooky.

'Don't tell me. There's a delay on the line and you want me to come and pick you up,' said Katherine.

'No. Why did you say that? I'm just about to catch my connection. I'll be at Truro station in a couple of hours. I wouldn't mind you picking me up from there though.'

'Sure, Patrick's not here.'

'Oh, should I have phoned Johnny? It's so confusing – where *is* Patrick living? With you or Johnny?'

'Both, really. He didn't exactly choose the best time to turn up out of the blue, so he's got to take what's going. Basically, when the children are here, Patrick is with Johnny, and when the children are with Johnny, Patrick is here. Listen, we're all going out for a meal tonight – Loveday, Beth, Patrick,

Johnny, and me . . . do you want to join us there or would you prefer me to persuade Patrick to take you straight home? I'm sure he could rustle up something from the sad contents of my cupboard.'

Dido laughed and decided she needed a bit of conviviality. 'You've tasted his efforts in the kitchen, have you? No, I'll get a taxi and join you there, if that's okay. Where will you be?'

'La Tienda, in Lemon Street. The taxi drivers will know it.'

'La Tienda? Okay, great. Are you and Johnny back . . . ?'

'No, no, we just thought we all needed a kick-start into Christmas. It'll be good to see you. We could do with a breath of fresh air.'

'You did get my message, didn't you? Last night, to say I was coming?'

Katherine only managed to say, 'Oh, gosh, no. I haven't checked the machine . . .' before the line went dead.

Only then did Dido question the wisdom of her snap decision to join them all at the restaurant, and Katherine wonder just how good it really would be to see her.

Evan Ross spent the early part of the evening drinking whisky on his own in an empty office. The most significant New Year's Eve he would ever live to see was only ten days away and as yet, he had no plans for celebrating. A refund for his ticket to go to the Isles of Scilly party had arrived in the post a week before, accompanied by a note from Johnny stating categorically that he would no longer be welcome. At first, he'd thought he might turn up anyway, but then he'd wondered who might be on his side if he did and he had quickly crossed it off his list of possibilities. The only other offer he had received so far was dinner with his unmarried sister in Bristol, and there was no mileage in that. Still, it was something.

He poured one more tot of whisky, knocked it back, and left the office. On the way out, he noticed his secretary's boyfriend's van on the private forecourt and stopped to write a rude note which he pushed under the windscreen wipers. He was angry with almost everyone at the moment, mainly because they all seemed to have a purpose and he didn't – unless it was to see Beth penniless and repentant.

As he turned into the one-way system that would take him past the cathedral and out on to the city's relief road, his simmering malice, triggered by Sarah Stokes' snub of yesterday and exacerbated by drink, eventually boiled over. An unmistakable red MG – unmistakable because he had chosen it and he had paid for it – was badly parked on the kerb outside La Tienda, the restaurant he used for client entertaining and had lately made his own. In front of it was Johnny's Triumph Daytona and Katherine's muddy estate, all chummily in line as if the vehicles too were in league with each other.

He drove slowly past, and looked through the large glass window to see if anyone was in sight. To his immediate satisfaction, the first face he saw was Dido's, gloriously stylish and as out of reach as ever. She must have come down in pursuit of Patrick. She had never hidden the fact that she disliked Evan, which had made him conjecture about her even more. Well, he could give her one more reason not to like him now, couldn't he?

As he accelerated, he took a last-minute decision and indicated right – not to join the lane that filtered traffic out on to the relief road as he had intended to a minute before, but to enter the one-way system once again. The driver behind slammed his foot on the brakes and his hand on the horn, and Evan lowered his window to thrust his middle finger into the air in a victory salute.

He was back outside the restaurant in a matter of minutes, riled to find another car parking in the space next to Katherine's, forcing him to put his down a side alley. There had been a satisfyingly vengeful symmetry in the idea of his car joining theirs, the first sign that the bad penny was about to turn up where it wasn't wanted.

None of them saw him standing in front of the window pretending to study the menu. If it hadn't been for the reinforced glass, he could have reached out and stroked Beth's back. She was wearing the black silk sweater he'd bought her for her birthday. How much had that cost him? She wouldn't be wearing stuff of that quality in a year's time, would she? No, she had some lessons coming, she did. She'd soon learn how he'd kept her in the lap of luxury. As he stood at the window, he took a few mental notes. Dido had a suitcase with her, and the clothes she had on – twill shirt, jacket, jeans – looked well-travelled. The realisation that she must have just arrived filled him with a hand-wringing pleasure, a pleasure which doubled when he saw Patrick at the other end of the table. She's arrived late, they won't have had any time to talk yet, there will be that awkwardness between them all, he thought, recalling he had seen both Katherine's car and Johnny's bike, which meant they still hadn't sorted their problems either. The perfect scenario, he smiled, going inside to retrieve some lost triumph.

He spoke to the waitress in a voice that was too loud and too familiar. She ran her finger down the bookings to see if she could help, but Evan was already on stage two of his plan.

'Bring me a double scotch to the table in the window, will you? I've just seen someone I know.'

To check her ears weren't playing tricks, Beth looked up.

'Oh, God. It's Evan,' she hissed to Katherine.

'Right. You don't even speak, okay?' said Katherine quickly.

Beth looked straight through him. It wasn't difficult because she suddenly realised there had never been much to him anyway, certainly no depth. His lack of presence shocked her, he was almost a non-entity. She suddenly remembered the conversation she'd had with her mother about people's gaps. Loveday was right. He had no core, no soul – and if you don't have a centre, how can it be filled?

'I saw you all through the window and I decided to come and wish you a Happy Christmas. Mind if I join you?' he boomed, taking the chair beside Patrick.

Patrick held it firm and said, 'Yes, we do mind.'

'Well, then, I'll just stand.' The waitress handed him his drink and he raised it to the group.

'Cheers!'

No one replied. It was as if they had already discussed that in the event of him turning up they should keep talking but give nothing away. Dido had been in the middle of describing her emergency on the Path underground and so she carried on, swapping the more personal bits to something more general.

'It was very claustrophobic in there – just how you imagine it to be, you know, when you're on the Tube in London and it lurches to a halt and you sit there waiting for it to start up again, only this time it didn't. Then after about half an hour, the doors opened. I'm not sure if they opened because two men had a shovel rammed between them or whether they were opened by the guards, but they opened anyway, and I got out.'

'Still in the tunnel?'

'Yep. Pitch black. I thought everyone would follow, but there were only three of us – the men with the shovel and me. And every time we passed another open door to another compartment, I expected more people to jump out, but do you know, not one single person did?'

'Maybe they thought you were staff.'

'Thanks!' Dido laughed loudly, encouraging them all to do the same.

Evan was waiting for his moment, but they were making it difficult for him.

'Apparently, you can divide the whole of society into rescuers and bystanders,' said Loveday. 'Imagine you're standing by a frozen lake and a child steps on to the ice and it cracks. Do you leap in to rescue him, or watch in horror while someone else does? You sound as if you would be a rescuer, Dido.' She spoke as if she hadn't even noticed the man who had so nearly ruined her daughter's life, but underneath, she churned with loathing.

'Give me a rescuer any day – eh, Patrick?' Evan roared. Patrick ignored him.

Dido spoke again. 'Maybe I am. I'd like to think I was. I was surprised more people didn't follow me. I mean, I know it looked pretty scary out there but it was a better alternative to staying inside. At least by doing something we were in control of our own destinies again, even if it did ruin my best-in-the-world silver skiing jacket.'

'I would have stayed, I think,' said Katherine, having no idea *what* she would have done but doing her bit to keep the conversation rolling. Beth had very wisely clammed up.

Evan made another bid. 'What about you, Patrick? Does it run in the family, this streak of daring?'

'Would you mind leaving us?' Loveday asked. 'You are

surplus to requirements as I am sure you must have realised.'

'Not for the moment, thank you, Mother-in-law. Being in
your company passes the time quite amusingly. What the hell
have you got dangling from your ears tonight? A couple of
lumps of mining waste from the last century?'

The group continued to ignore him and carried on talking,
skirting around anything too personal.

'Did you suffer any kind of delayed shock?' Katherine
asked Dido. 'You know, you cope with whatever is going
on at the time, and then later, when it is all over, you're
hit by it. I'm sure I did when I put our car over the hedge
last year.'

At the very moment Evan opened his mouth to speak
again, Beth suddenly realised why he was there and where
it was leading, that he knew he had hold of a fragile and
priceless bowl, and that he was going to let it go. There was
no time to do anything about it. All she could do was watch
him drop it, block her ears to the sound of the crash and
retrieve the bits to stick it back together once he'd done so.
Here he goes, she said to herself, here he goes.

'So, Dido, when did you arrive?' Evan asked slowly,
looking at Patrick.

'This evening,' she said, 'which is why it would be rather
nice if you pissed off and left us to talk.'

'Got a lot of talking to do, have you? Group therapy, is
it?'

'Evan, I think you . . .' With her eyes, Beth willed him to
shut up.

'Oh, good evening, darling, I didn't see you there. I was
just going to say how Dido seems to deal with shock well,
takes it in her stride, looks bloody good on it, wouldn't you
say? Not like her brother. He's had a shock too, but he

doesn't look so hot, does he? Mind you, it was a different sort of shock, wasn't it, Patrick? More stomach churning.'

'Evan,' said Loveday quietly. 'We've no idea what you're talking about, so do please shut up and piss off, like Dido said.'

'Piss off? *Piss off*? What kind of language is that for a woman of your age? I do wish you would learn to grow old gracefully, not that it affects me any more, thank God. Anyway, *you* may not know what I'm talking about, but Beth does – don't you, sweetie? And so does Patrick. Would you like to know, Dido?'

'Not really,' said Dido. 'I've heard you're not a terribly reliable source when it comes to the truth.'

'Get out,' said Patrick, standing up and shooting a look at Beth.

'It's quite okay, Patrick,' Dido said, leaning forward to try and let him see she knew what was coming. 'Evan is trying to embarrass us, aren't you? Get on with it then. Do your bit, and then bugger off. My food is going cold.'

'It should be your blood going cold, not your food,' said Evan. 'Beth here, my soon-to-be ex-wife, told me a secret about you, and I just feel you ought to be in on it too.'

Dido took a small gamble. She was almost sure Patrick did know the truth, but if he didn't, he soon would. Anyway, she could deal with all that later. First, she had to eliminate Evan from the equation.

'All I was going to do,' said Evan, 'was offer my sympathies to you both over the death of your father. It must have been bad enough losing him in the first place without discovering he had lied to you both all your lives. No wonder you both look so alike.'

Dido kept her voice on the level. 'What lie would that be then?'

'The one about him being Patrick's real father. There, isn't that nice to know? Keep it in the family and all that.'

'Beth told you that was a secret?' said Dido in her most astringent voice. 'How peculiar! I wonder why. Patrick, tell me, dear brother, are you shocked?'

He was convulsing with panic, but he was always absolutely on her wavelength and he managed exactly the right tone in his reply.

'When were we told that? Nineteen seventy-two, was it? Now, let's see, that gives us twenty-seven years to get used to the idea. Yes, absolutely, as you can see, I'm rigid with the shock of it.'

'Or was it seventy-one?'

'It could have been sixty-nine. It's one of those tricky ones.'

'Is there something else, Evan?' Loveday asked. 'Only you looked as if you had something important to say a minute ago.'

'Oh, sod you,' he spat drunkenly, 'you all think you're so bloody clever. I know bloody well you've only just found out. Did you two do it though? That's what I want to know. Did you do it *before* you found out or after?'

As he raged, he knocked a table lamp which rocked precariously. The group around the table, led by Beth who knew exactly where to find his Achilles heel, started to laugh loudly at him, and the louder they laughed, the redder he became. He only heard one level of laughter and that was mockery. Levels two, three, four and five – relief, nausea, shock and anxiety – were utterly lost on him.

Outside, he seethed with fury. Not at himself, because he knew he was right, but with his bitch of a wife, and with the rest of them too, just for being better at it all than he was. As he raced his BMW through the narrow streets, a blue light flashed, first in his rear window and then in his face.

'Good evening sir,' said the policeman through his open window. 'You took that corner a bit fast, didn't you? And is that alcohol I can smell on your breath?'

Evan's detestable cabaret had done what he intended it to because less than twenty minutes after he had staggered drunkenly out the restaurant door, his audience had followed – not en masse for further indulgence as they had planned, but two by two, to lick their wounds in separate corners.

The first response had been for them to draw closer together, united against a single enemy. Beth had cried and Patrick and Dido had held hands as the six of them collectively marvelled at what a poisonous man Evan was proving to be, but it wasn't long before a need to be away from the gaze of strangers overcame them all. Patrick and Dido were the first to leave.

'Katherine, perhaps Patrick and I could go back to your place for a while?' Dido asked with confident control, in great contrast to her brother who was just sitting there with his head down.

'Go to my cottage,' Johnny suggested, thinking of the babysitter and the children. 'Take the bike.'

'There's a spare crash helmet in my car,' said Katherine.

They immersed themselves in the practicalities of keys, cars, bikes and beds for long enough to allow the two protagonists to walk out of the door almost normally. Dido had even turned round and given them all a little wave with a promise to catch up with them the next day, just as if they had decided to leave early because of tiredness or some other innocuous reason. It was to her credit, and not Patrick's, that other diners barely took any notice of the departure, putting Evan down as nothing more than an embarrassing drunk.

'She's a rescuer,' Loveday vouched as soon as they were out the door. Loveday had always admired Dido. She didn't trust her entirely, but nor did she feel threatened by her, and she had seen through her veneer a long time ago.

'Adam was Patrick's real father?' Katherine asked Beth, desperate for the facts now that there was something concrete to go on and Patrick was out of the way.

'How long has he known?' said Johnny.' I can't believe he hasn't said anything to us.'

'Is that what all this has been about?' Katherine asked again.

Beth stopped biting her lip. 'I feel awful. It's all my fault.'

'No, it's not,' Johnny reassured her. 'If it's anyone's fault, it's Patrick's, for keeping something like that a secret.'

'Except he didn't, did he? He told me . . . and I told Evan.'

'Well, then it's our fault, for not dragging it out of him.'

'Well, *tell* us then,' said Katherine kindly, clutching her hand across the table.

'I wish I'd told you before, then you might have warned me to keep my big mouth shut. Do you think I should? I mean, would Patrick prefer to tell you himself?'

'It's a bit late to be the soul of discretion now, darling,' said Loveday. 'Hey, come on, no more tears. That's exactly what Evan wanted. Johnny, go and order everyone a brandy, on me. Beth, give me the car keys. I'll drive, I've been on water until now.'

Beth wiped her eyes and sniffed.

'Now,' Loveday began calmly, 'what's going on? It'll be much easier to help if we all know what the problem is.'

'Wait two seconds,' said Johnny, on his way to the bar, giving Katherine's shoulder a momentary massage as he squeezed past. 'Okay?'

She put her hand up to his and clasped it. 'Yes, fine. But no brandy for me, thanks.'

When he returned with the brandies and a coffee for Katherine, Beth took a sip, twisted her grey velvet scarf and her loose hair into a tight coil, and began.

'Okay, well, when we all went to St Mary's in October, Patrick and I nearly but not quite ended up in bed together, as I told you – remember, Katherine? But when we got to the crucial point, we both realised it wasn't what we wanted, so we started talking instead, and well, it was like opening the floodgates.

'Before Adam died in February, he summonsed Patrick to his bedside and told him that he was not actually his step-father after all, but his real father, and the reason he was telling him was because he thought Patrick might be harbouring the wrong kind of thoughts about Dido.'

'And he was probably right,' said Loveday. 'Go on.'

'And although Adam could barely speak, he managed to describe in some detail the affair he and Jean had during the time Don – that's the man Patrick *thought* was his father – was dying. And then he made Patrick promise never to tell Dido – and then he died.'

Beth looked at the other three with her red-rimmed eyes. 'How's that for thoughtfulness?' she asked.

'Shit,' said Johnny.

'Dido obviously does already know though,' said Loveday. 'And it looked as if she was coping with it a whole lot better than Patrick.'

'Let me finish a minute, Mum,' Beth interrupted, keen to get it all out now she could. 'And then I went and told

304

Evan. It was during our last row, just before I walked out. He found the pregnancy-test kit and because he knew he couldn't possibly be the father, he jumped the gun and accused me of sleeping with Patrick, and the only thing I could think of that would persuade him otherwise was to tell him what Patrick had told me, about the fact that he hadn't been able to make love to anyone, let alone me, since all this happened, that he was currently celibate, impotent, sexually disabled.'

No one noticed Katherine breathe in and hold it.

'Well, you can understand why, can't you?' Beth carried on. 'He gets that close with Dido, and then he discovers she is his real sister, his own flesh and blood and he is nearly sick with the thought of it, and so, well, sex for him isn't simple any more, is it? He told me he's given up on that side of life, that he hasn't been with another woman since Adam died, and I told all that to Evan, just to get him to see that accusing me of sleeping with Patrick was so off the mark.'

Katherine had turned pale as she began to appreciate what a major role she'd been playing.

'Don't beat yourself up about it, Beth,' said Johnny. 'Did you know any of that, Katherine?'

'No, no, I had no idea.' She shook her guilty head at the thought of how big a distance she had put between them since he arrived, being so busy either running from or towards the sexual tension he brought with him that she hadn't thought to look at the root of it. Three months living on and off with him, and his acute depression had barely touched her. What kind of friends must we be to provide nothing more than a roof, she asked herself.

'It doesn't matter who knew and who didn't,' said Loveday. 'We all know now, which will eventually be good news for Patrick.'

'I must call his mother,' Katherine said. 'She'll be going spare. He was supposed to meet her in Plymouth yesterday and he pretended to miss her. I don't think he even went, although where he was instead, I've no idea. Would anyone mind if I went home?'

'Yes, me,' said Johnny, taking his mobile phone from the deep pocket of his leather jacket. 'Don't leave yet, I can hardly go back to the cottage now, can I? Here you are, go and phone, and I'll order coffee.'

'Ask if they do tea,' said Katherine as she took her coat. 'I'll do it from outside. See you in a minute.'

She was sitting in her car reassuring Jean Seal above the noise of the pouring rain that her son was all right and that Dido had arrived safely, when Loveday and Beth came out of the restaurant. They mouthed something at her, but the telephone line was too bad for her to break her concentration and she made do with a quick raise of the hand. When she had finished, and she hoped she hadn't over-comforted Jean, she flipped down the sun-visor and looked in the mirror. Her hair hung in strips around her face and her mascara had smudged, accentuating the bags under her eyes. Her brush and emergency make-up was in her bag in the restaurant and she cursed herself for not bringing it out until she remembered she was not going in to share coffee with a potential boyfriend, but with her husband, who had seen her in states significantly less glamorous than the one she was in now.

Chapter 16

TEN DAYS TO GO

The Times, 21 December, 1999: Consumerism, the enduring social trend of the 20th century, has finally gone into reverse. Downshifting – simplifying one's life by earning and spending less – is now so prevalent in the Western world that the word has officially entered the *Oxford English Dictionary* and sociologists are calling it 'the universal religion for the 21st century'. The consumer society phenomenon that led to statistics like the typical American couple owning 21 times as much plastic as their parents did in 1950 is expected to disappear completely by the year 2050. According to the Institute of Retail Analysis, Downshifting will have such a profound effect on the way we live in the third millennium that consumerism is set to become seriously unfashionable.

'We're not staying here,' Dido had declared on arrival at Johnny's rented cottage after the abortive restaurant meal, 'it smells of depression,' and the next day, she secured a fortnight's let on a more optimistic-smelling house with its own waterfront on a peninsula ten miles from Tremewan.

The contrast between inland and coastal Cornwall was never so marked, but only Dido noticed how the smell of money got stronger and stronger the closer they drove to the sea. Patrick was too busy looking at his boots. No wonder the woman in the letting agency had been so desperate to hammer home the message that this was not bucket and spade country, she thought, as she passed yet another detached house in its own extensive grounds with yet another expensive-looking boat in the drive.

'We do have that on offer in Cornwall of course, if that is what you want, but this area of the south coast is much more suited to couples like yourselves who are in search of beauty, tranquillity and comfort,' she had gushed. 'A couple who honeymooned in this property in 1995 were so taken with the place they booked it there and then for the millennium, but they divorced a year ago and forgot to tell us until last week,' she'd prattled on from behind her computer. 'They've lost their deposit of course, which means you get it cheap.'

It still cost more than Dido's flight from New Jersey and that was before gas, electricity, and the rental car, but what price peace of mind? Someone had to pull Patrick from his whirlpool, and she was, after all, or according to Loveday anyway, a rescuer. Although now she was beginning to appreciate the strength of the undertow, she wished she could be a bystander instead.

What she did know was that she needed all the help she could get, and was embarrassed to find herself recalling a few basic rules of Feng Shui – the oriental art of arranging one's home for health, wealth and happiness. No one who was anyone in the States nowadays bought a house without having an individual consultation about the design of the garden or the layout of the rooms first, and Dido used to laugh at it. 'You should never be able to view the garden all at once, but be led from one part of it to another. It is considered auspicious to have a hill at the back of your home, and an element of water can improve your luck.'

Feng Shui counsellors took out full-page advertisements in Hoboken's free newspaper and she used to enjoy their advice in the same way that she enjoyed horoscopes, scoffing with disbelief at the number of people who set their lives by it, but then annoying herself later by remembering all the edifying bits. When she had seen the beach house with the grassy cliffs behind and its meandering path, narrower at the house end and widening gradually as you walked down the garden towards the sea, she had been stupidly bolstered by it and she took it not because it was cheaper than it should have been, or because it was beautiful, but because she really believed it might help them.

'Well, it's got to be better than that godforsaken little pit Johnny has been living in,' she told Patrick when he said he couldn't see the point of shelling out good money for nothing. 'I can't think how people sort out their problems in a hovel like that. No wonder he and Katherine can't straighten themselves out. He must be permanently discouraged.'

'Well, he wasn't exactly *en*couraged when he was living with her, was he? That's why he left. Your view of the world is so bloody simple, Dido.' He had been in a foul mood ever since she arrived.

'No it's not, it's just uncluttered. Or it is now that we've started to sort out the mess of a legacy left by our dear departed father.' She could speak about Adam in irreverent terms because she held nothing against him, unlike Patrick whose every syllable on the subject was forced. He watched her climb on a chair and cram garden greenery behind a mediocre picture.

'Couldn't we ignore Christmas, just this once? I can't stand all this compulsory cheer.'

'These things are sent to try us. We'll enjoy it once we get into it.'

'I won't.'

'Yes, you will. I'll make you.'

'I'm not in the mood for celebration.'

'No, I know, but I'm going to try and make it so you are. I want to see your smile again. I miss it.' She was fiddling with a trailing length of ivy and doing her best to appear nonchalant.

He grunted. Dido could be so annoying. When they'd first walked in through the door, you could smell the house's lack of permanence. Its musty air suited him fine. Now, with the fire roaring and holly everywhere, she'd gone and made it look like home. Patrick wanted an argument. He really wanted an argument with Adam, but since that was a non-starter, he thought Dido would do. If he saved it all up for when he finally met up with his mother again, they might never be able to repair the damage.

'Does it not bother you then?'

'Does what not bother me?'

'That you seem to be able to flick a switch. Lover, brother, eeny meeny miny mo. One minute you're on my doorstep in New Jersey telling me I am all you ever wanted, and the next, you've turned yourself into the common or garden supportive sister.'

'Well, isn't that what I should be now?'

'But shouldn't you be just a little confused? If you were normal, I mean? Should you really be decorating a rented beach hut with stupid little bits of tree and humming Christmas carols when you've just discovered your whole life has revolved around a central lie?'

'Hold on a second,' said Dido, climbing down from her chair and beginning to lose her cool. 'I've had two and a half months to get used to the idea. You haven't got a clue what I was like when I first found out because you weren't there, so don't go trying to make out I'm taking this lightly. We each deal with things differently, although I'm not even sure you're dealing with it at all, are you?'

Patrick laughed sarcastically. 'I know damn well you're taking it lightly. You never suffer, so don't pretend you do. I'm the one who suffers. I've had ten months of it, and I'm no closer to sorting it than I was when Dad first—'

'Oh, he's Dad now, is he? He's been Adam since you were fifteen.'

'Dido, I don't know who the fuck he is – or was – and I don't care.'

'Yes, you do,' she said, before moving to the door with the intention of getting out of his way for a while. 'I can see it in your eyes.'

Just as she reached it, he let out such a self-pitying sigh that she could hold on no more. She had tried for days to keep on an even keel, despite the way he spat back at her all the time, as if it were all her fault. She was not naturally passive, but Joe had suggested letting Patrick do the shouting and her the listening and so she had been trying, as hard as she could. Well, she could try no more.

'Okay, it's my turn to be unpleasant now,' she said, turning back. 'How about explaining why you didn't tell me, why you let me share your bed for seven weeks, led me to believe you just needed more time, left me there while you ran halfway across the world to get away from me? I had to fly home and confront Mum, when you could have told me six months earlier. How about explaining that, instead of sitting there and giving me dirty looks!'

'I didn't ask you to come and join me,' Patrick told her coldly.

Dido carried on. 'No, but I thought it was what we both wanted. Okay, so I got that bit wrong, and anyway, would we ever have taken the plunge? If we were going to, don't you think we'd have done so by now?'

'I've no idea,' he replied, his impulse for debate leaving him. It was the thought of how close he and Dido had got that made his guts turn, every time. He was lying on the sofa and he shifted his body round to face the wall which should have been indication enough, but she kept going.

'I was so busy trying to force our love into a shape it was never going to fit that I didn't stop to look at us from the outside. If I had, I doubt very much whether I would ever have come to America. We didn't think we were tied by blood so we wanted to be tied by flesh. The more I think of it, the more I'm convinced that's what it was – we wanted more of each other than we thought we had.'

He refused to respond.

'Can't you remember hating Will and Agnes for being able to lie all over each other, play with each other's hair, share each other's clothes? They were never questioned, were they? Because twins have a physical as well as an emotional bond, don't they? Well, so do we, as it happens.'

Still no reply.

'Come on, Patrick. You started this. Go on, get cross with me for coping. Shout at me. Don't just lie there looking at me. Talk to me. Do something, anything, just so I know you're still alive in there.'

So he did. He got up and walked out of the room.

An hour later, when he re-appeared, she tried again.

'Look, I'm sorry about earlier. Do you think it would help if you talked to someone else about this? Someone trained to listen?'

'I shouldn't think so.'

'Would you go if I arranged it for you?'

'Probably not.'

'Well, would you be cross if I sorted something for you? Then at least you could think about it.'

'I expect so.'

It was all she succeeded in getting out of him. 'I don't know, I don't care, maybe.' He had shut down and she couldn't find his reboot button. That night, she phoned Joe out of desperation from a call box, not just because he would know what to do, but because she missed the way he made her feel as if her feet were properly planted and pointing in the right direction. He'd never heard her so serious.

'I can't advise properly from here,' he said, 'but if you think he is on the brink of a breakdown, you should really try and get some help.'

'He isn't irrational. He's just silent.'

'Then don't be tempted to speak for him. He's got to fill in the silences for himself.'

'Joe, you're an oasis of calm.'

'Absolutely. Phone me on Christmas Day.'

'Where will you be?'

'That's a good point. I'm not sure. I'll phone you.'

'You can't. There's no phone at the beach house.'

'I'll give you my wife's number. If I'm not at my flat, I'll be there.'

'Can I say I'm your girlfriend?' Dido teased, pleased for the chance of some banter at last. Joe's wife suffered from the classic syndrome of not wanting her husband herself, but not wanting anyone else to have him either.

'Only if you promise to sleep with me first.'

'You turned me down the last time I offered.'

'That's because I can't bear charity.' he said. 'But this is no time to discuss it! Embarrassing stuff aside, you're okay, are you?'

'I am, but I really don't think Patrick is. I think he probably does need help, but he says he doesn't.'

'Well, just don't drag yourself down too, okay?'

'Okay.'

Immediately the line went dead, she wondered when she could call him again.

'Joe says you've got to fill in your own silences,' she told Patrick on Christmas Eve morning.

'Please, Dido, you're not really helping,' he replied condescendingly.

'And neither are you. Okay, so you have been lied to all your life. But you've also been loved all your life, and that should count for more. Begin by telling me exactly what have you lost here?'

'How about myself, just for starters?'

'But you're still the same man you were before Adam told you.'

'No, I'm not.'

'Of course you are.'

'I'm telling you I'm not. I used to feel justified in wanting you. I mean, after all, your father was attracted to my mother, wasn't he? So why shouldn't their children have an attraction for each other too? Because it would have been incestuous, that's why. Now tell me that thought doesn't make you sick to the core! And that's just a tiny, tiny part of it.'

'It doesn't. Answer me honestly. Did you ever *really* believe we would be lovers – in your heart of hearts? You didn't. I know you didn't, nor me you. We just thought that because there was no reason not to, we could. The disease of the late twentieth century – having it all.'

'I didn't want it all. I just wanted you.'

'I don't believe you. If you'd wanted me, you could have had me.'

'Yes, but by then, I knew I couldn't.'

'Patrick, we are thirty-five. We've been teetering on the brink of something for ten if not twenty years, and it hasn't happened. Why is that? Because something about it wasn't right, and now we know what it is.'

He got a glass from the cupboard and filled it with tap water, drinking half of it and sending the rest sloshing around the chunky corners of the square ceramic sink. She waited for him to say something but he remained silent.

'Do you still want me then? In that way?' she asked recklessly, desperate for him to say no.

'No.'

'Well then.'

'I don't want you at all. Not in my bed, or in my life. That's how much I have lost myself.'

'Why are you trying to make me suffer too? You won't let me be happy, will you? Tell me, apart from your own self-pity, is there anything else that you care about?'

'No.'

'Well, I still love you, as much as I've always done, maybe even more.'

'Aren't you the lucky one?'

'And I can stop comparing you to every man I meet now, can't I? Because you're not in the frame. It's all so much clearer.'

'Is that what I was then? In the frame? What as?'

'A life partner. It's what we're all looking for, isn't it?'

'Feng Shui? Life partner? Dido, go back to the States, it suits you.'

'Okay,' she said, 'if that's what you want. I'm sorry I came out to join you in August. I wasn't to know though, was I?

And if you *hadn't* been Adam's son, would there have been any harm?'

'I'm not getting hypothetical with you, Dido. It is how it is, and that's the end of it.'

If ever Beth had come up with a good suggestion, it was the one she produced in Katherine's kitchen on Christmas Eve 1999 where things weren't half so confrontational. She was sitting on the limed-oak surface of the units watching her friend try and cram a freezer bag of prepared vegetables into the already groaning fridge while Johnny, who had just arrived, was trying to compensate for being there when he hadn't really been invited by getting straight on with his famous midnight punch.

'Are the children going to be away for the whole day?' Beth asked hopefully.

'Until six,' said Katherine. 'The pantomime doesn't start until two, and then there's a party tea.'

'Can I have this lemon?' asked Johnny.

'Check that there's still one left for the stuffing.'

'Where are they now?'

'Lemons fridge, children farm,' Katherine laughed. 'I don't know whether to believe her or not, but Penny rang an hour ago to say there were three deer in their garden. I warned her that Seth was practically senseless with excitement but she took him all the same.'

'And do we know what Patrick is up to today?' Beth asked in the same hopeful voice.

'Yes, he's coming here. Things obviously aren't going too smoothly at their little hideaway because he phoned just after Penny did to say he couldn't face the thought of being with Dido all day, and could he come and do some work on the computer. I told him he could as long as he was

prepared to pick up the turkey for me on the way. I tried
to sound festive but I didn't get much response.'

'Well,' said Beth, amazed that circumstance was in her
favour for once, 'I was thinking, if we get everything done
by noon, how about an impromptu picnic at Landurgan
Gardens?'

'I'm on for that,' voted Johnny, taking a taste of his
brew.

'I think I could be too,' said Katherine, surprising herself
by feeling a rare burst of well-being.

The idea had actually presented itself to Beth the day
before when she'd been told in the village shop that the
vaulted barn in the grounds of Landurgan House had been
turned into a living nativity scene with donkeys from the
local sanctuary and a camel from Newquay Zoo. Mind you,
she'd also been told that the new-born grandchild of the
present incumbents was being forced to sleep in the manger
as a publicity stunt because the family was so hard up it
needed all the help it could get to encourage visitors through
the gates. Luckily, Beth knew her informant, Frank Pascoe,
of old, and she couldn't even be sure about the donkeys let
alone the camel, but whether it was true or not, he had
planted an image in her mind of happy times, and she'd
been wondering ever since if she had the power to make
those times happen again.

The principal task facing her, or so she thought, was to
find a humane way of discarding Dido and the children
since she had an absolute conviction that a picnic between
the four of them would work, but that a picnic between the
five or seven of them wouldn't. She still hadn't forgotten her
mistake in taking Evan along once, right at the beginning; he
had only paused once in his excruciatingly boring discourse
on architecture, to tell her off for swigging out of a wine

bottle, so she was more than aware of the dangers of appendages. It was a long time since the four of them had been together alone, if you didn't count that flop of a weekend on St Mary's in October, and not only did Beth not count it, she had actively banished it from her mind.

However, now that the orchestration had fallen so neatly into her lap, with the children at a pantomime and Patrick needing time without Dido, the picnic idea suddenly started to take on a different, unwelcome significance – that they were about to embark on some kind of urgent mission or bold crusade, a sort of pilgrimage to a monument of their past. The last thing they all needed was pressure to get it right. That way, they'd be on for another St Mary's.

'Some facile fun, brilliant plan,' said Johnny, casting out the shadow from her mind.

'Great,' she replied, smiling and jumping down from the units. 'Okay, you two do everything you've got to do for tomorrow, and leave me to worry about the picnic. See you in an hour.'

Landurgan Gardens was the most Cornish of stately gardens. It had all the usual towering glossy green rhododendrons, the rarer varieties of camellia and the oldest known magnolia in the country, it had palms and monkey puzzle trees, it had a pond surrounded by bamboo, and apart from its famous laurel maze, it held another secret in the crescent shape of its own private beach on an estuary banked by woodland and rock.

In winter, its variegated holly hedges dripped with berries, the red and yellow stems of the dogwood flashed their colour against grey granite walls and the coloured textured barks of the acers, the birches and the eucalyptus trees made spring seem just around the corner.

'Maze, picnic, beach,' Beth said, climbing out of Katherine's car and changing her shoes for wellies.

'We could always break with convention and do beach, picnic, maze,' Johnny teased.

'Ooh, I don't know,' said Patrick, breathing in doubtfully and giving the other three their first reason to believe that he might come out of it, one day. Maybe even this day, Beth found herself wishing, and then cursed herself for it. No pilgrimage, she remembered, just a silly day out.

The layout of the garden had changed slightly from their last visit, mainly to accommodate a commemorative millennium lawn in the centre of which was a weeping spruce. It was hardly a major alteration, but it was enough to throw their sense of direction and have them lost before they even reached the maze. The pasties were warm and heavy in Beth's rucksack and the smell was making them all hungry.

'Perhaps we're already in it,' Johnny ventured unhelpfully, 'which is why we can't find it.'

'Perhaps it only exists in our minds,' said Patrick, 'and we're really at a mind-expanding conference in Milton Keynes.'

'Excuse me, have you seen the maze?' Katherine asked an earnest-looking man as he passed.

'Yes, thank you,' he nodded, carrying on his way up the slight incline of the path. Beth started to giggle and then Katherine joined in. The joke got funnier and funnier the more they thought about it, until they were almost howling. Just as they were at their most uncontrollable, the man started to scurry back down the hill towards them.

'I must say, I do like the idea of garden guides. Could you point me towards the *Araucaria araucana*. I'm very interested to see it – it is the tallest in Britain, is it not?'

The girls could not speak for choking, although Beth managed to wave her hand in a vague north-westerly direction.

'Thank you,' he said. 'Keep up the good work. Merry Christmas to you!' and off he scuttled, muttering in Latin under his breath.

'You've both got the same bloody sweatshirts on!' Johnny laughed. 'Garden guides! More like garden gnomes.'

'You try it,' suggested Beth through tears. 'Go on, just ask the next person you see if they've seen the maze, and see what happens.'

A couple of well-dressed elderly women came up the path, their arms linked and Katherine gave Johnny a shove forward.

'Excuse me, have you seen—' he started before finding himself inexplicably strangled by a desire to explode. His eyes began to prick with the effort of holding it back and he bit his cheek.

'Maze . . . ?' he croaked, at which point Patrick did explode, his face bursting into rare vitality.

The older of the two women smiled. 'I expect you're excited about this millennium business, are you? I wouldn't mind being your age again!' She looked as if she might have had a rather wild time in her thirties.

Patrick, momentarily overwhelmed by an attack of goodwill, leaped forward, kissed her hand and apologised for his juvenile behaviour. Thankfully, she laughed, backing off slightly but glowing with pleasure.

'Well, that's stripped a few years off! Now, the maze is just down there, over the bridge and turn left by the winter flowering viburnums my husband is so proud of.'

'Is he a gardener here?' asked Beth, suddenly wanting to be polite.

'Sort of,' smiled the woman. 'We live here.'

'Have I just kissed the Lady of the house?' asked Patrick. 'I'm so sorry.'

'Don't apologise,' said Lady St Ives. 'Being embraced by a good-looking stranger in my own garden is just the sort of thing that reminds me what a joy it is to open one's home to the public. As long as you've paid your entrance fee, that is.'

'I did,' Patrick smiled.

'Jolly good. Happy Christmas!' replied Lady St Ives, striding off towards the house.

'Right,' said Katherine as they all picked up speed down the path. 'First one to kiss the Colonel!'

Johnny got to the centre of the maze first, and then had to spend a freezing ten minutes sitting on the icy stone seat in the peculiar little folly decorated with seashells, waiting for the others to get there too. He had run all the way and taken only two wrong turns, unlike Katherine who, at the time he'd let out his victory shout, was still wandering around the outside not even able to find the way in. Patrick kept his hands in his pockets all the way round, and when he came to his fifth dead end, he just stood there sighing at it until he saw a gap and climbed through. Beth pretended to be lost, because she thought it would be a shame if they all got to the middle without making the most of it, and she kept calling over the high hedges to her friends to see if they were near.

The crisp wintry air was pierced again a few seconds after Johnny's triumphant call when Patrick suddenly discovered he was enjoying himself and decided to pounce on an unsuspecting Beth brandishing a frozen dead bird.

'Get those pasties here NOW!' Johnny shouted, and within minutes, they were all sitting on the stone seats next to him, ripping open paper bags and uncorking the wine. It was Beth who raised the traditional toast.

'I'd just like to say how much you all mean to me,' she said, lifting her mug to lip level and trying to look at them all equally. 'And how fantastic it is to be here in the maze on Christmas Eve with you lot instead of at some god-awful function in Truro with Evan. So cheers, and thanks.'

'Ah,' said Patrick, hugging her, 'and we love you too.'

'I'll raise a toast too,' said Katherine. 'To friendship and its many complexions.'

'To friendship and its many complexions,' they all repeated, smiling at each other with a vibrant warmth before Johnny broke the spell with a delinquent shout.

'Let's eat these sodding pasties then, before they go cold!'

Later, when the light was already fading after the best day he'd had since his father died, as he parked the rental car outside the beach house, Patrick thought he would go in and try to talk things through with Dido. It was the first time he had felt remotely like sharing anything with her, and he was glad she was there. Only she wasn't. A four-line note on the kitchen table told him she had decided to leave him to his own wallowing, and if he wanted her, she would be with Jean in Oxford. She did say sorry, and that she loved him and she even ventured a Happy Christmas, although she must have known there was little chance of that.

Chapter 17

The day after that, 25 December, 1999 – the last Christmas Day of the second millennium – made its mark with sub-zero temperatures and brilliant blue skies. Patrick woke early and crumpled almost immediately. The winter sunshine winked at him through the thin material of his drawn curtains and brought with it a huge composite childhood memory, made up of years and years of Christmas mornings, the taste of orange juice and chocolate coins mingling in your mouth at breakfast, parents poking around with the turkey in between sips of champagne and saying, 'One more present each then, before church.' In one ear, he could almost hear all that going on everywhere around him, but in the other, he could hear almost nothing.

He got up, dressed in the clothes he had dropped on the floor the night before, and looked at Dido's note, in exactly the same place she had left it on the kitchen table, took his coat and went outside. Down the icy garden steps on to the brittle frosty grass, through the wooden gate with its peeling blue paint, and on to the dunes. The further he could walk, the more distant Christmas would become.

After ten minutes of concentrating more on the biting cold than his own despair, he was on flat damp sand that still bore the scummy foam of a recent tide. He imagined seeing himself from a great height, a tiny speck on a stretch of virgin sand, trekking pointlessly in one direction, leading nowhere, the only person in his world today without an obligation to fulfil.

As he walked, he tried to cast out the image of his family, of what they might be doing, or saying, and he focused instead on his own aimlessness. He could turn round and go back to the house, but for what? Or he could walk as far as his eye could see, but then what? And there were other choices – straight out into and under the freezing sea until the coldness killed all sensation, or simply lie down, on the wet sand, and wait – but for what? Everything ended in a question, and as Paul Grogan the Christian had once said, he didn't have the answers.

It would be good to have an answer. Any answer would do. It wouldn't have to be Paul's, or Dido's, or anyone else's, but to have his own answer would be good. The first thing to do would be to formulate a question. What should I do with the rest of my life? What is happiness? What's the point of it all? Do I care? What chance do I have of finding an answer if I can't even find the question?

The beach house disappeared behind the clumps of sea grass and he rounded a corner into a cove. Rocks had formed into an arch, which he passed under, feeling splashes of water drip down the back of his neck as he bent. A cave beckoned, but the wet discomfort of his collar persuaded him to walk on.

The tide was way out now, the beach was vast, and he felt even more irrelevant than before. He started to head towards the cliffs, climbing over a few slimy boulders, slipping on seaweed and jarring his ankles on barnacled rocks. One foot missed and took a dip in a small rock pool, but his boot kept out all but a sharp spurt of water.

A path led away from the beach and up through the cliffs,

but before he lost sight of the sand, he turned back to look at his footprints. One track, in a straight purposeful line, except there *was* no purpose to it. If someone was following him, where would they think he was going? He wished there had been *two* sets of prints, then the sight of them might be less disturbing, more companionable, but their singleness was threatening and he was frightened for himself. He had no idea where he was or how he was going to get back, but since there was nothing and no one to get back for anyway, he told himself it didn't matter.

Climbing uphill through the rough wintry vegetation made the blood pump around his body and he tried to make it the stirrings of endeavour. If he had a goal . . . but he didn't even have a destination. It wasn't a case of not having anything to do, it was not having anywhere to go either, and even if he did have somewhere to go, he would have nothing to do when he arrived. His life was an ever-decreasing circle and he had no desire to start walking against it.

The steps of the path were wide, cut into the cliff and edged with timber, but they had no rhythm to them. One, two, three steps up, and then a walk along the flat. The next step took two strides, and then there were two smaller ones he could take together. His breathing was deep and he could see it in the air – proof that he was still alive. He willed himself to meet the challenge, to begin the long haul back up to motivation, but it made no difference, it was all just too quiet everywhere, especially in his heart and head.

How easy would it really be to take the obvious step of suicide? What proof is there that it would work? If I hurled myself over these, he thought as he reached the top of the cliff and found himself in a field cut by a well-trodden footpath leading towards a road, what guarantee is there that I wouldn't end suspended from a tree with nothing more than a broken arm?

That is precisely the source of all my problems. I need certainties, I am no good with possibilities. But life isn't about certainty, as Adam proved last February, and as Katherine and Johnny are proving now. Nothing is certain. Not your lineage, not your marriage, not even your own capacity for survival or suicide.

So what are we then? he wondered as he took the wooden stile, shiny and smooth from years of being climbed over, and began to walk along a single-track road. Pawns? But who's the player? Or are we, as agnostics would have us believe, just material phenomena, the result of cell division?

He was pleased to be thinking, even if it wasn't a process that led to an answer. And at least he wasn't thinking about Dido, or Adam, or Jean, or trying to re-define them as he had for the last ten months. The air was full of Christmas, carrying in its droplets the anticipation of children, the birth of Jesus, and the smell of a cooking turkey, but to Patrick, it was just air. Air to breathe in and out, in and out, a regular, consistent breathing that kept him going, walking to nowhere along the lane that stretched for miles ahead, broken only by a few bare and wind-bent bushes.

In Oxford, Dido was busy justifying herself to the rest of her family. The empty place at the head of the polished oak table had stared at them throughout breakfast, but whether it was Adam or Patrick who was missing, no one quite knew. At least there was a chance Adam was at peace, somewhere away from the poking and prodding of doctors and the cloud of prognosis. There was no such comfort to be gained from thinking of Patrick, of where he was and what he would be doing, of what they could do to help, and whether or not he would phone them.

'You shouldn't have left him,' Agnes told Dido. 'He doesn't sound in any fit state to be on his own.'

'I've told you, I can't help him if he won't let me. You try commuting across the Atlantic on his behalf, holding the fort for him in New Jersey, dragging him off to an isolated cottage to force it all out of him. If you can get any further, then be my guest. It's all been a complete waste of time.'

'Have you actually taken any positive steps towards sorting this mess out?' Will asked his mother, who looked more drawn than she had on Adam's death.

'I've tried,' Jean said. 'I have phoned him and I have tried to meet with him, but he won't talk and he didn't turn up on our one arranged meeting, nor did he bother to apologise.'

'Have *you* apologised to *him*?'

'Shut up, Will!' snapped Dido.

'No, let him say what he needs to say,' Agnes said.

Jean thought how strange it was to hear the twins speaking out so authoritatively. All Will's life he'd been third in line in the male pecking order, but now with his father dead and his older brother AWOL, his voice could be heard. Agnes too had found a new opportunity. With Patrick gone, there was no one to jump on her when she criticised Dido. It was turning into something of a free-for-all.

'Of course, every time I have spoken to him,' said Jean. 'I've even put it in writing. I can't think what more to do.'

'There *is* no more to do,' said Dido. 'He's on his own. Anyway, stop worrying. He'll be at Katherine's, I bet you. I'll prove it to you.'

Katherine and Johnny's determination to spend Christmas Day as a family had raised a few curious eyebrows, but it would have raised a few more if it had been made clear he was staying, both on Christmas Eve and on Christmas night. Strangely, the children hadn't shown any interest in where he would be sleeping, and Johnny had left it until they were both in bed before unstrapping his leather bag from the back of his bike and dumping it in the den. He was keen for the signs of parental separation to be as inconspicuous as possible and promised himself he would get up early to make the bed back into a sofa and the bedroom back into a den before Hattie had a chance to get upset about it.

Katherine had initially told him not to be so stupid, and that the children ought to know exactly where the relationship stood, and he had said, 'So where does it stand?' When she hadn't been able to answer him, he did what he thought was right, and hid all evidence of confusion, and in the event, she had thanked him for it, particularly on Christmas morning as she'd lain in her double bed, bracing herself to get up in the painstakingly leisurely manner she knew she had to if she was to avoid being sick. Knowing she could send the children downstairs when they ran in, and that Johnny would be there, dressed and ready for the day as if nothing had ever changed, allowed her to breathe a little easier. If he'd noticed the ginger biscuits she'd armed herself with the night before or the way she'd nibbled cautiously on them before she rose, then he would know just as well as she did what was going on. She swung her legs out of bed, and planted them firmly on the floor. Her next move, after a minute or so in this position, was to stand up. Then, a slow walk to the bathroom, a gentle wash, and back to the bedroom where she had attempted to put on her pants without bending over. It was day four of the nausea, which meant it was probably week five of the pregnancy.

The morning passed harmoniously. Loveday and Beth had

been at church, popping in for a quick drink on the way home, and Johnny had been relieved when Katherine hadn't insisted they stay. 'This is great,' Hattie told him when he was concocting his famous stuffing. 'We haven't been like this since you and Mum—' and she screwed up her nose.

'Yeah,' he said, screwing up his in the same way.

'Where's Patrick?'

'He and Dido are having a quiet day together at their little beach hut.'

'Oh. Good.'

'Don't worry, he won't be coming here. Although you're going to have to start making an effort with him again soon, you know. He hasn't really done anything to deserve your cold shoulder, and believe you me, your shoulder can be very cold when you want it to be. But we'll talk about that another day, eh?'

'I was going to say that I hoped he wasn't on his own,' Hattie corrected him.

'Oh. He won't be. Anyway, he's a big boy.'

'Who is?' asked Seth, coming into the kitchen with his new basketball and net.

'Not you,' said Hattie.

'You can't fix that up in here,' Johnny told him.

'Where can I put it then?'

'In your bedroom.' The phone rang. 'Where's Mum?'

'Upstairs, in the bathroom. I think she's being sick.'

Hattie looked at her father, he looked at her, and they both screwed up their noses again.

'Answer that, would you Hats? It'll be Granny.'

'Happy Christmas!' Seth shouted into the phone, beating his sister to it. 'Oh, hello. We thought it was going to be Granny.'

'Well, Happy Christmas anyway. Is that Hattie?'

'No, it's Seth,' he growled, dropping his voice an octave. 'Who's that?'

'Dido.'

'Dad? It's Dido,' Seth shouted, letting the phone drop and skidding off to have a prod at a few more unopened presents, forgetting the offence taken at Dido's ineptitude.

'Hi, we were just talking about you two,' Johnny said. 'Been for a dip in the sea yet, have you?'

'What? Oh God, isn't he with you?' Dido answered, not as surprised as she sounded. Still, Oxford was too far from Cornwall to do anything about it.

'Isn't who with us?'

'Patrick. I'm in Oxford – I left yesterday. He was being so horrible, Johnny, he made it impossible for me to stay. I was sure he'd be with you. Maybe he'll turn up this afternoon.'

'Well, he's not here now and we haven't heard a word.'

'Don't worry. Mum wanted to wish him a Happy Christmas and the beach house isn't on the phone so I thought I'd try you, on the off-chance. If you see him, try and persuade him to call us, yeah?'

'Okay. He was in good spirits yesterday, so he might be on the up.'

'Oh good. I left before he got back, but I got the impression he'd rather be on his own, so I'm sure he's fine. I'm sorry to interrupt your day. Are you having a good one?'

'Not bad, all things considered,' Johnny said.

'Good. Well, if you see Patrick, bend his arm and get him to phone, and if I don't speak to you before, have a happy new millennium, won't you?'

'You'll see me at the party. I've got your ticket here.'

'Well, no actually, that was another thing I wanted to talk to Patrick about. I've just put the phone down from speaking to Joe – you know, the friend I was telling you about, in the States? He's bought me a flight to New Zealand as a Christmas present and I'm meeting him in the Visitors' Information Centre at Christchurch Airport on the twenty-ninth.'

'Really? Won't Patrick . . . ?'

'Probably, but he hasn't got a lot of choice. Listen, I'll leave you to it, Johnny. Give my love to Katherine. Happy Christmas!' And she put the phone down before she heard anything she didn't want to.

Johnny's face rarely changed colour through anger, but just then, his cheeks were red with it. It was quite apparent what Dido's game had been. She couldn't be bothered to worry about Patrick so she had given the worry to someone else, passing the buck as usual. Unbelievable.

Katherine appeared, looking pale. 'Who was that?'

'Dido.'

'They're not coming round, are they? We could really do without them today.'

'Hardly. She's in Oxford. She was phoning to speak to Patrick.'

'What, they're not together?'

'Apparently not. And she's not coming to the party either.'

'Oh, great,' said Katherine sarcastically. 'That's all he needs. That bloody woman! Just as I get round to thinking I quite like her, she persuades me not to.'

'I'm not sure I like her that much,' Hattie said cautiously.

'She's dire,' said Seth, coming back in, now sporting a pair of flashing sunglasses. 'Who are we talking about anyway?'

Patrick reached a small village that seemed to have more hotels and pubs than houses, and in one of the last few remaining red telephone kiosks in Britain, he put down the receiver and reclaimed his fifty-pence piece. Both numbers had been engaged. Dido had probably been calling her shrink in New York and Katherine was probably on the phone to her mother. It didn't occur to him that the two lines might be talking to each other about him.

He didn't know where he was or how to get back to anywhere either. He had a few pence in his pocket, an empty stomach, a sudden thirst and aching legs. He had walked so far that he had run out of choice. He could hardly knock on a door and ask for help, could he? Not on Christmas Day. 'Hello, sorry to trouble you, could I possibly have a drink of water?' And he couldn't phone for a taxi either, because he didn't even know the beach house address. There was nothing else for it but to keep walking until something happened. He'd got himself into this, and no one else could get him out. All he knew was that he didn't want to re-trace his steps. There was no going back now.

As he neared the church, the congregation began to spill out and he increased his pace. His black denim jeans and sand-covered boots would make too much of a point against all that cashmere and velvet, and someone might try and offer the hand of peace to him or something.

'Merry Christmas,' shouted a young girl and her brother as they skidded over the flagstones and into his path. I'd like to be a child again, he thought. All that unquestioned security. If I was, I'd find out who I really was and hang on to it. 'Merry Christmas,' he said back with an artificial smile. And he walked on.

Chapter 18

TWO DAYS TO GO

The Times, 29 December, 1999: Historians of the future will pinpoint the year 2000 as the beginning of the Information Age, according to the Institute for Employment Research. Nearly a third of Britain's full-time workers are now employed in data services – gathering, processing, retrieving or analysing information. Agriculture now involves less than two per cent of the workforce, and less than twenty per cent of UK employees currently work in production or manufacturing compared to forty-five per cent in 1950. This radical and speedy shift towards technology has forced businesses across the world to re-structure entire organisations at a global cost of billions. The research figures conclude that 'information is now the world's most important product and the Industrial Age is ready to be resigned to the history books'.

When Katherine had thought about it in church on Christmas Day, the total eclipse of the sun in August had seemed years, not months, ago. Back then, she and Johnny had been hanging on to an excuse of a marriage, Patrick had been incommunicado in the States, and Beth had been putting on a good show of appearing happily childless, circumstances now annulled by the simple passing of time.

And the traumas are probably all for the good, she thought now as she looked out through the windows of Penzance heliport into a dense blanket of fog. We weren't worth any more like that than we are today.

Fleetingly, she smelt all the oppression and suffocating unease of the eclipse again, and yet there was a difference this time, as though somewhere inside her there was comfort to be had, as if the cross to bear no longer had her name on it.

She looked around the room that passed as an arrivals hall, departure lounge, cafeteria and baggage collection point, and she wondered idly which one of the patiently waiting passengers it *was* meant for. Behind which brave smile did the personal fog lurk this time? And why should it not be her? Separated, pregnant by one of two men, and facing a future alone – hardly the first set of circumstances one would choose with which to sail into a new century.

It was unlike her to feel so strong in early pregnancy. She was usually much more likely to opt out and lie on sofas, moaning, and the only reason she hadn't this time was because *someone* had to cook the meals and be nice to the children, but all the same, it was something of a revelation to discover she could beat her hormones if she had to. When she had been pregnant with Hattie and Seth, Johnny had done almost everything since even walking into a supermarket had made her retch. It still did – only last week she had abandoned a full trolley to go outside for fresh air and a ginger biscuit, but she had felt better for it – well, emotionally better anyway. Physically, she was wrecked.

The last few days had just about put the lid on it for her, what with Patrick mooning around the cottage, Johnny winding himself up more and more as the party approached, and Hattie's incessant enquiries as to Katherine's health.

'Feeling better, Mum?'

'Yes, thank you, darling.'

And then an hour or so later: 'Are you still feeling better, Mum?'

'Yes, thank you, Hattie, still feeling better.'

It was bad enough being sick in the first place without having to do it surreptitiously. As for Christmas Day, the precarious harmony had hit a discord the moment Dido had phoned in search of Patrick. How they were all supposed to carry on with the festivities after that, imagining Patrick hanging from the rafters in his rented cottage or in a broken heap at the foot of cliffs, she didn't know, but she didn't suppose Dido had thought of that. Johnny had been so enraged by Dido's call, or the reasons behind it, that he had called her back and suggested she phone the police.

'I don't have the number,' she'd said. 'But if you're worried, I don't mind you doing it. It might be more sensible for you to anyway, given the distance.'

'No can do, Dido. He's your family's problem today, not ours,' and he had hung up just in time to run outside and stop Katherine getting in the car and driving to the beach house to find out. 'It is Patrick's decision how to spend the day, and if that includes taking his own life, well then it is none of your business. Your business is here, with your children.' And Patrick had turned up at nine o'clock that night anyway, almost delirious with exhaustion, needing to be fed, watered and wrapped up just like the broken-winged sparrows the children picked up in the garden from time to time.

Johnny had been so clear about the part the two of them should play in the saga. Of course, he didn't yet know that her role was so much more muddied, but then how could he, unless she told him? This weekend, she promised herself, come hell or high water, this weekend.

The helicopter fleet that had been booked in his name for the last eighteen months was just visible through the large misty windows. The two of them should have been at least halfway through their relay race to and from St Mary's by now, but there they were – or the vague outline of them anyway – skulking by the hangars, empty and silent, in direct contrast to the over-loaded shed that represented the heliport.

Katherine was forced to take back what she said about it being a guest-list of strangers. At least half of the one hundred or so present were friends, some firm, some casual, and the others all looked to be friends of those friends. There were bottles of champagne and boxes of orange juice balancing perilously on cushioned seats as a Bucks Fizz trend began mushrooming across the hall, and someone – a member of one of the bands, she realised later – had even brought along a saxophone.

Unlike Beth, Katherine had never been good at these kind of undefinable gatherings and so she resorted to small talk. It unnerved her that the absence of Beth's husband had a positive energy to it but the absence of her own was negative. People were coming straight out with it – 'Where's Evan?' – to which Beth would reply, 'Who knows? Who cares?' and then everyone immediately knew where they stood. When those people who hadn't heard about the state of her own marriage asked her where Johnny was, she skirted round it.

'Over there already, waiting for us lot to arrive and no doubt tearing his hair out,' she said more than once. It was the truth, but not the whole truth. And if she did mention his name to those people already in the know, everyone felt twinges of regret or bewilderment, including herself.

Beth's freedom of spirit since she had left Evan reminded Katherine of the way she had imagined she would be herself once Johnny left, revelling in the release. In the event, that hadn't happened at all, and the only thing she had really learned since living on her own was a feeling that things still weren't quite right.

She had been watching Beth from a distance, the way her eyes flitted from one face to the next and how, when she recognised someone she once knew, or someone she simply hadn't seen for a year or two, she alighted with kisses and noisy acknowledgments. She'd already had a cup of machine coffee on a bench with Dr Jeremy Shaw and managed to make it look more like a frothy cappuccino on a bar stool, but that was Beth for you, effortlessly lovely. Still, we can't all have everything, she thought, reminding herself of Loveday's favourite phrase.

When Beth had discovered from Johnny a few days ago that Jeremy Shaw was one of the party guests, she had demanded to be put next to him on the dinner seating plan.

'I'll damn well ask him to justify the wild-goose chase he had me on when he knew all along that Evan was shooting blanks.'

'Fine,' Johnny had replied. 'Nothing like a good row to get a party going.'

Tables turn so quickly, Katherine reflected, remembering the fragile Beth she had shared a room with on St Mary's in October, the falsely optimistic Beth who had so convincingly talked herself into being pregnant just afterwards, and the broken-to-pieces Beth who had walked out on her lying husband with a suitcase of clothes and a shattered dream and who had seemed all but washed up for the foreseeable future just seven weeks ago. And here she was now, the old Beth, apparently home and dry.

Johnny had left Cornwall for the Isles of Scilly the day before and taken Patrick with him, a decision not entirely his own. When Patrick had literally fallen through the cottage door on Christmas night, practically hypothermic and seriously dehydrated, he had effectively put an end to anything she and Johnny might have built up during the day. They had just embarked on their first useful conversation – she had been going to tell him about her pregnancy and how they ought to decide once and for all if divorce proceedings should be started, but then the knock had come, and there hadn't been a moment since.

'If you don't get him out of this house soon, I swear I'll walk,' she'd told Johnny on the day after Boxing Day, with a nodding salute to Dido for what she had put up with too. 'I can't suffer another moment of his self-indulgence.'

'I'll take him with me tomorrow,' Johnny had promised. 'But I don't find him any easier, you know.'

She imagined Johnny now, standing in the empty island airport trying to search the fog for clues as to the length of the delay and telling himself he could see a patch of blue sky, just there between the control tower and the tree, while Patrick ambled along some solitary stretch of sand thinking only of himself.

The questions had already started.

'Is there any overnight accommodation available in Penzance?'

'Is there anywhere nearby to grab a decent meal?'

'Is there any other way we can reach the island?'

Katherine was tempted to say she knew no more than they did, but that wouldn't have been true. Johnny had been trying to make contingency plans for exactly this kind of crisis for the last six months but there wasn't a bed to be had for love nor money within a ten-mile radius of the heliport and in the end he had just decided to take the risk, a risk that all of a sudden didn't look like it had been worth taking.

Perhaps she had better try and contact him, let him know how things were her end, that the atmosphere was far from the grumpy mix of frustration and boredom that it could so easily have been, and that the heliport staff were doing all they could to keep the party spirit up. Besides, he knew how much she hated flying and he would tell her all the right things, about the helicopters not flying unless the pilots were sure it was safe and all that. She'd heard it heaps of times before, and it always helped, a little. If she knew him – and she felt a confidence that she *did* know him – then he really would be where she'd imagined him to be – at the airport on St Mary's.

'Hello, I wonder, you should have a Johnny Bates with you at the moment, waiting for an arrival. Would it be possible to speak to him, please?' She felt nervous.

'I'll see if I can find someone with that name,' said a female voice. 'Who shall I say is calling?'

'His wife,' said Katherine, without even thinking about it.

She heard the tannoy go out. St Mary's Airport was so small, the receptionist could probably just have shouted. Johnny's voice came soon afterwards.

'Katherine?'

'Hi.'

'Is everything okay?'

'Fine, I just thought I'd let you know everyone seems happy enough my end, in case you were worrying.'

'Your end?' Johnny sounded puzzled.

'Yes, you know, Penzance.'

'Oh,' he said, with a relieved laugh. 'Right. Your end.'

'I'm at the heliport, along with all your other guests. Where did you think I was?'

'Yes, got you. I thought for one minute you meant your end as in home, and something had gone wrong that I should know about and you were phoning to say it was all okay again now.' He tried to stop his nervous gabble. 'Thanks, that's really kind. I've just heard that the fog is lifting and it should all be gone in a couple of hours.'

'Who told you that?'

'A pilot.'

'Great. Shall I let people know?'

'I don't know, what do you think? I don't want people to get their hopes up too much.'

'I think we should. It's actually quite good fun here, and if a pilot told you . . .'

'Okay, would you?'

'Sure.'

'Don't promise anything, but just say what I've told you. That would be good actually, yes.'

'Okay, I'll do that. See you soon.'

'Katherine?'

'Yes?'

'Don't worry about the flight. They wouldn't go up if they weren't sure it was entirely safe. Tell Beth if you're frightened. She'll talk you through it.'

'I'll be fine. Anyway, I've got the children to fret over, haven't I? They'll take my mind off me.'

'That's my girl.'

Too late for that, thought Katherine. They both stood there for a few moments after the receivers went down, wanting to be sure that the conversation had just happened. Johnny had heard her say 'her end' and Katherine had heard him say 'don't worry'. As they walked away, it occurred to them both how ironic it was to find a way back to each other just when it was all too late. His resignation, her pregnancy. The goalposts had moved a considerable distance since August.

Penny Shepherd came up, obviously under the gentle influence of one glass of afternoon champagne, her respectable face slightly flushed and not helped by the way her hair was pulled back by a velvet band.

'Good Christmas, Katherine? Or shouldn't I ask?'

'Ha!' Katherine squeaked. 'Ha!'

'That bad?'

'Oh, you know, suicidal house guest, estranged husband sleeping on floor, pregnant hostess with head permanently down loo, the usual kind of stuff. No, it was fine, lovely, how was yours?'

'Did you say pregnant?'

'No.'

'I didn't think you did,' winked Penny, even more flushed now with intrigue but having to leave it there with the arrival of the five Shepherd and Bates children.

'Dad says Johnny has organised an artificial snow machine and we're all going to ski down to the beach at midnight,' shouted Luke. 'Is that true?'

'You have got your skis with you, haven't you?' Katherine was beginning to feel a bubble of fun, despite everything.

'I haven't,' Seth said in a panic.

'You haven't got any,' Hattie reminded him, 'so how could you bring them with you?'

'Mum?'

Katherine winked.

'Oh, right, got it,' he said conspiratorially.

'Thicko,' said Hattie, and they ran off to find another victim for the same joke.

Penny resumed her line of questioning.

'Now, just run that past me again. Suicidal house guest, estranged husband sleeping on floor, and . . . what was the bit about the hostess?'

'Penny, I know you are absolutely brilliant at keeping your mouth shut, but on this one, perhaps I should have kept mine shut.'

'You are then?'

Katherine tried to look non-committal but the temptation to talk to someone had gained so much ground in the last few days that she surrendered.

'I think so.'

'You *think* so? Don't you know?'

'Well . . .'

'You are, of course you are, I can see it in your eyes now. Oh God, are you okay?'

'I'll get by. Please don't say anything, not even to Nick.'

'Of course not. We're not talking Johnny here, are we?'

'Very possibly, yes we are,' said Katherine, crossing her fingers behind her back. Well, remotely possibly maybe, she rewrote silently, although she knew her pregnant self too well to really think that.

'Oh!' Penny smiled, delighted at the thought. 'Tell me more. I knew you two couldn't stay apart for long.'

'No. I'm not telling you any more. I haven't told him yet. I'll tell him this weekend.'

'What a way to celebrate!'

'I can think of better.'

'Yes, but that's what started the trouble in the first place.'

'But all joking aside, he's not going to be overjoyed, is he?'

'Why not? I've never met a man more passionate about his children than Johnny. Can't you remember how much I used to moan when the children were little about how good Johnny was and how hopeless Nick was? He loves all that breast-feeding baby-rice stuff, you know he does.'

'But the burden of it all, Penny – the way a baby just throws everything into turmoil. Johnny left because he needed more order to his life, he told me he wanted less pressure. This is hardly going to make things easier.'

'That's what he said in August. You might be surprised what he says now,' but just as Penny was saying it, the confident lilt in her voice faded. She had just remembered the decision Johnny had taken a month before, one she and Nick had done their best to dissuade him from during those two or three long evenings at the farmhouse when he had evangelised about the wisdom of reviewing one's entire life at once. He'd been at a crossroads – Chief Officer, fat salary, comfortable pension one way – voluntary redundancy and back out into the uncertain market-place the other. Now that he had chosen the small farm-track instead of the dual carriageway, his reaction to Katherine's news just might not be so favourable. Her face fell.

'What's the matter?' Katherine asked. 'You look like you've said something you shouldn't have.'

'Not at all. But maybe you should tell him after the party, when his head is clearer. Now, apart from the fact that you are pregnant, is everything else okay?' Penny was trying to joke the moment away. 'Are you finally, after all your crabby cantankerous crotchety old bag-iness, coming round to the idea of enjoying yourself over the next few days, by any chance?'

'Well, maybe.'

'I thought so. What did it? The sperm and the egg?'

'No, that's had the reverse effect! It's been a mix of things, the children's excitement, and funnily enough, Dido, Patrick's sister. She's gone to New Zealand you know, and by the time we're all kissing and hugging and singing *Auld Lang Syne*, she'll be having her first lunch of the new millennium. It'll already be January for her by then, she'll have been there and done that, lived through this great frantic moment in time that we've all been working up to for so long. Doesn't that just put the whole crazy thing in perspective?'

'I suppose it does, although I've never thought of this as anything other than a bigger than normal New Year's Eve party anyway, have you?'

Katherine laughed. 'Er . . . yes!'

'Oh! In what way?'

'In an "I've got to get my life in order before the year 2000" kind of way.'

Penny laughed. 'But you've done the complete opposite, big time! Come on, there must be another reason for your optimism. You're not one for being happy for no reason.'

'Thanks, Pen. You know how to make a girl feel good.'

'No, but it's true. Come on, you're pleased about the pregnancy, aren't you?'

'Can I think about that and get back to you?' Katherine asked.

'I'll give you five minutes,' Penny joked, being dragged off by her youngest. 'And tell Johnny he'd better come up with something better than *Auld Lang Syne* for midnight or I shall be asking for a refund!'

Katherine wondered if she *was* pleased about the baby. It was such a radical idea, she hadn't even contemplated it. How would she feel if she lost it, if she started bleeding, or it turned out to be a phantom pregnancy brought on by stress? How would she feel then? 'Strange' was about the best answer she could come up with. She walked over to a drinks machine where Penny was taking out a can of orange fizz for a child.

'I've thought about it,' she said. 'Have you got a diary on you?'

'Funny you should say that.'

'Give it here then.'

Penny pulled one with a tan suede cover out of her bag and waved it pointedly in the air. 'Be careful – it's Gucci!' And then, more confessionally, 'Nick bought it for me for Christmas, and I can't bear it. How can I produce this at the next cattle-market ladies' lunch, for goodness sake?'

Katherine laughed. 'Look at all those gold zeros!'

'Has he left the price on?' Penny joked, trying to coax the dainty little tortoiseshell pen out of its holder. 'Two thousand? God, he never paid two thousand for a diary?'

She handed it to her friend who opened at random and flicked to August. On the space for the eleventh she wrote *Katherine's baby due.*

'There,' she said, handing it back. 'Maybe there is life in the year 2000 after all.'

'That's exactly a year after the eclipse!'

'Just a guess,' said Katherine, trying a Mona Lisa smile.

Penny's laugh was drowned by the voice over the tannoy. 'Will passengers for flight BS 1344 to St Mary's please go to the departure doors to board the helicopter. Thank you.'

A massive cheer equal to any local rugby derby went up around the hall. Over the tannoy, the owner of the voice found enough courage to lean a little further into her microphone and say with all the daring she could muster: 'And I wish you all a Happy New Millennium!'

There was no fog in Christchurch, New Zealand, at the same time – just the early morning skies of a promisingly sunny day, which meant that Dido's flight from Heathrow touched down on time and Joe's was due any minute. The Visitors' Information Centre, just as busy at 6 a.m. as it was at 6 p.m., was inside the main airport door, and she'd been there no longer than ten minutes when she heard his voice in her ear.

'That is some peachy little butt,' he said, giving it a soft pinch. She spun round on her Cuban-heeled boots and found she had to look down at him, not that it suddenly mattered to her in the slightest. It was the first time Joe had ever touched her below the chin. Not only that, but he was beaming and it had been the first time she had seen anyone beam since she'd left America nine days ago. Both events deserved recognition and so she put her arms around his neck, still not caring that she had to crook her neck, and gave him the sort of welcome kiss she had once thought she would give to Patrick.

'That was definitely not the kiss of an ambivalent woman,' he said when she had stopped for breath.

'Me? Ambivalent? Since when?' she said with conviction.

'Hello two thousand!' shouted Joe, picking her up and swirling her round the room, sending a pile of leaflets about Avis hire cars flitting to the floor.

'And about my butt?'

'Yes?' he said, putting one hand lightly on it again.

'You told me once I didn't have one, so how come it's peachy all of a sudden?'

'It's not all of a sudden. It's been a gradual peachiness, as you well know.'

Chapter 19

THE NIGHT ITSELF

The Times, 31 December, 1999: Population experts are forecasting a massive baby boom for September 2000 as couples celebrate the new millennium with midnight lovemaking. For those of you without a partner, you would be well-advised to follow the example of 16-year-old Gemma Brown who advertised her baby-sitting services in Bristol yesterday at £50 an hour. 'I left it till the last minute to make myself available because I knew the premium would be higher. There was a massive response and I've obviously taken the highest offer which should pay for me to go on holiday this summer.' London's Trafalgar Square has already been cordoned off by police who will spend the day carrying out security checks, but for those of you thinking of turning up impromptu, remember – it is a ticket-only affair this year.

From about seven o'clock onwards on the evening of 31 December, St Mary's main street was more akin to a badly lit catwalk. One of Johnny's greatest problems had been how to find enough accommodation on the island for his guests. The Cloudsley was St Mary's biggest hotel with a hundred beds, and since it was also the venue for the party, he had taken the precaution of securing every one of its rooms two years ago, with the help of a large deposit. The next two years had been spent persuading owners of the smaller hotels to let him do the same, but it had been much more difficult since the trend was to swap St Mary's for St Lucia during the winter months, so he had upped the incentive and offered to provide the staff as well.

As it happened, the allocation of party people in groups of twenty or more around the island and all within reasonable walking distance of The Cloudsley, turned out to be a sound move. A convoy of mini-buses had been organised to transport guests in case of bad weather but to Johnny's satisfaction, the evening was dry and everyone chose to promenade, like peacocks or flamboyant ants, depending on how confident they were. They all wanted photographic evidence of their historic night to wave in their grandchildren's faces in years to come and say, 'That's me on the eve of the new millennium,' as if it was a true representation of what they used to be like, and so they broke off their journey to position themselves by tropical trees or ancient buildings and smile self-consciously at the flashlight.

Even the most conventional women had shown a certain bravery, with a risky slit up the back of an otherwise safe frock, or a dress so clingy that underwear was evidently dispensable. If the clothes were wild, the hair was even more so, though not necessarily through choice. Island hairdressers were not in abundance and the four or five that there were had all been booked by the Scillonians months ago, so the look that night was home-spun, great bundles of hair and pins and spray, long locks plaited with braid, or an easy bob livened up with a confident hint of colour. The islanders gathered around their doorways and watched it all with an amused superiority, most of them having declined an invitation to The Cloudsley in favour of what would be going on in the bar of the Divers Inn.

The most unlikely people were already drunk by ten-thirty, with women falling first, their careful coiffures coming loose with excessive dancing, and their bare arms displaying wintery pallors as they flung them around virtual strangers in an exaggerated state of excitement.

Even the beautiful can come undone with a red wine moustache and burgundy teeth, thought Johnny, as he watched an army of staff clear the tables of pudding debris. If the punch had been excellent, the meal had been even better. There was quite a crowd round the ski simulator, shouting and cheering at whoever was currently hurtling down the computerised piste. No one seemed to care that for their £500 ticket money they might just have been able to ski for real if they had thought about it early enough, but then money seemed no object either, if the roulette table was anything to go by. He thought too how odd the women looked with their skirts hitched up and their elegant little shoes kicked to one side in favour of the simulator's ski boots, the same way the girl playing the electric guitar in one of the bands did – incongruous, somehow – not that he would ever voice anything as politically incorrect. He was bounced out of his contemplation by the pleasant feeling of a female form barging into his back.

'Sorry,' Katherine shouted over the music directly into his ear, laughing. 'I didn't *mean* to proffer myself just then, someone nudged me from behind. Just as well it was you, I suppose.'

Johnny wondered if they were both coming across each other with such regularity on purpose.

'How much did you pay them?' he shouted back.

We're actually flirting, she realised deliriously. She had always regretted the fact that their leap from the platonic to the physical hadn't been more memorable, a mere question of swapping kisses on the cheek for kisses elsewhere and sharing a bed instead of a house. How ridiculous then, that in the middle of this preposterous gala – the culmination of the very thing that had caused so much irritation between them – they were suddenly giving off such adolescent signals.

'I can't remember the exact sum,' she told him, 'but I beat them down, obviously.'

Johnny put his hand in his pocket and pulled out a ten-pound note. 'Here you are – that buys two.'

'Thanks,' she said, snatching it playfully and stuffing it between her breasts. Then she slid her hand under the flap of his dinner jacket and moved it across part of his buttock and a little way down his thigh before taking it away.

'You're still in credit,' he said, dizzied at the effect of her touch, but the moment had gone. A wave of nausea had just swept through her and she turned to rip the crust off an abandoned bread roll. Food was the only thing that stopped the sickness, which was why she usually carried an emergency rations bag with her. It had worn off around week twelve of each of her previous pregnancies, so if the life inside her was anything to do with the man beside her, she should be feeling better by now. If not, she had at least another seven weeks of it. Curses to her erratic cycle. Not only had it got her into this in the first place, it was now refusing to shed any light as to which first place it had been.

Johnny studied her. Her hair still looked like her hair, and she was wearing a dress he had seen before. All these other wives and women around with their hired costumes and alien head creations couldn't hold a candle to her. Her beauty happened somewhere underneath her pale skin and her brown hair, and it surprised you when you caught it, but he was catching something else as well – a greyness under her make-up and a certain dependency on the crust she was holding.

'Hungry?'

'Not really, just pigging.' She smiled weakly and changed

the subject. 'The children are having a fantastic time on that skiing thing. I didn't realise you were getting one for them as well.'

'Nor did I, but the ship turned up with two, so I got them to put one in with the kids just for somewhere to stick it. They'd better not charge me for it. Have you had a go yet?'

'No, have you?'

'Yes, but I made a complete dick of myself.'

'Never!'

'Ask Seth. He'd be more than happy to tell you. He was hardly what you'd call a sympathetic audience.'

'Do you know where is he now? Has their film started yet?'

'The last thing I heard, they were going to save it for after midnight, but half of them will never last that long.'

'I'm not sure I will. What should I do? Put them to bed after the fireworks?'

'We'll do it together, shall we?' he said, wanting very much to hold her but making do with a hopeful raise of his eyebrows.

'Is that a date?' she smiled. This is not wise, she thought. I should not be starting something I can't finish, but I can't help myself, I want him. I don't want anyone else in the entire room, I want him, and I can feel him wanting me. Maybe we could do just tonight.

'Your first of the new millennium,' he answered, thinking much the same.

'Probably my only.'

'You might not want any more.'

'You might not either,' when you hear what I've got to tell you, she added to herself. Had Johnny planned a reconciliation this way, just like he'd planned the casino, and the bands and the fireworks? The clock strikes midnight and they both fall into each other's arms for ever after? Because if he had, he was in for a big disappointment. Come to think of it, so was she.

Patrick's whole evening came to him in snatches as he wandered from room to room in search of a crumb of optimism. What he found instead was a barrage of noise, some background and some in his face. The sound of the band starting up again, or a cheer from the ski-simulator as someone took a corner too fast and crashed into the flags was easier to deal with than the direct hits. It was when someone tried to engage him in conversation that he felt the urge to run. A ten-minute chat with a person he hadn't seen for fourteen years here, a drink with another who was married to someone else he hadn't seen for fifteen years there – his entire adult life was being stitched up around him like an unsightly patchwork quilt that had taken an age to make but that, when it came down to it, no one actually wanted to have on their bed. He wondered why Johnny had kept in touch with so many people for so long and could only think that ultimately, Johnny must possess a quality he did not, since he found the prospect of swapping addresses with anyone tonight so utterly odious.

He found Beth sharing a bottle of wine at a table in the corner with a man he didn't know. They spoke briefly, and then he ambled off again on the pretext of going somewhere to see someone.

'That's him,' Beth said to Jeremy Shaw, worrying as he disappeared into the crowd, 'the lovely Patrick who is shot to pieces over his sister.'

'Is she here too? You said she was drop-dead gorgeous and I've only seen one woman of that description here tonight.'

'And don't tell me, she's sitting next to you?' Beth laughed.

'No, she's over there,' Jeremy teased, pointing in a vague direction to a large woman who was shimmering rather too much.

Beth laughed again and looked at her watch. 'No, Dido's well into the twenty-first century by now.'

'I'm sorry?' said Jeremy. 'You've lost me.'

'Dido, Patrick's sister. She's in New Zealand. She phoned Patrick tonight. I was in his room, doing up his bow tie, and the phone went. She was having breakfast at a party in Christchurch – they're thirteen hours ahead or something. She told him she could hardly tell the difference between the two centuries and so far she hadn't seen one single alien, but Patrick didn't really seem that amused when he was re-telling it all to me.'

'Well, no, he wouldn't.'

'I thought it was quite a good line, much as I loathe to give her any credit. It's typical Dido. She loves being the centre of attention, and flying off to the other side of the world at a moment's notice to beat us all to it is just the kind of cock-a-snook stuff she likes.'

'You're fond of her then?'

'Er . . . I could live without her.'

He filled her glass and laughed, but then, straightening up, he asked: 'Is Patrick still as depressed?'

'Terminally, I think,' said Beth. 'I mean, he's always had it in him and now he's got a pretty good excuse. I'm losing patience with him, he's dragging it out so long.'

'And what about you?'

'What about me?'

'Can I ask if you're still depressed?'

'You can if you need to.'

'It really bothered me when you cried in my surgery. I couldn't shake you from my mind. I was going to ask you the same question a month ago but you never turned up for your appointment.'

'Should you be asking me things like this at a party? I mean, isn't it against the Hippocratic oath or something, asking a patient personal questions?'

'Sorry, Beth. I didn't mean to pry.'

'Oh, I don't mind really,' she said hurriedly. 'It's nice to know you care.'

'Good, because I do. It's difficult though, trying to find out how you are without sounding like a doctor.'

'Is that what you're doing now?'

'Not exactly. I was just, er, wondering what had happened to your husband,' he replied, trying to find some courage to steer the conversation where he wanted it to go. 'He's not here is he?'

'I hope not,' said Beth assertively.

'That sounds like you and he have parted company.'

'Didn't you feel that sudden surge of angry energy in Truro around November the tenth then? You didn't have a power cut or a mini-thunderstorm or anything?'

Jeremy laughed. 'I must have been out of the county. It was bad, was it?'

'I'm sure you can imagine.'

'Can I? Do you want me to guess? It would be easier if you could tell it to me straight.'

'Like you did, you mean?'

'Like I did?'

'Sarcasm, Jeremy. Think about it.'

'I don't want to – it all sounds too cryptic. I think I'd rather have a dance, wouldn't you?'

'I might. But I'd like you to explain something to me beforehand.'

'Would you? Is this leading somewhere?'

'Yes,' Beth said in a half-tease, 'outside. I'm seething with resentment, and if we dance before we talk, I'm liable to step on your toes pretty bloody hard. Can I drag you into the garden and give it to you there?'

'It's an interesting offer,' he replied, raising those sandy eyebrows again.

'You're a gentleman. Come on then.' And she got up from her chair and walked out of the room, saying over her shoulder, 'I am going to let you have the complete works, and then I'll forget it ever happened.'

'God, it sounds terrifying,' he said lightly, but his heart was beating too fast to feel comfortable. He knew exactly what she was alluding to, and he had to admit he had been compromised, but her marriage was obviously over and she seemed the stronger for it. Well, he thought, looking at his watch and realising there was an hour to go, I'll take whatever is coming to me. She might just thank me for it one day.

Hattie Bates and Luke Shepherd had a bird's eye view of it all from the balcony. Seth had pretended he was keen to watch the film – an Oscar winning re-make of *Lord of the Flies* which had become something of a cult among the early teens – but he was already asleep in the front row of the makeshift cinema along with at least six other ten-year-olds. In the back row, something more exploratory was going on, but whatever it was, Hattie and Luke decided they weren't ready for it. The one decisive moment came when they either had to join in or leave, so they left.

'Have you ever seen that film before?' Luke asked, too flustered to say what he wanted.

'No, but everyone talks about it so much I sometimes think I have. I'll probably see it one day. I'm in no rush.'

'Me neither.'

'I don't think I'm quite ready to watch it just yet,' Hattie replied enigmatically. 'What about you?'

'I would if you would, but I can wait.'

'You don't mind?'

'Course not.'

'But I would quite like to see it one day.'

'With me?'

'If that's okay.'

'That's okay.'

'Great.'

'Good.'

Their mature handling of a situation so complex would have been a fine example for any one of the so-called grown-ups below.

The two children leaned over the balcony railings and tried to spot their parents in the mêlée. Nick Shepherd in his red satin waistcoat was about as far away from his wife as he could have been, propping up the bar and talking to another man Luke didn't know about the workforce of the future. Nick had heard an American professor on television the day before say something profoundly funny about factories in the twenty-first century having only two employees – a man and a dog – and had been determined to use it during the party. 'The man will be there to feed the dog and the dog will be there to stop the man touching the equipment.'

He laughed so loudly that Luke and Hattie heard him above all the other laughs. So had Penny, who was dancing embarrassingly in the halter-necked low backed dress she'd had made specially for the occasion, and who was beckoning her husband to come and join her.

'She'll never get him up there,' Luke told Hattie. 'She's mad to even try. He's a terrible dancer.'

'Does it matter that they're not together?' asked Hattie.

'They are together.'

'I mean now. Your mum is there, and your dad is over there. Have they had a row?'

'No, I shouldn't think so. They hardly ever row. Anyway, look at your parents. That's the second time your Dad has gone back to your Mum's table.'

'I know, I've noticed.'

'What do you think is going to happen?' Luke asked.

'I don't know.'

'I do.'

'You don't.'

'I do.'

'What then?'

'They're going to get back together.'

'You're just saying that to make me feel better,' she said in a little voice.

'I'm not. Don't you, then?'

'I'm too frightened to think about it.'

'Ah, poor Hattie,' Luke said, and put his boy-meets-man arm around her shoulder and gave her a squeeze, half wanting to ask her if she'd changed her mind about watching the film.

Neither of them noticed Patrick approach a solitary man standing behind an amplifier by the band and say a few words before walking inconspicuously away again. He had dipped his toe into the berserk pool of controlled substances a few times before, mainly out of curiosity, and, like even the most casual drug-users, he had it written all over his face. The dealer had caught his eye at the bar earlier and said, 'You look like you need a helping hand with Spirit Big Shift,' and offered him a choice of powder or pills. At first, Patrick declined, but an hour later, as the man knew he would, he'd been back. He put the small white tablet on to his tongue and swigged it back with the wine he was carrying, nodding in recognition to the stranger who had given it him. Spirit Big Shift. Cheers. Happy Third Millennium.

Katherine and Johnny were dancing together, much to the delight of their daughter who was too far away to see the pessimism etched on their faces. Over their shoulders, they were both thinking this might well be the last dance. In six weeks' time, Johnny would be officially unemployed. When he said the words 'voluntary redundancy' to himself now, they sounded much less brave and liberating than when he'd first practised them. His decision had been taken alone because at that time, he thought he would have to carry the consequences alone too. The ways out of his crisis had been thin on the ground – the one back to his marriage had been well and truly bricked up – and in his agitation to go forward somehow, he had chosen the only available exit. Now, he wasn't so sure, and yet the deed was done. 'Yes, darling, I'll come back and we'll live happily ever after,' he was envisaging himself saying. 'Oh, by the way, we'll have to sell the house and live on the breadline for a bit.'

Supposing he *had* applied for the Chief Officer's job and was facing a rock solid future, would he now be running into her arms for ever more, offering to provide everything they ever needed for the rest of their happy lives together? No. He'd be back where he'd been in August. This way, his way, was at least the beginning of a solution.

Katherine was imagining a scene too, in which she lay in his arms and whispered in his ear, 'I forgot to tell you. I'm pregnant. It could be yours, but it's probably Patrick's. Now, when did you say you were moving back in?'

The slow number came to an end and Hattie watched for a kiss but there wasn't one, just a smile, and a walk in opposite directions.

At a quarter past eleven, the clamour got too much. Patrick took a quick look around to find the faces that mattered, and once he had seen them all, he left.

As he walked out of the hotel by the garden entrance and on to the rough stone balcony hewn from the cliffs, he was aware that people would be wondering where he was going so close to the witching hour, especially on his own. But he was also aware that they wouldn't be caring much. They would probably comfort themselves by saying he was one of the organisers off to check the firework display, and how hard it must be, to be working on a night like tonight. They wouldn't find the compassion to worry if he was running away, or if they did, they'd make sure they soon lost it again.

It occurred to him that it might as well be the middle of a working day in London for all the peace and privacy this particular night had to offer. Was there anyone – apart from the very young and the very old – who wasn't up at this hour, squeezing everything they possibly could out of this moment of a lifetime?

He took the three steps on to the hotel lawn, which curved round either side of an ancient sundial and he walked across it, in between the twelve super-rockets in their purpose-built launchers that would be lit in forty minutes' time, and that Johnny had been so proud of when he brought them back from the Birmingham Trade Fair, and then he turned sideways to slide through a gap in the row of ragged palms.

The change in temperature from the stuffy ballroom to the clear cold night, coupled with the effect of the little white pill that was now coursing round his bloodstream, had heightened his senses. The pebbles on the beach path were in fact calcified shells which cracked and shattered as his size elevens strode with purpose over them, and he concentrated on how good it was to hear that level of noise again after the blaring cacophony of the last four hours. Soon he found himself standing on top of a low wall that separated the beach from the garden and he jumped down, landing on harder, bigger pebbles, jarring his knee and making an altogether different sound from the cracking of the shells.

A small rowing boat was tied to a rusty ring cemented to the wall. It looked as if it had been dragged up the shoal not so long ago. Its rope when he felt it was wet and the pebbles underneath looked recently disturbed. He assumed it was a tender for a larger boat and that someone at the party had arrived by sea.

He untied the single knot, surprised that it was secured so superficially, and he dragged the boat down to the water. The rumble and crunch as it almost slid by itself cut out the distant hubbub and for a second, he felt relief, but then the laughing and the music wafted back, and he pushed and heaved more than he needed to, just to dominate the air. It was as freezing a night as any other New Year's Eve he'd known, and as the sea slapped over his leather shoes and into his socks, his toes were desensitised by the ice. The part of his brain that normally dealt with pain had shut down, as had the part that dealt with rational behaviour. All he could hear now was the enticing rush of salt water and the howling of a winter wind. The fear of hearing anything else as midnight struck was motivation enough to get him in the boat and out to sea, to become a part of the deep, not the shallow.

As soon as he was out there, he knew it was where he

wanted to be – an insignificant speck of mankind, bobbing aimlessly on an ocean wide enough to swallow a continent. Now, when the meaningless tick of the clock that had lately been given such epic status propelled the world forward another nonsensical second in the race towards nothing, he wouldn't have to ring any bells or fire any pistols, he could just shut it all off and no one would be around to ask him why.

The tide took him out, and he picked up the oars to row as fast as he could. He was shivering but there was no need to worry about the cold, because human comfort didn't matter to him any more. All he wanted was to be away before the first rocket hit the sky, too far from land to jump and swim. His body moved rhythmically backwards and forwards, echoing the times in his teenage years when he had rowed for his school, but he pushed the memory away because it was too full of the kind of regatta and celebration he was trying to escape, and yet somehow he couldn't help finding that trained pattern of lean, pull, lift. As the sandy outline of the beach merged with the sky, and the rocks withdrew into the darkness, he took a lungful of the sea air, clean of smoke and drink and man-made agitation.

Suddenly, a great searing scream scorched through the sky and blew itself up into hundreds of orange falling stars, each one exploding with a sharp report and consuming his peace. So it had happened. The first moment of the Third Age had arrived and gone again, just like that, taking with it years of preparation, miles of travel, huge reserves of cash, and God knows how many afflicted souls. Then another screech, and another, and another, each choosing different trajectories, criss-crossing his empty navy sky, each agonising squeal piercing his ears like the sound of a mythical beast writhing in agony to the gouging of a warrior's spear.

The human cheers fell away into the expanse, then eight more scorching trails and eight more cheers followed. Patrick lay back in the boat and stared above him, watching the traces of fire the rockets left, wondering if it might be the last thing he saw before death.

Half a mile away on land, the blaze of colour that had flashed and shimmered and sparkled so climactically to spell out the year 2000 was dying. Number Two was already ash and the first nought was only just hanging on in there, phutting grey smoke and threatening to die, but the last two – Beth's dreaded double zero – were still burning merrily, like the wide eyes of a fabled monster staring incredulously at the inordinate amount of kissing going on.

Katherine noticed how the huge amorphous crowd had re-grouped into smaller parties, families and couples, or smaller circles of friends, and she looked for Patrick, but of course, he was nowhere, because if he wasn't with them, he wouldn't be with anyone.

Hattie lifted her head back and smiled up at her father who stood behind her on the granite balcony. Johnny thought then how big a smile it was, and how it wasn't entirely the smile of a child, and he planted his lips on her forehead. Katherine caught the mutual well-being as she stood next to them both, her arms around the neck of her exhausted ten-year-old son. Johnny was standing very close, their shoulders touching, the residue of a deep midnight kiss that had tried to say it all. But there was one more thing to say, Katherine reminded herself, one more thing that would change it all once more and that had to be said before morning.

'Isn't it odd?' she said to Johnny. 'The four of us were so sure we'd spend this moment together ten years ago, weren't we? And now look at us. No Patrick, no Beth, and but for the grace of God, go we. Where *are* they?'

'We don't own them, Katherine. Let them go. Beth looked more than happy the last time I saw her. Anyway, the four of us that matter *are* spending this moment together,' he replied, putting his arms round Hattie.

Patrick lay still on the bottom of the boat. The oars were by his side, waiting for him to take them up and start rowing again, but instead, he picked them up with his freezing hands and dropped them over the side, hearing the heavy splash and visualising their journey down to the ocean bed.

'Do what you want with me!' he said out loud, his voice cracking. 'Do what you want.'

He was challenging the sea, or the wind, or any other power or force that might be out there that he imagined could claim lives when it so desired. The floor of the boat was puddled and his clothes were sodden but he lay down again all the same. Every now and again, a wave or a gust of wind blew in some more water, on to his face, or across his front, plastering his thin cotton shirt to his hairless chest.

When he had been a child, his mother had painted a verse around the top of his bedroom wall, ten lines from the *Hymn of St Patrick*. He used to recite them every night before he went to sleep, and sometimes again in the morning before he got up – not as a prayer, but a chant, another element of his complicated bedtime routine, his version of a security blanket. The words had been covered over long ago, as soon as he'd been allowed to impose his own taste, but now they came floating back to him, drifting through his mind in a ribbon of prayer.

> *I arise today*
> *Through the strength of heaven;*
> *Light of sun,*
> *Radiance of moon,*
> *Splendour of fire,*
> *Speed of lightning,*
> *Swiftness of wind,*
> *Depth of sea,*
> *Stability of earth,*
> *Firmness of rock.*

They held no meaning for him as a child, although they were lyrical and he had seen a sort of power in them that belonged more to the mystery and magic of the land of dragons and brave knights, and when he thought about them, he used to feel proud that his name was Patrick, but that was it, there was nothing else in them for him, not then. Here, out on the dark watery expanse, he imagined they were saying something else.

He thought about heaven and wondered if that was where he was bound. The water would swallow him up, freeze him rather than drown him, and then would he, through the strength of heaven, rise up? Is that what was happening to him, why he felt anaesthetised, because death was already upon him?

Radiance and Splendour were strong words, but he was frightened by what they conjured up, and he wished he hadn't thought of them. It was the rockets bursting their man-made flashes into the sky that had done it. *Splendour of fire*. Then, as he'd remembered the prayer, the depth of the sea had beckoned to him, called to him to get in and go under. He opened his eyes and looked above him into the nothingness, and his voice filled the air, even though he fought not to speak.

> *Radiance of moon,*
> *Splendour of fire,*
> *Speed of lightning,*
> *Swiftness of wind,*
> *Depth of sea,*
> *Stability of earth,*
> *Firmness of rock.*

The little wooden craft was moving faster than he thought, dragged by the swiftness of wind in search of the stability of earth. Patrick gave himself up to the emptiness around him. 'Take me,' he called. 'Do what you want with me. I have no direction of my own.'

When the very last firework had fizzled to nothing, Katherine and Johnny joined in the mass exodus from the hotel lawn to the bedrooms. The adults were keen to continue the party and the children were just as pleased to be told they couldn't, especially Seth who was asleep within minutes of his head hitting the pillow in the room he was sharing with his father. Hattie hovered next door in her nightshirt.

'Mum?'

'Yes?'

'Shall I sleep in Seth's room?'

Katherine was immediately both proud and ashamed. Here was her daughter, not yet a teenager, offering to ease her parents' path towards sexual reconciliation.

'Do you want to?'

'If you think it would help.'

'Oh Hattie, do you know how much I love you? I think I'm as nervous about this as you are.'

'I was just thinking that if you're going back down to the party, I don't want to be on my own. Dad can kick me out when he comes to bed if he wants to.'

'Okay. Good plan. You'll be all right up here, won't you? You know where we are if you want us.'

'Of course. We're not babies, you know!'

'I know, you've just proved that.'

'Goodnight then,' Hattie said, almost running out the door. 'I love you too. Happy New Millennium.'

Johnny met her in the corridor.

'I'm sleeping in with Seth,' she said. 'Mum says you'll have to sleep with her, okay? Goodnight, Dad.'

As she crept into bed she knocked once on the wall between her room and the one where the Shepherd children were sleeping.

'Good plan, Luke,' she whispered, before taking up her huggie and closing her eyes.

Next door, Katherine remembered the last time she and Johnny were alone in a hotel room together – this hotel, ten weeks ago, same curtain material and bedspreads, a brief togetherness, a possible armistice and then a row. The only thing that separated the two moments, then and now, was the baby inside her.

'I haven't thanked you for my midnight kiss,' he said when he came in. 'It was perfect.'

'Thank *you*,' she replied, 'I quite liked it too.'

'I'm up for a re-run if you are.'

A smile flew across Katherine's face which made her look all the more serious once it had gone. 'You might not be. I don't know how to say this.'

'Don't say anything yet,' Johnny entreated, putting a finger to her lips. 'Let's change into something more sensible and go for a walk. It's wild out there.'

'No, there's something I need—'

'Please, Kath – outside, under the moon. I can take anything in moonlight. We can't talk in here with the ghost of October hanging over us.'

'You're right,' she agreed, relieved to have a few more moments before she spelt it out.

He watched as she found her favourite jumper and pulled it on over her bronze silk full-length dress, took off her strappy sling-backs and put on a pair of leather boots, and then topped it all off with the black woollen reefer jacket she had had since college.

'Ravishing,' he said. 'Let's go.'

'What about you?'

'My clothes are in with the children. I'll just have to freeze.'

'Right, so I go down looking like a bag lady and you stay like that?'

'Okay, chuck us another jumper.'

Katherine threw a red cardigan with a tie belt and a collar at him, and he put it on.

'There. Now we've both got something to be humiliated about.'

With a scrape and a crunch, the little wooden craft lurched on to the shore and jerked Patrick out of his semi-consciousness. Instinct made him jump out into the shallow water and begin to pull the boat up the slight incline. Only once it had cleared the hump of pebbles and he had turned it up to sit on its underbelly did he begin to wonder where he was. Holding his head tightly in his hands and catching his quickened breath, it dawned on him as he looked out across the moonlit sea and saw the lights of St Mary's twinkling at him that he had not gone full circle and ended up on the same beach he had been so determined to leave, but that he had crossed the water somehow and found a new land.

Or had he? Was he alive? Was this the twenty-first century, or was it an afterlife? Could it be that it wasn't the water he had just crossed but the timelessness between life and death? Was his mind simply playing tricks, trying to make a physical coherence out of a spiritual climax? He lay back on the painted hull and let his thoughts wash over him to the sound of the sea sloshing against the shingle, waiting for the truth to show.

The air temperature had dipped even further and in danger of hypothermia or worse as his saturated evening trousers stuck to his frozen legs, he lay there, staring into the stars, trying to deny the multiple certainty that had penetrated to the very core of his being, that he was alive, that he was not alone, and that he was not insignificant. For a while he struggled to deny it, believing it was too late for all that now. He willed himself to find the preference to crawl back inside himself and re-discover the reassuring irrelevance of it all, the pointlessness that had led him to get here in the first place, so that it still didn't matter if he lived or died. He reminded himself that he had taken the boat because he had wanted to die, and that he still had that choice. How easy it would be just to roll off the hull and fall on to the sand. The water would inevitably come to meet him sooner or later, and if it was later, he could well be unconscious through cold by then, and so it could take him bit by bit. It would be a painless way to opt out – he was already numb and it wasn't an entirely unpleasant sensation – and dead people didn't have to explain anything.

But none of these arguments worked – they were hypothetical, academic and abstract, and they had no place in his head because suddenly, passionately, Patrick wanted to live out his future.

In a state of unnerving exhilaration, he sat up and in one movement swung his exhausted legs to one side of the hull and hurled his body into the night, making the first effort towards survival. As he stumbled on to the wet ground his knees gave way and unable to support himself, he fell stomach-down on to the coarse grains, not seeing the rusty mooring post sticking awkwardly out of a lump of concrete hewn into a hundred jagged edges by the sea, nor feeling the warm trickle of blood escaping from under his curls and on to the sand.

Dido's face passed across his mind, then his mother's, then Adam's. He was already all but senseless, but he could just about feel or see something peaceful beckoning him, as if the decision had already been made for him. He opened his eyes, took a look at the starry sky and closed them again, wondering how he could have believed that if he wanted to live, it was up to him.

The band was still playing as Katherine, in her jacket, jumper, boots and bronze silk skirt, tried not to clomp too heavily across the floor. She was following the bright red woolly back of her husband who was beaming at everyone he saw, including an omnipotent Beth who had just made her own private resolution never to let a man mould her against her will again. She gave them both a wink and mouthed, 'Happy New Millennium!'

'Where's Patrick?' Katherine mouthed back, but Beth just shrugged.

'You'll get struck off!' Johnny shouted at the doctor,

leading Katherine by the hand out on to the balcony. 'You should never mix business and pleasure, everyone knows that!'

Outside, it felt a few degrees colder than it had done during the firework display, but that could have been the absence of mass anticipation in the air. There was no hot exhilarated breath here, only the empty cartridges of spent explosives and the controlled suspense of two people, waiting to hear what the other had to say.

They walked to the sundial in the centre of the lawn and Katherine started to trace her finger nervously over the brass characters. She didn't look up as she said, 'I wish I didn't have to break the spell.'

'It's not a spell. It's how we are,' he said. 'Magic is a here today gone tomorrow kind of thing, and we're more of a here today and here again tomorrow and the next day and the next day and the day after that. Even when we're apart, that's how it feels.' He sounded romantic and reliable at the same time.

'Which was maybe why we parted. Too much of a good thing and all that,' she replied, finally lifting her eyes to see his face looking into hers.

'But nothing is irretrievable.'

Katherine sighed and then immediately took another deep breath. 'Johnny, we're not as close to getting back together as you might think. My life has gone off on another tangent.'

He didn't speak until he saw she needed encouragement. 'Go on,' he said softly, 'tell me.'

Her whole body wore the look of apprehension. 'I don't really want to. If I go on, I'll spoil it. Why don't we just agree to be good parents to our children and love each other from afar? No picking over the bones.'

'Because there won't be a reason big enough,' he told her, holding her with his eyes.

'But there is,' she said, staring back into him but rubbing harder at the brass to take away the pain.

'I know what you're going to say,' Johnny said quietly, stopping her hands from their frantic buffing by taking them and squeezing them in his. Katherine gave small shakes of her head.

'No you don't, you couldn't.'

'I think I do, and for me, it isn't reason enough.'

She wanted to cry with frustration. He wasn't listening, he couldn't be.

'Tell me then.'

'That you're pregnant, and I might not necessarily be the father.'

He squeezed her hands again to pull her out of her dazed panic, to let her know he was there, and was telling her he would be there, regardless. She couldn't speak, but looked at him with hesitant tears rolling down her cheeks.

'Hey, come on,' he said, so tenderly it made her cheeks even wetter. 'It's okay. It's life. Do I know my own father? Does Beth know hers? Did Patrick really know his? Does all that really matter?'

He remembered how much he'd had to wrestle in the last week or so to get there himself and his heart even stung a little as he braced himself to hear the part he'd fought with most.

'It does when the father could be Patrick,' she spluttered. Her whole world went quiet, as if nothing else would happen anywhere until he spoke. They had been each other's exclusively for fifteen years until she had let in their best friend – and not only that, she had let him in for good. No man, not even Johnny, she thought, could live with such a truth.

'Well, thank God for that,' he whispered, managing to find the words he'd hoped he could. 'For one moment I thought you were going to tell me there was someone else.'

It wasn't meant entirely as a joke. His embrace as he took her was unconditional, and when they pulled away, he put her hands up to his mouth and blew through them to revive them from the biting cold.

'Tell me it doesn't mean I've lost you,' he said.

'It's me who should be asking that,' Katherine said. 'I can't believe you're taking it like this. Well, I can, because you're you, but . . .'

'It's because I love you.'

She wanted to hear it again and again, and she wrapped herself back into him, but he was already saying something else.

'I need to tell you something too. My life has also gone off on another tangent.'

Their worlds were suspended again.

He breathed in.

'I've chucked in my job.'

He waited for her arms to withdraw and the questions to start, but she stayed there with her head on his chest listening to his pounding heart.

'But that's great,' she said. 'You hated it.'

'And I haven't got another one,' he told her, re-lighting the touch paper.

'Wow. Unemployed and pregnant,' she murmured. 'Can we do this?'

'We can do anything,' he said euphorically, sounding convincing and focused and strong and soft and all those other things she loved him for so much.

They stood there a while longer, burying their faces in each other, looking up at the moon and the stars and then back to each other, until their lips finally came together in a kiss that said it all.

'Bed?' Katherine whispered.

'Bed,' Johnny agreed, and they started the short walk back to their marriage.

How long Patrick stayed face down on the sand and when the blood stopped running from his head, he didn't know, but slowly and undeniably, he came to. His ankle throbbed and the open gash in his head stung and stabbed him, but the invitation to give up his life had been withdrawn, and he suddenly knew with a conviction not only that he was alive, but that he had been saved. The spiritual vacuum that had sucked and sucked away at his insides until there was no space left to put anything there even if he had tried had been broken, and he could feel a heart beating in there instead.

Words started to spill from his mouth – forgive me, show me, thank you – but they were not the prayers he'd heard as a child nor the private and intense mutterings he had caught as an adult. Whatever they were, they were coming from him and they were shot through with a certainty that he had heard the voice of his God.

Patrick pushed his elbows and knees, then his hands and his feet into the wet sand and he stood up. Putting one sodden shoe in front of another, the moon moved out from behind a cloud and showed him a clear path ahead. He was on Bryher, on the beach where he had lain with his friends in October, and in front of him was the boathouse where they had sheltered from the rain.

POCKET
B O O K S

A SELECTED LIST OF TITLES AVAILABLE FROM POCKET BOOKS

THE PRICES SHOWN BELOW WERE CORRECT AT THE TIME OF GOING TO PRESS. HOWEVER POCKET BOOKS RESERVE THE RIGHT TO SHOW NEW RETAIL PRICES ON COVERS WHICH MAY DIFFER FROM THOSE PREVIOUSLY ADVERTISED IN THE TEXT OR ELSEWHERE.

☐	0 671 85578 6	Sentimental Journey	Juliette Mead	£5.99
☐	0 671 01778 0	Intimate Strangers	Juliette Mead	£5.99
☐	0 671 85418 6	Foreign Correspondents	Cindy Blake	£5.99
☐	0 671 85417 8	Second Wives	Cindy Blake	£5.99
☐	0 671 01017 4	Reading Between The Lies	Lynn Peters	£6.99
☐	0 671 01832 9	Chat	Nan McCarthy	£3.99
☐	0 671 01833 7	Connect	Nan McCarthy	£3.99
☐	0 671 01834 5	Crash	Nan McCarthy	£3.99
☐	0 671 85471 2	Real Women	Susan Oudot	£5.99
☐	0 671 85470 4	Virtual Love	Susan Oudot	£5.99
☐	0 671 01568 0	All That I Am	Susan Oudot	£5.99
☐	0 671 01802 7	That Devil Called Love	Lynda Chater	£5.99
☐	0 671 01602 4	Ordinary Miracles	Grace Wynne Jones	£6.99
☐	0 671 85518 2	Wise Follies	Grace Wynne Jones	£6.99

All Pocket titles are available by post from:

Book Service By Post, P.O. Box 29, Douglas. Isle of Man IM99 1BQ

Credit cards accepted. Please telephone 01624 675137, fax 01624 670923, Internet http://www.bookpost.co.uk or e-mail: bookshop@enterprise.net for details.

Free postage and packing in the UK: Overseas customers allow £1 per book (paperbacks) and £3 per book (hardbacks).